ALSO BY
DARCY COATES

The Haunting of Ashburn House
The Haunting of Blackwood House
The House Next Door
Craven Manor
The Haunting of Rookward House
The Carrow Haunt
Hunted
The Folcroft Ghosts
The Haunting of Gillespie House
Dead Lake
Parasite
Quarter to Midnight
Small Horrors

House of Shadows
House of Shadows
House of Secrets

Black Winter
Voices in the Snow
Secrets in the Dark
Whispers in the Mist

WHISPERS
IN THE
MIST

DARCY COATES

Published by Poisoned Pen Press, an imprint of Sourcebooks
P.O. Box 4410, Naperville, Illinois 60567-4410
(630) 961-3900
sourcebooks.com

Library of Congress Cataloging-in-Publication Data
Names: Coates, Darcy, author.
Title: Whispers in the mist / Darcy Coates.
Description: Naperville, IL : Poisoned Pen Press, [2020] | Series: [Black winter ; 3]
Identifiers: LCCN 2020007176 | (trade paperback)
Subjects: GSAFD: Horror fiction. | Dystopias.
Classification: LCC PR9619.4.C628 W48 2020 | DDC 823/.92--dc23
LC record available at https://lccn.loc.gov/2020007176

Printed and bound in Canada.
MBP 10 9 8 7 6 5 4 3 2 1

CHAPTER 1

CLARE CLUNG TO HER seat as the minibus rocked through the city. Abandoned cars littered the streets like the fallen on a battlefield. A path had been carved through them using brute force, but it was irregular, weaving in sharp angles and often forcing them to rise onto the curb.

Every time the bus jolted over some obstacle, Dorran's shoulder bumped hers. Clare felt pure elation rush through her. They had gotten out of Helexis Tower and away from the scientist who had created the thanites that destroyed humanity. Dorran was with her. Dorran was *safe*.

She looked up at him, grinning. He tried to return the expression. Clare's heart sank.

They might be free, but Dorran hadn't escaped the tower unscathed. Even though he matched her smile, it was obvious that it took him effort. He braced one hand on the seat ahead to absorb the shocks. His fingers trembled. His skin was ashen, his dark eyes had lost their familiar brightness, and every jostle seemed to drain more of his strength. Black hair, slightly too long, was damp with sweat.

He needs rest. A few days of good food and sleep, and he'll start to heal. She wanted to believe the idea. She was desperate to. It seemed too cruel to escape the tower—to escape Ezra and his experiment—only to lose Dorran.

She took his free hand and pressed it gently. He threaded his fingers between hers. His thumb grazed over the ring he'd given her.

Hold on a little longer, Dorran. I'll do whatever it takes to make this right.

Two rows ahead of them, Beth sat in the driver's seat, navigating the congested roads. It felt like a dream. Clare had clung to hope for her sister longer than any rational part of her could justify. She had traveled across the country only to lose her again. To find Beth by what seemed like pure coincidence was more good luck than Clare dared trust in. But she was there, within touching distance, alive and real.

Clare swallowed, trying to find her voice. "Beth—"

"Not now," she barked, her eyes fixed on the path ahead as the minibus screeched around a tight bend.

Ten years her senior, Beth had become a surrogate mother to Clare after their father left and their mother passed away. Beth had taken her to school programs, swimming lessons, and camps and watched her like a hawk the entire time. There had been doctor visits over mild coughs. No swimming in pools unless both Beth and a lifeguard were present. No sleepovers unless Beth unequivocally trusted the families.

The old Beth, naturally cautious, had never sped in her life. She'd once told Clare, "Driving is one of the most dangerous things a person can do, second only to eating undercooked meat."

But the new world had changed Beth. Even with the road choked, she was over the speed limit. The minibus scraped half the cars it passed. She drove aggressively but efficiently. The chattering screams from the hollow ones pursuing them were already fading.

That wasn't the only part of Beth that had changed. Her fine, wavy blond hair had grown out a little since Clare had last seen her, and it grazed her shoulders. Her face looked harder. Leaner. Fresh scars marked her delicate features.

Clare leaned forward to try to see her sister more clearly. If Beth was aware of the scrutiny, she didn't acknowledge it. They rose onto another curb and clipped a light post, and Clare dropped back into her seat to avoid being rattled any more than she already was.

The scars were fresh. One ran across Beth's nose, starting near her eye and arcing down onto her cheek. Another mottled patch stood just above her temple. Three small marks showed where something had sliced into her jaw.

They were recent but already sealed over. Clare knew the thanites would be responsible for that. Airborne, nanoparticle-size machines designed to heal the human body but gone terribly, horrifically wrong. Like Clare, Beth would have been spared a full dose. She'd had her bunker, an airtight fortress that had saved her from being converted into one of the twisted, mindless creatures during the hours the thanites had been active.

The bunker would have limited Beth's exposure to the thanites but not eliminated them entirely. And now the tiny machines were inhabiting her body, healing her injuries. It was one of the reasons Clare had survived so long. Poison, blood loss, and infection were all being treated by the same creations that had grown out of control and mutated most of humanity.

Beth wrenched the wheel to navigate a tight angle. Clare hit Dorran's side, and he hit the window. The bus rose onto two wheels, and for a moment, Clare was afraid they were about to tip. Then the bus lurched back down, sending shock waves through them as it reconnected with the road.

This reckless, energetic Beth was a sharp contrast to the woman Clare knew. Her wardrobe had changed, too. All black swaddled her from the scarf around her neck to her boots. If she wore a mask, there wouldn't be a scrap of skin visible. Covering skin was a defense against the hollows, but it still left Clare disconcerted. She'd never seen Beth wear black before. It was as though all of Beth's soft sides had been sharpened into angles.

Clare supposed it was hard to stay static in the new world. She wondered how much *she* had changed in the past weeks.

The minibus's windows had been covered with plywood. Narrow gaps existed around the boards' edges. When Clare was close to them, she could see the businesses and vehicles they passed. She caught sight of movement inside many of the cars. Hollows, trapped, pressed their hands against the closed windows and hissed in frustration. Each nightmarish face was only visible for a split second, but the images haunted Clare. Deformed mouths. Missing teeth. Bulging eyes. Sparse hair.

She tried to imagine what their lives would have been like before the stillness. People on their way to their jobs, parents dropping their children off at day care, an elderly couple driving to an early morning breakfast date. Those were the monsters that now surrounded them.

Stop. Focus on what's good. Because there's a lot of good to be found today.

Dorran was safe. Hurt, but still alive. Clare tightened her hand around his. Against all odds, they had found Beth. Or, rather, Beth had found them. She'd gotten them out of Helexis Tower. And now they were leaving the city. The high-rise buildings were being replaced by homes and old trees as they entered the outer suburbs. The country wasn't far off.

The tires screeched as Beth pulled off the road. It wasn't the first time she'd taken a shortcut across a parking lot, but this time, she didn't floor the accelerator. She let the minibus rock to a halt, pulled the hand brake, and jumped out of the driver's seat.

"What the *hell* were you doing in the city?" She stood in the aisle, her face made of sharp angles and her eyes doused with fire. Then the expression softened, her jaw unclenching and her eyebrows rising, and she reached toward Clare. "Thank goodness you're okay."

Clare crossed to her in two quick steps. Beth's hug was fierce as she half cried, half laughed into Clare's wet hair.

"I didn't think I'd get to see you again," Clare managed.

"Neither did I." Beth leaned back far enough to see Clare's face and used her fingertips to brush wet hair off her cheek. "You're not hurt, are you?"

"I'm not, but…"

Clare turned to look at Dorran. He stood a few steps behind them, one hand braced on the back of a seat for support, watching cautiously. He was trying not to look intimidating, Clare knew, but that was hard to avoid when his head grazed the ceiling.

Beth's eyes fixed on Dorran. The hand on Clare's shoulder tightened a fraction. "This is the man you've been staying with?"

"Yes." Clare reached toward him. "I'm really glad you get to meet him. Dorran, this is Beth. Beth, Dorran."

He dipped his head in a respectful nod, his eyes not quite meeting hers and his voice subdued. "A pleasure."

"Mm." Beth's lips pressed into a tight line as her eyes ran over him, from his black hair to his broad shoulders, across the muddied lab coat he'd borrowed from Ezra, down to the boots. Clare wished she would be more subtle about it.

"He figured out how to repair my car." Clare spoke too fast as she tried to soften some of Beth's hostility. "I'd never have gotten this far without him—"

"Outside," Beth said abruptly and tugged on her arm.

"Ah…what?"

"Come on. We'll talk outside."

Clare stared at the windshield. Light reflected off the water flowing over the surface. "It's raining."

"You're already drenched." Beth hit a button and the door hissed open, letting the steady drum of rain inside, along with the faint scent of smoke, oil, and hollows. "Come on. I want to talk in private."

Clare sent Dorran an apologetic glance as she was dragged out of the bus. He looked conflicted, one hand reaching toward her, and Clare mouthed, *Don't worry*. Then the door creaked closed behind her, sealing him inside the bus.

Beth kept her hold on Clare's arm as she dragged her away from the vehicle. The rain, vicious in its intensity at Helexis Tower, had reduced to a drizzle in the outer suburbs.

Clare blinked at the space, surprised. Beth had stopped the minibus in the center of a shopping mall's parking lot. They were well-lit, as gigantic bulbs washed the area with harsh white light. Clare didn't know how the lights could still be running four weeks into the stillness. Even if the center had a generator—and she guessed it must have for emergencies—it would need to be refueled. The area seemed deserted except for their vehicle.

"Beth?" Clare was already wet from the run out of Helexis Tower, but the new wash of rain drained another layer of warmth. Her sneakers sank into a puddle two inches deep and she shivered. Beth stopped a dozen paces away from the bus, facing the deserted shopping mall, arms crossed. Clare hunched her shoulders. "Is everything okay?"

Beth dragged her hands over her hair, plastering it back, and then turned to Clare. "I don't like the way he looks."

She was used to Beth's wariness. "He's a good man. He's kind and patient, and he saved my life. Multiple times. I can't even begin to tell you how much I owe him."

Beth paced across the asphalt, arms folded, expression tense. When she turned back to Clare, there was fresh suspicion in her eyes. "He looks sick."

"He…" She could tell Beth exactly what had happened: about how Dorran had been coerced into becoming part of Ezra's experiment to destroy the thanites and how they didn't know what the consequences might be. But the way Beth was talking about Dorran—like he was an unwanted liability—made Clare swallow the story. She couldn't afford to give Beth any more reasons to mistrust him. Instead, she opted for a half-truth. "It's been a weird couple of days. He didn't sleep last night."

"Uh-huh." Beth's eyes narrowed in the way they did when she was skeptical. Her jaw worked as she stared at the bus, chewing something over. Then she took a deep breath. "We'll drop him off with some other survivors, then get back on the road."

"What?" Clare blinked water out of her eyes.

"Don't worry. I know some groups that would take him in."

"No." Clare took a step back, her heart thundering. "We're not going to abandon him. We're a team."

"He's a *stranger*."

"To *you*." She hated how defensive she sounded, but she couldn't stop. "He's *my* best friend."

Beth's lips twisted. "Oh really? After knowing him for, what? A couple of weeks?"

"After having to rely on him for my survival, repeatedly, through some of the worst moments of my life, yeah. And I think I'm a good enough judge of character to say I trust him. Why can't you believe that?"

"Oh, I don't know." Beth's voice rose, and a harsh note entered it. "Maybe because I can't even trust you to follow basic instructions."

It took Clare a second to catch the implication. "Are you angry because I came looking for you?"

"What did I tell you the last time we spoke?" Beth lifted her eyebrows to arrest Clare with one of the sharpest looks she'd ever experienced. "*Stay where you are.*"

"Your generator died. Was I supposed to just leave you there to suffocate?"

"Yes." Beth held her hands out to the sides, her open palms catching the rain. "It would have been better than traipsing across the country just to find my bunker was empty. And if that wasn't bad enough…what the *hell* were you doing in the city? The single most dangerous place in this part of the country."

Clare was used to her share of lectures from Beth. She'd hated them as a teen, but as she grew older and moved into her own home, she'd learned to see them for what they really were: an expression of love. Beth cared about her; therefore, Beth worried about her; therefore, Beth lectured her.

But this felt different. There wasn't any concerned tilt to her sister's eyes or pleading note in her voice. This Beth, the Beth that had been hardened and sharpened by the still world, was full of fire and wrath. Clare took a half step back.

"We—" *Were lost. Became trapped. Ran out of options.* None of them sounded good. She swallowed. "We found the tower by pure luck and recognized the address, so we took a chance on it."

"And how were you planning to get out?" Beth's piercing blue eyes were relentless. "You ran through the horde with no weapons. No protection. Not even a mask. If I hadn't been there, what would you have done to escape the hollows?"

The rain drenched Clare's skin. Her hair stuck to her face. But for all the external cold she felt, it was nothing compared to the lump of ice that was forming deep in her stomach.

She'd been desperate to reunite with Beth. She'd taken risks she shouldn't have just in the hope of finding her. But Beth was furious. And, unlike a normal lecture, she didn't know how to stop this new anger.

Beth took her silence for the answer it was. "You had no way to get out of that tower, did you? You're only alive right now because of pure, miserable luck."

Angry tears were building, and she was grateful that the rain would stop Beth from seeing them.

"I told you all of this *so* clearly." Beth's voice dropped until it was almost inaudible through the rain. "Don't take risks. People who gamble on the odds eventually lose. And what did you do?"

"Whatever it took to try to find my sister."

Beth's face stayed hard for all of a second, then the expression crumpled. She exhaled, head drooping and shoulders bowing.

For a moment, they stood together, letting the rain beat on their backs and drip off their chins. Then Beth lifted her head, her expression soft again.

"That was really dumb, Clare."

"Okay."

"But thank you anyway."

"Yeah."

Her sister's arms wrapped around her again. Beth's jacket was thick and cold, but her body was warm. She squeezed Clare tightly, swaying with her like she used to when Clare was a child.

"I'm happy to have you with me again," she murmured. "I didn't think I'd ever get the chance."

"I missed you, Beth."

"Mm." She pulled back, blinking rapidly. "Me too."

Thunder crackled in the distance. Clare turned to look behind them, toward the minibus. Its windows were blacked out, but she could imagine Dorran sitting inside, anxious and uncertain, alone in the dark as he waited for them to return. Her heart ached for him. "I'm not letting you kick Dorran out."

Beth chewed on her lip for a second, then sighed. "He can stay. For now. But if he wants to split up, we let him go, okay?"

Clare still didn't like her sister's tone, but she nodded. It was probably the best concession she could get. And she already knew Dorran would stay.

Beth squinted up at the sky as lightning arced above them. "Rain's nasty today. Come on. Let's get dry. We shouldn't linger here anyway. The hollows are growing impatient."

CHAPTER 2

BETH WRAPPED ONE ARM around Clare's shoulder as they moved back toward the minibus. Clare frowned, trying to understand what her sister had said. "The hollows?"

"Yeah. I parked here because it's the closest haven to the city. The light keeps the hollow ones at bay. But they'll only stay on the outskirts for so long before the hunger gets the best of them."

Clare squinted at their surroundings and took them in properly for the first time. The parking lot stretched around them in all directions, empty except for a handful of overturned shopping carts. The lights above them flooded the area for a hundred feet in each direction. But, if she stared at the shadows on the edges of the asphalt, where the light was thinner, she thought she saw bulblike eyes glowing in the bushes.

The shopping center stood not far behind them. Single story, designed in a long boomerang shape, she guessed it would house at least eighty stores. She'd thought the windows and doors were dark, but as she looked again, she realized they'd been boarded up. Through the planks and sheet metal, she thought she saw spots of light. "Beth…are there people in there?"

"Yeah."

"Should we—"

"No." They were at the bus's door, and Beth pushed the handle to open it. With the windows covered, barely any light reached inside the vehicle, and Clare had to blink as her eyes adjusted.

The minibus had probably been used for tours at one point. Six rows of seats, made of mottled blue-and-gray fabric, ran either side of the aisle. Metal baskets suspended above them were full of luggage. It wasn't exactly luxurious, but it was modern and clean.

Dorran still stood in the aisle, one hand braced on a seat for support, shivering as his clothes dripped onto the floor. His expression was unreadable, which Clare had learned was a defense mechanism when he felt uneasy.

"Hey," she called, injecting some brightness into her voice. "We're all good. Beth, do you have towels by any chance?"

"In the basket to your right." Beth dropped into the driver's seat and turned the key in the ignition. Lights flickered to life above them and the door slid closed, muffling the rain.

Clare found a black plastic bag full of towels in the storage compartment Beth had indicated. She pulled two out, checking they were clean, and passed one to Dorran. She couldn't stop herself from glancing back at the door as she squeezed water out of her hair. "Uh, Beth was just saying that there's someone in the shopping mall back there. And I'm really hoping she'll tell me more about that."

Beth sat crossways in her seat, one arm leaned on the dash, facing Clare as she peeled off her gloves. More fresh, barely sealed cuts marred her hands. "I stopped here before traveling into the city. They call it a safe haven. There are a few dozen havens just like it dotted around the country. Survivors who have found a place to hole up, somewhere with resources and adequate protection. Shopping malls are popular. Especially the more modern ones that have implemented antiterrorist precautions. There are larger safe havens in the country, some that boast actual democracies, though I'll believe it when I see it."

"They live here?" Clare wiped water out of her eyes. "How many?"

"About twenty in that center. They advertise their presence; I heard about them from a traveler on the road. It's the closest shelter you can get to the city center. They run the lights constantly to keep hollows away and welcome travelers…as long as you have something to trade."

"What do they trade for?"

"Things they have a finite supply of: food, water, fuel. In return, they'll let you spend the night there and you can take any nonnecessities from the other stores. I traded four liters of fuel for as many clothes as I could carry." She pulled a face. "Starting to regret it, to be honest. Fuel will be in short supply in the coming months."

Clare leaned close to the door, trying to glimpse the center through the rain. She caught sight of movement near one of the loading docks. It was impossible to tell whether it was human or hollow. "And you don't want to stay there again tonight?"

"No. They're a bit too zealous for my tastes. A lot of surviving bands are. They set up their own rules, their own hierarchy, their own little kingdoms. I know the cliché is survival in numbers, but in this kind of environment, I think we'll be safer just the two of us."

"Three of us," Clare said. "Don't forget Dorran."

"Hmm." Beth's eyes narrowed as she glanced at their silent companion. He ran the towel through his hair, tousling it, but kept his eyes on the floor.

She's just wary because he's a stranger. She was always overprotective like that. She needs some time to get used to him.

But the cautious part of her mind warned that this new Beth was different. The days of fretting over curious boys was over. This Beth was focused on survival.

"What have you been doing since we last spoke?" she asked Beth. "I want to know everything. How did you get out of the bunker? Where have you been? And your scars—"

"Later, maybe." Beth rubbed her neck, shaking droplets of water off her chin, as she leveled a cold gaze at Dorran. "So, you've been keeping my sister company these last few weeks, huh?"

He blinked but didn't meet her eyes. "Ah…yes."

"Well, I guess I owe you some thanks for that."

Good. Good. Clare glanced between them, hopeful.

15

"And I want to give you something to show my gratitude," Beth continued. "You're probably ready to get some agency back, right? Name a location. I'll drop you off there and set you up with good supplies."

"Hey," Clare snapped. "We agreed he was staying."

"We agreed *he could leave if he chose to*." Beth didn't take her eyes off Dorran. "Look, you've traveled a long way, and you're obviously tired. Clare and I might be on the road for a while before we settle down. Pick somewhere to stay and I'll give you supplies to last. What do you say?"

"Beth—"

"Let him answer."

Dorran allowed the towel to fall around his shoulders. His dark, deep-set eyes barely flickered, and Clare wondered if Beth could pick up on the quiet panic that was settling into him. His voice remained steady, though, even as he struggled to phrase himself diplomatically. "That is a kind offer. But I would be grateful for the opportunity to accompany you further. I hope I can continue to assist you and Clare."

Beth's lips twitched down. "I'll let you take some of our fuel. It's worth more than gold these days."

"Stop it." Clare stepped forward, planting herself between Dorran and Beth. "He's not going anywhere. We're a team."

Beth huffed. She didn't look happy, but she rolled her shoulders in something like a reluctant shrug. "All right. Fine. You said he's tired, right? He can sleep in the back of the bus. There's a bed set up there. But get some dry clothes on first. They're stored in the racks above your heads." Beth swiveled to face the dash and put the bus into gear. The engine rumbled as she eased them back toward the street. "We're far enough from the city that we don't have to rush, but we can't afford to sit here all day, either. The hollows get antsy around nightfall, and I want to be in the country by then. So you better figure out how to sleep while I drive."

"That's fine," Dorran said.

"Clare, get changed, then sit up front with me. I'll need you for navigation."

"Okay." Clare, relieved that Beth had let the argument drop, turned toward the racks and began looking through them. They held not just clothes but cartons of fuel, water, and cardboard boxes full of long-life food, as well as weapons suspended near the bus's rear. She pulled stacks of clothes down as she found them. Most of the outfits were small sizes that would fit the sisters. She had to dig to find clothes large enough for Dorran.

Beth had been sensible about the outfits she'd brought, though; there were extra-thick, insulated shirts and jackets, along with rainproof overcoats and sturdy leather footwear. Most still had their price tags attached, which identified them as coming from a high-end hiking store.

"Try these," Clare murmured, passing shirts and pants to Dorran. She snapped the tags off clothes for herself and sat in one of the seats to change. Her hair was still damp, but there wasn't much she could do for it, so she tied it into a messy bun as she approached Beth at the bus's front.

"You're looking better." Beth remained facing the road, but her eyes flicked up to the rearview mirror to watch her two companions. "We can't afford to waste fuel to heat the bus, but there are blankets in the basket under your seat."

Clare pulled the fleece bundle out, then settled into the seat beside the driver's console. It had been set back a little to make room for the door, but kept her close to Beth and allowed an unobstructed view of the twisting road ahead. She glanced behind. The row of seats at the back had been converted to a bed, stacked high with pillows and blankets. Dorran sat on its edge and gave her a small smile. He looked better wearing proper thermal clothes and with his hair brushed back, but the grayness hadn't left his face. Clare motioned for him to relax. He settled back in his seat, legs crossed ahead of himself, but didn't seem ready to sleep.

"Let's get out of this mess." Beth coaxed the bus around another sharp angle. Its rear bumper scraped against a fallen tree. "The map's in the side pocket there. If I show you where we are, can you help with directions?"

"Sure." Clare took the map from the compartment beside the driver's seat. The paper folded out to take up her whole lap and seemed to have been designed for tourists. Emblems dotted notable locations, and a beaming bird mascot gave them a thumbs-up from the map's corner.

Beth had drawn across the map in red pen. Thick X's covered many of the roads.

"That means the street is impassable," Beth explained, seeing

Clare looking. "Circles are for possible resources. Some of those are just hearsay from the people I've passed, though; no guarantee they're still intact. Triangles are safe havens. We'll be avoiding those. Stars are hazards."

Clare gazed across the dozens of marks. "You've been around."

Beth chuckled. "It took a while to get into the city. Lots of detours, lots of impassable roads."

"Okay." Clare traced a red marker line through the suburbs until it ended in the countryside. "Where are we going?"

"Just *out*. Somewhere we can set up camp and heat some food without these ghouls jabbering at us."

A taxi stood to their left. The driver, still wearing scraps of his uniform, clawed at his window, saliva dripping from his missing jaw. Beth sent it a derisive glare, then put some pressure on the accelerator to pass it.

"Did you clear the roads with this?" Clare nodded to the bus.

"Part of it. The part that goes up to the tower. But there are cleared roads like this snaking through the city and suburbs. They were made by people who came looking for their families." Beth sighed. "People who *escaped* the changes but had children, parents, or spouses living in the city. Hope is a brutal thing. It will carry you further than your feet ever wanted to go."

Clare knew how that felt. Hope had pushed her to drive to Beth's bunker even after the radio went quiet. She couldn't imagine how it must have been for the people searching for their lost loved ones, knowing the city was overrun, knowing that there was next to no chance of their family still being alive, but not being able to stop hoping because it was the only thing that kept them waking up in the morning.

"What happened after I lost contact with you?" Clare's eyes flicked to the scars marring Beth's face. "We saw the dead hollows inside your bunker. You must have opened your doors—"

"And fought my way out, yeah." A wolfish smile stretched her lips. "I never imagined I was capable of surviving something like that. But I did. I guess it was a...catalyst. I didn't *need* to be afraid any longer."

It had changed her; that was certain. Even though Clare was struggling to adjust to the stronger, harder version of her sister, she was still grateful for it. Beth hadn't cowered. And that had allowed her to survive.

"And you built this bus?" Clare indicated the modifications.

"No. This, I found. Some poor soul had obviously planned to be a hero. I found it on the side of the road next to a demolished campsite. As far as I can tell, he was attacked while cooking dinner and decided to stand and fight instead of hiding in the bus. There was nothing left except some blood soaked into the ground. The hollows even eat bones."

Clare shivered. She'd witnessed the creatures' all-consuming hunger.

Beth shrugged. "I feel bad for the guy, but I'm grateful, as well. He did a good job of getting this thing hollow-proof. There are even shutters you can pull over the front window. If they can't see you or hear you, eventually they lose interest and wander away. I mean, it takes hours. Sometimes all night. But it's better than trying to escape while they're crawling all over your windshield."

"I'd be worried about it chewing through fuel too fast."

"Oh, it does, but it gives me enough brute force to get through almost anything, and that's worth it."

The rain continued to drizzle throughout the afternoon, and thick clouds hid the sun. If not for the clock on the dash, Clare could have been lulled into thinking they were trapped in perpetual twilight. Their bus didn't make much noise beyond the motor's purr, the quiet thudding of their windshield wipers, and Clare's occasional directions.

Beth seemed to be mulling something over. She kept glancing at the rearview mirror. With the windows boarded up, the mirror wouldn't help her see the road. She had to be watching Dorran. He'd lain down, one arm folded under his head, breathing slow and heavy as he slept. "Tell me about him."

"I meant what I said earlier. He's a good man. Kind, smart, and loyal. I wouldn't have made it this far without him."

"There aren't many kind people left in this world," Beth said.

Clare started to nod but stopped herself as her sister continued.

"And there are a lot of bad people masquerading as good."

"What does that mean?"

Beth lifted her shoulders in a shrug. "Lots of people will pretend to be your friend if they need something from you."

Clare couldn't stop herself from bristling. "Well, I can vouch for Dorran."

"We're family. I know I can trust you, and you know you can

trust me. Come hell or high water, we'll stick together. But you can't expect that kind of loyalty from anyone else you meet on the road. Maybe this man is one of the better ones. But even he will leave if he decides you're weighing him down."

He won't. He didn't. Clare pressed her lips together. She couldn't tell Beth how wrong she was, not without telling her about some of the things that had happened in Winterbourne. Weak from blood loss and poison, convinced that she was going insane, she'd been nothing but a physical and emotional burden. But Dorran had carried her without any trace of reluctance or revulsion, no matter how bad it had been. She'd never believed a person could be so patient.

Clare looked down at her hands again. Her thumb grazed over the ring Dorran had given her. Beth hadn't noticed it yet. If she had, there would have been a comment. Making sure Beth's eyes were on the road, Clare slid the ring off and tucked it into a pocket.

Beth already mistrusted Dorran. Telling Beth they were married—or, at least, as close to married as they could be in a world without marriage registrars or ceremonies—would be like trying to extinguish a bonfire with gasoline. She'd give them time to get to know each other and develop some trust before taking that step.

The outer suburbs gradually faded into rural land, spotted with sickly plants and occasional sheds. Clare tried to watch her sister without being obvious about it. Something must have happened to Beth to make her so bitter. Something that hardened her against every other survivor. Clare wanted to ask her about it but didn't know whether that line of questioning might be safe.

"We'll stop here while we figure out where we're going next." Beth pulled off the road in a field. "Come on. Help me set up some shelter."

CHAPTER 3

THE SHELTER TURNED OUT to be a cloth overhang that extended from the bus's roof. Retractable tentpoles anchored into the wet ground, creating a six-foot-by-eight-foot sheltered area. Beth had parked in a weedy field away from any settlements. The grass was dead, but it was higher ground than the areas surrounding it and relatively dry compared to the fields that had been turned into shallow ponds.

Beth opened a compartment on the bus's side, and Clare stared in awe at the extra storage. The bus really had been fitted for self-reliance. The compartment carried a portable cooker and tank of gas, foldable chairs, more food and water, and an assortment of weapons, including axes, shovels, and a homemade pike.

Beth carried the camp stove out and placed it under the awning. "If your friend wants to eat, you'd better wake him up."

"On it." Clare jumped back into the bus. With the lights off, Dorran was almost invisible in the back seat. He lay with one arm under his head and the other fallen over the edge of the bed. He didn't quite fit. Even with the blankets, he'd huddled over, arms wrapped around himself as though cold.

"Hey," Clare murmured. She knelt beside him and ran her fingers through his damp hair. His eyebrows pulled down, but he didn't wake. Clare checked behind them, making sure Beth hadn't appeared in the doorway, then leaned closer and kissed his cheek. "Can you wake up? We're cooking some food."

He stirred and squinted up at her. She'd hoped the rest would help him, but the dark circles still lingered around his eyes. "Mm. Clare."

"How do you feel?"

He smiled, but even in the dim light, Clare could see his skin was gray. "Better."

"Do you want to stay here? I can bring you some food."

"Thank you, but I'll get up." He blinked, apparently trying to clear his head. "Are you eating outside?"

"Yeah. Beth has some shelter and a portable cooker, so the food will be warm."

"That sounds nice." He sat, moving gingerly. Clare wished she knew what was wrong with him. Even more than that, she wished there was something she could do to make it better.

She found a second jacket for Dorran in the overhead compartments and helped him pull it on. He let her fuss around him, adjusting the insulated fabric over his shoulders and zipping up its front. While she worked, his dark eyes watched her, gentle and inexplicably sad.

Clare finished adjusting the jacket but left her hands resting on Dorran's chest, unwilling to let him go so quickly. "What's wrong?"

"I am fine."

Clare raised her eyebrows.

He sighed and tried to smile. The expression came out crooked. "I don't think your sister likes me."

Oh. Clare opened her mouth, but the reassuring words she wanted to give died on her tongue. She patted Dorran's chest. "Beth takes a while to warm up to new people. She'll like you once she gets to know you."

"What should I do differently?" He was struggling to make eye contact.

Clare's heart ached. "Nothing. You're perfect as is. She just needs time."

Dorran nodded, but there wasn't much conviction in it. He stepped back so she could lead the way to the bus's front, and Clare, feeling helpless, followed the path to the outside.

The scent of rice and curry wafted around them as they stepped through the open doorway. She pushed some enthusiasm into her voice. "That smells great."

"It all comes out of cans, but it tastes almost as good as the real thing." Standing by the pot, the scars on her face lit by the portable stove's gas flames, Beth looked like something out of a book of myths. Fierce, strong, powerful. "I thought I'd make tonight a celebration. Our curry contains real chunks of reconstituted meat."

Three seats had been arranged around the camp stove: two close together, one set a little apart. Dorran hesitated but mutely took the isolated chair. Clare frowned. She grabbed the second seat and dragged it around, putting herself closer to Dorran.

Beth watched them, her lips pressed together, as she scooped curry into bowls that already held rice. She passed a serving to Clare first, then offered one to Dorran. As he took it, she said, "You're looking worse."

Clare glared at her sister, trying to telepathically tell her to be friendly.

Beth caught the look and shrugged. "Maybe some food will help."

"Thank you," Dorran murmured.

Beth removed the pots from the stove but left the flame running to warm them like a makeshift campfire, and dragged the third seat closer to Clare. As she sat, she scooped food into her mouth, swallowed, then leaned forward. "Now that we have a moment, why don't you tell me what happened? How did you end up in the city? Or in the tower, for that matter?"

"I have a very similar set of questions for you." Clare ran her spoon through her curry but didn't eat. "Why didn't you call me after the last time we spoke through the radio? Why did you go into the city instead?"

Beth's mouth twitched. "I lost my radio when I escaped the bunker. I was looking for a replacement."

"Still, though—the city was dangerous. Couldn't you have found one closer to your home?"

"That's the problem. Radios are in high demand since they're the only way humans can communicate now. A lot of the really remote houses have already been cleared out—not just of radios, but of food, bottled water, batteries, fuel, and anything else useful. There are still plenty of supplies in the suburban developments, but there are also hollows. The more populated an area, the better the chance of finding what you're looking for, but it's also overrun with ghouls."

"Huh. I guess that makes sense."

Beth tilted her head to the side. "Your turn. Why don't you tell me about what happened at Helexis Tower? I won't lie, after spending days trying to reach it, I want to know who, or what, was inside. Everyone on the road was talking about the bizarre radio transmission advertising its address."

Clare glanced at Dorran, and he nodded back at her. She took a bite of the curry as she tried to gather her thoughts, burned her tongue on it, and choked. Beth chuckled as she found a water bottle in the bus's external compartment and tossed it to Clare. She opened it and took a grateful sip.

The burn wouldn't bother her for long. The thanites would take care of it within a few hours. That thought was more disturbing than comforting.

"Okay." Clare clutched the bottle between her hands, staring into the stove's flames. "It's hard to explain the tower without telling you about everything else."

"Go ahead." Beth nodded, her expression intent.

Clare started from the morning when the quiet zones had

swept the world. She explained what had happened after her car crashed, how Dorran had found her and saved her, and then her experience inside Winterbourne. She left out key details: the poisoning incident, some of the riskier adventures that Beth would disapprove of, and how deeply she and Dorran had begun to care for each other. She dreaded Dorran's response to the last omission, but when she glanced at him, his expression was unreadable.

From Winterbourne, Clare briefly recounted the journey to Beth's bunker. Explaining what they'd found at Marnie's house was the hardest part. Clare's eyes burned at the memory of her aunt bloated, distorted, inhuman. Her voice wavered as she told how they'd put Marnie to rest. Beth remained quiet, but she bowed her head. Clare moved on to the events that had brought them to Helexis. Then came the encounter with Ezra, who had introduced himself as Peter.

She noticed Beth's eyes narrowed during that part of the story. To Beth, that encounter would simply be reinforcing what she already believed: strangers couldn't be trusted.

You weren't there, Clare wanted to say. *If you'd talked to him, I bet you would have believed him, too.*

But Beth didn't make any comments, and Clare pushed through it as factually as she was capable of. She did her best to explain the thanites. Beth interrupted occasionally with questions.

"Let me get this right, there are more machines still floating through the air?"

"Yeah." Clare swallowed a mouthful of curry. "But they're inactive. The only ones doing anything are the ones inside our bodies."

Beth nodded slowly. "So that's why we're resistant to infections."

"That's right." Again, Clare's eyes were drawn toward Beth's scars. They couldn't be more than a few days old, but they were already sealing over. That had to be the thanites speeding up her recovery. Clare's own cuts were healing themselves nearly as quickly.

She finished the story by telling how Ezra had tested his so-called cure on Dorran. She stressed the sacrifice he'd made for her sake, but Beth failed to look impressed.

"Does this mean he's the only human without thanites now?"

Clare shrugged. "It's possible. *Something* happened. But Ezra didn't share his results with us. We don't know if the treatment worked the way it was supposed to."

Finally, she talked about Ezra's death and how they had hidden in the elevator. As she spoke, her mind wandered to the last thing Ezra had ever said to her.

Give it to me!

Clare trailed off midsentence. There had been no time to examine his words when hollows were swarming up the stairwell, but for the first time, Clare had a chance to recognize what he'd meant.

Ezra had been looking for the USB stick containing his code. She couldn't remember what had happened to it after freeing

Dorran from the experiment chamber. Clare closed her eyes and tried to think back.

I shut off the system... I hit buttons to open the door...and I pulled the USB stick out of the port so Ezra couldn't start it up again.

Her eyes shot open. Both Beth and Dorran were watching her, equally confused and curious. Clare put her bowl on the ground and stood, feeling unsteady. "Hang on. Just a moment. I need to check..."

She jogged back into the minibus. Her and Dorran's old jackets—the ones Ezra had lent them—were hung over the backs of seats as they dried. Clare found hers and hunted through the pockets. In the second one, she found something small, solid, and metallic.

Oh. She hadn't been thinking when she'd taken the USB. She'd never intended to put it in her pocket, but somehow, she had. Clare's throat was dry as she returned to the outdoor seating area and held her hand out to show her companions.

Dorran's eyebrows rose. Beth's lowered.

"Is that the USB with the code?" Beth asked.

Clare nodded.

"And you didn't think to tell us before now?"

The tone was sharp. Clare closed her hand around the USB. Dorran glanced between them and silently put his bowl to one side.

"I forgot I had it. It was a tense couple of hours."

Beth leaned back in her chair and pressed her hand over her eyes. She was quiet for a moment, then said, "Well, what are we going to do with it?"

Clare sank into her chair. As night fell, the small amounts of light that made it through the rain clouds vanished, leaving her feeling vulnerable and cold. "Ezra said there were scientists at a research station in Evandale. He said they would be able to work on the code—"

"No, absolutely not." Beth's expression hardened. "We don't know anything about Evandale or this supposed research center. I can't justify traveling across the country for that."

"But if we don't—"

"We'll drop the USB off at one of the safe havens. They can worry about it in our place. Then we can focus on getting somewhere secure and protecting ourselves."

The USB felt much heavier than it had before. "I don't know if that's the right thing to do."

Beth lifted an eyebrow. Clare knew the expression: Beth wasn't happy with her dissent. She forged on.

"Ezra said the code would kill the hollows. Without it, the thanites will keep them alive for the next ten or even twenty years before their mutations finally destroy them."

"I still prefer those odds." Beth's jaw was tight. "We'll find somewhere secure and shore up our supplies to outlast this."

"That's not what I meant. The other survivors—" Clare's voice caught, and she had to swallow. "People are dying every day. The only chance humanity has against the hollows is to kill them."

"We don't even know it will work. That code was designed by a madman—"

"I don't think he was actually insane. He was fanatical. And smart. And jealous. He designed the thanites, so he's probably the only person who knows how to destroy them."

Beth leaned back in her chair, a muscle in her throat twitching. "We don't even know if the research facility exists or if anyone there is still alive. Survivors like to share the addresses of safe havens, and no one I've met has mentioned Evandale. Besides, from what you told me, Ezra lied about literally everything else."

"I'm sure he was telling the truth about this. You should have seen the way he reacted when I said I would take the USB to Evandale. He panicked. He was afraid they would steal his credit—"

"Clare, enough!" Beth slammed her bowl into the ground. "This is your problem. This is why I can't trust you on your own. You don't *think things through*."

Heat rose over Clare's face. "What—"

"How many times do I have to tell you this before you hear it? The heroes are dying. If you want to survive—if you want *me* to survive—you have to be careful. And you're not. You get an idea and just gleefully follow it with no idea of the consequences. 'Let's go visit Beth's bunker.' 'Oh, look, there's that tower we heard about. Let's stop there.' And I can already see where this is about to go. 'Hey, Beth, I found the USB. Let's drive across the country looking for a research station.'"

Clare clenched her teeth, her pulse thundering. "I—I'm doing the best I can—"

"No, you're not. You're acting like a child. You do whatever you want, then expect other people to clean up the mess you create."

"Don't speak to her that way."

Dorran's voice wasn't loud, but it held an intensity that made both Clare and Beth stare at him. He stayed in his chair, but his eyes were hard as he watched Beth.

Clare felt a swell of gratitude and guilt all at once. She didn't need him to defend her—she could hold her own against Beth—but it warmed her that he was willing to. Where he'd come from, confrontation never ended well. Even now, away from his mother and her sadistic tendencies, there were signs of stress in the way he held himself: head tilted, hands clasped, shoulders tight. Subconsciously, he was prepared for retaliation.

Beth narrowed her eyes at him. "What?"

His posture tightened further, but his voice remained steady. "She is an equal in this party. Speak to her with respect."

"Don't you dare lecture me," Beth spat. "You're not even supposed to be here."

Clare held the USB so tightly that it made her fingers ache. "Beth, stop."

Beth stood, breathing heavily, her face twitching. She looked from Clare to Dorran and back again. Clare lifted her chin, resolute. Beth's lips pulled back into a grimace. "Fine. Fine! Looks like we're done with dinner."

She snatched the half-eaten bowls off the ground and stacked them harshly enough that curry sloshed out. Then she grabbed a raincoat from the back of her chair and, holding the bowls under one arm, stalked into the night.

Clare followed her as far as the shelter's edge. "Where are you going?"

"To wash up."

Within seconds, Beth had vanished into the mist and the rain. Clare folded her arms across her chest and stepped back, her throat aching as she fought against the building tears.

CHAPTER 4

"CLARE, I AM SO sorry." Dorran's fingers grazed her shoulder. He was hesitating, speaking softly. Clare turned and wrapped her arms around him. He hugged her back. Gentle hands stroked her hair.

She tried not to cry. Beth was right. She was acting like a child, letting her emotions get the best of her and crumbling under pressure. Knowing that made the frustration even worse.

"Shh, it will be all right. I'm here for you." Dorran rocked her, kissing the top of her head. The hands kept moving in long, slow strokes.

"I'm sorry, Dorran." She leaned back to look up at him. "She's not normally like this. I mean, she never *acted* like this before. I think...I think the stillness has been hard on her."

"Understandable."

Oh, Dorran. You're patient, almost to a fault.

Clare rose onto her toes to kiss his neck. He leaned into the touch and finally smiled.

"It'll get better," she promised. "I'll keep working on her. Just...try to protect yourself. You don't have to stand up for me if we get into arguments. Leave Beth to me."

He lifted her hand and kissed the fingers tenderly. Then, abruptly, his smile faded. Clare pressed closer to him, trying to understand the sudden change in atmosphere. He was looking at her hand.

"Sorry! The ring! I have it here." She rushed to pull it out of her pocket. "I just—I—"

He smiled, but there was no joy in the expression any longer. "That's fine."

A cold rush of guilt filled her stomach. "I only took it off because Beth, with the way she's been acting... And I didn't want to make anything worse—"

"Clare, it's all right." He took her hand and wrapped the fingers around the ring. "I understand."

"Do you?" She blinked up at him, searching his expression, but it was as though he'd shuttered his face. She couldn't read his eyes any longer.

For a moment, Dorran didn't speak. He was looking down at their hands. Both of his were wrapped around hers, with the ring inside. Then he took a breath and spoke softly.

"You gave me your word inside an elevator, with monsters surrounding us and no hope of escape. It was not a fair situation to ask you in. And not a decision I would hold you to."

She shook her head, not sure she understood him. "Dorran—"

"I heard what your sister said earlier today. About how relationships are tenuous at best in this new world." His eyes flicked up to meet hers briefly, then dropped back down to their hands. His words were growing quicker, tighter, more formal—the way they did when he was under stress. "I do not wish you to stay with me because of a hastily made promise that you now regret. If you wish to give the ring back, I will understand. I would not resent it."

Their hands were still wrapped together. Clare pulled them closer so she could kiss Dorran's. Then she glared up at him, infusing all of the conviction she felt into her words. "No chance in hell."

The tightness in his expression broke. He blinked at her, shaken.

Clare pushed forward. "I fully intend to make good on that elevator promise, no matter how hastily made it was. You're stuck with me now, buddy. Till death do us part."

Laughter rose out of him, rolling through his chest first, then shaking his shoulders, and finally spilling into his face. He bent forward to touch his forehead against hers. Clare matched his grin, enjoying his delight.

"Truthfully?" His hand came up to stroke her cheek. "Are you certain you don't…have any regret?"

"Out of everything I've done in the last week, I regret this the least."

He wrapped his arms around her. She felt him lift her and

leaned up to meet his lips. He was still chilled. The darkness hadn't left his eyes. But in that moment, he seemed more alive than he had in the past days. Clare kissed him hungrily, fingers tangling in his hair. He hummed happily. When he finally let her down, she was breathless.

Clare realized she still held the ring. She made to put it back on her finger.

"It's all right." There was a smile in his voice. "Keep it hidden for the time being. I have enough handicaps to winning over your sister as it is. I do not mind a secret engagement."

"Sure." She tucked it back in beside the USB. Dorran bent quickly to kiss her again before finally letting her go.

Clare felt her smile fade as she stared outside their little square of shelter. Beth hadn't returned.

She needs time to cool off.

Fog swirled around them in little eddies as drizzling rain coursed through it. She could barely see more than thirty feet away. It made her skin crawl.

It's not safe to be alone. Especially not with visibility this low. I shouldn't have let her leave.

"Clare?" Dorran watched her, then glanced into the mist.

She took a step toward the shelter's edge. "I'm going to look for her. I'll be back in a moment."

"I will come too." He pulled his jacket's hood up, then moved to do the same to Clare's.

She cast a quick look at his pale skin and shadowed eyes. "You should wait here. I'll be quick."

39

"No. This is a foreign environment, and we don't know what is out there. I won't let you go alone." He lifted his eyebrows. "It is nonnegotiable."

"Hmm. Okay." She tried not to let him see how grateful she was. The mist played tricks on her eyes, building up shapes that vanished within a second. She wanted Dorran to rest, but she also didn't want to walk into the unknown alone.

Dorran turned off the stove and retrieved weapons from the bus. He took a metal pipe, while Clare picked up the baseball bat Beth had kept beside her chair. Then, together, they stepped out from the shelter.

The rain wasn't heavy, but it was persistent. Even with the water-resistant coat, trickles crawled in under her jacket and dripped down her cotton top. Clare shivered.

The mist had grown thicker as early night dropped the temperatures. She thought she could make out a small patch of straggly trees and, farther ahead, clumped boulders. In the low light, they could have been anything.

"Beth?" Clare raised her voice as high as she dared. The word seemed to sink into the fog, swallowed, unanswered.

She checked Dorran was still at her side. He swung the pipe in slow arcs, eyes narrowed as he tried to see through the haze.

Clare thought she could hear sounds. She tilted her head, trying to pinpoint their direction, and stumbled toward them. Her shoes sank deep into the spongy ground as they moved downhill.

She risked calling out again. "Beth!" Just like before, the

word was snatched away and muffled by the endless white. Clare strained, but the only sound she could make out was a low, rhythmic noise. *Like stones being scuffed. Or like a gathering of hollows chattering.*

Stress wound Clare's nerves tight. The longer she went without a reply, the more afraid she felt.

Beth wouldn't have gone far, would she?

It had been a mistake to let her leave on her own. Clare forged ahead, anxiety making her move faster than was wise. The noise grew closer. Trees, barely clinging to the slope, had grown lean and spindly from years of harsh winds and poor soil. Several had lost their grip on the hill and lay with their roots exposed.

Then a shape appeared through the fog. A silver ribbon, shimmering. Clare slowed. It took a second to realize what she was looking at.

A river had developed in the valley to carry the unprecedented deluge. It was recent enough that straggly, brown grass still lived in the riverbed, being unrelentingly pulled downhill. The water sloshed and jostled over itself, creating the noise that had drawn Clare's attention. She looked behind them. She thought she could still see a hint of light from their camp, but it was so faint that it was almost invisible.

Clare cupped her hands around her mouth. All pretense at noise moderation vanished as she yelled, "Beth!"

This time, she had a reply. A chattering, gibbering howl rose from the hills. It was answered by a second and then a third hollow.

CHAPTER 5

"OH." CLARE TOOK A step back.

Dorran's hand touched her shoulder. "We need to get back to the bus."

She shook her head furiously. "Beth's still out here."

He hesitated, his lips pulled back from clenched teeth. Then he gave Clare another push. "I'll search for her. Run for the bus and get inside. Don't open the door unless you hear our voices."

"Dorran, no—"

The words broke off as she saw movement behind him. Clare grasped Dorran's jacket and wrenched him toward her. A hollow's jaw snapped through the air where his shoulder had been a second before.

The hollow had four arms: two longer, thinner protrusions growing directly below its original pair. All four of them snatched at Dorran as it rocked past, carried by its momentum.

Dorran swung the pipe past Clare. It made a heavy cracking noise as it hit a hollow Clare hadn't seen.

She caught spots of white spiraling past her as the hollow's teeth broke out of its jaw. Then Dorran grasped her arm and swung her around to face the bus. "Run!"

Instead, Clare put her back against his. There were at least two hollows and more coming; she wouldn't let him sacrifice himself for her again. Dorran planted his feet, weapon raised, but she could still detect a sway in his stance that hinted at his exhaustion.

A creature came at her through the mist. Its lopsided head rocked with each step. It opened its mouth, and its jaw was filled with row upon row of teeth. Hundreds of them, jammed into its maw in uneven lines.

The shock slowed Clare's reflexes. She swung a fraction of a second too late. Instead of her bat connecting with the monster's head, the wood caught in its jaw. The rows of teeth tightened over her weapon, splintering it. Clare tried to pull back. The hollow wrenched its head to the side, and Clare gasped as the bat was dragged out of her grasp. Her palms smarted from where the fractured wood scraped.

Dorran staggered, bumping into her back. Clare looked over her shoulder and saw the creature with four arms had returned. Dorran held the pipe ahead of himself with both hands, trying to force some distance between him and the monster. It loomed over him, two of its hands holding the metal pipe, the other two reaching past it to grasp at Dorran's face.

Clare was unable to help without her weapon. She crouched, hands running through the mist, and found a rock the size of her fist jutting out of the marshy ground. She wrenched it free and raised it, and was just in time to see the many-toothed hollow returning.

Splinters from her broken bat poked through its face. They pierced its lips, its cheeks, one even jutting out from just under its eye, dripping dark blood over its jaw. Clare, choking, hurled the rock at it. She hit its mouth and flinched as one of the splinters was forced deeper into the creature's throat. It didn't stop coming, though. Clare braced herself and raised her arms.

A blur of motion came from the side. The many-toothed hollow froze as a metal bar ran through its head. Its jaw hung open, twitching. Then the bar was pulled back and the hollow dropped with a gush of dark blood. Beth stood over it. Her blond hair was plastered down by the rain, but fire blazed in her eyes.

Dorran grunted as he threw the four-armed creature to the side. It howled as it hit the ground and scrambled back up, ready to strike. Beth intercepted it. Teeth bared, she swung again and again, using the metal pole to bludgeon and impale indiscriminately. Dorran moved forward, guarding her back, with Clare positioned between them.

The four-armed hollow fell away, limp. It tumbled down the slope until it plunged into the river, where the current dragged it away. Beth stepped back, eyes hard as she scanned the mist.

"Into the bus," she snarled. "More will be coming."

Dorran kept one hand on Clare's back as they ran up the hill. The bus emerged from the fog, the light acting as a beacon.

The camp was still set up; the bus's compartment hung open and the shade cloth was still extended. It meant the bus was anchored to that spot, and they were out of time to pack the equipment away.

Dorran shoved Clare through the open door, then turned. "I can—"

"In," Beth nearly screamed. He jumped after Clare, lips pressed tight together.

Clare was shaking. She held her hands out to Dorran. "I'm sorry—"

"It's all right. You're all right." He reached for her, and she fell into the hug, grateful. "Are you hurt?"

"No, no, I'm fine." His shirt was wet, but she could still feel the warmth of his body underneath. She closed her eyes, just glad to be able to hold him.

The bus door slammed. Clare and Dorran jumped apart.

Beth stood by the driver's seat. Her eyes were wide, but her expression was unreadable. For a second, they were encased in perfect, horrible silence. Then Beth whispered, "Get into some dry clothes."

Clare took a half step forward, a hand held out. "Uh, Beth—"

"Try to be quick. More hollows will be coming. The faster we can be quiet, the sooner they will leave." She turned to the front window, unfastened a clasp, and pulled a thick metal shutter down over the glass.

In the distance, a hollow screamed. Clare backed away from the bus's front, trying to focus through the shivers. She felt sick to her stomach, but she knew Beth was right. They could talk once they made sure they would live through the night.

She reached into the racks above their heads and pulled towels and fresh outfits down. That was one thing Beth had in plentiful supply: clean clothes. Finding a second set to fit Dorran was a challenge, but she managed it.

He hung back, shrouded in darkness near the bus's rear seats, swaying slightly, his breathing ragged. Clare held a towel up to him. She dropped her voice to a whisper that she hoped Beth wouldn't hear. "Are you okay?"

"Yes." He took the towel and the clothes and stepped away from her.

Beth sat in the driver's seat and faced the closed metal shutters. She was soaked, her clothes dripping on the floor, but she made no move to change. Clare wanted to reach out to her but didn't know what to say. Instead, she crept in between a row of seats where she would have some privacy and rushed to change into a drier outfit.

There was no better option, so she hung the wet clothes over the back of the seats, next to the outfits they had shed earlier that day. A muffled noise dragged her attention to the nearest window. Something moved beyond it. Clare gave up on the wet shirt she'd been trying to spread out and silently dropped into a seat.

Fingernails dug into the bus's panels. Teeth clicked. Something heavy scrambled up over the windows and thudded onto the roof.

Clare pulled her legs up underneath herself, her back to the window. To her left, Dorran sat near the rear of the bus. His back was straight and his dark eyes glinted in the low light. To her right, Beth remained in the driver's seat, unmoving. Clare had never felt more isolated. She hugged the new jacket around herself and squeezed her eyes closed.

The hollows picked at the bus for what felt like hours. Their low, curious chattering echoed from every direction. Clare hated the noise, but it never seemed to stop. She clenched her teeth to hold back the scream that wanted to escape.

Occasionally one of the hollows would pass next to Clare's windows. Through the tiny gaps around the boards, she could see gray fingers prying at the structure, picking at the screws, trying to poke through to touch the glass. Once, an eye appeared in the gap. Clare held perfectly still, breath frozen. There was barely any light inside the bus, but she didn't know how well the hollows might be able to see in the dark. The eye rolled in its socket, passing over her, the seats, the ceiling. Then it disappeared, replaced by the too-long fingers once again.

She couldn't speak and couldn't move. Any hint of noise would only make the hollows redouble their efforts. The only thing she could do was sit as still as possible and pray the creatures left quickly. Feet thumped above her head. Something hissed.

An itch started below one of Clare's shoulder blades. She couldn't scratch it. Her eyes burned from tiredness, but she couldn't let them close, or else she might roll over and make noise in her sleep. Sometimes, she tried to watch Dorran. All she could make out in the gloom was the silhouette of his wet hair and sometimes the flash of his eyes. She thought he might be watching her, too.

Eventually, the chattering noise softened. Dorran finally moved. He leaned over to rest his head against the window. The motion was small, but Clare still flinched at the rustle his clothes made. She waited for the hollows to howl, but they didn't.

She turned toward Beth. Her sister remained ramrod straight in the driver's seat. Clare made to rise, to approach her. One of Beth's hands rose, silhouetted, and the finger pressed over her lips. The hollows might have left, but they still couldn't afford noise. Clare nodded and settled back into her seat.

Rain continued to wash over them. The sound was soothing, but Clare thought she could hear distant chattering through it. She leaned her head back and closed her eyes. To the sounds of the rain's tapping and the near-inaudible breathing of her companions, Clare fell asleep.

She didn't know how much time passed before she cracked her eyes open. Her neck was stiff from the angle she'd slept at, but she wasn't as cold as she'd been the night before.

The lights at the front of the bus were on. Beth had left the rest of the van dark, but the warm glow floating out from the driver's seat helped to dispel some of the shadows. The engine was running and the heater on. Beth had said it was a waste of fuel the day before. But now, a gentle warmth radiated around them.

Sunlight came through the gaps in the windows. It was insipid and gray, but she didn't care. It was the first natural light she'd seen in days.

A thick blanket had been draped over Clare. It had been tucked around her chin carefully, the way Beth had done when Clare was a child. Clare slowly, groggily sat up and looked to the back of the bus. Dorran still slept. A blanket had been placed over him, too. Beth hadn't tucked it in, though; instead, she'd tossed it over his form, almost carelessly. Despite that, Clare hoped she could take it as a good sign.

"Morning."

Beth sat in the navigator's seat, her legs propped up on the armrest as she examined the map. Her tone was clipped but not angry.

The last scraps of sleepiness faded from Clare. "Good morning."

"What do you want for breakfast? We have cereal or canned fruit."

Beth kept her attention on the map. Clare licked her lips. *Are we just going to ignore last night? Ignore the fight, ignore that she saw me hugging Dorran? Just...pretend none of it happened?*

The surrealism was too much for her to handle. The question—*What do you want for breakfast?*—was a familiar morning greeting. Beth had to know she was harkening back to old days. But the words were said with none of the cheerfulness Beth had once embodied.

"Um, either is fine. Whatever you have more of."

Finally, Beth looked at her. The expression was strange. There was sadness and resignation but something else mixed into it, too. She folded her map and put it aside. "Hell, we made it through the night. That means today is a good day, and we deserve good food. I'll get you some of both. Wake your friend."

Beth opened the door and stepped outside. Clare hesitated a second, then stood, folded her blanket, and approached Dorran.

He was already awake. He rolled to his feet as she neared him, a silent question dancing in his eyes. *Is everything all right?*

She didn't know how to answer that. She took his hand and squeezed it. Then they paced down the bus's aisle to reach the door.

Cold air gusted around them as they stepped outside. The cloth shelter was still out, but there was no rain to warrant it. Clare blinked in the early morning light. Mist coiled around the hill, moving in slow, lazy bands as weak puffs of air disturbed it. Condensation rose from her mouth with every exhale.

"Shut the door to keep the warmth in." Beth had already turned on the portable cooker and was heating water over it. She nodded. "Then go get yourselves a seat."

"Is it going to be safe to sit out here?"

"Yes. The sun's up. They won't come back into the open unless we make too much noise."

As Clare closed the bus door, she saw the vehicle had taken a beating from the hollows' exploration. The foldable chairs had been knocked over and dragged a dozen feet away. The plywood over the windows was marred with scratches and, in some places, dark blood from where a hollow's nail had been broken off. The wet ground had been churned into mud in a ring around the vehicle, and even its white sides bore more scrapes than Clare remembered.

She went to retrieve the chairs that had been knocked over and, with Dorran, set them up in a circle around the stove. Beth poured the boiled water into three mugs and used a single tea bag to infuse them all. She passed the cups out without saying a word, then slid into her own seat, staring at the steam rising from her drink.

The silence lasted a minute. Clare couldn't bear it. She scuffed her shoes over the ground. "So, um—"

"I'm trying to apologize." Beth looked up from her cup. Tight creases surrounded her eyes, and Clare realized they were rimmed with red. "I've been…having a lot of trouble handling the still world. I'm sorry for the way I've spoken to you. *Both* of you."

Dorran's eyebrows rose. He glanced at Clare, then cleared his throat. "Thank you."

Beth pursed her lips as she shuffled her grip on her cup. "I guess I got caught up in the way things *used* to be. When I could tell you what was best for you, Clare, and you'd listen. But you're not a child anymore. And I can't treat you that way."

Beth saw me with Dorran last night. She thinks I'm building a life without her. She's scared I'm going to leave her.

Clare swallowed around a lump in her throat. "I know. Everything's different since the stillness…including us, I guess."

"Yeah." Beth's eyes drifted from Clare to Dorran. "I guess we all change."

In the distance, a hollow howled in the mountains. Clare flinched at the noise, but it didn't seem to bother Beth. She took a slow breath. "Last night, I wanted to be angry with you for running out into the rain and yelling like that. You were basically a beacon for those hollows. I was furious at first, but then I thought about whose fault it really was—mine, for going into the rain first. If our positions had been reversed, would I have waited quietly for you to come back? I don't think so."

More hollows answered the first call. Even though they weren't close, the noise left Clare uncomfortable.

Beth scratched the back of her neck. "Then, I thought some *more*. Was it really fair to get mad at you for visiting Helexis Tower when I did exactly the same thing?"

Clare struggled to find her voice. "It's okay."

"No. It's not. I'll be better from now on." Beth sighed and swallowed a mouthful of her tea. When she lifted her head, it held a look of deep resignation, as though she dreaded the response to what she was going to say next. "We still have to decide what we're going to do with that bloody USB. After talking about how few true democracies exist in this new world, I should put my money where my mouth is and give you both equal rights. We have three parties here. We vote on what we should do with the stick."

CHAPTER 6.

CLARE'S STOMACH WAS IN knots. She squeezed her mug even though it was hot enough to almost scald the skin. The USB held incredible potential. And the right choice seemed clear to her.

But what was right for the rest of the world wasn't going to be what was best for her own little group. Beth's words from the day before echoed in her mind: *You do whatever you want, then expect other people to clean up the mess.* She deflected. "Beth, you first."

"I don't want to have anything to do with it." Beth shrugged. "Give it away, burn it, bury it, build it a little boat and let it sail down the river. I just don't want that thing on our shoulders."

Clare squirmed. She looked at Dorran. "What about you?"

"You first," he said.

He's going to match my vote.

At any other time, his loyalty would have warmed Clare. In

that moment, though, it filled her with quiet dread. It essentially negated Beth's vote entirely and gave Clare all of the power.

The trip to Evandale would be dangerous. It was days away, and they didn't know what obstacles might stand between them. Dorran was sick. Beth didn't want to go. The best thing for all of them would be to return to Winterbourne and shore up their defenses.

The USB waited in the bus. It seemed insane that something so small and innocuous could change the world. *Save* the world.

Maybe. If Ezra was right. If Ezra's code has any value. If the Evandale station still has people living in it. If they know what to do with the code.

That's a lot of ifs.

She tapped her fingers over the smooth ceramic mug. The cold air was burning her cheeks and nose, but at least her hands were warm. "Dorran, if it were just you and Beth—if I didn't even exist—what would you do? Please. Be honest."

His eyebrow quirked up. He chewed on his thoughts for a moment before answering. "That's a difficult question. If I removed you from the equation, if it were just Beth, myself, and this bus, I suspect our paths would diverge quite soon."

Clare tried not to let her disappointment show. *She doesn't like him. And now he doesn't like her.*

"On my own, I would probably try to take the USB to Evandale," Dorran continued. He shrugged, his eyes on the stove's small flames. "Winterbourne has never held much affection for me. If I were on my own, there would be no point in returning to it. What would I find there? Just loneliness and bad memories. But I would not like to wander the countryside aimlessly, either. The USB would give me a purpose. Something to travel toward, even if I wasn't likely to survive the journey."

"That's grim," Beth said. For the first time, she was watching him with a hint of curiosity.

Dorran chuckled. "She asked for the truth. If Clare were gone, if I were on my own, I would have precious little to tether me here. I would take the USB to Evandale simply to have a purpose."

"All right." Beth leaned back in her seat. "Let me pose you a different hypothetical scenario. Take me out of the picture; it's just you and Clare again. Except, in this case, Clare has no opinions about the USB. None at all. She would be equally happy on the road or going home. What do you do?"

"Then I would travel back to Winterbourne," he answered without hesitation. "I would try to pass the USB on along the way. But my first priority would be to get us home, where we would be relatively comfortable and safe."

"Ha," Beth said.

Clare closed her eyes. *I knew it. He'll match my vote, but deep down, he just wants to get home.*

Dorran continued, "But all of that is ultimately irrelevant."

"How?" Beth narrowed her eyes.

"Clare *does* have an opinion about what we should do. And it is a fiercely strong opinion."

"She *thinks* she knows what she wants," Beth said. "But that doesn't mean it's what's best for her."

He tilted his head, his eyes still on his mug. "I've seen her like this before. When she heard that your air filtration system had broken, she wanted to travel to you, but she tried to give me an equal say in our decision. I could have convinced her to stay at Winterbourne. I could have talked her out of looking for you. But the guilt would have eaten away at her day after day for the remainder of her life. So we left."

Beth's eyes were cold as ice. "And that decision could have killed her. From the sounds of it, it nearly did."

"Some things are more important than simply staying alive."

"That's insanity and you know it."

Clare stared at Dorran. His words clicked into place, and it made her heart hurt. *Some things are more important than simply staying alive.* He'd experienced that firsthand. Living under his mother's tyranny, with no freedom and no future, he had learned that sometimes life itself was not enough.

Dorran shrugged. His expression was mild, but Clare was surprised to see he wasn't trying to hide his emotions. The shutters were gone. "It does not matter. I know how Clare wants to vote, and based on that, I know how *I* want to vote. We will travel to Evandale. You can join us or you can wait for us at Winterbourne. I will give you directions to find it, if you like."

Beth gaped at him. She was sheet white. Furious tremors ran through her, and she squeezed the mug so tightly that Clare was afraid it would crack. "You're enabling bad decisions."

"Decisions that she is entitled to make. Just like it is my choice to travel with her."

Beth stood. She seemed to be fighting to keep some exceptionally harsh words inside of her. She upended the mug over the mud, emptying the last of her tea, then stalked back into the minibus. The door slammed behind her.

Clare felt as though she'd been caught in the middle of a hurricane. She sat, quietly shocked, then turned to Dorran. He sipped his tea. Clare needed a moment to find her voice. "Where did that come from?"

"I realized a few things." He spoke with his usual gentleness, but there was a renewed confidence in his eyes. "Last night, I realized I needed to fight for you."

Clare's mind jumped back to the ring. It was still tucked into the coat's pocket in the bus. "No, Dorran, I promise, I'm not—"

"Shh, do not worry. I understand *that*." He reached over the space between them and took her hand. His voice dropped, and his eyes focused on the ground, and Clare knew he was admitting something painful to him. "I am...not *used* to fighting for things. Once, wanting something was synonymous to being denied it. Fighting for something meant losing, and losing badly. And I am so used to it that it is hard to change."

She pressed his hand, and in return, he ran his thumb across her fingers tenderly, as though savoring the way they felt.

"I value your affection more than anything, but I have held you gently, ready to let you go the moment you wish to be free. But what message does that send to you?" His eyebrows pulled together, and his voice dropped even lower. "How many times can I offer you your freedom before you begin to feel you are not valued? Do you know how intensely, how ferociously you are wanted?"

"I do."

"Not enough." He chuckled, then raised her hand and kissed it, his warm lips lingering over the skin. "I am going to fight for you, my darling. It does not matter if Beth does not want me here; I *will* be here for as long as you allow me."

Emotions struggled through her. She loved Dorran. She also loved Beth. Feeling them pull against each other was more painful than she had ever imagined. The words came out before she could stop them. "Please don't be angry with her."

He looked surprised, then smiled, kissing her hand again. "I am not. Of course I am not. That is the second thing I realized, and it took me until this morning to understand it. Beth and I are two sides of the same coin. We both care about you deeply. We just have different ways of showing it."

Heat rose over her face. "It's just… I don't want her to feel like I'm cutting her out of my life."

"No. She will be coming with us. I'm sure of it." He tilted his head toward the bus. "She can't conceive of staying at Winterbourne without you any more than I can."

"But she's going to hate this. It's a huge risk. And she hates risks more than anything."

"Does she? She drove to Helexis Tower's doorstep based on curiosity. If all she wanted was to find a safe location, she had many opportunities. But it seems to me that safety has only become a priority since she was reconnected with you."

"Oh." Clare blinked. "That's…"

He chuckled and brushed stray hair behind her ear. "I think all three of us are surprisingly similar in that regard. Left alone, with only ourselves to think of, we would all take the USB to Evandale. It is only when others' safety is brought into the equation that we start doubting our choices. Now, would you like to sit outside a little longer, or would you be happy to drink your tea inside? I suspect Beth will want to start moving quickly now that our decision has been made."

Clare shook her head, incredulous. "Since when do you know my sister better than me?"

The bus's door slammed open again. Beth stood in the entryway. She still looked pale, but the anger seemed to be under control. She stared at Dorran's hand, still wrapped around Clare's, then mutely began to pack away the equipment and retract the shade cloth. Dorran rose to help, but she shot him such a murderous glare that he backed up, hands held out placatingly.

It only took a few minutes to pack up their campsite, but as Beth worked, Clare heard another batch of chattering rising through the mist. She shuddered as she folded the chairs.

"Don't worry. They're still a while away." Beth took the last chair and stowed it in the bus's side compartment. "We'll be gone before they reach us."

"Beth, are you okay about"—she shifted her weight uneasily—"everything?"

Beth turned to face her, wearing the most starkly deadpan

expression Clare had ever seen. Then she sighed. "Nope. But the democracy voted, and I'm not going to contest that."

"Right." More chattering rose from the wooded part of the hills. Clare stared toward it, trying to pick out shapes among the mist. "So…"

"Get in the bus." Beth slammed the hatch, and the noise was responded to by a dozen screeches.

Clare leaped into the vehicle with Dorran close behind. Beth stepped in last, shut the door, and slid behind the wheel. "Put your seat belts on. Our first step will be to find a map that shows where Evandale actually is."

CHAPTER 7

DORRAN AND CLARE SAT together near the front of the bus. Beth waited until their buckles clicked, then turned the key and put the bus into gear. As they pulled back onto the road, Clare caught a glimpse of shapes racing toward them through the fog. One hit the front bumper and disappeared under the wheels. The bus bounced, rattling them. Beth showed no reaction as she applied more speed. Then they were back onto clear road, the shapes disappearing behind them.

"Map," Beth said, tossing the folded page to Clare. "It only covers the city and surrounding area. We'll need something more comprehensive to find Evandale. Pick one of the towns to search. Something touristy but not too big."

"Got it." Clare unfolded the map. It took a moment of hunting to find where they were. Then she traced outward from it, following the roads to all of the nearby habitations. She rejected any that were just suburbs with small shopping malls. Then she saw a familiar name. "Hey, what about Little Leura? It's close."

Beth cracked a smile. "I remember that. We drove through there when you were twelve."

"I wanted an ice cream."

"But it was Sunday and the ice-cream parlor was closed."

"So we stopped in at that little service station, and they were having a special on half-gallon tubs…"

"We both gorged ourselves on ice cream on the drive home." Beth laughed. "Oh, that was a good memory. I'm surprised you didn't get sick from eating so much."

"I was too full for dinner." Clare grinned and shuffled the map around so she could read it more easily. "That service station we stopped at had maps. If they're still there, maybe it would be a good place to try."

"Yes. That's a smart find. It was near the edge of town, so we won't have to travel too far into an infested area. And it's just obscure enough that anyone else looking for maps is less likely to have raided it already. Tell me where to go."

"Left turn up ahead."

The town was nearly forty minutes away. Clare alternately traced their progress on the map and watched the changing landscape outside. The mountains were fading behind them. Intermittent fields gave way to uncultivated hills. Once, she saw a hawk circling above. She pointed it out to Beth and Dorran. "I haven't seen many animals since the stillness."

"No." Beth sighed. "The hollows eat anything that moves.

Wildlife is becoming harder and harder to find, but it's a good sign when you do. It means you're in an area with fewer of the monsters."

"Do they travel far?"

"Yes. Sometimes. A lot of them just hang out in the area they once lived in, using the buildings for shelter during the day. They hate moving in the light. If they're going to roam, it will be during the night, or when there's a heavy storm."

As they neared Little Leura, Clare began to recognize some of the scenery. The town was situated in a valley, and the roads ran through light woodland as they led down toward it. Beth slowed the bus as they neared the outskirts of the town. Once, they would have seen a scattering of house lights glowing through the mist. Now, they had to strain to make out rooftops.

"We need to talk about our strategy." Beth coasted along the road, squinting into the trees on either side of them. She evidently found what she was looking for because she abruptly pulled the bus to the left.

A gap in the trees formed a natural tunnel running alongside the road. Beth reversed into it, easing back as far as the bus could go, until branches scraped over the roof and doors, and the main road was no longer visible from the front window. She parked, then turned around in her seat to face them. "Here's the plan. At least one of us is going to get a map. Someone else stays here to guard the bus."

"Okay." Clare unclipped her seat belt. "You don't want to drive closer to the service station?"

"No. Hollows will be drawn to the engine. Our best chance is if we're quiet. With luck, we can slip in and slip out without their notice. I've gotten supplies that way. It works well as long as you don't make any noise and don't accidentally bump into one of them lurking around a corner."

Clare rubbed at her sore neck muscles. "I'm not sure we need anyone guarding the bus, though. It's not like hollows will hang around it if it's empty. We should stay together."

Beth shook her head. "No. We're not guarding from hollows. This close to town, with the sun out, all of those creatures are going to be indoors, not hiding in the woods. The trees are too sparse to give them the cover they want. But we still need to guard the bus from other survivors."

Clare grimaced. She hadn't thought of that as a possibility.

"If anyone finds this bus abandoned, they'll do exactly what I did and take it. The last thing we need is to be stranded out here with no transport, no food, and no shelter."

"Okay. Which of us will stay?"

"I vote Dorran," Beth said. "If anyone finds the bus, there's a fifty-fifty chance how they'll act. Some people are decent. They'll see the bus is occupied, say hello, trade a story or two, and be on their way. Other people will see an opportunity. If they think they have a decent chance of winning in a fight, they'll try to knife you." She turned to Dorran. "Are you any good in a fight?"

"Ah...I suppose?"

"Well, either way, you're intimidating enough that most solo travelers won't even try." Beth shrugged. "He's the best choice to stand guard."

Dorran gave a small nod. "That makes sense to me."

"Clare, you should stay with him," Beth continued. "I've done this kind of supply run before. I know how to avoid the hollows."

"You shouldn't go alone. Especially in the fog. You need someone to watch your back."

"Don't you worry about me. I can handle myself around those monsters."

Clare looked over her sister—the scars on her face, and the scars on her hands—and knew Beth was telling the truth. But a horrible sense of misgiving had solidified in her stomach. "You keep saying we need to minimize risk. *Don't gamble*. Well, going in there alone is gambling. We stack the odds in our favor if we go together."

Dorran touched her shoulder. "Clare, I agree with your sister. You'd be safer in the bus."

She narrowed her eyes. "What was that about letting me make my own bad decisions?"

He half sighed, half laughed. "Well…"

Beth rolled her head, stretching her neck muscles. "Okay, Clare. You can come. But you have to follow my instructions. Deal?"

"Deal."

Beth stood and fished through one of the compartments near the driver's seat. She passed Clare a pair of thick gloves and a wooden mask that looked like it had once been a part of a theater production. The eye holes, already small, had fabric glued over them. When Clare put the mask on, it was like staring at the world through a dark, blurry filter. "This isn't great for visibility."

"Yeah. But you won't need perfect sight. You only need to be able to watch where you're walking." Beth put on her own protection, a beekeeper's helmet, and checked both of them to make sure no skin was exposed. Then she opened a box near the driver's seat and retrieved two objects: a small red stick, which she pocketed, and a large hunting knife.

"Just in case," she said, as she passed the knife to Dorran. "We'll be back within the hour."

Dorran tucked the knife into his jacket pocket, then took Clare's hand. He pressed it gently, his eyes earnest. "Be safe."

"You too." She didn't want to let him go, but Beth was already at the door. Reluctantly, she released his hand, then stepped up behind her sister. Beth, her face inscrutable under the mask, unfastened the lock and pushed the door open, and Clare sucked in a lungful of mist as they stepped outside.

Their boots crunched over dead grass as they retraced the path to the road, staying close to the sparse trees, then began following it as it trended downhill toward the town. As far as Clare could tell, Beth was right. She couldn't see or hear any trace of the hollow ones among the trees. They had parked far enough out from town that nothing living there would hear them. As far as remaining discreet, the plan seemed to be working.

Clare wished she could see more easily. The mask was more stifling than the fencing guard she'd worn when leaving

Winterbourne, and it only took a few minutes for its edges to stick to her face from condensing mist and her own warm breath.

Beth walked at her side, hands thrust into her jacket pockets. "The masks will buy you time, but don't rely on them to keep you safe," she whispered. "If we're spotted by a hollow, we either kill it, silently, or run. If it makes any noises, our time is up, and we get out and try a different town. If we become split up for any reason, we meet back at the bus. Understood?"

"Yes." Clare kept her voice low. The mist seemed to swallow any noise she made, which meant it would mask any creatures around them, as well. She didn't like the way it isolated them.

Winter had set in weeks before, but the days still felt abnormally cold. She hoped they wouldn't have to deal with any more snow on their trip. It could close up the roads within hours, and even the bus wouldn't be able to handle them.

Beth's mask perfectly hid her face. Clare wished she could see her sister's expression. That morning's argument had left her uneasy, and she couldn't shake the feeling. She cleared her throat. "Apparently the thanites were responsible for destabilizing the weather and bringing on early snows. I wonder what they will do to summer. Will it be warmer than usual or colder?"

"My bet is on colder." The path was growing steeper, and Beth kept her head tilted to watch her feet as she navigated the debris cluttering the asphalt. The fog became thicker the farther into the valley they walked. "Not all of the weather's issues would have been caused by those machines. We were spared the worst of it in our colder areas, but I've heard stories of immense fires in the regions that didn't get snow."

"Oh?"

"Yeah. Entire towns and forests burning. People thought it might be a way to kill the hollows, which, technically, it is. But it kills everything else at the same time. The urban fires especially were devastating—all of that plastic turns into black smoke, which chokes the sky. I wouldn't be surprised if a lot of this"— she indicated the pale sun—"is smog from those fires."

Clare shivered. She didn't like to think about what summer would be like with the sun dampened like that.

She tried a different topic. One she'd been curious about since being reunited with her sister. "Did you meet up with many other survivors on your way into the city?"

Beth was quiet for a moment. When she spoke, her voice was oddly devoid of emotion. "I stopped at a couple of safe havens. We traded stories."

"You didn't want to stay at any of them?"

"No."

A note of terseness had entered her sister's voice, and Clare knew she was pushing a line of questioning Beth wanted to leave dead. *This is why she's so hostile. This is why she mistrusts Dorran and why she doesn't want to meet any other humans. Something happened at those safe havens.*

Beth had talked about how democracy was in short supply in the new world. About how friendships counted for nothing. Clare's stomach coiled. She wanted to press Beth for more, but she sensed any further questioning would be rebuffed with increasing sharpness. *Give her space.*

Beth tapped Clare's arm. Buildings were emerging from the fog. She nodded to let Beth know she understood and began stepping more carefully.

If the hollows were staying indoors, then the walls and windows would muffle sound, but even one slip—a rock kicked accidentally or a snapped branch—could end their sojourn in Little Leura.

Clare alternated her focus from the ground ahead to their surroundings. Houses drifted in and out of the smothering white. There was no sign of motion. She squinted at the buildings, searching for names or designs that might be familiar. It had been ten years since they'd stopped in Little Leura to buy a giant tub of ice cream, and her memories of its layout were sketchy.

Beth tugged her sleeve and pointed to the left. Clare squinted through the rolling white. There was a curb. Beyond that, some kind of sign. And…

Gas pumps. The service station.

She moved toward it, but a hand on her chest halted her. Beth backed up as she pulled the red cylinder out of her pocket. Clare realized what it was: a flare. This was one part of the plan Beth hadn't thought to share with her. She backed up, frowning.

The fuse hissed to life. Beth turned, pulled her arm back, and hurled the flare away from the station. It arced through the mist, and bright-red light burst from its end as it bounced across the street a dozen meters away.

It was a clever plan, Clare knew. The flare would act as a distraction: noise to attract any nearby hollows, and light to keep them at a distance until the flare burned itself out.

They backed toward the service station, moving carefully in case hollows emerged from behind them. Clare finally had a chance to see the station properly. Two wrecked cars were crumpled near the door. Empty containers lay across the ground near the pumps. Other survivors had come to the station looking for fuel.

Clare glanced behind them, toward where the fuse hissed in the street. Dark shapes darted around it. None were looking in their direction.

Beth reached the station doors and pulled on the handles. They shifted half an inch, then froze. Something metal clinked on the inside. Chains, Clare thought.

The station's still locked. The stillness must have passed through here before its owner opened for the morning.

Beth backed up. Clare wished she could see her face to know what she was thinking. They stared at the door for a moment, then Beth crossed to the cars. They lay butted up against the pumps, fracturing the concrete around them. Beth crouched and picked up one of the loose concrete pieces.

Clare held out a hand, but it was too late. Beth slammed the concrete into the nearest window. The glass shattered. Clare flinched as the jarring crash of breaking glass echoed around them.

She twisted to look toward the flare. The shadowy shapes had frozen. She thought they might be staring at them.

Beth paid the hollows no attention. She used her elbow to knock panes of glass free from the frame, then jumped through. Glass crunched under her shoes as she landed inside the store. Clare swore under her breath and leaped in after her sister.

The store was dark. Empty fridges lined the back wall. Magazine racks flanked the door, and bare shelves still held stickers advertising discounted snacks. In the rear corner, near the backroom door, stood a rack filled with maps and tourist pamphlets.

Yes.

Clare took two steps toward the maps, then stopped. The hairs rose on her arms. Something was wrong.

The doors had been locked. She'd assumed the station had never opened on the day the stillness spread. But that couldn't be right, she realized. The town was small. The thanites targeted heavily populated areas first. Based on Little Leura's size, it wouldn't have fallen until near midday.

Someone was working in the morning and saw what was happening on the news. They left the store and locked the doors behind them.

She blinked at her surroundings. The magazine rack was overflowing. But the fridges and the food shelves were all empty. The store had been raided for supplies, probably many times, just like how people had tried to get fuel from the pumps.

Except looters wouldn't lock the doors when they left.

Beth yanked her back. A gunshot exploded through the room. The flash came from the back corner, near the maps. The staff room.

Someone lives here.

71

A click. The gun was being cocked. Beth's hands were on Clare's back, forcing her to the window. "Run!"

Clare skidded over broken glass. Through the window, she saw the flare spluttering in the distance. She prepared to leap. Silhouetted shapes appeared in the opening. Bald heads, painted red by the flare's glow. Grasping fingers. She reeled back, trying to stop her momentum. That was the only thing that saved her from the next bullet. It went past her shoulder, so close that she felt a tug as it pierced her jacket sleeve. One of the hollows jerked back as the bullet entered through its open mouth. The others scattered at the gun's crack. Clare leaped, clearing the window, and staggered over the broken curb.

"Run!" Beth yelled again.

There wasn't time to look back. Clare held her body low, but she no longer tried to be stealthy. Gravel crunched under her feet. Her breathing was ragged. She aimed for the brick wall at the edge of the service station's parking lot, knowing it would give her at least a little cover. Beth's footsteps rang out just behind her. The gun went off again. She flinched, but there was no sting of being hit. They were at the wall. She dove around it but didn't dare stop moving. She kept the pace as she dashed past the houses on the town's outskirts and along the road.

Clare's lungs burned. She dragged in gasping breaths. They were all she could hear, mingled with the crash of her feet across the ground and the stress-fueled ringing in her ears. She couldn't hear the hollows. She couldn't hear the stranger. There was no time to look back to see if they were even being followed.

Then the gun cracked again. It was no longer on their heels. In fact, the noise was nearly swallowed by the mist. It sounded like it was still in the service station. Clare finally allowed herself to slow, shaking and gasping as she tried to get oxygen into her lungs. She pressed one hand to the stitch in her side as she turned to face Beth.

"Are you okay—"

The road was still and quiet, save for the rustle of a cold wind shaking the trees.

She was alone.

CHAPTER 8

"NO, NO, PLEASE, NO." Clare moaned as she pulled her mask off and dropped it to the ground. Trees banked both sides of the road. Mist drifted between the trunks, leaving a bright dew on every surface. There was no sound of footsteps. No sign of Beth.

Where did I lose her? I was sure I heard her footsteps just behind me as we rounded the brick wall.

Clare tried to swallow. Her throat was raw and held a bitter taste.

Were the footsteps even Beth's? There were hollows everywhere. Some of them might have been dogging me. What if I left Beth in the service station?

The gun had fired four times. One bullet had grazed Clare. The stranger had been shooting to kill, or at least to maim. Clare wrapped her arms around her chest as terrified shivers rocked her.

No one was coming up the road. No noises came from the

town. Clare looked behind her. The bus was waiting for her just fifteen minutes away. Ten, if she jogged.

If we become split up for any reason, we meet back at the bus.

That had been Beth's instruction. *But what happens if I return to the bus and Beth never shows up? How long do we wait in that little alcove, listening for footsteps that might never arrive? What do we do then? Go on a search party to the town to see if Beth is still there, to see if Beth can be saved?*

"No," she moaned again, digging her fingers into her sides. "Please, Beth, please."

If her sister had been shot, if her sister had been caught by one of the hollows, there would be a limited time to help her. Minutes. Seconds. Clare's heart thumped painfully. She scooped the mask back up and fit it on as she retraced the path she'd just taken.

Her lungs were dry and her legs ached, but she moved as quickly as she dared. If the flare hadn't woken up every hollow in town, the gunshots certainly would have. It was near suicide to use such a loud weapon in the stillness. But then, the person in the service station obviously hadn't been thinking rationally.

We rattled the chains on his doors. We broke his window, breaching his security. We don't know how long he's been alone there, or whether he was starving or had lost his sanity in the new world. Even a normal person can become paranoid under this kind of pressure.

That didn't absolve them of the blame. They'd inadvertently breached his home. Perhaps he'd attached chains to the doors after being looted, but he'd had no way to board up the windows without making noise.

Clare was forced to slow down as she reached the outskirts of town. Her breathing was too loud. Her legs were unstable, and it was harder to place each step carefully. Through the mist, she thought she saw shapes moving between the buildings. The flare had gone out.

Clare retraced her steps around the brick wall. As she moved, she hunted for any sign of a body lying on the ground or spatters of blood or signs of life. All she saw were her own shoe prints in the mud, left during her escape. One pair. Beth hadn't made it that far.

She passed the wall and approached the service station. A glimpse of movement startled her. She froze, breath held, as she watched shapes dance inside the broken window.

Please, no, not Beth.

Clare crept nearer, rolling her feet. The station was full of hollow ones. Wet smacking noises floated toward her through the cold air. Chattering. Hissing. Chewing.

Her ears were ringing. Dizziness rose over her like a wave. She forced herself to take a breath. It whistled through her too-tight throat. The nearest hollows heard. They lifted their heads to stare at her. Clare froze. A second passed. They dropped their heads back down.

Down to eat from their feast.

It was a man. The gun lay useless, forgotten, near the counter. One of his legs was being shared by two of the creatures near the rack of magazines. An arm and shoulder were being dragged away to the store's opposite corner. The rest of the hollows bent over his open stomach and face. The body twitched, and for one horrific second, Clare thought he might still be alive. But it was only the hollows, jostling his body as they tore lumps of flesh free.

I'm sorry. She felt on the verge of being sick. She couldn't afford to be.

Something large bumped her arm. She flinched. Fingers, coming from behind, fell over her shoulder and tightened. A hollow one stepped into her narrow band of vision. Its distended mouth widened, elongated teeth glistening as it stared at her. Clare didn't move. Didn't breathe. The creature locked eyes with her for a second, then the hand moved off her shoulder as it turned toward the thick, sickly smell of blood. It crawled through the open windows. A fresh set of snapping jaws joined the muffled cacophony.

Clare turned. She'd pushed her luck as far as it was ever going to go. Her legs were like paper, ready to crumple, as they carried her back past the brick wall and onto the path that led out of town.

The service station had been drenched in blood. She'd seen the man's head, but not her sister's. *How many limbs were there? Just four? Or were there more?*

"Please, Beth, please." Her tongue felt too heavy to form the words. Her sister had said to meet back at the bus if they ever became separated. She needed Beth to be there. She didn't know what she would do otherwise.

Her unsteady steps lengthened as she exited the town. She was exhausted, but she made herself move faster. Uphill. Through the mud. Toward the little offshoot where Dorran would be waiting. Her vision was blurred, her thoughts a mess. She didn't allow herself to cry. Crying would be an acceptance of grief.

And then she heard Beth's voice. It was full of fire and fear as she screamed, "I don't know!"

Dorran responded, his own voice rising in desperation. "Where did you last see her?"

"I don't know! *I don't know!*"

The cloud of terror lifted from Clare. She dragged in a giddy, disbelieving breath, then pulled off the smothering mask and broke into a run to reach the bus. Before she could touch the door, it was thrown open.

Dorran leaped from the bus, colliding with Clare. She would have been knocked to the ground if he hadn't reflexively grasped her arms. He gaped at her, face pale and eyes wild.

"Hi," Clare hazarded.

Shock flashed through his expression, closely followed by relief. His arms wrapped around her, holding her so fiercely that she struggled to breathe.

"You're all right. You're all right!" He pulled back far enough to search her face. Hands patted over her, touching her arms, her neck, and her back. Then he was kissing anywhere he could reach, peppering her cheeks and forehead with affection.

"Clare!" Beth had followed Dorran out of the bus, her own face pinched with worry. "Where did you *go?*"

"Where did *you* go?" Clare retorted.

Dorran moved back, allowing her a little more space, but kept one arm around her. He was shaking. Clare took his hand and squeezed it. If Beth had been harboring any doubts about their relationship, it would be thoroughly gone by that point.

Beth ran her hands over her face as she exhaled. "I split away from you outside the service station. He couldn't chase two of us at the same time. I thought you'd understand to meet me back here. I just about had a heart attack when I realized you weren't coming."

Clare let herself lean against Dorran as he held her possessively. Her heart hurt from the stress. "I couldn't see you on the road. I was scared you were trapped in the service station."

Horror flashed over Beth's face. "You didn't go back there, did you?"

"I didn't know what else to do."

Beth opened her mouth, then clamped it down and closed her eyes. When she looked up again, she had the anger under control. "Okay. That's all right. You're here now. You're safe. Get into the bus. Let's get on the road before we tempt fate any longer."

Clare let Dorran guide her back into the vehicle. He fussed over her, wrapping a blanket around her shoulders and fastening her seat belt for her. They took the seats closest to the driver's compartment, and Beth watched them through the rearview mirror for a second before she put the bus into gear. Branches scraped over the vehicle's sides as they pulled onto the road, and Beth navigated a tight U-turn to face them away from the town.

Clare felt a tug of regret as the town disappeared behind them, vanishing into the mist and the trees. She blinked and saw the final scene from the service station again. The blood, the hollows, the feast. It was their fault the man was dead. He'd survived there for weeks and might have continued to survive except for their invasion.

We couldn't have known. She could still see the scene on the backs of her eyelids. A dark part of her mind whispered, *Better him than us.*

"What's wrong?"

Clare realized she was still being watched through the rearview mirror. Beth wouldn't know what had become of the man, and Clare didn't feel it was right to put his final moments into her head. In some cases, ignorance truly was a blessing.

She forced herself to smile. "I was just thinking. All of that effort, and we still couldn't get a map."

"Don't be so sure about that." Beth flashed her a grin as she reached into the compartment beside the driver's seat. She brought out a thick, book-like object with a bright-yellow cover.

Clare stared at it, stunned. "You… What…"

"There was one near the front door. I managed to grab it on the way out."

"Beth, you're amazing."

She laughed as she tucked the map back into its slot. "I know. Let's get away from that damn town. We'll have plenty of time to leaf through this thing once we're somewhere more remote."

"Sounds like a plan." Clare tried to settle herself at Dorran's side. She held the smile, but even though the map was a relief, it didn't absolve the guilt. The innocuous yellow book had been bought at a high price.

Beth seemed content, but Clare thought Dorran could feel some of her disquiet. He gently wrapped one arm around her back, holding her close, fingers tracing over her jacket's stitching. He smiled whenever she looked up at him, but the lingering stress was still clear in his eyes.

They drove until the woods turned back into fields. The sun, already distant and cold, drifted in and out from behind patchy clouds.

Beth leaned forward in her seat, searching for a stopping point that met her standards. She evidently found one in a gently sloping hill that meandered down to a river. Tangling fig trees grew in clumps, their roots weaving above the earth like snakes. The ground was solid enough that the bus's wheels didn't chew it into a pulp as they navigated between the trees.

Beth positioned the bus so it was concealed between several clusters of trees, then sighed. "This will do for a while. Clare, do you want to sort something out for lunch? Dorran, get the chairs and cooker out of the hatch. I'll be back in a minute."

Clare rose as Beth pulled an off-white bag out of one of the overhead compartments. "Where are you going?"

"Just scoping around." Beth adjusted her scarf around her neck.

"You shouldn't go alone." Clare followed her to the door, earning herself a glare. "Remember last night? It's too dangerous to split up."

A hint of warning entered Beth's voice. "I'm not going far. I just want to clean up at the river."

"Then I'll go with you."

"No. I need some space, okay?"

As Beth turned away, her scarf swung. One loop slipped down, and Clare caught a glimpse of red. Her eyes trailed down Beth's arm to the white bag she carried. A medical bag, clutched in a hand stained by fresh blood.

Her heart flipped unpleasantly. "You're hurt."

"I'm *fine*," Beth said.

Clare jogged after her, boots sinking into the wet grass as she reached a hand toward her sister. "Was it one of the hollows? What happened? Is it—"

Beth swung back to face her, adjusting the scarf around her neck. "It's none of your business. I'm dealing with it, so kindly do the job I gave you and stop pestering me."

Clare pressed her lips together. Her eyes were burning. She wouldn't let herself cry. "Stop freezing me out. If we're going to survive together, we have to *talk*."

Beth sighed, then closed her eyes, resigned. "A bullet clipped me. I didn't want to tell you because it sounds much worse than it is."

The fear redoubled, clawing at her insides, filling her with ice. "Beth…"

"It grazed my shoulder. Nothing life-threatening, I promise. The thanites will deal with it anyway, right?"

"Doesn't it hurt?"

Beth laughed. "It sure does. But I'm dealing with it. Adrenaline's a hell of a drug."

Clare took a step closer. "Let me help. I can wash it. Or"—she knew this was a risk, but couldn't stop herself—"let Dorran take a look. He trained with a doctor. He's really—"

Beth lifted her hand, her expression cold. "Nope. I wasn't lying. I'm in dire need of some space. If you want to help, get lunch. I'm hungry."

Clare took slow, deep breaths as Beth stalked toward the river. She was trying to calm her racing heart and ease the cold in her stomach. It didn't help much. Slowly, she turned back to the bus.

Dorran had set up the seats and was firing up the cooker. His expression was calm, but there was a tightness around his lips that Clare recognized.

"You heard that, huh?"

He straightened and let the tightness spread to his eyes. "Oh, Clare…"

"It's fine." She tried to smile. "Families argue sometimes, that's all. We're good."

He didn't say anything, but he followed Clare into the bus as she went in search of food.

CHAPTER 9

CLARE PICKED AN EASY meal: pasta with sauce and a can of tuna flaked through it. She cooked the food over the stove, keeping one eye on the tree line Beth had disappeared behind.

She was bleeding enough for it to drip down her arm. It probably soaked into her jacket and scarf, as well. I can't believe I let her drive like that. I can't believe she didn't say anything.

The pasta was cooked. Still, Beth hadn't returned. Clare divided the food into three bowls, trying to keep her hands and mind busy. Still no Beth. She couldn't eat and left her bowl on the dead grass as she began pacing. Dorran stood behind a chair, hands braced on its back, watching her. The awful, sad tightness remained around his eyes. She knew he would help if he could, but at that moment, his concern only made it worse.

Movement came from behind the trees. Clare took a sharp breath, then let it out as Beth stepped into view. Her sister still wore the jacket and scarf, but now a white bandage peeked through at her throat.

"I'm great," she said before Clare could speak. "Just hungry. Pass over my food."

Clare handed her sister a bowl. As she sank into one of the chairs, Beth nodded toward Dorran. "Get the map, would you? Now's a good time to figure out where we're going."

Dorran disappeared into the bus. When he returned, he carried the book close to his side, along with extra blankets to ward off the cold. The three of them scooted their chairs closer together, blankets around their shoulders, with Clare holding the map in the middle. Beth ate while she peered over Clare's shoulder. Dorran remained quiet, but curiosity lit his eyes as Clare flipped to the map's directory.

The map was an old-fashioned model like Clare's parents had used before mobile phones and GPS simplified traveling. Hundreds of pages each held a segment of the map, tiny numbers on their sides indicating which pages they connected with. Clare ran through the list of suburbs. She found Evandale and turned to page 273.

As far as she could tell, it was a small suburb. Two main streets ran through it, with a couple of small side roads branching off. There was no sign of any kind of major research center.

"The map might be outdated," Clare said. She had to fight to not sound defensive.

Beth didn't seem bothered. "Or the research station could be omitted for security reasons. Go to the overview map. I want to see how far away it is."

Clare flipped to the book's start. A large map represented most of the country, with only the major roads visible. It was divided into a grid with a small number for each corresponding page. She found 273, then traced back to the largest mark on the map, the city they'd come out of.

"Hmm." Beth scratched the back of her neck. "Well, it could be worse."

Clare searched for other locations she knew in an attempt to get a sense of scale. "We might be able to make the trip in a single day—"

"If the freeways were clear." Beth tapped a finger on the map and traced it up to Evandale. "We'll need to take the back roads. It'll be slower but safer."

Clare knew Beth was right. Freeways would be too much of a gamble. The rural roads could be hit-and-miss, as well, but at least they presented less chance of becoming cornered as hollow ones descended on them.

Still, she hated seeing how much their path had to diverge. Using the rural roads would bump the journey out to at least three days. The USB in her pocket felt like it weighed a ton.

Beth thinks it's wishful thinking. She thinks the USB won't be able to change anything. But we have to try, don't we?

They washed their plates in the river, then packed the equipment back into the bus. Beth resumed her place in the driver's seat with Clare and Dorran sitting in the closest row of seats. Clare held the map, leafing through pages as they crossed the countryside.

At first, they talked. Clare answered Beth's questions about the time she'd spent at Helexis Tower. Clare tried to ask her own questions about Beth's journey, but her sister was quick to change the subject back to Clare's encounters.

The road led them through a hilly region around the mountains' foothills. As a bridge between two major towns, it was dotted with vehicles. They passed vans, cars, and even a taxi. Most of the vehicles had either parked off the side of the road, or been pushed there by other travelers. Most looked as though they had been looted. Some had doors and trunks hanging open; others had windows smashed and tires removed.

As they skirted around the mountains, Clare caught sight of motion in the distance. She leaned forward and squinted. "Is that someone else driving toward us?"

"Yep," Beth said. Her face was emotionless.

"Should we—"

"We're going to pass them by. We don't need anything from them, and I won't let them take anything from us."

Clare chewed her lip as she settled back in her seat. The car, a silver sedan, was smaller than their vehicle, and scratches along its sides told her it had been through hollow-heavy areas. It slowed as it neared them but didn't try to stop. Beth kept her bus on one side of the road, the stranger moved to the other side, and they passed.

Clare craned to see the occupants. The glimpse lasted no longer than a second, but the image froze in her mind like a snapshot. A man drove. His stubble was developing into a beard and a healing cut ran through one of his eyebrows. He gave a small nod of acknowledgment as he passed them. In the passenger's seat was what looked like a hiking backpack—his, or taken from someone less lucky, Clare couldn't guess. Two children slept in the back seat. They couldn't have been older than six. The younger girl had a bloody patch fastened over her eye.

Something small, golden, and shiny had been suspended from the rearview mirror by a ribbon. Clare's mind blanked on what it might be. As the stranger's car disappeared behind them, she finally made the connection. A wedding ring.

Who are they? And where are they going? Maybe they had been camping when the stillness hit. Maybe the father was now driving, searching everywhere, desperate for a place that would be safe enough for his children. Somewhere they wouldn't be hurt again.

"Focus, Clare," Beth called.

She jolted and quickly flipped through the map to follow their path.

The afternoon hours passed peacefully. Their path inevitably carried them through towns. Clare had been careful to direct them toward smaller hamlets, and the caution paid off. The streets were wide and relatively clear of debris. Beth kept the car at a steady speed as she passed through. Shapes moved around the buildings, but they passed through the towns before anything could try to slink into the light.

Dorran fell asleep leaning against the window. Clare rose as quietly as she could and fetched a blanket from the overhead compartments, then draped it over him. Beth had turned the heater off before lunch, and the bus was nowhere near as warm as it could have been. Dorran shifted, eyebrows pulling together, then relaxed again.

"Hey," Clare whispered, approaching Beth's side. "Do you want to swap? You must be tired, too."

"Clare, I love you, but if I gave you the wheel, there is no way in hell I could sleep." Beth flashed her a smile.

Clare ignored the jab. "Isn't your arm hurting?"

"Yeah. And it'll hurt whether I sit here or back there." Beth drove one-handed, leaning her right arm on the armrest. "At least this way I have something to keep my mind busy. Ish."

The road ahead was straight, clear, and entirely void of stimulus. Empty, brown fields bridged either side, with gray mountains rising on their left. Clare thought she would be at risk of nodding off if she had to stare at it for as long as Beth had.

But as she settled back at Dorran's side, she realized Beth wasn't driving passively. Her sister's eyes were constantly roving, moving over the mirrors, across the fields to either side, and scanning the road ahead.

Clare suddenly understood what she'd meant about not being able to sleep. She wasn't just driving; she was on watch, at high alert, constantly looking for threats. And she couldn't stop.

The dashboard read nearly three in the afternoon by the time the first fleck of sleet hit the windshield. Clare had gotten used to how cold the bus was and, wrapped in layers of jackets and insulated boots, had barely felt the shift in temperature. But as she sleepily blinked at the view, she realized the world was changing around them.

The mountains had been gray just hours before. Somehow, without her even noticing, their caps were starting to turn white. The sky had taken on a bitter shade of slate. Lightning crackled across the horizon. Clare sat up in her seat, suddenly intent. "Beth."

"Yeah. I see it." Beth didn't change their speed. Her face remained as expressionless as before.

"Do you have a plan for what we'll do if it starts to snow?"

"Of course. We'll look for somewhere to bunk down. A shed, probably."

"Can't we pull over and stay in the bus?"

"Not without risking carbon monoxide poisoning, which is what we'd be facing if the snow coated us. We need proper shelter."

Clare's anxiety returned with a vengeance. She joined her sister in watching their surroundings, alternately staring at the windshield ahead, peering through the gaps around the windows to either side, and eyeing the clock. The sun was failing quickly. As the last rays battled through the clouds, the snowstorm descended on them.

The bus didn't have snow tires. Beth drove well, but she could only mitigate the slipping, not stop it entirely. Clare clutched the edges of her seat. Abruptly, the bus lurched off the road and into a field. Clare gasped.

"Relax." Beth's voice was just as calm as ever. "There's a building up ahead. We'll stay there."

Clare had to fight to see through the snow. Ahead, a blocky structure emerged from the blur of white. A farmhouse, she thought. The windows were dark and no smoke rose from the chimney, but the structure, positioned between several old oak trees, at least seemed intact. She prayed it would be uninhabited.

Clare gently shook Dorran's arm to wake him. He'd been in a deep sleep and it took him a moment to emerge. As he sat upright and squinted through the windows, the tiredness fled from his eyes. "Oh."

The house was near the top of a hill. Behind it were solid wooden fences that must have been used to house cattle before the stillness. The bus wheels skidded on frozen mud as Beth pushed it up the incline. They crested the worst of the rise and slowed as they neared the dirt parking area ahead of the house's front door. Beth pulled on the handbrake and turned the engine off.

"It looks unoccupied, but that doesn't necessarily mean it's empty." She drummed her fingertips on the wheel. "If there are humans inside, we'll leave. If they're hollows, we'll kill them. Agreed?"

They both nodded. Beth, one eye on the front door, rose and began to sort through the storage compartments. She tossed them each an extra jacket, then dished out weapons: a broom handle sharpened into a stake for Dorran, a crowbar for Clare, and Beth carried the piece of rebar she'd used the previous day. They gathered at the bus's front. Beth glanced over them, checking that they were protected well enough, then pulled the bus's door open.

CHAPTER 10

CLARE HAD THOUGHT SHE was prepared for the cold, but she was still shocked by its severity. She clenched her teeth as ice scraped across her cheeks and tangled in her hair.

The snowfall was already deep enough to leave depressions when they stepped in it. Clare squinted up at the house. It wasn't luxurious, but it was large for a country home. Beth pulled her scarf over the lower half of her face as they approached the front door. She tried the handle. It turned, but the hinges were stiff, and she had to put her shoulder into it to get it unjammed.

They stood on the front step while the door swung open. They each held their weapons at the ready, squinting to see through the gloom. Nothing moved. Beth lowered her rebar a fraction as she stepped over the threshold. Clare exchanged a glance with Dorran, then followed.

The structure creaked as winds tore around it. A hallway stretched ahead, winding to the right, into what had to be bedrooms and bathrooms. To their left was a dining room. Its floor was speckled with snow coming through a large broken window. To their right was a living room with fabric couches and a fireplace in the back wall.

As she stepped deeper into the house, a familiar smell filled Clare's nose. Sticky. Musty. Oily. The hairs across the back of her neck rose as she recognized the scent of hollows. It permeated the new world, even clinging to their bus, but it was stronger in the farmhouse. "There's something in here."

Dorran took Clare's empty hand and squeezed tightly. Beth stared along the hallway, toward where the wood flooring and wood walls vanished into shadows. "Scout the house," she whispered. "Keep your backs to a wall."

They stayed as a tight group. Dorran used his stake to nudge a door open, revealing a bedroom, its walls painted in bright blues. The next room along was filled with dark colors and two electric guitars. Then a bathroom, its medicine cabinet standing open. The laundry had a pile of clothes in a basket waiting to be washed. Then, finally, they reached the room at the end of the hall.

The door had been left closed. An elastic cord was fastened from the door handle to a hook on the wall, effectively locking it from the outside. The stench was stronger.

Dorran moved forward first, but Beth put out an arm and swept him back. She unhooked the elastic rope. It made a rough snapping noise as it sprang free. She turned the handle, raised her rebar, and pushed the door inward.

The master bedroom's shutters were drawn. Only thin slats of light were allowed in, and they ran along the floor and up the walls like prison bars.

That's what this was. A prison.

A body crawled toward them. Broken arms dragged across the floor. A filthy nightgown hung from narrow shoulders. Bones strained against emaciated flesh at every angle. The head lifted, long strands of thinned hair sticking to a spit-dampened face, and the hollow hissed at them.

Clare took a reflexive step away, but she didn't need to. The hollow's head snapped back as a shackle around its neck pulled taut. The chain ran to the corner of the four-poster bed, where a thick padlock hung, key still embedded.

"I'll take care of this one," Beth said. She shifted the bar into her left hand as she stepped forward.

Clare couldn't tear her eyes away from the woman. She was thoroughly and entirely removed from her humanity, but hints of her former life still hovered around her like ghosts. A delicate gold necklace hung around her neck. Her nails had been almost entirely torn off, but the two that remained had scraps of a pastel-pink nail polish.

Beth noticed her staring and frowned. "If you're squeamish, wait outside."

"No. It's not… I just…" She stared into the hollow's eyes. The hollow stared back.

Dorran's arm moved around her shoulders and gently guided her back into the hallway. "It's a kindness," he murmured. "She wouldn't have wanted to be like this."

Clare tried to nod. She *knew* that. But the reality never felt as simple as her mind wanted it to be. It hadn't been simple at Marnie's. It was no easier now.

A loud *thwack* sounded from the room behind her, and she flinched. The noise was followed by another and another, until it no longer sounded hard, but wet. The hissing chatters fell quiet. A moment later, Beth stepped out to join them, using a T-shirt she'd taken from the closet to dry her rebar. She nonchalantly kicked the door closed behind them. "Did we miss anywhere? I don't want to be woken by any surprise guests at two in the morning."

"I think that was it," Dorran said.

"All right. You'll help me seal off that broken window somehow. Clare, build us a fire. Once we have a bit of heat in this place, we'll get some food."

Clare felt as though she should do or say something more. They had just ended a life. It didn't seem right to brush past that.

It was a hollow. You've killed them before. You will probably kill more before you get home. You can't grieve for them.

The vulnerable hollows were always the worst, though. The aggressive ones—the ones that hunted and howled and were consumed by hunger—they were easier to kill. It was purely a matter of survival. The hollow in the bedroom hadn't been a hunter, though. It had barely been able to crawl.

Dorran was watching Clare. His strong features were full of quiet concern, one hand lingering over her shoulder in case she needed support.

Both of her companions were more adept at handling the new world than Clare. She was too quick to grasp for empathy. She let it hurt her.

Dorran held compassion. He didn't enjoy killing the hollows, but he could see it as what it was: necessary. More importantly, he could separate what the hollows had become from what they once were.

Beth was something different. *Callous*, the voice in the back of her mind whispered. *She never used to be callous.*

As they reached the front hallway, Beth and Dorran went right, toward the dining area and the broken window. Clare turned left, following the open archway into the living room. Cozy, well-used chairs and a rugged coffee table were spaced around the fireplace. The metal box was less elaborate and less grand than Winterbourne's stone hearths, but it would be enough to warm them.

The fireplace hadn't been touched in a long while. Dust coated the handle. Clare opened the glass door and coughed as she inadvertently disturbed layers of soot. The nearby wood bracket held several logs, and a box of matches waited beside it, but there was no kindling. Clare muttered under her breath. She picked through the logs, trying to work out if there was a way to break one of them into smaller pieces, but all she achieved was embedding a splinter into her palm. She sucked on it as she rocked back onto her heels.

Behind her, Beth and Dorran were in the dining area, arguing over the broken window. Stark-white light fell across them, and Clare felt an unpleasant shock. Dorran looked gaunt. The bus had been dim enough to disguise it, but standing in the harsh light, Clare couldn't believe she'd missed it.

Beth was directing Dorran to drag one of the china cabinets across the room. Dorran let it go, and the plates inside rattled. Frustration lay across his features in hard angles. "I'm telling you, the windowsill—"

"It'll fit. Just push it over."

"We need to seal the hallway instead—"

Clare bit her lip. She didn't know how the two people she loved the most could be so incompatible, but Beth and Dorran seemed to bring out the worst in each other. The argument was swelling, but she had the awful feeling that any interruption would only make it worse.

We need a fire. And that needs kindling. What here is flammable?

She turned in a slow circle and stopped facing the bookcase. Her heart sank. Before the stillness, reading had been one of her favorite pastimes. Setting books on fire felt like heresy.

But they needed warmth if they wanted to get through the night. They did not, technically, need the books. Especially not when there were now many more libraries than library owners. If she wanted to collect books, she could fill the bus with armfuls every time they passed a house.

That didn't make her feel any better. Clare leafed through the bookcase, trying to choose volumes that she didn't care about as deeply. She couldn't touch any of the classics. There was an assortment of nonfiction on the lowest shelves, and Clare picked through them to pull out volumes without any plastic covers or laminated pages. She settled on a self-help book, a biography, and a physics textbook. She still felt compelled to apologize as she tore pages out of them, scrunched them up, and used the matches to set them alight.

Something heavy scraped behind her, and Clare turned to see the china cabinet and a second bookcase had been used to seal off the opening to the dining room entirely. It looked like Dorran had won the disagreement. The exertion hadn't been kind to him, though; he was pale as he leaned against the archway, breathing too quickly.

"How's the fire looking?" Beth thrust her hands into her jacket pockets as she came up behind Clare.

"Getting there." Thicker and thicker portions of the books went over the infant flames, gradually growing the blaze and heating the metal.

Beth made a faint noise of approval. "Good. Don't let it go out. Dorran and I are going to bring some food inside, then I'll see if this place has its own water supply so I can wash up and make us some dinner."

As Clare hovered over the flames, coaxing them to catch on a piece of wood, the door behind her opened and slammed repeatedly, each time inviting in a gust of icy air. Dorran and Beth dropped armfuls of supplies onto the coffee table, then Beth stalked into the hallway to look for water.

Dorran crouched down beside Clare. "Can I help?"

"Thanks, but I think I'm good." Clare frowned at the creases around his eyes. "You look tired. If Beth is bossing you around too much—"

He chuckled. "She's fine. Just stubborn."

"Isn't she?" Clare gently bumped his shoulder. "Almost as stubborn as me, huh?"

"Mm. Though I would much rather face off against you."

"Oh yeah?"

His eyes were warm as he smiled down at her. "You are so pretty when you are angry."

"What? No. No I'm not." She narrowed her eyes in a mock glower to demonstrate.

His smile only grew. "You are. You become full of fire and life. If I loved you less, I might provoke you more, just to enjoy it." He pressed his lips together as he glanced toward the hallway. "When Beth is angry, I fear I am about to have my head bitten off."

Clare laughed, but there was a little too much truth in his observation.

Dorran ducked closer to kiss her cheek, then gently pressed her shoulder before moving away and settling in one of the fireside chairs. Clare fed an extra slab of the biography under the log to make sure the fire wouldn't go out, then rose to look for blankets.

The storm whipped frantic flecks of snow against the windowpane, and Clare's breath sent up plumes of condensation. Beth and Dorran had brought food and cooking utensils inside, but no cloths. Clare guessed they must have planned to use what the house offered. She returned to the hallway. Sounds of splashing water came from the bathroom, telling her the house had tank water. Clare tapped on the door. "Beth? Everything all right?"

"Yep." The word came out shaky. The water must have been freezing.

"I could look at your cuts—"

"Nope."

Clare was tempted to try the handle regardless but forced herself to step back. *Be patient. She needs more time to open up.*

She found a linen cupboard partway along the hallway. It was stocked with blankets, towels, and cleaning supplies. Clare pulled down one blanket and saw it featured brightly colored rocket ships. She swallowed thickly and put it back, instead pulling out a thick, gray blanket that was sized for an adult.

As she moved back down the hallway, she noticed a piece of paper nearly hidden under a side table. Clare shifted the blanket under one arm and bent to pick it up.

From what she could tell, it had come out of a notebook. Perforations ran down one side and blue lines scored the white. A dark pen had been used to write a brief, sloppy message.

Mum,

I've gone to get help. Don't try to leave the house. I'll be back soon.

I didn't mean to hurt you. I'm sorry.

Josh

Clare slowly turned to look at the bedroom at the end of the hall. The note wasn't recent. Water had stained one corner, near some kind of smear that looked like blood. The paper had curled around the edges from exposure to moisture in the air. It must have been there for weeks.

He must have woken on the morning of the silence to find his mother had been transformed. He chained her up, to keep her safe, to keep himself safe. And he went to try to get help.

Clare's eyes stung as she reread the note. She hadn't seen anywhere in the house that could be airtight. Josh must have been infected by the thanites, too. But unlike his mother, he'd kept his mind.

People with AB-negative blood are protected against the insanity. That's what Ezra had said at least. Josh might have woken up late that morning, after his mother had already begun to change. He wouldn't have understood what was happening. Inside the silent zones, there was no TV, no phones, no way to contact anyone. He restrained his mother where he thought she would be safe. Then he'd left the key in the lock and wrote her a note in case her mind returned.

Clare wondered how far Josh might have gotten before his own body started to change. Maybe it had only been in the early stages for him, before it was easy to notice. He'd gone for help.

Maybe he went to his neighbors or drove into the nearest town and fell to the hollow hordes.

Or maybe he'd survived long enough to realize what was happening. To see his own body begin to deform, to watch the people he'd once called friends turn into mindless, soulless monsters. To realize there was no help for his mother. No help for *anyone*. Maybe he'd gotten back into his car and driven to the nearest lake, where he could end his existence and escape the all-consuming despair.

Clare's hands shook as she slipped the paper back under the side table. There was no use keeping it. Beth wouldn't care. Dorran would be sad but resigned. The intended recipient was now dead. The note wouldn't matter to anyone in the new world.

Her eyes burned as she crept back to the living room. Dorran was already asleep, curled up in the chair, one arm hanging over the edge. The fire bathed him in a warm glow but enhanced the shadows around his features. She draped the blanket over him, taking care to tuck it in, then kissed the cool skin on his cheek before settling back down in front of the blaze.

The logs had caught, and Clare used the poker to nudge them around into a better arrangement. Even with the layers of thermal jackets, she still felt cold.

A floorboard creaked behind her. Clare turned. Beth stood in the hallway opening, a towel around her wet hair. She still wore the familiar thick jacket and scarf, hiding the injury on her shoulder. The corners of her mouth twitched up, then dropped back down as her eyes drifted to Dorran. "We need to talk."

Clare thought she knew what was on her sister's mind. She didn't feel ready for it.

"He's sick."

Clare squeezed her hands together. "I know."

"And he's not getting better."

"He just needs rest."

Beth let her breath out slowly as her eyes drifted back to Clare. "He's had rest. I don't think any more will fix this."

Clare tried to swallow, but it was as though her muscles had forgotten how to work. Perspiration glistened on Dorran's face. He wasn't overheated, though. Anytime Clare touched him, he felt cold. His color was bad. Even asleep, his breathing was still labored.

She'd tried to tell herself that he just needed time. That whatever Ezra had done to him would be temporary, that a long sleep and some good food would return his strength. But it had been two days. And Beth was right. He was growing worse.

Dorran's hand hung over the chair's side, and Clare took it. He didn't respond. Clare blinked furiously, trying not to let any of the building tears spill over as she looked up at her sister. "What can we do?"

CHAPTER 11

BETH'S FEATURES WERE SHADOWED as she leaned against the archway. "I don't have any antibiotics. But we can try to find some."

Clare looked up from Dorran's gaunt face. "Will antibiotics help?"

"No idea. But we can try." Beth shrugged off the doorway and sauntered into the room. She took the second chair, the one opposite Dorran. "I don't know anyone with medical expertise. Short of that and failing an obvious cause, antibiotics are probably the best we can do for him."

"What about the research facility? They might have doctors on staff—"

"Don't count on it. There's a wide gap between theoretical medicine and practical. If it's not an active hospital, I doubt they'll be much help." Beth chewed on her lip. "Evandale is days away as well. Our best chance is finding something local. I already checked this house's medicine cabinet. If it had anything stronger than eye drops, it's already been cleared out."

The fire crackled behind her, but Clare couldn't feel its warmth. She tucked her knees under her chin. "Where's the best place to look for antibiotics?"

"There's a town nearby, right?"

Clare struggled to remember the map. "Yeah. It shouldn't be more than an hour away."

"Then we'll try there. The pharmacies will be emptied. Those and the groceries stores would have been the first to go to looters. But we can try some houses, maybe get lucky."

"Okay. Okay. We…we'll do that." Clare looked toward the window. Ice, funneled against the house by ferocious winds, plastered over the glass and hid the outside world. "It's not safe to go now, is it?"

"No. The snow's too thick to drive in. We'll have to wait until the storm is over." Beth sighed and curled deeper into the chair. "At least, in this weather, we only need to worry about hollows, not other survivors. Let's have some dinner and get some sleep. Tomorrow might be better."

It was a somber, subdued night. Beth cooked canned stew over the fire while Clare scouted the rest of the house for anything that might help them. She found candles in a cupboard and brought them back to light the living room, along with more blankets from the linen closet.

As night set in, Clare stopped by the bathroom. Beth had said she'd already searched it, but Clare couldn't stop herself from double-checking. The medicine cabinet was open, with a bottle of eye drops, a manicure set, and lotion the only remaining goods. She still scoped through the rest of the room, opening the cupboards under the sink and sorting through the shampoo bottles.

The bathroom trash caught her eyes as she passed it. It was full of scraps of cloth and used bandages, all stained red. Clare stared, horrified. Beth's injury had to be worse than she was letting on.

Dorran needs help. Beth's hurt. And we don't know how long the storm might last.

It had raged around Winterbourne for weeks. Clare tried to imagine what they would do if they were trapped in the house for that long. She wasn't sure they even had enough food to survive.

The idea haunted her, and instead of returning to the living room, she followed the hallway into the kitchen.

Freezing air snapped at her, gusting through the dining room's open window. She squinted to protect her eyes as she searched the cupboards. They were almost completely bare. All she found were sponges, food coloring, and an empty bag of oats.

Someone raided this house after all. She closed the cupboards and leaned her forehead against the wood as she tried to calm the panic rising through her.

Clare woke Dorran for dinner. He didn't talk much and barely ate, his bowl still half-full when he put it aside.

"Sorry," he mumbled at Clare's worried look. "Just tired."

"Sure. Get some rest." She adjusted the blanket over him as he drifted under.

Beth lounged in the second chair, stirring her own food absentmindedly. Her expression was unreadable. "You should sleep, too, Clare. Dawn will come sooner than you expect."

The storm continued to batter the home during the night. Clare, sleeping in a nest of blankets by the fire, woke repeatedly as windows rattled and wood creaked. The house still smelled like dead hollow. Disturbing dreams threaded through reality, leaving her clammy and frightened every time she woke.

Dorran didn't stir through the night. Whenever Clare looked at her sister, she saw Beth was still awake and staring into the fire. The dancing light played over her sharp features, lighting her eyes and building shadows around the scars.

By the time morning's light began to pierce through the snow-caked windows, Clare felt no better rested. She sat up, groggy, and rubbed sleep out of her eyes with one hand and clutched the blanket around herself with the other. It was cold.

"Morning," Beth said. She stood at the window, hands in her jacket pockets, staring into the haze of white beyond. She'd pulled her scarf high around her throat to ward off the chill.

The fire was down to embers. Clare looked at the wood basket, but it was empty. Beth must have fed logs into the fire during the night. Clare turned to Dorran's chair. It was empty. She felt her heart skip a beat. "Beth? Where's Dorran?"

Beth only shrugged.

A loud cracking noise came from deeper in the house. Clare threw the blanket aside. Her legs were stiff and unsteady as they carried her into the hallway. She caught herself on the bookcase, trying to orient herself as to where the noise had come from. It was repeated, echoing out of the first bedroom. Clare crossed to it in two steps and shoved the door open.

Dorran bent over a wooden rocking chair. The back had been broken, and as she watched, he placed his boots on one of the slats and stomped down until it cracked.

"Hey, there you are. What's happening?" The room was colder than the main part of the house. Clare shuddered and folded her arms around herself.

Dorran's breath misted in the air as he turned toward her. His smile seemed horribly strained. "Ah, Clare. I didn't mean to wake you. We just needed some more wood for the fire."

"Don't worry about that. I can take care of it." Clare crossed to him and threaded her arm around his, trying to pull him back toward the door.

He didn't budge. Instead, he placed one hand over hers. "I don't mind. It's good to be useful."

"You need to rest."

He chuckled and tugged her a fraction closer so he could kiss the top of her head. "I'll rest later."

Her throat ached. She hugged him fiercely. Even through the coats, he felt thinner than she remembered. A deep fear froze her insides, making it impossible to think or to speak. She just held him.

Dorran ran his fingers over her hair. He made soft humming noises as he rocked her. "Don't be afraid. This will be all right."

She leaned back to read his face. His eyes had seemed dull

before, but now they appeared too bright. Glassy, even. She touched the side of his face, where the skin had turned gray.

He smiled. "You have Beth now. She'll keep you safe."

Clare shook her head furiously. "Please. Come back to the fire. We can take care of the wood later."

"All right. Let me just get this." He bent to gather the pieces he'd broken. Hacking coughs shook him. He turned away, bracing one arm on the wall as his body convulsed. Clare held a hand out to him, petrified in her helplessness. When Dorran straightened again, he was shaking. His face held something she wasn't used to seeing in him. Fear.

Clare grabbed his hand and hauled him back into the hallway, toward the living room. He tried to speak, but she just held up a hand. She didn't let go until he was in front of the fire, then she pushed him down into his chair.

"Sit there," she said. She tried to put force behind her words, but they still broke. "Beth, get him some more food. I—I'll get the firewood."

Hot tears streaked down her face as she jogged back to the spare bedroom, to the chair Dorran had been dismantling. Silent tears dripped from her chin as she clenched her teeth, eyes squeezed closed and shoulders trembling. Then she swiped her sleeve across her face, drying it, and picked up the firewood.

Snow continued to fall all through that day. Once an hour on the dot, Clare crossed to the window and stared into the expanse beyond their house. The storm had passed, at least, but the white flakes continued to blur the landscape and stick against the panes.

Their minibus waited on the lawn, less than a dozen paces away, but it was half-hidden under a dense layer of white.

A somber atmosphere had fallen across the house. They were all feeling the isolation and the imprisonment. It shortened tempers. Clare found she had to constantly watch her tongue. Beth rarely spoke; when she did, it was to give commands. Dorran was the quietest of all of them. He slept sometimes. When he was awake, he watched the fire with glazed eyes. Several times, he tried to rise to fetch something or do some kind of work. Clare didn't let him leave. He didn't argue with her, but she could see in his eyes that he hated being tethered to the fire. He wanted to feel useful.

Clare tried to pass the time by reading. The house had plenty of books at least. When she'd read so long that a migraine throbbed behind her eyes, she gave up and instead stared at the ceiling as she counted seconds in the back of her mind.

They gradually worked through the house's wooden furniture to keep the fire alive. Luckily, the family hadn't been a big fan of paints or varnishes. The dining table kept the fire going through the evening and night.

Dawn on the second day brought rain. Clare stirred out of her sleep, faintly aware of the heavy tapping across the roof. The noise had followed her in her dreams, making her feel hunted, her mind bringing up images of hollow ones crowding around her and tapping on her meager defenses. It took a second to separate reality from her nightmares. When she did, she bolted upright.

"Yes," Beth said, seeing the look on her face. She stood at the window, the trails of rain reflected like a map across her features. "We can risk the roads again."

Dorran was already awake and sitting up in his chair, one leg pulled underneath himself, holding a mug. Heavy-lidded eyes watched the fire. "We should wait for the snow to clear further. There's no guarantee the temperature won't drop again, and we're safer trapped here than trapped on the road."

"I want to go today," Clare said. Her heart thundered. "Right now."

Beth chewed her lip. Her eyes moved from Dorran to the view outside, and Clare knew she had to be calculating the risk. She clenched her fists at her side. Dorran needed medicine. An extra day waiting inside the house could be a day too long. Beth lifted her eyebrows, then shrugged. "Okay, I vote we go, too. Democracy wins. Pack up and get ready to move out."

Any other day, Dorran might have argued more. He looked like he wanted to. Instead, he just sighed and said, "Very well."

There wasn't much to collect. Both Clare and Beth had scouted the house for useful supplies, but they hadn't found much that the minibus didn't already have. They bundled their clothes and a few extra blankets up, packed up the last of the food, then faced the door.

Clare sent one final look back at the door at the end of the hall, where a lost son had chained his mother to her bed while he went to get help. She knew it was just one tragedy in a world that now held billions of them. That didn't make it hurt any less. Then Beth opened the door, and all of Clare's thoughts were snatched away by the icy wind.

CHAPTER 12

THEY JOGGED TO THE minibus, heads bowed against the downpour. Its headlights flashed as Beth unlocked it, seeming strangely cheerful for the environment. Clare was shivering by the time they got inside and shut the door behind them. Beth slid into the driver's seat, and Clare took her familiar place in the closest passenger row.

"Can we have the heater on?" she asked.

Beth's voice was emotionless as she turned the key in the ignition. "It wastes fuel."

Dorran settled at Clare's side. His posture was an imitation of relaxation. Even though he leaned back in the seat, he'd set his jaw and clasped his hands to hide how much he was shaking.

"I'm sure we can afford it for a few minutes," Clare pressed. "Just to take the chill off—"

"I said *no*." Beth's voice developed a vicious bite.

Clare bit her tongue. The incarceration was to blame, she knew. It had whittled all of their tempers down. Dorran touched her arm, gentle, a wordless question over whether she was okay, and she made herself smile. She wouldn't let it hurt her. She wouldn't let their little group tear itself apart with infighting.

Beth put the van into gear. The wipers' muffled thumps floated around them as they worked on clearing the view. As she pulled onto the muddy, snow-choked driveway, Beth glanced into the rearview mirror. Her eyes tightened with something like remorse. Then, to Clare's surprise, she switched on the heater.

"Just for a moment," she said.

"Thanks," Clare whispered.

Clare waited until they were safely away from the farmstead and back onto the rural road to pull the map book out from where she'd tucked it under her seat. She had dog-eared pages to track their progress. She traced the road they were following, examining all of the towns they could stop at. That part of the country had very few settlements that would count for more than a few hundred houses, and most of them were spaced apart. They would need to travel closer to the city to happen upon real, tightly packed suburbs.

"There's a town two hours away," Clare said. "It's not large, but it's still one of the bigger ones in the area."

"We'll try there."

Dorran blinked, seeming to collect himself. "Are we stopping?"

Clare cleared her throat. She didn't know how to broach the subject. *I'm scared. I don't know how to help you. This is the best plan we could come up with.*

Beth answered on Clare's behalf. "We're looking for antibiotics."

Dorran's mouth tightened. "I am fine."

"Ha. You sure about that?" Beth sent him a searching glance through the rearview mirror.

"I am *fine.*"

Beth lifted a hand from the wheel, then let it slap back down. "I'm just saying, *one* of us lost their thanites, and it wasn't me."

Clare opened her mouth, hot anger rising as she prepared to defend Dorran. She stopped as warm chuckles rose from the man beside her.

It had been a joke. A joke that Dorran had appreciated. She looked up at him, surprised and relieved to see good humor in his expression.

"*Allegedly* lost their thanites," he corrected. "I hope this world is not so far gone that I cannot be considered innocent until proven guilty. We do not know whether Ezra's experiment had the intended results."

"Well, either way, you need to put your ego aside for a moment," Beth said. "As much as I'm sure you'd like it, this isn't about you. Antibiotics are as good as currency in the new world, and I want some in case we need to make an emergency trade. Plus, we still don't know how the thanites actually work or what their weak spots might be. If one of us gets an infected cut, I want a backup solution."

Dorran thought it over for a moment, then nodded. "That makes sense."

"Of course it does. I said it, didn't I? Clare, keep feeding me directions."

Thank you. Clare kept her head down to the map but smiled. *Thank you, Beth, for making this easier for him. Thank you, Dorran, for not trying to fight.*

They had plenty of warning as they neared the town. Cars lay neglected in the road, tipped into ditches, or tangled into one another in the relics of a gruesome crash. Clare craned her neck to look among the swirling fog. She thought she saw shapes darting between the vehicles.

Beth swore under her breath. "There's not going to be anywhere safe to park. At least, not within an hour's walk."

Clare gripped the edges of the map. Between the half-melted snow, the rain, and the thickening mist, the cars were barely recognizable. They floated out of the ether like some science-fiction artist's nightmare. She couldn't imagine trying to walk among them.

"We'll coast through the town," Beth said. "See if there's anywhere safe to stop. I doubt we'll find anything, though. If the sun were out, at least the hollows would all be inside. Weather like this turns the world into their playground."

Houses rose out of the fog. They were grim sights. Broken windows and broken roofs, surrounded by dead gardens. It would have been a beautiful place once. Now, the environment felt as though it had been exhumed straight out of her nightmares.

Beth's head moved continually, twitching left and right, scanning their surroundings as she drove through the town. She'd been correct; the creatures were active. They stepped out of open doors and from the spaces between buildings, eyes glowing in the minibus's beams.

They passed a playground. The swings rocked in the breeze, still carrying a lining of snow-soaked leaves. Two paces away stood a figure, horribly tall, its head towering above the swing's highest bar. It turned lazily, eyes tracking them.

"This won't work," Beth said. "The place is lousy with them. There's nowhere to park. We'll keep driving and try the next town."

"There's nothing else for ages." Clare scowled as she flipped through the maps. "Just farmsteads."

"And those will all be cleared out. Damn." Beth chewed on her lip.

"Can we do without antibiotics?" Dorran lifted his head from where he rested it against his window. "I understand they would be helpful, but they aren't strictly necessary, are they?"

Beth only hesitated a second. "No. We need to get them. Either here or somewhere else."

"Very well. I might have a solution." He ran his fingers through his hair, tousling it. "You need someone to watch over the bus. You need to keep the hollows away from it for twenty minutes. And you need a distraction. Correct?"

"I'm listening," Beth said.

"I could drive the bus while you search the houses. I'll circle around the block—not too close, but close enough to pick you up if you need a quick escape. The hollows should be attracted to the noise, which will clear them away from your area. When you're ready, find a way to signal me, and I'll collect you."

"That…" Beth shook her head. "That is not a half-bad idea."

Clare frowned at Dorran. "The hollows will try to swarm you."

"That is fine. I can drive fast enough to stay clear."

She took his hand. It felt cold. She blinked furiously as she nodded. "Okay. Okay."

"If we're doing this, we need to be quick," Beth said. "Swap with me, Dorran. Drive us around a bit while we get our masks on. Clare, get a thicker jacket."

Dorran pressed Clare's hand, then he slipped away. The changeover was seamless. Beth jumped out of the driver's seat and Dorran took her place within a second. The bus, which had been coasting, picked up speed again.

"Be careful." Beth narrowed her eyes at Dorran as she stepped back from him. "This bus is too valuable for me to let you wreck it."

"Understood." He turned a corner, leading them back toward the center of town.

Clare had already retrieved their masks and gloves from one of the overhead compartments. They pulled them on with quick efficiency, Beth speaking as she worked.

"We're spreading our luck thin just by being here, so we can't afford to push it much further. We'll visit a maximum of four houses. Two minutes in each, tops." She snapped her fingers at Dorran. "Keep the car no more than a block away. Keep it moving. The engine has to be loud enough to distract anything in the area. Clare, you search, I'll cover your back. Understood?"

"Yes," they both chorused.

Beth tossed Clare an empty backpack. "Search kitchens and bathrooms. Medicine is almost always kept in a high cabinet. If you can't find anything with a quick look, cut your losses and move on. And when you find some, don't bother sorting through it, just dump it all into the bag. We're measuring our time in seconds. We'll have a flare, partially for light and partially to blind them if they get too close. I want to be back in the bus before it runs out."

Clare pulled her mask down to cover her face. "I'm ready."

"Let's hope you are." Beth lifted her rebar and stood by the doors, squinting through the glass to watch the streets. "This area looks good. Houses are nice and close together. Dorran, I'll throw the flare into the road when we're ready for pickup. Will you be able to see it through the fog?"

"Yes. I'll watch for it." Dorran looked back at Clare, his face tight. "Be careful."

"We will." She approached the door, carrying her crowbar. Dorran hit the brakes, pulling the bus to a sharp halt. Clare braced herself to stay upright. The bus doors flew open. Beth leaped out first, Clare close behind. She'd barely touched the asphalt when the engine roared and tires wailed as the bus skidded down the street.

"He'd damn well better not crash my bus," Beth muttered.

Clare grabbed her arm and yanked her toward the nearest house. The mist was horribly thick. In among it, she could see long, thin shapes skittering between the yards. Some of the eyes followed the bus. Some followed her. *Damn it.*

They ran along the pavers leading to the first house. A large white door with glass decor greeted them, nestled between two massive pots holding dead shrubs. Clare tried the handle. It was locked. Beth pushed her out of the way. She rose onto her toes as she punched a hole in the glass, reached her gloved hand through, and unhooked the lock.

Chattering rose from the yards behind them. Clare tried to watch for movement. She couldn't see any. Her heart skipped as they pushed the door open and stepped through.

The house's curtains had all been drawn, and the hallway was aggressively dark. Clare could barely see the edges of the doors ahead. A red glow fizzled around them as Beth lit the flare. Beth pushed it into her hand, and Clare stretched it ahead of herself, using the hellish red light to ward off the shadows. It wasn't strong, but it was better than darkness.

"Fast," Beth whispered.

Clare forced herself to move. Their footsteps echoed over the wood floor. It seemed too loud. Beth stepped ahead of her to shove doors open one at a time, rebar held at the ready. They found the bathroom on the third door they tried.

"Go," Beth whispered. She stepped aside to stand next to the door like a bouncer.

The bathroom window didn't allow any light in. Clare raised her flare to illuminate the room. The sink had a mirror, but no medicine cabinet. She opened the cupboards below it. They held an assortment of children's bath toys and scrubbing brushes. She snapped the cabinet closed and moved back into the hallway. "Master bedroom."

Beth shook her head. "Not as likely. Next house."

Clare ignored her as she moved down the hallway. She couldn't spare the seconds it would take to explain that the main bathroom had been the children's domain. The parents would have an en suite.

The master bedroom was at the end of the hall. Clare paused inside the door just long enough to see that the curtains above the window had been wrenched down. The wooden rod was broken, and the fabric lay in a pool on the floor. Clare barely glanced at it as she opened the doors, first to the closet, then the bathroom.

The en suite was smaller, but when Clare opened the cabinet, her heart rose. They'd found medicine. A lot of it, both bottles and cardboard boxes with pills. She grabbed them by the handful and pushed them into her bag.

Behind her, metal connected with something solid. The *thwack* rang through the cold air. Clare shivered but stayed focused. She dumped the last of the boxes into the bag and moved back into the bedroom.

Beth was waiting for her there. Her mask had a streak of red liquid running across it, and she was wiping the rebar on a corner of the fallen curtains. A gray limb was visible reaching around from behind the bed. Wordlessly, they turned back to the hallway and jogged for the open front door.

CHAPTER 13

COLD MIST STUNG CLARE'S throat as they exited the house. As far as she could tell, the street was empty. In the distance, the bus's engine roared, disturbing the silence. Wheels screeched. Clare prayed that Dorran was safe as she followed Beth across the front yard and onto the neighbor's property.

They had found medicine, but there was no guarantee antibiotics were among it and no time to read each box and bottle to check. Their best chance was to keep moving, keep gathering, and hope to get lucky.

The second house was smaller and unlocked. Like before, Beth swept ahead of Clare, opening doors and standing guard as she searched. She tried the main bathroom, the en suite, and the kitchen cupboards with no success. There were stacks of food in the cupboards—pasta, canned fish, canned vegetables, and packets of crackers. Clare dragged a handful into her bag but had to suppress her instinct to take more. They weren't close to starving yet, and speed was more important than resupplying.

Back into the yard, the bus sounded more distant. Beth had given Dorran instructions to stay no more than a block away, but Clare thought he'd strayed beyond that. She was afraid of what that might mean. They jogged to the next house along. Its front door was locked. There were no glass panels, and decorative metal bars guarded the closest windows.

"Next one," Beth hissed. They left the house and continued along the street, cutting across the front yards. Something moved out from behind a row of shrubs. Beth lunged forward, rebar extended. Her aim was good. Clare squinted against the gush of blood that burst out of the creature's open mouth. It crumpled. Beth wrenched her rebar free and shoved Clare's shoulder. "Keep moving."

She was shaking as she neared the next house. Its door already hung open. Inside was chaos. Furniture had been overturned and holes put into the walls. Clare tried not to think about what kind of fate the occupants had met as she ran for the bathroom.

There was a stack of bottles in the cupboard. Most of them seemed to be herbal. Clare didn't discriminate and used an arm to drag them into the bag. It was starting to grow heavy. She hitched it over her shoulder and nodded to Beth.

They returned to the street once again. As they moved toward the next house, a horn rang out in the distance, followed by the screech of tires. Clare bit her lip as she stared through the haze of white. The horn sounded again, closer, and Beth pushed Clare away from the houses and toward the road. "I think our time's up."

Clare glanced back at the fourth house. They'd found medicine, but the anxious part of her mind was terrified it wouldn't be enough. The horn sounded again, almost deafening. Then the bus emerged from the mist, its tires screaming on the asphalt as it scraped to a halt. The doors flew open.

"In!" Dorran barked.

Clare discarded the flare as she leaped up the step. She was faintly aware of a howling noise behind them. Beth jostled her shoulder as she pulled the door closed, then the bus skidded forward, black smoke rising from its wheels.

"What's happening?" Clare grabbed the nearest seat to hold herself upright.

Dorran leaned over the wheel, his dark eyes thunderous as he strained to see through the fog. "One of them is smart. And it has influence over the others. They've been trying to corral the bus. Trap it."

"Damn," Beth muttered.

The street met a crossroad ahead. As they drew near, Clare's heart dropped. The paths to their left and straight ahead were blocked by debris, leaving them no choice except to turn right.

The blockades didn't look like the previous obstacles Clare had encountered in the silent world. They weren't simply a fallen tree or a car wreck that had occurred naturally. Vehicles and cast-off furniture had been stacked into walls, and as she peered at them, she saw pallid heads rising above the piles.

They did this, Clare realized as the bus's headlights glowed across countless eyes. *They're funneling us. Toward what? A trap? A dead end?*

"Brace," Dorran called. The engine roared as he fed it more energy.

Clare's mouth turned dry as she realized they were forging straight ahead, toward the barricade. As the headlights pierced through the mist, the creatures' faces became clear. Their wide eyes watched the bus while unnatural, pale limbs clung to their structure.

The bus's front had been modified. Metal plates were fastened in a wedge shape, like an improvised snowplow. It served them well then. They crashed into the barrier. Fractured furniture and dented metal exploded away. Hands beat against the windows and walls as hollows latched on to the vehicle. Clare, feet spread wide for balance and one hand pressed to the door, stared upward as fingernails scraped across the roof.

Dorran swerved sharply enough for the bus to rise onto one set of wheels. Clare gasped and clutched the nearest seat. The bus touched down again, and Clare felt objects bang across the bus's length as the hollows clinging to it were knocked off.

She leaned close to the window, trying to see around the barriers. Three gray fingers appeared in the gap around the boards, horribly close to her face. Clare pulled away, calling, "On the right."

Dorran turned the wheel again, teeth bared. The bus jolted as it rose up onto the curb, and Beth gasped as she lost her footing.

Trees had been planted along the sidewalk. Dorran aimed for the nearest one, turning aside at the last possible moment. The branches scraped along the bus's side. The hollow howled. One of the pieces of plywood drilled over the windows splintered. Then they were back on the road, free from the hollow, and Dorran increased their speed as they raced toward the town's edge.

Houses thinned as they left the suburb, and Clare began to breathe a little more easily. She released her death grip on the seat as Dorran slowed to a less reckless speed.

He turned to Beth. "Do you want to take over now?"

"Yes," she snapped. She'd ended up on the floor, clutching one of the seat's bases to keep herself from being shaken too much. She clambered back to her feet as Dorran set the wheel straight, then they switched just as efficiently as they had before.

Clare took Dorran's arm. "That was amazing."

"Oh." He looked surprised and faintly pleased. "Not really. I'm sure Beth could have managed it better if she'd been driving."

"Damn straight I would have," Beth growled from the driver's seat.

Clare laughed as she and Dorran moved into their usual spot. "Well, I think it was amazing."

Houses disappeared from around them as they left the town's border. Clare waited just long enough to know they were free from its confines, then dragged her backpack into her lap and unzipped it.

She quickly tossed the long-life food she'd claimed into the racks above them, then began pulling bottles out. The last house had held mostly herbal complexes. She read their names, but they weren't familiar, so she was forced to put them aside.

Underneath those was the store from the first house. She sorted through several packs of painkillers. Laxatives. An antidepressant. Clare's desperation rose as she discarded each half-used box.

Please. There must have been some antibiotics. Please!

Then she found it, tucked in the bottom of the bag. A box of high-strength antibiotics. Its seal had been broken, so she opened the cardboard container and shook the little foil cases out. There were only four capsules left. She was just grateful to have any.

"Did you find some?" Beth was watching her through the rearview mirror.

Clare nodded.

"Good. Follow the instructions on the packet and make sure he takes them on time."

At her side, Dorran's lips pulled back in displeasure. "This *was* all because of me, wasn't it?"

"Shh, just take this." Clare's relief spilled out as a smile. She popped one of the capsules out of its foil case and pushed it into Dorran's hand, then offered him a bottle of water from the overhead baskets.

"Liar," he said, and begrudgingly swallowed the capsule.

Clare watched him wash it down, then turned the packet over to read the instructions. It said to take a dose every twelve hours, and to finish the entire course. They only had three left. That wouldn't be enough, but it would buy them time. A day and a half. Long enough to find more.

CHAPTER 14

THAT AFTERNOON WAS THE happiest they'd spent together. Dorran seemed more lively than he had before. It was too early for the antibiotic to be helping him, and Clare couldn't tell whether the adrenaline from escaping the town was lending him more life or whether he'd realized just how worried Clare was and was putting in more effort to compensate. Either way, she clung to it, hope fluttering inside of her. Dorran chatted and laughed easily, and held her hand, their fingers laced together.

Beth seemed brighter, too. She sang an old song she was fond of, and Clare joined in. They were both off tune. Neither of them cared.

They stopped twice to refuel the bus from the casks stored in the bus's back and once to eat. The portable stove's gas canister fizzled out near the end of lunch. Beth examined it, then huffed a sigh as she tossed it aside. "That was my last one. We either need to find more gas, or we're cooking with fires from now on."

When they returned to the road after lunch, Dorran slept against the window while Clare poured over the maps. The region was flooded with new waterways thanks to the recent snows and rain, but their route kept them mostly on high ground. The bus was tall enough and heavy enough to handle the shallow streams that were popping up everywhere, and on the two occasions they had to cross rivers, the bridges were still intact.

Clare was starting to feel as though their luck might hold. They were making good progress. If they could keep it up, they would be at Evandale by the following evening.

The spitting rain cleared, but the clouds remained thick by the time the sun started to fail. Beth stretched, flexing her neck, and wriggling the fingers that held the wheel. She had to be sore after days of solid driving. "We'd better stop and get some dinner before it's dark."

"Mm." Clare's hair had been falling in her face, and she ran her fingers through it to push it back, cringing as she snagged tangles. She needed a shower—a proper one, not just being drenched by the rain. "And it'll be easier to find a good location to spend the night while we can still see."

She glanced at Dorran. He'd been sleeping for hours by that point, a spare jacket rolled up against the glass for a cushion. Long eyelashes twitched above pale cheeks as he dreamed. Clare hoped whatever was running through his mind wasn't unpleasant. She slipped her hand around his. The fingers were cold, almost cold enough to belong to a corpse, but they curled at her touch.

They were traveling through a region filled with twining rivers and patches of sparse, dead trees. That was a risk. Cover meant hollow ones, even thin cover like what they were driving among. Beth scanned the environment, searching for a good campsite, and Clare did her best to trust in her sister's judgment. The clouds had developed the sickly orange tint of a masked sunset before Beth sighed and said, "This'll do."

She pulled off the road and drove through the scrubby bushes and stunted trees. Dead branches scraped at the bus as they trundled down a light slope. Then Beth pulled up sharply as they reached a clearing.

The jolt was enough to disturb Dorran. He took a sharp breath as his eyes opened, and his fingers tightened around Clare's.

"Hey," Clare whispered, gently rubbing his hand to make the transition back to wakefulness less jarring. "We think we're going to stop for the night."

"Ah. Good." He blinked, pushing away from the bus's wall. Despite the sleep, he didn't seem any better rested, but he still smiled at her. "I'm looking forward to stretching my legs."

His words were encouraging, but Clare had the sense he was only saying what he thought she wanted to hear. She held a running timer in her head of when his next dose of antibiotics would be due. They would help. He would get better. She had to believe that.

Beth scanned the environment from her perch in the driver's

seat, then pulled the brake on, her face grim. "We'll light a fire tonight. That'll make us a bit safer from the hollows, but we'll be more vulnerable to any humans who see the light and decide to check us out. Don't take anything out of the bus that we can't afford to lose. We might need to leave at short notice."

They'd stopped in a ragged clearing twenty feet wide and thirty feet long, surrounded by rings of dead, tangled plants. Beth exited the bus first, and as Clare followed in her wake, her sister held up her hand in a wordless request for silence. They held still. Clare couldn't hear anything except dry branches scratching against each other. Then, in the distance, a bird screeched.

"Nature," Beth murmured. "A good sign. Start looking for kindling. I'll work on the fire."

Finding dry wood was not an easy task. As Clare scouted through the dense tangles, she sometimes found branches that had been shielded from the rain by leaves or outcroppings of rocks. Even then, it was the difference between damp wood and drenched wood. Their only saving grace was that most of the branches were long dead.

She and Dorran brought armfuls of material back to Beth, who picked through it to build her fire. She'd cleared a patch of dirt in the middle of the clearing and had brought fire starters out of the bus. Soon, a plume of thick smoke began to rise as the fire caught.

The sun had nearly vanished. Beth beckoned to Clare as she stopped to drop off wood. "Do you remember where you put those candles you found?"

"Yeah. Would they help?"

"They should. Light them in a circle at the edge of the clearing. It won't be much, but it'll buy us some warning if anything tries to sneak up on us."

Clare leaped back into the bus and found the pack of twenty tall, narrow candles she'd taken from the farmhouse. They wouldn't be able to light the area thoroughly, but they would do a better job than the struggling campfire. She paced around the clearing's edge, digging the candles into the ground at even intervals and lighting their wicks before moving on. By the time she returned to Beth with an empty box, they had a weak ring of light surrounding them.

Beth had worked miracles with her fire. It still released billowing smoke that stung Clare's eyes and scratched her throat, but it was warm and growing.

"Keep an eye on this," Beth said, stretching as she stood. "And start dinner. Whatever you feel like. I'm going to go clean up."

"I'll come—"

"You'll cook dinner, end of discussion. I'm not going far."

Clare bit her lip. "How's your shoulder doing?"

"Fine." She sounded indifferent, but the corner of the medical kit poked out of her jacket pocket. "I'll be back in twenty minutes. Yell if you hear anything approaching."

Beth sauntered downhill in search of one of the temporary rivers funneling water away from the higher ground. The candles painted a yellow sheen across her hair and jacket as she passed between them, then she vanished into the night. Clare released a slow, measured breath and focused on the fire.

131

Dorran brought out the folding chairs and set one up for Clare. His movements were steady and assured, but Clare had the sense it took him effort to make them that way.

He's not used to being vulnerable. Because in his old life, vulnerability was punished.

Clare pulled her chair closer to his until she could hold him. She threaded one arm around his and leaned against him. His muscles relaxed, and the smile looked a little less forced.

"How are you feeling?"

"Better."

She wished she could trust him. Clare reached up to touch his face. His eyes closed as she ran her fingertips across his skin. Cold and clammy. She didn't pull away but rested her palm against his cheek as he leaned into the touch.

Give the antibiotics time. She tried to match his smile. *He'll be all right. He* has *to be all right.*

Her thoughts switched to the backpack. She'd been so focused on finding antibiotics that she'd all but ignored the rest of the contents. "Wait. I forgot. We have painkillers now. I'll get you some."

"I'm fine, Clare."

She was already out of her seat and climbing through the open bus door. Dorran called after her, trying to insist that he didn't need them, but Clare ignored him as she found the small blue box where she'd stashed it in the luggage compartment.

Why didn't I think of this before? Beth's been driving with an injured shoulder, too. There's not much I can do for either of them, but I can at least make sure they're not hurting.

She returned to the fire with the tablets and a bottle of water, and popped two into Dorran's hand despite his sustained objections, along with his due dose of antibiotics. As he reluctantly swallowed them, Clare glanced toward the clearing's edge. Beth was trying to clean her shoulder. It had to be painful. A couple of painkillers might not completely stop that, but they would at least make the ordeal more bearable. "I'll run some to Beth. Be back in a moment."

Dorran began to rise out of his chair. "I'll come with you."

"No, you'll stay here." Clare put a hand on his shoulder and gently pushed him back down. "Remember what Beth said. We need someone to watch the bus."

He pressed his lips together, glancing at the twisted, black branches surrounding them. "Hmm. Don't go far."

"I won't."

"Stay within calling distance. Shout if you see or hear anything unusual."

"Okay."

"If you don't return within three minutes, I'll come looking for you."

Clare laughed and squeezed his shoulder. "Beth wouldn't have gone far. Besides, you've seen how she handles the hollows."

He sighed, his eyes tight and worried. "All right. Just be safe."

"I will." Clare raised a hand in goodbye as she jogged away from the fire, toward where Beth had disappeared.

Stepping through the ring of candles was a surreal experience. One moment, she was surrounded by light—it wasn't strong, but it was enough that she could make out the ground and the shapes around her. As soon as she put the candles at her back, the shapes began to blend together, bleeding into one another like an optical illusion. Clare slowed and reached one hand ahead of herself as she waited for her eyes to adjust to the dimness that came from the last moments of twilight.

The trees were short, barely reaching above her head, but their limbs were tangled and thick. Some natural disaster had killed them years before. Drought, Clare suspected. It had left the branches bare and sharp. They snagged her jacket and scratched at her exposed skin as she wove her way between them.

She caught the sound of rushing water in the distance and followed it. The ground tended downward and became spongy. It only took a minute to reach the river, which had overflowed its usual bounds and gurgled around the closest trees. Clare reached the water's edge and squinted as she looked in both directions. The trees encroached on the bending river, masking its shores from her sight. She couldn't see Beth. Knowing that Dorran wouldn't wait for long, she turned left.

Not far away, the river curved sharply, creating a shore. A figure knelt there. Clare quickened her pace to a jog and opened her mouth to call to Beth, but her voice caught in her throat. Something was deeply wrong.

CHAPTER 15

BETH CROUCHED ON THE riverbank holding a blood-tinged cloth in the water to rinse it clean. She'd removed her jacket and scarf to strip down to just her bra. It was the first time Clare had seen her without the layers.

The bullet wound was like a red stain on her shoulder. It looked swollen; the hole itself was small, but a discolored tinge spread out from it. The thanites were efficient, though. The mark was already scabbing over.

Clare's eyes were irrevocably drawn away from the bullet hole. Without the jacket, Beth's back was visible for the first time. Nausea rose through Clare. She dropped the painkillers and clamped her hand over her mouth to muffle a cry.

Beth heard. She turned, eyes flashing in the low light. Her expression froze into something wild. Slowly, she rose out of her crouch.

Her spine rippled under her skin as she moved. The vertebrae were overgrown, poking up like spines. The highest two had sliced through the skin. They were what Beth had been cleaning.

Clare couldn't breathe. She locked eyes with Beth, her hand pressed over her mouth, every hair on her body standing up. Around them, the dead branches creaked. A bird cried in the distance. The river gurgled as it snatched at dead trees. Clare barely heard them.

The ferocity in Beth's features melted into sadness. She held out one hand, then let it drop. "You weren't supposed to see this."

"You…" The words felt as though they were choking Clare. "You're a…"

"I don't know what I am." Beth bent to pick up her shirt. Clare flinched at the movement. Beth noticed, and her face tightened further as she held the fabric over her chest. Clare still couldn't stop staring. Staring at her back. Staring at the spines. Staring at the hollow one she called her sister.

"The day the stillness arrived, I waited too long to shut the bunker door." Beth closed her eyes. The corners of her mouth pulled down. "You know how I keep telling you not to gamble with your safety? Well, I gambled that day. I kept hoping you might arrive. Even though our phones had been disconnected, even though I saw on TV that the world was falling apart, I waited at my open bunker door, watching the street, *hoping*, just in case…"

Her voice broke. She dropped her head. The fingers clenched her shirt, pulling the fabric until it threatened to tear. Then she took a breath and continued, voice shaking.

"I wouldn't stop hoping, so I ignored the warning signs. I kept the door open when the sky turned from blue to black and it started pelting snow. I kept it open when I heard people screaming in the distance. I didn't shut the door until my own lungs started to burn."

Cold prickled at Clare's cheeks as tears raced toward her chin. Beth's hair hung over her face, hiding her expression, but the pain was still clear in her voice.

"I wasn't fully infected. Not like the other people on my street. Shutting the bunker door limited how many of the machines could reach me, I guess. But…it was enough. I could feel myself changing in the dark of my bunker. I knew I wasn't like the creatures outside—the monsters that kept clawing at my door, making that awful clicking noise as they tried to get in. I still had my mind. But I was changing, and I couldn't stop it." She took a shuddering breath.

"You…" Clare lowered her hand, trying to pull her mind back together. "You're AB negative, right? I couldn't remember your blood type, but…" *But AB negative is the only blood type that lets crawlers keep their mind.*

"Yeah." Beth's shoulders sagged. "Clare, sweetheart, I'm so sorry. I should have told you sooner. But I knew it would mean I would have to leave, and I couldn't stand to let you go. I just wanted to be with you for a little longer."

Clare took a step back. Her shoulders bumped into one of the trees. She folded her arms across her chest as she tried to breathe enough to resupply her mind with oxygen. It was starting to work again, to catch up to everything, to process what she was seeing. Her eyes flicked back to the spines. She forced them down to the ground.

"Beth…" She didn't want to ask the question, but she had to know. "Is…is it changing your mind?"

Her sister's eyes were flat. "Yes."

She's been so different since the stillness. Sharper. Angrier. Clare swallowed. "How much is it changing?"

Beth looked aside, toward the river, and her features softened with grief. "I still feel like a person. Most of the time. It's easier when I'm around you. Seeing your face reminds me of my old life, of who I was. Sometimes I can forget what's happening completely. But you said the thanites make you mad…and I can feel it."

Clare pressed her lips together, waiting for Beth to continue.

"I don't sleep anymore. I don't like the light. I can't feel pain. This bullet hole in my shoulder? I've had to pretend like I can feel it, just so you wouldn't suspect anything." Her expression abruptly darkened, losing some of its humanity, and Clare caught a glimpse of the monster inside. "And I'm hungry all the time. Oh, Clare, I'm so hungry. Food isn't enough. I've kept the hunger under control until now. But the others…they like human flesh. And I keep thinking… I wonder what it would taste like. I wonder if I could finally feel satisfied…"

Shivers ran through Clare. Beth's face was still familiar, with all of the angles and slopes she knew well. But it was like the soul behind it had been taken away, leaving it alien.

Then Beth blinked, and the familiarity was back. Her lips twitched into a bitter mimic of a smile. "It was my plan to get you somewhere safe. Then I would leave. But I think our time is up."

Clare closed her eyes. Her heart was like a drum, drowning out all other noises. Her limbs felt too heavy. She forced her feet to move her forward and raised her arms. She swallowed the repulsion and horror and embraced Beth. Her sister stiffened and tried to pull back, so Clare hugged her more tightly.

Beth remained frozen for a second, then slowly, cautiously relaxed. She lifted her own arms around Clare in turn.

"I don't want you to leave," Clare whispered. "You're still my sister. No matter what. We'll figure this out."

Beth's shoulders shook. She dropped her head to rest it against Clare's. Her breaths were cold as they ghosted across Clare's neck.

Hugging Beth, Clare could feel the awful spines under her hands. They were sharp, at least two inches long each, straining against the skin. She could see gore glistening around the two that had punctured through. She forced herself to hold on.

"Thank you," Beth whispered, her voice raw with emotion. "I'm so sorry."

I should have noticed earlier. Clare closed her eyes so she wouldn't have to look at the spines. *I never saw Beth sleep. She used her bad shoulder to drive the bus for hours without complaint. She never let me see her without the jacket and scarf.*

She dreaded the answer to her next question, but she had to ask. "Is it getting worse?"

"Yes. Not quickly. But it gets a little worse every day."

Clare nodded. She hated the answer, but she'd expected it. The thanites continued to mutate their hosts, redesigning over their own work in escalating layers.

Beth pulled back first. Her cheeks glistened with moisture, but her expression was set, and some of the hardness had returned to her face. "I don't expect you to be nice to me, you know. I'm halfway to becoming the enemy. And it's going to get worse."

"We'll..." She swallowed, tucking her arms in under her shoulders. "We'll deal with that. You're my sister. A few extra bones doesn't change that."

Beth pulled a wry smile. "It's a bit more than some extra bones, love. But I appreciate it."

Behind them, a voice floated through the fog. Dorran, sounding stressed, called, "Clare?"

Beth jolted backward and clutched the shirt tightly against her chest. Her eyes widened as the remaining color vanished from her face.

"Oh, damn it." Clare ran her hands through her hair. "I promised him I wouldn't be long."

"Don't tell him." For the first time, Beth looked frightened. "Please."

"But—"

Dorran called again, closer. "Clare! Answer me!"

"Put your shirt back on," Clare hissed, then raised her voice. "I'm here! Everything's fine!"

Beth rushed to tug her shirt on as the sound of snapping

branches drew nearer. Clare snatched the jacket off the ground and held it out for her, and Beth yanked it on over the top. The thick fabric disguised the spines, and the scarf wrapped over the top hid the highest protrusions.

Dorran emerged into the clearing. His dark eyes darted from Clare to Beth, then scanned the surrounding environment, searching for danger. When he looked back at Clare, he lifted his eyebrows pointedly.

"Sorry." She sent him a sheepish grin and scuffed her shoes across the dirt. "We started talking and I lost track of time."

He exhaled. "As long as you're safe. Everything fine, Beth?"

"Yep." Her voice was tight.

Dorran nodded. "Are you ready to come back to camp? I started dinner."

"We'll be right behind you," Clare promised.

Dorran hesitated, and Clare knew he must have guessed that something had happened. He glanced over them again, his eyes questioning, but didn't press the issue. Clare waited until he'd turned and disappeared into the trees before leaning close to Beth.

"I have to tell him."

Her expression hardened. "He's not going to be as forgiving as you are."

"He's a good man. I promise. You can trust him."

Beth grabbed her sleeve. She leaned in close so her voice wouldn't travel. "He has one focus in this world: killing any monster that threatens you. And, baby, I am a monster. He doesn't have the benefit of nostalgia to cloud his judgment."

"Firstly"—Clare grabbed the wrist that held her hand and leaned in just as far as Beth had—"my judgment isn't clouded, thank you very much. You've been infected, but you're *not* a monster."

Beth's laugh was rueful. "Oh, you sure about that?"

"*Secondly*," Clare charged on, "I'm not going to lie to Dorran. He's an equal party. And the only way we're going to be safe out here is if we trust each other. I trust him. I trust you. And I expect the both of you to show each other the same level of respect."

"All right. Have it your way." A flash of danger passed through Beth's eyes. "But don't be shocked if he doesn't take the news as kindly as you did. And don't blame me if I'm forced to run."

They let go of each other. Dorran had gained so much distance on them that Clare could no longer hear his footsteps. She licked her lips and found they were dry. "I'll talk to him alone. It might be easier that way."

"If you think so." Beth pushed her hair away from her face. "I'll meet you there in a few minutes."

As Clare stepped back into the woods, she had a chance to take one last glance at her sister. Beth stood on the riverbank, staring down at the water, her back straight and proud, but her head bowed.

CHAPTER 16

CLARE'S MIND CHURNED AS she hiked back toward the bus. Beth expected Dorran would try to drive her off. Clare knew better. Dorran was strong and he could be aggressive when he needed to be, but he was also deeply empathetic. He would understand Beth's situation. He would be kind to her.

Won't he?

She hated the doubts that crowded in at every side. She hated the way her own misgivings blended into them.

She couldn't reject her sister. It wasn't Beth's fault that she was infected. She hadn't *asked* for this, and she was fighting it as much as she could. That was all anyone could expect of her.

But questions still swarmed through Clare's mind, stinging her like wasps. *How long does she have before the rest of the spines break out of her skin? How long will her mind stay intact? How long will she survive? And how long will she still be my sister?*

Already, the changes were immense. Clare had credited the new hardness to a latent survivor's instinct kicking in. Now, she could see it was the thanites. Just like Dorran's mother, and just like every other hollow they had encountered, Beth was having her humanity stripped away. She'd lost her natural fear. She no longer felt pain. And her gentle nature was being replaced with an obsessive resentfulness Clare had never seen in her sister before.

She needed a long walk to get her thoughts into some kind of order, but the trip back to the bus was painfully short. Too soon, she stepped through the candles spaced around the clearing and was faced with the bonfire they had built.

Dorran stood next to the flames, hands in his pockets, his back to Clare. He cast a long shadow across the ground as he shifted his weight. He tilted his head toward her as she moved to his side.

"Did something happen?" Dark eyes filled with worry searched her face. Clare nodded. She hadn't rehearsed this part. She didn't know how to start or what to say. Dorran's hand rose to graze along her cheek in a gentle caress. "Did you have an argument?"

He thinks that's the worst that could happen. Until ten minutes ago, I thought the same.

"Dorran, something happened with Beth, and I'm going to ask you—I'm going to *beg* you—to please be patient."

The worry in his eyes deepened. He kept his hand on the side of her face, soft and comforting, as he turned his body to face her, giving her his full attention. A small nod encouraged her to go on.

The words tumbled out, jumbled and chaotic, a mirror of her

thoughts. She was aware she was trying to apologize for Beth, but she couldn't stop. Dorran didn't try to interrupt, but his eyebrows gradually fell lower, and that only increased Clare's desperation.

She stopped herself when she realized she was repeating things she'd already said. She took a sharp, gasping breath and finished with, "We have to stick together. I'll figure out how to help her. Just, please, don't be angry with her, because she can't change what happened."

Dorran appeared to be struggling with his thoughts. It took him a moment to voice them. "She is…infected."

"Yes."

He turned back to face the fire, his expression grim. She could see the same questions she'd had darting through his mind. *Is she dangerous? How much worse is it going to get? Where's the line between human and hollow?*

"Please." Her voice broke. She swallowed, trying to control her emotions. "I can't give up on her."

Branches snapped behind them. They both turned. Beth stood at the edge of the clearing, poised between two candles. The wan light bathed her features and shone over the ridges of her scars.

Beth and Dorran stared at each other over the expanse. The silence stretched, unbearable, so awful that Clare wished she could scream just to break it. Then Dorran took a slow breath. He tilted his head toward the campfire, his eyes not leaving Beth's. "Dinner is ready. Come and have some."

Hot gratitude flooded Clare, and she felt like she could breathe again. *Thank you, Dorran.*

Three chairs were already set up and a pot of stew hung over the flames. Clare moved to find bowls and fill them. She felt as though, if they could just sit together and have dinner, things might be better. Not normal. They were past normal, and she didn't dare ask for it. But she needed things to be better.

Beth hadn't moved from the edge of the clearing. It wasn't until Clare held a bowl out to her that she cautiously stepped closer. Even when Clare and Dorran had both sat, she still hesitated before slinking into her own chair.

"Here." Clare's smile was painfully wide as she added a spoon to Beth's bowl. Dorran, on the other side of the fire, kept his expression blank at he watched Beth. Beth looked like she was one sudden move away from flight. Clare returned to her chair between them, hoping the unyielding panic wouldn't be visible in her face. "I think we could all benefit from some good food."

Beth didn't touch the spoon. She kept her attention trained on Dorran as she spoke carefully. "I don't think I need to eat anymore. I did before, to make the both of you comfortable. But I don't need to. I'm not hungry for this kind of food."

She's testing him. She wants to see how he'll react to a more obvious display of the infection's symptoms.

Dorran stared back, his expression unreadable. "You *can* eat, though. And I think I would prefer it if you did."

Beth still made no move to lift her spoon. Clare sensed how much tension was contained in her body. And it wasn't just Beth, she realized. They were all wound as tight as springs, ready to explode at the slightest wrong move.

"It would be wasteful." Beth's words were soft and measured. "We don't know when we'll get more food. We should conserve it for the people who still need it."

Dorran looked aside, then turned back to her, rolling his shoulders. "The hollow ones out there are almost always bone thin. They grow too fast and don't eat enough. If you're going to drive me across the country, I'd rather it if your stomach, at least, weren't hollow."

"Ha." Beth's stony expression cracked as one corner of her mouth quirked up. "Was that a joke?"

"A bad one, admittedly." His own mouth broke into a smile, then all of a sudden, they were both laughing. Beth cackled giddily, then dropped her head to drink her soup. Clare suspected it was a deliberate move to hide the fact she was crying. She drank straight from the bowl, draining half of it in one go. Clare, grinning, raised her own soup. It was hot enough to scorch her tongue, and she sat back, gasping.

Beth can't feel it. That was another reminder of how badly her sister was being twisted. Clare tried not to think about it and blew on a spoonful of her stew to cool it.

Dorran stirred his own soup for a moment, then cleared his throat, glancing at Beth. "I would like to ask some questions."

"Sure. I thought you would." Beth shrugged. "And I'll be truthful now. I don't have anything else to hide."

"May I see it?"

Beth placed her bowl on the ground, stood, and shrugged out of her jacket. She turned her back to Dorran and pulled her hair out of the way. He stared at the spines raising bumps in her tank top, his expression shuttered. After a moment, he said, "All right."

Beth shucked her jacket back on and resumed her seat. Her eyes were hard. Testing. "Thoughts?"

He countered with another question. "It doesn't hurt?"

"No."

"But you wash it daily."

"Mm." She rolled her shoulders, then leaned back in the chair. "At first, before you told me about the thanites, I was trying to stop infection. Now, it's to keep my jacket clean. And to stop the smell."

The hollow scent. Clare knew it too well. It turned her stomach and sent fear through her nerves. She'd caught traces of it in the bus. She'd thought it was residue from the creatures that had tried to dig their way inside.

Dorran paused to drink more of his stew. Clare thought he was rehearsing his next question. "Does the infection make you less likely to be targeted by other hollows?"

"It does more than that." Her lips quirked up into a wicked smile. "It makes me invisible to them."

Clare frowned, thinking back. Beth had never been concerned about wandering into the mist alone. She'd never shown any fear of the monsters. And on the first night, when the pack of hollows had attacked Clare and Dorran, Beth had swooped in and killed them with no resistance. They hadn't even reacted to her presence.

They recognize her as one of their own. She can walk among them no matter how many there are.

"That's why you were traveling to the tower," Clare said, breathless. "People had heard the broadcast, but no one knew what it was about because no one could reach it. There were too many hollows for anyone to try unless they were suicidal."

"Or unless they were me," Beth said. "You got it in one. I could walk right between the hollows. I thought I might be the only person alive who could see what was actually in the tower, and…well, it seemed a better way to spend my last days than any alternative."

"Mm. I had wondered about that." At Beth's questioning look, Dorran lifted his shoulders in a shrug. "Clare spoke about you so fondly, and I felt as though the two of you would be inseparable. But in the days after you left the bunker, you made no attempt to reconnect. You did not seek out a new radio, and you did not try to travel to Winterbourne, even though Clare had told you where it was located. You never had any intention to see her again, did you?"

Beth glanced at Clare, her eyes sad. "I'm sorry, baby. I wanted to. I missed you more than anything. But—" She lifted a hand, indicating herself and the world around them. "I thought it would hurt you less if it was a clean break. If you never knew what I was becoming."

"That wasn't your plan initially, was it?" Dorran's eyes seemed very dark in the firelight. "Otherwise you wouldn't have been so distressed in your last radio message."

She chuckled bitterly. "Right again. Up until I opened my bunker doors, I thought I really, truly was as good as dead. They were right outside, howling, screaming. Clawing to get in. I welcomed death when I opened that door. And they swarmed right past me."

"You killed some."

"I did. They were in a frenzy, and I was terrified. I killed two. They didn't fight back. So I ran. Every minute, I expected to feel teeth dig into me as they caught up. They never did. They didn't even try to chase me. And it wasn't until later that night, when I tried to hide in the forest and one of the hollow ones walked right in front of me without reacting, that I realized what must be happening. And that was when I decided I would rather Clare think I was dead than know what I really was."

"Stop talking like that." The words came out louder than she'd meant, and Clare frowned at her bowl as she tried again. "You're still human. You might be more than that, too, but you're still—"

Beth's laughter was rough. "I'll tell you this much. The hollows accept me more readily than the humans do."

"Can you control them?" Dorran asked. Both Clare and Beth stared at him, and he dipped his head, his gaze piercing. "The other intelligent hollows we've encountered—the ones who are AB negative, the ones who kept their minds—they seemed to have some power over the lesser hollows."

Like Dorran's mother, Madeline, and her maids. It couldn't have been just prior loyalty that kept them tethered to her when they changed.

Beth looked intrigued. "I've never tried. I don't think I'd know how to. But that would be a useful skill to have. We wouldn't have to worry about being attacked ever again."

"That's what I assumed. If you knew how to, you would have used it already to protect Clare." He tilted his head. "I'd suggest we try practicing, but I'm not sure how we could without exposing ourselves to more hollows."

"Well, it's something to keep in mind, at least. Hopefully it's an instinctual thing. If they have some kind of language, I have no idea how to speak it."

Clare swallowed the last of her stew. Her insides ached, but it wasn't entirely grief. Now, the emotions were tempered with relief. The awful atmosphere had been dispelled. Dorran was treating Beth like an equal. Beth was acting like herself. And, in a rare display, they were getting along.

Dorran waited until Clare had finished her meal before clearing his throat. She looked up, expectant.

"We have a decision to make, I'm afraid." He put his bowl aside and folded his hands in his lap. "It doesn't have to be made tonight. But we will need to know by tomorrow. Do we continue to Evandale?"

"Of course," Clare said. "Why wouldn't—" Understanding hit her. Beth met her horrified look with a grim smile.

"That's why you voted against traveling to Evandale," Clare said.

Beth shrugged and stared down into her empty bowl. "I've reconciled myself to the idea. Maybe it's the best way to go. Wiped out instantly by some code, rather than having the responsibility of killing myself, being bludgeoned by some other well-intentioned survivor, or waiting for my mutations to finally destroy me. It actually sounds humane compared to the alternatives."

Clare's mind turned to the USB in her pocket as the weight of the choice registered. *The power to save humanity. The power to kill my sister.*

"I've changed my mind." The words hurt, but she didn't stop. "I want to go back to Winterbourne."

Beth actually laughed. "I thought you might do this. In that case, I change my vote, too. Onward to Evandale. Long live democracy."

"Dorran." She grabbed his arm. "We can't—"

Beth pointed her spoon at him. "Don't you dare change your vote."

"Ah…" He swallowed as Clare tightened her grip on his arm. "Clare, I wonder, if Beth is happy to take that route—"

"No." Clare pushed away from him, horrified. "No, no! She's my *sister*!"

"I know. I understand." He reached out, trying to comfort her. "Do not be alarmed. We don't need to make this choice immediately."

"I won't let you." She shook her head as she reached into her pocket. Her fingers tightened around the USB. It was so small. So delicate. Ahead of her, the fire crackled. All she needed to do was open her hand over it, and in a single moment, the code would be lost forever.

"Clare." Beth shuffled her seat slightly closer. "Sweetheart, listen to me. I'm okay with this."

Clare continued to shake her head.

"What's the other path?" Beth spread her hands. "We all go back to Winterbourne. I'll be there with you for a few days, or a few weeks, or maybe even a few months. But I'm slipping. What would you do? Would you keep me after I've lost my humanity? Chain me up, like that mother we found in that house? I would rather be dead."

"Stop!" Clare stood so quickly that the chair was knocked over behind her. An urgent need to escape consumed her, so strong that she felt like she was choking. She took one step toward the forest, but both Beth and Dorran rose, prepared to follow her. She grit her teeth and turned in the other direction, toward the bus. She jumped on board and slammed the door behind herself.

"Sure, go ahead, throw a tantrum," Beth yelled. "I'm so *sick* of dealing with your moods."

It's just the thanites talking. Tears dripped down her face. She scrubbed them away furiously as she stalked to the back seats. Farthest from the windows, the bed was the darkest part of the bus. She curled up on it, facing away from the door.

She was angry with Beth. But she was angry with herself as well. Because she knew Beth was right. Ultimately, her death was inevitable. Only the path that lead to it could be altered.

But she wouldn't agree to it. She couldn't be responsible for killing her sister.

Quiet voices murmured outside the bus. Clare closed her eyes, trying not to listen. She heard Beth say, "I'll talk to her," then a moment later, the door creaked as it opened.

153

"Clare?"

She pressed her eyes more tightly closed, hoping Beth would take the hint. Her sister sighed, then the edge of the bed depressed as Beth sat on it.

"I'm sorry I yelled."

"It's fine."

Beth's fingers traced over her hair, very lightly, then disappeared again. She didn't speak for a moment. When she did, her voice sounded strained.

"I've been thinking about it a lot over the past few days. You were right. When I first heard about the USB and what it might mean, my gut reaction was to make sure it never surfaced. Even now, my instincts are telling me to destroy it. But I think that's the machines in me. It's erasing my morals, slowly, one by one, and replacing them with nothing but the will to survive. But that wasn't who I used to be. And I'm trying, as hard as I can, not to forget that part of me."

Clare rolled over so she could see her sister. The pale light grazed over her fine, shoulder-length hair, her delicate nose, and the scars marring her face. The hardness and angles were still there. But a sweetness had appeared that Clare hadn't seen since before the stillness.

"I don't want to lose you," Clare whispered. "We only just found each other."

Beth smiled. It was a bittersweet expression. "I know. And I'm grateful for it. We got to see each other again. Spend time together. Make things right...as much as we could."

"Maybe there's something we can do to slow it down." Clare swallowed. "Maybe the people at Evandale will be able to figure something out—"

"Clare, no. If the code works, it will save what's left of the world. We can't delay that just for one person…and a person who isn't even really human anymore."

"Stop saying that. You're still human."

Beth chuckled, then her smile faltered. "That's kind. But other people don't think the same way."

"You don't know that. Dorran accepted you. Others will, too—"

"Clare, you wanted to know why I don't trust safe havens." Beth's smile was fading, and her jaw tightened as she stared at the opposite wall. "I visited one on my way to the city. At first, they welcomed me. They were happy to meet another survivor. They were kind and more generous than I had expected. I was given a bed and food, and many of them wanted to talk to me and hear my story. They were so nice…" She sighed. "I started thinking maybe I could live there for a while. They were looking for people who could help maintain the building."

Clare bit her lip. "Did you…tell them?"

"No. I'd meant to keep it a secret. But I dropped my guard and let one of the women there hug me. She was older, with beautiful graying hair and a kind face. At least, it was kind up until she felt my bones."

Beth lifted her hand to trace along the scar that ran from her nose to her cheek. "She did this. With one of the machetes they kept in every room." She touched the mark near her forehead. "That was from the man who helped set up my bed." Then, the scratches on her chin. "The woman who brought me dinner. I couldn't see through all of the blood. All I could do was run, and run, and run. I'm faster than I used to be. And I don't get tired. I was able to lose them."

Outside the bus, the sound of the crackling fire intensified as Dorran threw more wood onto it. Dead trees creaked as the wind picked up.

Beth tilted her head back, her expression unusually serene. "I don't blame them. They were frightened. They didn't know if I could infect them or if maybe I was leading more hollows into their midst. They just wanted to survive. But I know now—there isn't room for me in the human world."

"Beth, I'm sorry."

She blinked quickly, and the smile reappeared. "Let's take the USB to Evandale together. I think that would make me happy. At least that way, I will go down doing something good. I won't be *remembered* as a monster."

Clare found Beth's hand and squeezed it as tightly as she could. Her throat felt too raw to talk, but she gave a small, resigned nod.

I'm sorry, Beth. I wish I could do better for you.

"I'll pack up," Beth said. She rolled her shoulders, and Clare had the impression a heavy burden had fallen from her. "You and your friend try to get some sleep. Now that I'm not pretending to be human any longer, I can drive through the night."

CHAPTER 17

THE ROCKING BUS HELPED stir Clare awake faster than she would have wanted. The internal lights were off, but the glow coming through the front window still felt unpleasantly invasive against her eyes. She squinted, mumbling under her breath.

"Good morning." Dorran rested in the nearest seat, one arm slung over its back so he could face her. He'd changed into fresh clothes and Clare thought he must have washed up as well; his long hair was still damp. The effort he'd put into cleaning up didn't entirely hide the dark shadows under his eyes.

"Morning." Clare sat up, shivering as her feet slipped out from under the blankets. She'd slept on the layers of blankets spread on the row of seats at the back of the bus. It was the vehicle's only designated bed, and even though it was too short to stretch out on it properly, it was still more comfortable than trying to doze against a window. Clare had originally wanted Dorran to sleep there. He'd refused, saying he'd already slept enough and that Clare needed the rest more. The argument had escalated until Beth, bearer of the shortest temper out of all of them, snapped, "Someone get into the damn bed before I dump you both on the side of the road to be hollow food."

Clare begrudgingly took it, but only after pulling piles of blankets out of the overhead baskets and building a second bed on the bus's floor. Dorran had already packed it up, she saw; the blankets were all refolded and stored away. He must have been quiet to avoid disturbing her.

She had the awful suspicion that he'd done it, not because he felt better, but as a way to prove that she didn't need to worry. *He's not used to being cared for. He's still afraid of being seen as weak.*

The thoughts faded as Clare looked toward the windshield. They were moving through a gently hilled wooded area. The horizon was hazy, but the texture didn't match the blanketing fog they had been driving through for days. She leaned forward, frowning. "What's wrong with the sky?"

"Hmm?" Beth sounded distracted.

"That doesn't look like fog to me." It was too dark. Too ruddy. Clare slowly rose from her seat and moved up the aisle.

Beth raised her shoulders and let them drop again. "Dust maybe?"

They dipped into another valley, and the sky became obscured as branches passed over the bus. Clare stopped a few paces behind Beth, swaying lightly as the bus rocked on the dirt road.

"Where would dust be coming from?" Dorran asked. He'd

followed Clare, and shivers ran along her back as his voice came from just behind her ear.

Clare said, "It's been raining for days. The humidity's still through the roof. There shouldn't be dust storms, and especially not in this part of the country—"

They crested another hill, and the trees around them parted. A gray-brown haze spread across the sky. Clare saw the sun to their left, an hour or two above the horizon. It was putting out no more light than the moon would have.

The bus slowed as Beth took her foot off the accelerator. She worked her jaw as she stared at the blur. "Thin clouds, maybe? The sun might be giving them that color. It hasn't been up for long."

"I guess." Clare looked up at Dorran and saw doubt in his face as well. She found his hand and pressed it. She'd seen clouds that spread out until they became a thin blanket across the sky. She'd never seen them take on that shade before, though.

"I'll keep an eye on it," Beth said as she pushed the bus back up to speed. "In the meantime, can you two sort yourselves out for breakfast? There's nowhere to stop, and I doubt there will be for a while to come."

"Yeah." Clare reluctantly turned away from the view. The trees around them weren't densely smothering the way Winterbourne's forest had been, but they offered too much cover for Clare to think they didn't harbor any hollow. Beth had the map open on the dashboard. From what Clare could make out, the dirt road wove for miles with no variation. "Do you want me to take over driving for a bit? You must be exhausted."

"You'd think so, wouldn't you?" Beth's lips quirked up with bitter humor. "But no. I'm not sleepy. My muscles aren't fatigued or sore. I haven't left this seat in twelve hours, and yet I don't feel anything from it. So I might as well keep driving and let you conserve your energy."

"Right." Clare's skin crawled, but she could feel Beth watching her through the mirror, so she hid it as much as she could. It would take her a while to become used to the new Beth and to understand her needs and limitations.

As they ate bowls of dry cereal and canned fruit, Clare couldn't stop picking at her hair. It was greasy and itchy, and flecks of dirt had become trapped in it. Dorran watched, thoughtful, then put his bowl aside. "Would you like to wash your hair?"

"Yes. Yes please." Clare took a deep breath. "Can we? I'm about half a day away from shaving it off."

Dorran arranged her on the bus floor, sitting on one of the blankets. He reclined on a chair behind her, his legs at her back, a comb and a two-liter bottle of water at his side.

Beth didn't have any shampoo, and they couldn't waste enough water to rinse it out even if she did, so Dorran washed her hair a patch at a time with just the water and comb. Clare braced herself for pain as Dorran tried to work through the tangles, but she'd underestimated his patience. He worked meticulously, taking as long as he needed to pry through the snags.

She tilted her head back to see his face. His brows pulled low in concentration, his jaw set. The expression wouldn't have looked out of place if he were defusing a bomb.

"Okay?" he asked.

"Fine. You don't have to be so gentle."

He made a noise in the back of his throat, something between a laugh and a scoff, and kept working at the same cautious pace.

It took the better part of an hour before Dorran was satisfied. As he ran the comb through her damp hair, checking for any missed patches, he exhaled a deep breath. "Done, I think."

"I can't even begin to tell you how good that feels." Clare grinned as she shook her hair. She'd need soap to eradicate the excess oil, but at least it no longer felt grimy.

Dorran's fingers stayed at the back of her neck, as though he was reluctant to let her go again. Clare smiled up at him. His eyes reflected deep affection. The fingers began to move in small circles, hypnotic, as he bent forward, pressing a kiss to her lips. Clare arched her back and tangled her fingers into his shirt collar to hold him there. He groaned into her mouth, melting into her.

"We'll need to stop to refuel soon," Beth said.

Dorran snapped away, a flush of color rising over his throat. Clare stared at her sister. Beth's eyes were on the road, but the rearview mirror was still angled to see the bus's inside. She sighed and looked up at Dorran. He avoided her eyes, lips pressed together sheepishly, as he made a show of screwing the cap back onto the bottle of water and folding the towel.

A bus that seats twenty-four, and it's still not big enough for three of us.

Clare rolled to her feet, stretching. "It's not going to be safe to stop in the forest. How low's the tank?"

161

"Low, but the fuel light isn't on yet." Beth's voice betrayed nothing. "If we pass through a town, we should be able to find some clearings or parkland on its outskirts, but the nearest one is at least an hour away, and I don't think we'll make it that far."

"Mm." Clare rubbed at the back of her neck. The road was narrow; trees grew less than ten feet to either side, and they provided enough cover that she couldn't see far between them. She had no idea how dense the hollow population might be, but stopping for any longer than a few seconds would be a risk. It seemed as though they wouldn't have much of a choice, though.

"Look for any areas with thinner trees or more light," Dorran said. "Clare can refuel the bus. Beth and I will stand guard. If we can't fill the tank, we can at least give it enough to carry us to the town."

"That's not the worst idea, I guess," Beth said.

Clare approached the bus's front. The trees were thick and blocked a lot of the light, but as she caught glimpses of the sky, the uneasy prickles intensified.

The muddy haze hadn't abated. It was worse. She licked her lips and imagined she could taste it: dry, bitter, toxic.

She didn't like knowing that they were driving toward the haze. But there weren't many alternatives. They couldn't turn back; there was nowhere to turn back *to*. The discoloration spread across the sky, and unless they knew its cause, they couldn't avoid it or protect against it.

What could look like a dust cloud but exist in an environment that's too wet for dust?

She measured her movements, trying to stay calm, as she plaited her damp hair to keep it from tickling the back of her neck. The bus's dashboard said it was nine in the morning. They had another hour before Dorran was due for his next dose of antibiotics, but she wouldn't be able to stop thinking about the little capsules until he'd taken one. An hour early wouldn't hurt. She crossed to the basket holding their medical supplies, found the right container, and popped out one of the capsules. That was at least one source of anxiety she wouldn't have to obsess over.

Dorran stayed where she'd left him, sitting sideways in one of the seats. She pressed the capsule into his hand, along with a fresh bottle of water, and he murmured subdued thanks before taking it. Clare rested a hand on his cheek as he swallowed it. Dark eyes gazed up at her, a little brighter than they should be. He still felt cold. Clare, ignoring Beth's silent but judgmental presence, bent to kiss Dorran's forehead. He smiled.

Clare returned the packet of antibiotics to the overhead basket, then staggered. The bus's wheels screeched as it abruptly pulled to a halt. Clare swung, heart pumping, searching for what might have caused their abrupt stop.

"Quick decision," Beth called. "There's a freeway. If we get onto it, we might have some space while we refuel. But we might also become cornered if anything follows us up there."

Clare jogged back to the front of the bus, Dorran close behind her. Clare rested one hand on the dashboard and bent close to the window to survey the scene.

Ahead, a side road split off from the one they were on. An old, weather-faded sign pointed toward it, advertising a freeway. She could see the road curving away for a few dozen meters before it was swallowed by trees.

Up ahead, the freeway cut across the sky in a sharp, straight line. It ran diagonally to their road and was raised above ground level. If they continued ahead, their road dipped down slightly to carry them through a tunnel below.

The freeway's railings were too high for Clare to be able to see how heavy its debris was. She could make out the white roof of a truck to their left, but nothing else. She bit her lip, mind racing.

The trees around the freeway are dense enough that the hollows should prefer them to the relatively sparse shelter on the freeway. Any creatures that came out of the cars will have migrated away by now. If we can get up there, we should be alone, and we'll have a good view of anything that tries to follow us up.

She glanced to her left. Tree branches bowed in the steady breeze, dead leaves rattling. They would have no advance warning of an attack if they tried to refuel on the narrower dirt path. That made up her mind.

"I vote yes. The freeway might be blocked, but even if there's no room to drive up there, we should still be able to reverse back down the path we took."

"I agree," Dorran said.

"Glad we're on the same page." Beth hit the accelerator and they surged forward, following the offshoot to the freeway. "We'll still need to be quick. Both of you, get some protection on. Take my mask, Dorran; I don't need it. But get me a weapon. The rebar is good. Clare, gather the fuel near the bus's doors. This beast eats a lot, but I want to give it as much as we can before our time runs out."

"On it." Dorran had already brought their leather gloves, jackets, and scarves down from storage. Clare took her set and pulled them into place, then retrieved cartons of fuel from under the seats and dragged them to the door.

The bus swayed as the ramp carried them up. The freeway had been designed to compensate for the area's naturally undulating landscape. As the on-ramp brought them level with the freeway, it created a lane of its own that gradually merged with the four existing channels. The temporary lane was clearer than the others. Cars, most empty, some with their doors hanging open, were jammed across the road, but there weren't as many as Clare had feared. Beth slowed the bus, directing it closer to the freeway's center to buy them some space from the railings, then pulled to a halt.

"Ready?" She retrieved a tie from her pocket and used it to fasten her mane to keep it out of her face. "I want us back in the bus in less than four minutes. I'll guard the bus's front. Dorran, you take the back. Yell if you see any hollows."

"Understood." Dorran pulled the beekeeper mask down over his face. He held the hatchet in one hand and the rebar in his other, which he offered to Beth as she approached the bus door.

Clare pulled on her own mask. The visibility wasn't good; the eyeholes were too small, and with the fabric fastened over them, it dulled the world into a blurred monochrome. It would be enough, though. Dorran and Beth, on watch, needed to keep their vision clear. Clare just needed to focus on her job.

She lifted a jug in each hand as Beth pushed the door open. The three of them swept out, moving quickly. Beth speared toward the bus's front. Dorran lifted two of the fuel jugs and moved ahead of Clare toward the bus's rear. He placed the jugs beside the fuel hatch.

"Be safe," he whispered. "If I yell, get back inside the bus immediately. All right?"

"*You* be safe," Clare countered.

He chuckled and switched the hatchet into his right hand. His left hand squeezed Clare's shoulder, just for a second, then he disappeared around the bus's back.

Clare bent at the fuel intake and worked on unscrewing the cap with feverish haste. Even with her vision compromised, it was hard to ignore her surroundings. The freeway held tangles of cars, vans, and trucks. The gaps between them were just wide enough that Clare knew they wouldn't be hospitable to hollows seeking shelter from the sun, but that didn't mean the freeway was empty.

Creatures had become trapped in their cars. Those that hadn't opened the doors before the madness overtook them had lost the knowledge of how to do so. The dull thud of hands against glass rang around her, not quite masking the endless scrape of fingernails against leather. One of the monsters to her left howled, its voice breaking as the note rose.

She couldn't guess how many there were, only knew that they

were a multitude. Perhaps one in every fourth car. Maybe as many as one in three. They never cohabitated inside vehicles. Hollows in the wilderness ignored each other, but in enclosed spaces, the weaker ones fell victim to their companions' hunger.

But the hollows weren't the only distraction. Clare's throat burned. As the cap came away from the fuel intake, Clare had to turn aside to cough. An acrid taste coated her tongue.

What is that? It has to be related to the smog, doesn't it? Some kind of chemical maybe. She lifted a fuel jug to the intake and tilted the bottle. Her throat itched like a thousand insects were crawling down it and creeping into her lungs. She braced her feet and adjusted the jug's angle, feeling it lighten as the precious fuel flowed into the tank. Her eyes burned, and blinking didn't help. The last of the fuel emptied, she dropped the jug to the ground before unscrewing a second.

Her mind continued to race, trying to pinpoint the odors in the air. It felt like a bad omen, but she just couldn't make sense of it. She couldn't imagine anything man-made that had the power to cover the horizon like the smog did—especially with how few humans were left.

The thanites could. Fear coiled through her stomach. According to Madeline Morthorne, burning air had been the first symptom of the end of the world. Thanites still floated through the atmosphere. After the stillness event, they would have begun self-replicating, building up their numbers in anticipation of a second activation.

But they couldn't have been activated. That knowledge died with

Ezra. No one else knows about the thanites. No one else knows how to switch them on.

She was hyperaware of every limb, every bone. Her tongue ran across her teeth, tasting the toxic bitterness. *Were they always this sharp?* Her fingers ached as she gripped the canister too tightly. *Were they always this long?*

Clare leaned her masked forehead against the bus, fighting against the panic rising in her as she waited for the second jug to empty. If she really was feeling the nanobots activating in her lungs, it was already too late to save any of them.

To her right, Dorran paced away from the bus, his head lifted as he looked at the horizon. As he reached the nearest car, a sedan, he placed one foot onto the tow bar and used it as a step to climb onto the trunk. From there, he stepped onto the roof and removed his mask.

Does he feel it, too? The jug was empty. Clare dropped it and fumbled for a new canister without moving her eyes from Dorran.

"Clare. Beth!" He reached one hand behind himself to beckon to her. "Come here. It's urgent."

CHAPTER 18

CLARE ABANDONED THE FUEL canisters beside the bus. Footsteps crunched through broken glass as Beth loped toward them. Frustration pulled her face into hard angles.

"I said *no delays*," Beth hissed.

"He wouldn't unless it was important." Clare turned back to Dorran. Flecks of something small and pale were spiraling past him. *Snow? Surely not. It's nowhere near cold enough.*

She used the trailer hitch to climb onto the trunk, just like she'd seen Dorran do. He remained facing the horizon but offered her his hand. She took it, and he pulled her up to stand beside him.

At first glance, Clare thought she was staring into a vivid sunset. The dusty haze grew more saturated toward the skyline until it became a streak of golden red.

The mask blurred Clare's vision too badly to make out any details. She pulled it off and let it hang at her side.

The mask had dulled her vision, but not entirely, she realized. The sky was blurred. The distant golden-red streak shimmered. She inhaled and tasted the toxic prickles in her lungs. "Is that…"

The car listed as Beth climbed up beside them. Her lips flattened into a line and her eyebrows pulled together. "Fire."

Not just fire. An inferno. Clare's eyes watered as she followed the trail of color across the horizon. It went for miles.

"How?" Her voice caught. "It's been raining for days—"

"If a fire becomes hot enough, dampness ceases to be a hindrance." Dorran's voice was tense. "We had to be aware of this at Winterbourne, where we were surrounded by trees. If a fire grows out of control, it will consume anything in its path, old and fresh growth alike. Even a snowcapped forest can burn."

"I bet we have other survivors to thank for this." Beth's lips peeled back into a grimace. "Someone came up with the bright idea to use fire to chase away the hollows. Purge them from your area by burning a town or burning a forest. Use accelerant to help it grow. Don't stop to consider what will happen if it gets too big."

"Oh," Clare groaned. Off-white flakes spiraled past them. Soot was funneled in their direction by a sharp breeze. Funneling the *fire* toward them. Her palms were sweaty. "We…we need to go…"

"Yes." Beth worked her jaw. "We need to get off the freeway."

"Wait." Dorran grabbed her arm before she could leap off the sedan. Beth glared at him, and he quickly let go of her. "Where does the road we were on lead? Right now, it's parallel to the fire and surrounded by trees. If we stay on that course, we won't have long before the blaze reaches us."

"Can we take shelter inside the bus?" Clare asked.

Dorran shook his head. "The walls are too thin. A fire this large will be hot enough to make flammable material combust without even a spark."

Hot enough to cook us inside the bus like bread in an oven.

Beth's eyes flickered strangely in the faint orange glow. Clare thought she saw a trace of fear, but then it was buried under anger. "Damn it. Damn it! Dorran, take over refueling. We can't afford to run dry while we're outmaneuvering this thing. Clare, get the map."

Dorran slid off the sedan first, his boots thudding as he hit the concrete. Clare leaped off after him, and he caught her, swinging her around to set her down gently. "Go," he whispered, and pushed her toward the bus's door.

Her patience for masks was gone. As she leaped into the bus, Clare tossed it onto a seat. She scrambled for the map Beth had left on the dashboard, then slipped back outside. She flipped through pages as she jogged to Beth, who held her position on the sedan, watching the skyline.

"The road goes on for maybe an hour before it reaches town." Clare flipped another page as she clambered onto the trunk, then the roof. "But a town will burn just as easily as a forest, right?"

"Yeah. We need a barren field. Or a very large parking lot. Just…any sort of large space without much flammable material. The fire will still travel through it, but it should pass quickly enough that we can survive it inside the bus." Beth took half of the map. They moved feverishly, paging through the patchwork grays and greens. Beth ground her teeth, and Clare repressed the impulse to lean away from the noise. It sounded too much like the hollows. More than she liked to think about.

"Damn it," Beth muttered. "He's right. The road we were on just keeps going straight for ages. There aren't any offshoots."

Clare turned to look along the freeway. From their elevated position, she could make out the jigsaw of tangled, abandoned cars stretching away for miles. "How far before the freeway has another turnoff?"

The sound of grinding teeth intensified. More pages flipped. Then Beth blew a breath out through her nostrils. "Twenty minutes at full speed."

"That's too far." Soot landed on Clare's neck. She flicked it off, imagining she could feel latent heat transferred from it. The ribbon of golden light on the horizon looked larger than it had two minutes before.

Beth's eyes moved from the skyline, to the bus, to the freeway. Her tongue darted over her lips. "Maybe not."

"What are you thinking?"

"The freeway carries us away from the fire. That in itself will buy us time. The bus is big enough and heavy enough to win a fight over most stationary vehicles. It can take a beating; I've already tested that. If we get some momentum behind us, we should be able to carve a path through this mess."

Clare didn't like the way the plan made her feel. Once they left the on-ramp, they'd arrived through, there would be no chance to leave the freeway until the next exit. "If we get stuck…"

"We die," Beth confirmed. "But if we get back onto the other road and don't find a clearing in time, we die. If we stay where we are, we die. This way at least gives the possibility of a different outcome." She turned the map back to an earlier page. "If we can make it to the next turnoff, we're only ten minutes from farmland. All we need is a field big enough and barren enough to starve the fire of fuel and we can outlast this thing."

Clare turned toward the bus and saw Dorran waiting just a few paces away, his dark eyes narrowed against the soot. "Dorran—"

"I heard. And I agree. It is perhaps the least awful out of a bad set of choices."

"All right. How are we looking for fuel?"

"The tank is full."

Clare slid off the car roof and onto the trunk, then clambered to the ground while Dorran threw the empty fuel containers into the bus. Beth tucked the map under one arm and leaped from the sedan's roof. Her movements had developed an animalistic litheness, and she loped to the bus's door without even pausing to catch her balance.

"Let's go," Beth called. "We have an inferno to outrun."

CHAPTER 19

"SEAT BELTS." BETH JUMPED into the driver's seat. The door snapped shut as Clare and Dorran took the row of seats second from the front. Clare hoped they wouldn't need it, but the row ahead of them would give them something to brace against if the drive was too rocky.

Clare's hands shook, and it took two attempts to clip the seat belt buckle. Dorran, at her side, was steady and silent except for his breathing, which came a little too quickly. Flecks of soot stuck in his dark hair. His eyes were still too bright, and Clare was glad she'd given him the antibiotic when she'd had the chance.

"Ready?" The engine roared to life. Beth's hair shimmered in the overhead light, her eyes flashing as she put the bus into gear. "Hold on. We're not stopping for anything."

The floor vibrated under Clare's feet as the bus lurched forward, its wheels fighting for traction on the broken glass and cracked concrete. The vehicle wasn't designed to be driven like a race car, but that was what Beth asked of it, twisting the wheel to take advantage of a gap in the vehicles.

The plan was to carve a path through brute force. That would only work if they could get enough momentum behind them. Clare grit her teeth, her knuckles white as she gripped her seat and their speed increased. Faster and faster, the engine rumbled as gears changed, the ground disappearing under them. A hatchback blocked their path less than thirty feet away. Clare closed her eyes.

The impact shook her. The seat belt bit into her lap. She opened her eyes just in time to see the hatchback spiraling away. It hadn't just been pushed aside; it had been shoveled into the air, where it twisted, poised for a beautiful second before gravity pulled it back down. A small smile broke through the tightness around Beth's lips, and the engine roared again as she pushed into the accelerator.

They hit a second car that had been hidden behind the hatchback. It had been at an angle and exploded away in a shower of broken glass and dust. The road was clear. The rumbling grew as they passed the speed limit and kept climbing.

Dorran's hand brushed against hers. She fastened her hand around his, and they held each other, fingers aching from how tight the grip was, damp with sweat, terrified to let go.

A sedan skidded away and crumpled to a halt, wedged between two other cars. The road only stayed clear for forty feet; a sports car was propped across lanes, its driver's side door open, sunroof retracted. It looked light, but Clare still braced for the impact.

A bang was followed by the wail of bending metal. The sports car, too low to the ground to be lifted away by their plow, jammed against the bus's front.

Their momentum was immense, and they pushed the sports car ahead of themselves like a toy. Its sleek blue-gray metal twisted, curving against the bus's front. The wheels lasted all of four seconds, then burst with deafening bangs. Sparks showered around the windshield. It was slowing them. Every foot drained their energy, sapping their speed, grinding them inevitably closer to a standstill.

"Come on, come on," Beth growled. She flexed her grip on the wheel, her jaw working, as she hunched forward.

Then the sports car's rear bumper clipped a truck and it twisted, the front wheels rising up to pirouette on its end. The scream of twisting metal ran along the bus's side, and Clare knew their own transport hadn't escaped unscathed. But they were free and back onto a clear stretch of road. Their speed began to rise again.

Clare realized she'd forgotten to breathe. She sucked in shallow, ragged gasps of air. It burned. She pressed a sleeve over her mouth to muffle her coughs.

The noise seemed to make Dorran realize how tightly he was holding her hand. He adjusted his grip, rubbing her fingers instead, a silent apology. She pressed in return. She didn't care how hard he held; she needed it. Just as long as she didn't feel alone.

Beth found an equilibrium on the road. Poised between lanes, the white, dotted line disappearing under the bus's center, she hit twice as many vehicles but met half the resistance. The cars sluiced to either side of the bus, no longer working as blockades but as bumpers.

Clare wished she could see the fire behind them. Or even just know how far the orange glow had spread across the sky. With their windows blocked, her only choice was to watch the road ahead. It was gradually darkening. The air tasted worse. Flecks of ash landed on their windshield, only to be buffeted away a second later.

The steady channel Beth had been following became broken. A wreck appeared ahead. Two cars had collided, covering the highway's width, one vehicle rising up to become stuck on its partner. It was going to be another hard hit, Clare knew, but they were traveling too fast to turn aside. Her muscles tensed, every part of her body from her feet to her jaw preparing for the impact.

She saw the hollow a second before they hit. The car on top of the pile was occupied; its driver scrambled over the seats, screaming, eyes bulging. It had heard their approach. It was excited.

They collided with the wreck, and Clare was slammed forward in her seat. The lower car spun in a half circle. Its brakes had been engaged and the tires left black lines across the concrete. The top car impacted their windshield. Instead of rolling up to disappear over their heads, it fell down, jamming against the metal plow. It didn't stay there for long. They hit another SUV, and the car broke in two, splitting at the driver's side door's seam in a shower of glass and debris.

The hollow one came free. It slammed into their windshield. Long fingers, eight on each hand, splayed over the glass as it tried to find purchase. It stared inside, not at Beth, but at Clare and Dorran two rows behind. The jaw opened and the teeth scraped against the window.

Then the hollow disintegrated as they hit a camper van. The impact was brutal, jarring Clare and throwing her head forward so fast that she bit the inside of her mouth. She pressed her forearm against the row of seats ahead. Both her neck and head ached. When she looked up, the crawler was gone save for a smear of thick liquids and a distended shape that she thought might be its lower jaw.

Beth simply turned on the windshield wipers. Soapy water sprayed over the mess as it smeared in thick, sickening streaks across the window. She kept the wipers on until the water reservoir was empty and the gore only blurred their view, instead of obscuring it.

Clare's heart felt like it was going to fracture from the stress. She trembled. Dorran was quiet, but she knew that didn't mean he was calm.

A sign rose up by the side of the road. Arrows indicated an upcoming turnoff.

"Two minutes." Beth, breathless, was hard to hear underneath the rhythmic bangs and grinding metal. "We're almost there."

Please. Let it be enough. Clare thought she could feel the heat. The change in temperature was subtle enough that she could almost believe she was imagining it, except that she had the urge to take off her jacket. For the first time in weeks, she could no longer describe the air as chilled.

A motorbike disappeared underneath them, and Clare felt each distinct bump as it passed below their wheels. The cut on her lip filled her mouth with the astringent tang of blood.

Then, up ahead, she caught sight of the turnoff. Clear white markers indicated where cars could form a new lane and merge out of traffic. Her heart skipped.

A truck blocked the exit. A car had tried to cut in front of it, desperate to escape the freeway on the last normal day. The two had collided, tangling against concrete railing, creating a barrier across their exit.

A faint choking noise came from Beth. She took her foot off the accelerator as she faced the exit. It was coming up on them blindingly fast. They would be at it in seconds, but they couldn't slow down; slowing would mean losing momentum at the risk of never gaining it again.

We can't keep driving. There's no time to get to another exit. But we can't get past the truck without leaving the bus. And we can't leave the bus if we want to survive. There's no way. There's no way... unless—

"The on-ramp!" Clare yelled.

Beth's eyes flashed with understanding. She put pressure back on the accelerator as a sedan spun out of their path. She rose up in her seat, leaning forward, as she searched the scene.

Only one road leads off the freeway. But there'll be another chance. A road that leads on.

The on-ramp would be hard to see. It would come after the off-ramp funneled cars toward the town; their first warning would be the appearance of a new lane. And if they wanted to use the on-ramp, they would have to be facing the opposite direction.

Can't lose our speed. Can't miss our one chance. No room for even a single mistake.

"There," Dorran called.

A shoulder-height concrete wall bordered the road. A flash of red appeared over its top: the roof of a car. Clare craned her neck and saw where the concrete blockade tapered into nothing as the new lane merged onto the freeway. The area held clusters of cars. It was going to be tight.

"Brace!" Beth yanked the bus's wheel. Clare grabbed the seat ahead of her as gravity tried to drag her into the aisle. Dorran hit her shoulder with a gasp as the minibus rose onto two wheels. The angle was too sharp; they were going to topple, but Clare had no breath left to make any noise. She tried to prepare herself for the stab of fractured glass, the wrenching pain of her belt tying her to the seat as the bus rolled, the impact of their luggage becoming projectiles…

The bus hit a camper van. Beth had timed it impeccably. The camper van skidded away, rocking, but the impact had been enough to tilt the balance back into their favor. The bus crashed back onto the road with a bone-shaking *bang*. They were still moving, but now the bus's rear was fishtailing as their front turned toward the on-ramp.

The turn brought them around to face the fire. It was no

longer limited to a distant glow, ominous and unreadable. It consumed the sky. Plumes of toxic black smoke spewed above them as trees and buildings alike were devoured. The smoke was painted orange by miles of licking fire, the flames rising higher than the houses, higher than the trees, towering above everything in their path. The ash was no longer a dusting; it snowed.

The bus wheels screamed as they completed their arc, leaving lines of black behind them. The on-ramp had concrete barriers edging it. They hit the blockades on the outer side, rattling them, then they were free and running down the slope to the ground below.

For a second, fields were visible in the distance, then the trees rose up to block the view. The forest still surrounded them. The engine roared as they entered a narrow road surrounded by craggy growth and leaf litter, not much different from the road they'd left twenty minutes before.

Get out of the trees. Get out of the trees...

A shape lurched out of the forest to their left. A hollow one, massive and bloated, folds of skin swollen with fat or fluids. If it had been upright, it would have been at least ten feet tall. It lumbered on all fours, its body rocking wildly, its vacant eyes gazing into the distance as a bellow came from its slack jaw.

Beth yelled. She hit the brakes, throwing Clare forward in her seat. The crawler collided with the bus near the door, and Clare was jerked back. The momentum that had acted as an advantage moments before robbed them of control. The bus fishtailed again, front wheels spinning off the road. Beth swore. She swung the wheel, trying to correct them, but the road was dirt and offered precious little traction. The bus nearly completed a full revolution, and Clare thought they might actually make it out of the encounter. Then the front wheels left the edge of the road. The bus tilted down as they plunged into the ditch, branches fracturing against their windshield, bringing them to a grinding halt.

CHAPTER 20

THE CRAWLER HADN'T MADE it out of the collision unscathed. It rolled across the path, limbs clawing up the dirt as it bellowed, pus seeping out of a split in its bulbous chest. Then it gained its feet and lurched across the road, disappearing back into the forest.

Clare was panting, leaned back in her seat, both arms pressed against the chair ahead, every muscle tight. Her head throbbed, pulsing red and black across her vision. Her neck ached. But, otherwise, she thought she was okay.

At her side, Dorran stared ahead, eyes wide. He looked shocked: not at what had happened, but at the fact that they were still alive.

For a heartbeat, none of them moved. Then Beth slowly turned in her seat. Patches of hair had come free from the tie and hung about her face. A line of red traced over her forehead and dripped into her eyebrow; the impact had thrown her forward and cut her. She didn't seem to notice it. "Clare? Baby? You okay?"

"I'm good," Clare managed. She was pretty sure she had whiplash. And possibly a mild concussion, if the throbbing headache was anything to go by. But that wouldn't kill her. The thanites would take care of it all in a matter of days.

Beth's throat bobbed as she swallowed. Then she added, her voice faint, "Dorran?"

"Fine." His voice was remarkably calm, in the way that only Dorran's could sound. His arms remained ahead of him, holding on to the seats in front for support, as though frozen. Clare realized she was still in the same position, elbows locked and hands braced. She tried to let go, but stopped when she felt herself slide.

Her world was tilted. The bus hung at an angle. Not enough to throw her out of her seat, but enough that the floor was no longer horizontal. The bus's rear wheels would have to be in the air. The front was buried in the bracken and dead branches of the trees ahead of them.

Clare tried to moisten her mouth. It tasted of fear and smoke. "Beth...the fire..."

"Right. Yeah." Beth turned back to face the wheel. They would have time to collect themselves and lick their wounds once they were out of the fire's path. The engine still rumbled. No matter what other damage the hollow had done, it hadn't been enough to kill the minibus.

Beth shifted into reverse. The bus shuddered as it tried to

climb out of the ditch, but they made it no more than a couple of inches before sliding back down, wheels spinning. Beth swore. She pushed harder, until the engine roared and the shuddering made their luggage shake in its compartments.

"Stop." Dorran's voice was soft and without anger but held an intent focus. Beth eased off the accelerator. "The bus isn't going to move. Continuing will only dig ruts under the wheels."

Beth swore with conviction. She put it in Park. "We can't stay here."

Dorran's seat belt clicked as he unfastened it, and before Clare knew what was happening, he'd climbed over her. He used the seats for support as he skidded toward the bus's front. "Do you have a shovel?"

"Yeah. In the outside compartment."

"Good." He forced the door open and disappeared outside. His words were mild and his voice was gentle, but Clare knew him too well to think that translated into complacency. He was moving with the sharp urgency of a crisis.

She struggled with her own seat belt, fighting against numb fingers. The second it unfastened, she tried to jog toward the bus's front. She underestimated the angle, lost her balance, and hit the dashboard with a grunt. Beth was already in the open door and offered her hand to Clare. Together, they stepped outside.

The smoke was suffocating. Clare pressed her sleeve across her mouth, her eyes burning, her throat convulsing. She caught a glimpse of the damage as she clambered over fallen branches and rocks to reach the bus's front. The hollow had left a wicked dent beside the door and fractured one of the pieces of plywood nailed over the windows. The freeway hadn't shown them mercy, either; both sets of headlights were gone, and although the vehicle's structural integrity wasn't compromised, the metal wedge they had used as a plow was covered in dents.

Clare raised her head. The sky was full of ravenous oranges and poisonous blacks. The fire roared. It sounded like a plane flying overhead, except instead of growing fainter, it grew louder with every second. Sparks mingled with the falling ash.

Get out of the trees, her mind screamed. *Get out of the trees!*

She turned in a circle, her head pounding and her body overridden with panic. They were in the depths of the forest. For a wild second, she wanted to grab her companions' hands and run with them along the road, aiming for the fields, but that would be tantamount to suicide. There were no clearings within running distance. Their only chance was to drive—and drive fast.

Dorran crouched at the bus's front. He had one shoulder against the metal, testing, seeing if he could push the bus out of the ditch through sheer force. The structure creaked as he lifted, but it didn't move. He released the pressure, and as he stepped back, he swiped his hand across his jaw. A smear of red came away from his nose. "We need to get wood under the wheels. Quickly."

The instruction took a second to sink in, then Clare shot into action. At least that was one small mercy; there was no shortage of wood in the forest.

Dorran used the shovel to clear loose dirt away from the front tires and jam branches under them. As Clare dropped a load at his side, she turned to face the forest. A strange noise came from between the trees. It was higher than the fire's roar. Closer.

A hollow burst out of the tree line. Clare barely had time to react. Her back hit the bus, and she raised her arms defensively. Beth appeared out of nowhere, stepping between Clare and the hollow, teeth bared and eyes wild.

The creature darted aside a second before collision. It galloped along the bus's side and across the road, disappearing into the forest on the other side. Clare cautiously lowered her arms. She had never seen a hollow willingly relinquish a meal before.

The large hollow, the one that hit the bus and forced us off the road…it wasn't trying to attack us either, was it?

The impact had been too sudden to be planned. The hollow's eyes hadn't even been focused on them; it had been staring blankly into the distance. And it had scrambled away after it derailed them, not even stopping to examine the bus.

It's the fire. They're fleeing, just like we are.

More shapes darted out of the tree line. Clare stared in wonder as hollows flowed around them, not even sparing the humans a glance. Jaws hung open. Eyes stared vacantly. They were terrified.

Dorran stepped away from the wheels. His breathing sounded painful as he threw the shovel aside, dark eyes darting across his work, scanning for weaknesses. "Clare, take the driver's seat. Be ready to reverse on my signal."

She nodded, mouth too dry to speak.

"Beth, get behind the bus. Hold on to something at its back; try to use your body weight to pull it down."

"What are you going to do?"

"I'll stay here and push."

Beth glanced at the horizon. It was growing bright. "Swap with me. You're heavier." Dorran opened his mouth to argue, but Beth put a hand on his arm and shoved him away. "Don't worry. I've got strength. Maybe more than even you."

He gave a single tight nod and left at a jog. Clare jumped through the bus's open door, staggered on the uneven floor, and dropped into the driver's seat. It was her first time piloting the minibus, but if Beth had figured out the controls, she could as well.

More hollows were racing out of the forest. She caught flashes of wild eyes and faces twisted with pure terror. Their chattering, screeching cries rose in volume.

Beth shed her jacket and braced her hands against the bus's front. The cut on her forehead continued to bleed, dripping over her eyebrow and staining her chin. The bus groaned, and Clare knew Dorran had found his grip at the back. Beth gave her a small nod, and Clare pulled the gearshift into reverse.

The engine rattled. She lightly touched the accelerator, testing it, and felt the vehicle shudder as it sought purchase. Beth put her head down, feet braced, and pushed. Her only form of exercise before the stillness had been yoga, and Clare would have never labeled her as physically strong. Now, defined muscles tightened like ropes under her skin. Her body curled, all sleek, raw power, and the metal groaned under her hands.

The bus shuddered backward in fractions. One inch, then two. Clare gave it slightly more gas. One of the branches they'd used for traction was spat aside and the wheel began to spin. But they were tilting back. Metal creaked as the bus's structure was strained beyond what it had been designed to handle. Then the tires caught on the edge of the road. The back wheels touched down.

Beth lifted her head. Victory twisted her features into those of a monster. Her eyes were too angular. Her mouth too wide. Clare's foot twitched on the accelerator, and they shot backward.

She slammed on the breaks, panic stabbing into her nerves. Dorran was still behind the bus. *Did I hit him? Would I have felt it if I had?*

She was at the open door before she could breathe. Dorran appeared at the bus's side, jogging toward her, and Clare's legs turned weak. "Are you okay?"

"Of course." An easy smile, so beautifully familiar, warmed his face. His arm slipped around her and he pulled her back onto the bus, not even breaking stride. They had barely cleared the entryway before Beth leaped up behind them, slamming the door.

"Move." She shoved past them to reach the driver's seat. "We've already lost too much time."

Beth's face looked familiar again. The angles were a little harder, and the scars were a constant reminder of what the stillness had done to her, but behind them was the same Beth she had always known. The Beth from outside the bus had not been familiar. It was as though a mask had slipped over her sweet features.

A horrible suspicion rose: that Beth did have a mask. That she wore it constantly. That, in that moment she had been outside of the bus, she had let it slip.

Clare had come to a halt. Dorran's hand rested on her back, a silent question that she had no way to answer. She moved automatically, retracing the path along the aisle. The bus began to move before she had a chance to reach her seat.

Dorran didn't sit next to her, like she'd expected. He continued along the aisle to reach the bottled water. She watched with growing concern. His movements remained steady, but getting the bus back onto the road had drained him. The wash he'd had that morning was undone by a layer of soot and dirt. His breathing was rough. He was running on empty.

"Come and sit," Clare said. "If you need something, I'll find it."

"Just one moment." The exhaustion was starting to bleed into his voice. He found dish towels in the compartments, cracked open the bottle, and used it to dampen a cloth. Then he crossed back to Clare. "Here. It will filter the worst of the smoke."

Dorran helped tie the fabric around the lower half of her face. Just the touch alone was a balm; the heat was increasing, the humidity evaporating, and Clare's airways were scorched dry. She pressed the damp fabric over her mouth and nose, grateful.

The bus rocked as Beth took a sharp turn. Dorran caught himself on the seats. The view outside the window changed; they were still surrounded by trees on both sides, but now the boughs held flames. Sparks danced around their bus, spiraling on the heated air like vivid red snowflakes. The spot fires were small but many, and growing on both sides of them. Black smoke flowed across the road. Clare couldn't stifle a dread-filled moan.

Dorran stared at the flickering, blurred scene, then drenched a second towel in water. He approached Beth and moved to tie it around her face. She held up a hand to block him. "I don't need it."

"It will help—"

"Nope. Get back to your seat."

Her voice was raspy. But unlike Clare and Dorran, she didn't seem to be fighting the urge to cough. The thanites had to be protecting her throat from the smoke, or, what Clare thought was more likely, they dulled the sensation.

Dorran tied the cloth around his own face and lurched into the seat beside Clare. She found his hand, more from reflex than clear thought, and he enveloped it in both of his.

The flames on either side of the road were becoming more frequent. Entire clumps of trees were being swallowed. Deep crackling made itself heard above the bus's engine. Perspiration evaporated as soon as it beaded on Clare's exposed skin, but underneath her jacket, she was drenched.

This isn't the worst yet. The blaze she'd seen on the horizon wasn't slow moving or made up of spot fires. It was an inferno, a wall of fire, consuming everything in its path.

Beth drove like hell itself was on their heels. Tires shrieked as she clipped the bends on the winding road. They had to be moving toward farmland; Clare had seen it from the freeway. But every turn only exposed more trees. Burning, alive with twisting reds and whites, the leaves curling under the onslaught of sparks.

Then they cleared a hill, and the trees vanished. Farmland spread out ahead of them. Fields of gray weeds, neglected before the silence, then killed by the snow, were already smoking as sparks ignited the flammable stalks. Not far past was a segment of dead grass. It had been kept well trimmed, possibly by cattle, and Beth's gaze fixed on it. They roared past the smoking fields. A fence made of wood posts and barbed metal blocked their path, but that was the least the bus had been through that day. Beth veered off the narrow road, rocking them as they tilted down the shallow incline, and pointed them straight at the fence. Splinters of wood burst past their windshield. A line of barbed wire managed to hang on, dragging posts out of the ground behind them, before snapping free. Beth didn't stop moving until they ground to a halt in the field's center.

"Will this be enough?" she asked Dorran.

He swallowed. "I hope so."

CHAPTER 21

BETH WAS OUT OF her seat in a heartbeat. Clare held the cloth tight against her face as she and Dorran rose. The front windshield held a view of the farmhouses dotting the fields and the distant rooftops of the town, but they were rapidly being swallowed by a blanket of black smoke.

Clare stepped toward the window and suddenly felt dizzy. Beth had parked at an angle where the forest was visible to their left. The trees were vanishing under the roaring wall of white and red. It was advancing on them, slicing through the forest faster than she had imagined was possible, raw and beautiful and brutal all at once.

Until then, she'd believed that the field could protect them. But at that moment, the fire seemed to be something unnatural, something that did not abide by physical bounds, that did not care how little fuel there was, that was destined to consume the earth.

Beth dragged the bus's metal shutter down to cover the windshield. Darkness swallowed them, hot, cramped, and claustrophobic. Dorran was at her side. Beth was somewhere ahead, breathing quickly. Clare closed her eyes. She wished she could close her ears as well. The fire was deafening and growing louder. She reached one arm out and touched the bus's side. It was hot. She recoiled. Dorran's arm moved around her. Then a hand touched her other side: Beth. Clare pulled them both close. They formed a circle, standing in the center of the bus, heads down, holding each other.

Dorran's forehead grazed hers. She could just barely hear his whisper. "I love you."

Clare mouthed the words back. The cloth he'd tied around her face was no longer wet. She was too hot. Every breath felt like it was suffocating her. Beth was shaking; Clare tightened her hold on her.

She had no moisture left in her body to sweat. Her skin crawled. Her lungs burned. Her legs turned weak, but Beth's hold on her was a steel grip. The heat was relentless, growing hotter, unbearable, and she couldn't take even another second—

"I think it's passed."

The words echoed through Clare's head. They didn't make any sense. She held her mouth open as her lungs, starved for oxygen, tried to find air. Beth's steel grip pulled her, making her stumble. She tried to speak. Couldn't. Her sister's hand kept pulling, and Clare, afraid of losing either of her companions in the dark, followed.

A door banged. Fresh air brushed across Clare's face. It wasn't *cold*, but it wasn't suffocating her, either. Beth had the bus door open and was trying to pull her outside.

She nearly lost her footing as she took the step down onto the earth below. Her limbs felt boneless and the world tilted sickeningly. She didn't realize she was still holding on to Dorran's arm until he lurched to a halt beside her.

"It's over." Beth's face was painted in strange shadows. Hair stuck to her forehead and neck as she unzipped the jacket and pulled the scarf free. A thin, crooked smile appeared as she gazed around the field. "We're all right."

Clare, dazed, stared at their environment. Flames still surrounded them, but they were no longer all-consuming. Patches of fire clung to the last sources of fuel in the field: branches, thicker clumps of grass, roots half-embedded in the ground. The fire's front had passed them in a matter of minutes as the small amount of fuel was decimated. The earth was scorched black, the dry grass reduced to ash, and choking smoke rose from the still-hot soil. She looked to her left. The forest continued to burn. The flammable leaves and smaller branches were gone; now, only trunks remained as fuel, and they smoldered.

She turned in the other direction. The farmhouse she'd spotted earlier was now a pillar of whites and yellows as it succumbed to the fire.

We made it. We're safe. The idea seemed hard to believe as the smoke blocked out the sky and heat radiated from every direction. But they were free. The fire would continue traveling, but it wouldn't pass over the ground it had already charred.

Dorran pressed one arm across his face as he coughed in violent spasms. He let go of her arm and collapsed to his knees.

Clare reached for him. She wanted to help. She didn't know how. Her mind was empty and dull, as though the fire had consumed everything inside, too. She didn't know what else to do, so she lowered herself to her knees beside him as his coughs subsided. Flecks of blood stained the sleeve. Beth stood over them, and Clare blinked up at her, feeling frightened and lost. "Beth?"

The word didn't come out properly; her tongue was dry and refused to move. Beth swore under her breath. She jogged to the bus's door, leaped inside, and a moment later, returned with two bottles of water. She unscrewed the caps with feverish haste and forced one into Clare's hands. "You're dehydrated. Drink."

Clare stared at the bottle blankly. Her throat ached. Her nose and eyes burned. But she didn't think she needed the water that badly. Dorran's head was down, his breathing coming in thin gasps. She found his hand and pressed the bottle into it.

Beth muttered something furious. She unscrewed the second water and held it out to Clare. She didn't take it. She was too busy watching Dorran.

"Fine, we'll do it the hard way." Beth tugged the cloth away from Clare's face, put one hand under her chin, and tilted her head back as she poured water into her mouth. Clare wasn't ready; she choked and reeled back, gasping and coughing as liquid flooded her nose.

"Ow," she said as she righted herself, water dripping off her chin.

"Are you going to be sensible now and drink?" Beth asked. "Or do you want to be waterboarded again?"

"You get cranky when you're scared," Clare mumbled. She took the bottle. Beth's force-feeding hadn't been gentle, but just the taste of water had awakened a deep craving. She tried a sip, testing her ability to swallow, then tilted her head back as she drank deeply.

Dorran mimicked the motion beside her, draining his bottle in seconds. Beth watched them both, and she wasn't able to fully conceal the fear underneath her icy glare. When she saw they were going to finish the bottles, she disappeared back into the bus to retrieve more.

Sitting in the ash-crusted field, watching streams of smoke drift away on the wind, Clare felt her mind creeping back to her a fraction at a time. She tilted her head to see the man beside her. "How are you doing?"

"Tired. But alive."

Beth reappeared, opening three more bottles and passing them out.

Clare had to stop herself from draining the second bottle. Her throat was still dry and her body begged for more water, but she knew if she drank too much too quickly, she would be sick.

Beth crouched near her. She'd kept one of the bottles for herself but only sipped it as she gazed at the smoldering forest.

"Aren't you thirsty?" Clare asked.

Beth's glance was sharp, but her shrug felt casual. "Not really. But I figure, if you need water, I must, too."

"Mm." Clare rolled her tongue around her mouth. It was tacky, despite what she'd already drunk, and held the bitter taste of smoke and blood. She tipped some more water into her mouth, swirled it around, and spat it behind her.

"The tires are still intact." Beth seemed to be trying to make conversation. "That's a mercy. And the fuel didn't leak, either, which is always a good thing."

The mental image of the fuel containers stored in their bus's luggage compartment exploding into balls of flame made Clare's skin crawl. She pulled a face. "If you're trying to be comforting, you're not doing a great job."

Beth's lopsided smile widened. "I thought you *liked* good news. If you want some more, we won't have to worry about being interrupted for a while. That fire's going to torch everything in its path, hollow and human alike. We're probably the only things alive for hours in any direction."

Clare shuddered. Beth had failed to keep the glee out of her voice. A clear path didn't feel like it should be something to celebrate if it came at the cost of lives. Her stomach turned queasy, and she closed her eyes as she waited for the world to stabilize. The throbbing headache wasn't abating as quickly as she'd hoped.

"We'll be fine," Beth continued. "I'll give the bus a bit longer to cool. Wish I could open the windows. Regardless. Fifteen or so minutes should be enough, then we can get back onto the road.

We lost ground outrunning the fire, but it's nothing we can't make up. We should be at Evandale before midnight."

Clare pictured it: back on the bus, her world swaying with constant motion. The headache swelled. She turned aside and was sick.

"Hey, baby." Beth's smile vanished as she reached toward Clare. "Come on, you need that water. You need to drink."

Clare tried to answer. Her stomach turned over again. She retched, but she'd already brought up everything she could. Shivers traveled through her in waves.

"Clare?" Beth sounded truly worried. "Talk to me. What's wrong?"

She slumped back, praying the ground would stop tilting. A hand, large, gentle, and familiar, rested on her back.

"Concussion." Dorran's voice was strained as he spoke through a raw throat. "Hit your head. I saw. You need to lie down. Beth—pain tablets in the bus."

"Okay. Right." Beth was up before Clare could draw breath. She returned within seconds, rattling bottles as she sorted through the bag of medication.

"Drink," Dorran whispered. "Just a little. It will help."

A bottle was held up to her mouth. Clare didn't trust herself to hold anything down, but she didn't have the energy to fight, either. She swallowed a mouthful, then someone pressed two tablets onto her tongue, followed by more water. She tried to open her eyes, to focus on the world, but the endless field of grays and blacks and flickering reds washed together. Dorran's arm wrapped around her as the shades faded into gray.

CHAPTER 22

THE HEADACHE CONTINUED TO throb, but it no longer overwhelmed her other senses. Her tongue tasted like death. Her nose and throat stung. The smoke was so overwhelming that it turned her stomach, but at least she thought she was in control again.

Clare opened her eyes a fraction at a time. Nearby light hurt her retinas. She squinted while her head came to terms with it.

She was outside. Clare's first thought was that the smoke had covered the whole world, but as her eyes focused, she realized she could see pale stars through the patches of smog. She squinted, not sure she could trust her vision. "What time is it?"

There was movement at her side, and Beth's face appeared above her, smiling. "Hey, there you are. Can you sit up? You need to drink more water."

The words were kind, and the smile tried to match them, but there was something distinctly unsettling about it. Clare struggled to identify what had gone wrong. It showed too many teeth, or it was too wide, or it didn't move her cheeks right, or maybe a little of all three. The eyes were unblinking as they gazed down at her, expectant, and Clare was suddenly struck by the feeling that she was locking eyes with a predatory animal.

Beth tilted her head, then made a strange chuckling noise in the back of her throat. Her hand moved under Clare's shoulders and, before she could object, Clare was pulled up.

"Oh…no." She clenched her teeth, eyes closed, as the headache boomed through her skull and nausea returned with a vengeance.

"*Gentle*," Dorran said. He sounded frustrated. "She's hurt. You can't throw her around like a doll."

"She needs…to…drink." Beth's voice took on a strange singsong lilt, bouncing through different tones, unnaturally happy. A hand patted Clare's back too hard.

"Gentle, gentle," Dorran repeated.

Beth's voice abruptly twisted into a snarl. "*Back off.*"

For a moment, everything was quiet. Clare cautiously opened her eyes. Beth crouched at her side, the manic smile still in place, her eyes perfect circles as she stared at Dorran. He was on his knees at her other side, one hand frozen midair as he'd moved to touch Clare's shoulder. His expression seemed mild, almost pleasant, but Clare recognized the look. It was the mask he wore when he was stressed.

Her eyes adjusted as she squinted at their camp. They were still close to the bus and had made a kind of nest in the ashes. Someone had scraped a stretch of ground clear from the worst of the ash and lit a fire in the center. They had to be using the wood they'd kept in the bus. There would be virtually no flammable material for miles.

Blankets had been draped over Clare and folded under her head. Ash transferred readily, and it was in the process of turning every surface gray, including her companions.

Dorran slowly lowered his hand. His voice was level and calm, but he didn't take his eyes off Beth. "I am here to help her, just like you."

"Ha." Beth's gaze flicked back to Clare. The smile trembled. "I-I—"

Clare tried to find her voice. "Beth."

"I'm fine. I just…" Beth blinked aggressively, then shook her head, as though there was some kind of irritant sticking to it. "I know I'm overreacting. It's the fire. I hated it. We all hated it, right? But it wasn't just *fire* to me. I wasn't afraid of dying. I was afraid of—of—"

"Hey." Speaking made Clare's throat ache worse. She rested one hand on Beth's shoulder and felt as Beth's body rocked with every breath.

"It was the heat and the light. I could feel it behind us. I could tell it was coming closer, even when I couldn't see it. Every atom of my body was screaming, telling me to run, to run fast and run far. But I didn't leave you." She laughed, but the sound broke with fear and stress. "I stayed, didn't I? And we're fine. You're fine and I'm fine and you just need to drink some water."

She abruptly stood and paced away from Clare, panting. She

hadn't yet put her jacket back on and the spines created bumps across her tank top's back. Red halos circled the three highest bones where they cut through her skin. She paused, facing the darkness, swaying lightly, hands buried in her hair. When she turned back to Clare, her face seemed a little more familiar.

"It's the night, too. It always gets worse at night. I'm going to take a walk, okay? A walk will help. Give me time to think…and breathe."

Clare didn't know what else to say. "Don't go far, okay?"

Beth's barking laughter seemed shockingly loud. "I'll be back by dawn. You should be safe enough here. I don't like being in the ashes; I don't think the others will, either."

She didn't give them a chance to answer, moving into the darkness at something between a jog and a lope, and vanished like evaporating mist.

Dorran exhaled deeply. His head drooped, and Clare realized he'd been holding more tension than she'd thought.

"Are you okay?" she asked.

"Yeah." He rubbed his palm across his eyes, leaving smears of ash, then picked a bottle of water off a small stack beside them and opened it before offering it to Clare. She took it, grateful, and downed as much as she thought she could handle. The headache continued to throb. The fire's light hurt her eyes, but at least its warmth was welcome. She hadn't thought the temperature would drop so quickly after the blaze, but she wouldn't be surprised if frost dotted the ground by dawn.

Dorran wiped his hand on a cloth before popping two pain

tablets out of his packet. Despite his best efforts, they still had a smudge of black on them when he placed them into her palm.

"Sorry," he murmured. "The soot is somewhat endemic."

"Mm, I don't mind." She swallowed the tablets and breathed slowly as she waited for the swelling dizziness to subside. "Was I out for long?"

"A few hours." He shuffled closer to sit at her side. She leaned into him, appreciating the feel of his arm at her back. "You needed it."

"What about you? Did you sleep?"

"A little." To Clare's surprise, he looked ashamed. "I tried not to, but—"

"Why wouldn't you want to sleep? You were exhausted." She tilted her head back to read his expression, but he wouldn't meet her eyes. Something cold and unpleasant settled in her stomach. "Was it…because of Beth?"

He started to answer, stopped himself, and licked his lips.

Clare still had half of her water left. She held it up to him. "What did she do?"

"Nothing bad." He took the water and sipped. "She was just… well, like you saw. She was worried for you. The fire made her anxious, and I think she felt helpless as well. Unable to travel, unable to make you better. She couldn't keep still. I'm sure she'll feel more like herself when she comes back."

He was trying to play it off like it wasn't a big deal, but Clare knew it must have been bad for him to fight to stay awake. She rested her head against his chest, searching for his heartbeat, and found it. "I'm sorry for leaving you alone with her."

"Don't be. I'm just glad you had a chance to rest." His chin touched the top of her head. "Do you still have a headache?"

"Not bad."

"Mm. Symptoms may take a while to ease, even with the thanites. I'll talk to Beth about taking it slow when we return to the road."

Clare frowned at the fire. They were supposed to have been at Evandale by that evening. Hours were stacking onto their arrival time. And Dorran only had one dose of the antibiotics left.

"Wait." Clare sat up, frowning at the pale, sparse stars above them. "What time is it?"

"Close to midnight, I believe."

She muttered furiously under her breath and grabbed for the bag of medicine. "You should have had this sooner."

Dorran took the final antibiotic and swallowed it without arguing. That worried Clare. It meant he truly thought he needed it. The fire's light ran wild across his features, changing and discoloring them, and a coating of soot made him even harder to read. But she thought he was growing gaunter. The grayness around his eyes was more than stray soot. She pressed her hand to his throat, but the skin was cool.

"Have you had something to eat? Are you drinking enough?"

He chuckled and rested his hand over hers. "I am looking after myself. Do not worry."

"Don't tell me what to do," she retorted, and Dorran's chuckles deepened. That warmed her inside. She made him drink the last of the water, then pulled him closer to her side. "I'm up now. That means you can sleep."

"I'll stay awake a little longer. It is a nice night, despite the dusting of ash."

"Let me rephrase myself. I'm awake now, which means I'll *make* you sleep." She planted her hands on his shoulders and pushed, and he let himself be shoved back into the makeshift bed. His hair tousled as he smiled up at her. Clare leaned over him and pressed a gentle kiss against his lips. He tasted like char and blood, but she didn't care. It was good just to be close to him. "Sleep."

His smile faltered a fraction. "Stay with me?"

"Of course." She nestled down at his side, resting her head on his shoulder, an arrangement that had become familiar at Winterbourne. His hand curled over her head, fingers lacing through her hair, and he made a faint, regretful noise. "I'm sorry. I'm making you dusty."

"I think I'll be about fifty percent dust by the time we get out of this place." Clare wrapped her arm across his broad chest and felt it rise with every breath. "A little more won't hurt."

"Mm." His eyes closed. She'd guessed right; he was desperately tired, and already, he was slipping away. "Thank you, Clare."

"I love you."

She'd planned to stay awake and keep watch in case anything disturbed the camp. She shouldn't have been tired after sleeping through most of the afternoon and evening. But as the fire burned itself down to embers and the headache ebbed to a barely perceptible throb, tiredness came to pull her back under. In the surreal moments where her mind hung between wakefulness and dreams, she thought she heard a hollow in the distance, chattering in a voice that sounded unpleasantly like Beth's.

CHAPTER 23

"GOOD MORNING."

Clare groaned. Sun pierced through her closed eyes. She was cold; her prediction of frost hadn't been far off, and there weren't enough blankets between her and the ground. The only saving grace was Dorran; they'd stayed together as they slept, both seeking out each other's body heat. As Clare woke, he stirred at her side.

"I said *good morning.*"

She forced herself up to sit and squinted her eyes open. Beth sat on the other side of the revived fire. She leaned her back against a canister of fuel and had both legs stretched ahead of herself, crossed at the ankles. The jacket and scarf were back in place. So were the parts that made her Beth: the quirked eyebrows, the wry humor around her mouth, the spark of humanity in her eyes.

"Hey," Clare managed. Memories from the previous night

filtered back to her in drips. Beth's voice. Beth's appearance. They were unnatural enough to feel like a dream. She swallowed, felt how dry her throat still was, and looked around for water.

"Here." Beth tossed a bottle to her. Clare caught it clumsily and mumbled her thanks. "All good. Drink that, then we can get back on the bus and on the road to Evandale. We lost time, but I've been reading the map, and if we keep breaks to a minimum, we'll be there by four this afternoon without a problem."

"Oh…okay…great." Clare was still half-asleep. She drank to buy herself a moment to think and frowned at the way her fingers left black prints across the bottle's label. She was filthy. All of Dorran's work on her hair the previous day had gone to waste, her clothes barely looked like their original colors, and the dust continued to burn her airways. Beth might not notice the effects, but if Clare was struggling with it, it had to be even worse for Dorran. He had a persistent cough that frightened her. And the box of antibiotics was empty.

Beth drummed her fingertips on the fuel canister under her arm. "Ready to go? I'll drive so you can finish waking up on the road."

"No. Actually. Hold on a moment." Clare put the bottle aside. "We need breakfast. I'm starving. And we can't drive straight to Evandale; we need to look for antibiotics first. The next dose is due by eleven."

"Damn it," Beth muttered. "Food. Medicine. Sleep. You're both *really* needy, you know that, right?"

"I'm glad your newfound powers didn't make you disdainful

toward your mortal colleagues," Dorran said. He sat up beside Clare, bleary eyes narrowed against the invasive sun.

"You look awful," Beth noted.

"Thank you. I truly appreciate it."

Beth took a deep breath and let it out in an exaggerated sigh. "Fine. Okay. We can afford some delays. Food first, since we have the fire to warm it. Then we'll try to figure out where in the hell we're going to find antibiotics."

"Thanks." Clare, relieved, rolled onto her feet. She dusted her hands on her jeans, realized it only made matters worse, and resignedly turned toward the bus's food compartment.

What time is it? His next dose is due by eleven. That gives us maybe two, three hours?

She found a pot large enough to cook for all three of them and squinted into the distance as she carried it to the fire. The farmhouse she'd seen the previous day was gone. A stack of charcoal and blackened bricks marked its location. Beyond that, she could barely make out the town's roofline through the hazy smoke.

Will anything in town have survived the fire? If Beth's right, it should be clear of hollows, but that doesn't help much if the houses are all gone.

"Hey. Clare. Turn your brain on, please."

She startled and realized she'd been staring at the empty pot as it heated over the fire. She gave Beth a tight-lipped smile as she returned to the bus's side compartment and dug out more water and a cardboard box of instant food. The cardboard had become warped from the heat and had probably been no more than a few minutes from catching fire. It was another reminder of how close they had come to losing everything, and Clare chewed on the inside of her cheek as she shut the hatch.

The bus itself looked significantly worse. The smoke had darkened it by several shades until it appeared a deep, dirty gray. The plywood over the windows was badly singed. The damage they'd sustained between entering the freeway and escaping the ditch was hard to see under the discoloration, but Clare knew it had to be extensive.

But we're alive. As she carried packets of just-add-water-and-heat pasta meals back to the group, she tried to remind herself of everything she had and how grateful she was for it. They were alive. They were still together.

Beth shook out and folded the blankets. She wanted to be back on the road and wasn't trying to hide it. As Clare cooked the food, she remembered a throwaway comment Beth had made about the ash making her uncomfortable. The hollows had to be hardwired to dread fire; that was probably why it had been lit in the first place. A town—or even a lone human—had seen a chance to drive the monsters back. Maybe they'd been hemmed in on all sides, too desperate to see or care about the consequences. It could have even been an accident—a campfire someone hadn't put out, a generator sparking an electrical fire, a lightning strike.

So much destruction. So much lost. There were no firefighters to keep the flames contained. No infrastructure to even pump water out to slow it. The inferno could have swallowed hundreds of miles of land before it hit natural barriers like mountains or rivers.

The region would probably be considered barren for a long time to come. Not because the ground was bad—the ash would feed future generations of plants. But because the houses were gone. That meant there was no food, no clothes, and no fuel for desperate travelers. Beth's bus was stocked with supplies. Clare tried to imagine what they would do if it wasn't. She imagined driving through the desolation, searching for just enough sustenance to stay alive, while the fuel needle inched closer to empty.

"I swear, Clare—"

"Sorry, sorry." The pot of pasta was steaming. Clare found a rag to protect her hands as she divided the meal into bowls. Beth took hers, not noticing that the dish was hot enough to scorch her fingers, and swallowed mouthfuls in between attempts to force the dirty blankets into the bus's hatch.

"We could leave those," Clare suggested. "I don't know if even three rounds through a washing machine could save them, and we have enough spares—"

"They're flammable enough to be useful to light fires." Beth used her boot to squash the package into a narrow gap, then slammed the hatch closed over them. "You're right that we're not hurting for bedding material right now, but we might need the fuel. A storm's coming."

Clare looked at the sky, but except for the blanketing layer of smoke, it seemed clear. The sun was brighter than it had been for days. She turned slowly and finally noticed the bank of darkness growing over the smoldering remains of the forest.

"Another?" Clare glared at the clouds as she blew on a spoonful of her breakfast. "I was really hoping we would have at least one or two clear days."

Beth rubbed at the back of her neck. "Honestly, I won't mind so much if it washes some of this ash away."

"I would have to agree." Dorran leaned his back against the bus. His voice was raw and his expression was weary, and she knew his sleep hadn't been as restful as he needed. "The landscape is depressing."

Clare couldn't see anything but shades of gray and black on every horizon. She'd done her best to keep ash out of their breakfast, but she could still taste it with every bite. The sooner they moved out of the fire's destruction, the easier it would be for all of them.

But even that wasn't their first priority. "Beth, you said you had a chance to check the map earlier, right?"

"Yep. Spent a few hours going over it while I waited for you to wake up."

"Where's the closest place that has a reasonable chance of antibiotics?"

"Huh." Beth tilted her head back, working her jaw. "I guess a lot of that depends on how far the fire will have spread. But... let's try that town over there first."

"You sure?" Clare examined the distant roofline. Faint smoke rose from the jagged edges.

"Yup. I didn't go into it last night, but I skirted around the edge. Parts were still burning, but I have the feeling some areas might have been sheltered from the flames. We need to travel in that direction anyway, so we might as well stop by."

Dorran tilted his head. "You made it that far on foot?"

"I had six hours to burn. That was enough time to scope out the town and the major roads nearby." She shrugged. "I was still back well before dawn."

Clare had trouble estimating the distance to the town with the cloud of smog disguising landmarks, but she was fairly certain it was farther than she could get in a night. Beth must have jogged the entire way.

It was somewhere to start, though. Beth's judgment hadn't led them astray before, so she was prepared to trust it then. If the town was entirely burned out, they would just keep traveling until they found one that wasn't.

They finished their meal in silence. With water limited for the foreseeable future, they couldn't afford any to wash up, and instead dropped the dirty bowls and pot into a bag to worry about later. Beth then led the way back onto the bus. After watching the world around them transform into something unrecognizable, Clare felt surprised by how little the bus's insides had changed. A thin powdering of the ash lay across the floor, and the space was dimmer thanks to a dirty windshield, but everything else had been preserved like a shrine. She and Dorran took their seats near the driver's compartment. Some of the tension that had been hovering around Beth faded as she slid in behind the wheel.

The engine clicked over for an agonizing second, then caught. Beth pulled a lever to spray soapy water over the windshield, but since she'd used the entire reservoir the previous day, only a spritz came out. The wipers grated over the grime, smearing it into streaks, but Beth evidently thought the narrow bands of visibility were enough and pulled the bus onto the road.

Thunder disturbed the unnatural stillness. It crackled behind them, seeming to emerge from the forest like some abhorrent child of the scorching fire. Clare was grateful the windows were blocked. It kept her eyes on the one thing that mattered: the distant remains of the town.

CHAPTER 24

THEY HAD BEEN ON the road for less than twenty minutes when the first spot of rain hit their windshield. It was so large and dark that, for a second, Clare thought they must have hit an insect. Then a second drop came down, and a third, and within a minute the downpour was so loud that Clare couldn't hear anything else.

Black water washed over the window. Beth put the wipers on their highest speed but still had to slow to a trundle as she struggled to see the road. Clare waited for the window to clear as the rain washed the soot away, but it didn't. It wasn't the bus that was dirty, she realized; it was the rain itself. It was catching the smoke still suspended in the air and bringing it down in a deluge.

The bus jolted as Beth misjudged the road's direction and nearly ran into the ditch. Dorran turned aside as another coughing fit hit him.

"Maybe we should stop and wait it out." Clare yelled to be heard over the rain. "It's too heavy."

"I doubt it's going to improve anytime soon." Beth tapped the accelerator again, and their speed inched up.

Clare clenched her fists in her lap. The headache was breaking through the painkillers' numbing effect. She would have argued, except they couldn't afford to delay much longer. They were rapidly approaching the twelve-hour mark for the antibiotics. She wanted to trust her sister, but at the same time, she couldn't tell if Beth was acting in their best interests or out of a desire to escape the fields of ash.

Dorran's coughing subsided. He'd wrapped one arm around his chest as though he needed to hold his ribs in place. A quiet, panicked voice in the back of Clare's head asked what would happen if the antibiotics didn't work. If Dorran was sick with something worse.

Then we keep driving. Evandale is less than a day away. They're a medical research station; surely they'll know how to help. Her eyes ached. She blinked furiously to clear them.

The rain continued, furious and unrelenting, as they passed a sign welcoming them to town. Black water washed across the road in streams, spraying behind them as the bus's wheels sliced through it. Clare struggled to make out the structures surrounding them. Everywhere she looked carried a crushing sense of desolation. Burned-out cars clung close to the skeletal remains of houses. The trees that once would have provided shade for the roads were scorched black and reduced to stumps.

It was hard for Clare to imagine anything in the town could have survived.

Their crawling speed slowed even further as Beth tried to navigate the streets. Neither of the headlights worked, and she had to rely on the bus's internal lights to wash out of the windshield combined with frequent bursts of lightning. More than the usual array of debris blocked their path. Along with abandoned vehicles and fallen trees, there were entire sections of collapsed houses. The drains were already overflowing, choked beyond capacity as they regurgitated the dark water back across the streets. It was a nightmare maze of invisible hazards. And yet, Beth kept driving.

Clare jammed her hands under her legs to stop herself from picking at her nails in anxiety. She could barely think over the rain's drumming and the unending crackle of thunder. In the distorted shadows of the overhead lights, Beth's face held an unsettling intensity that did not welcome interruption. Her eyes scanned the road and buildings with quick flicks, her nostrils flaring whenever she saw something she didn't like. Occasionally, her tongue darted out to taste her cracked, ash-blackened lips.

The lightning hurt Clare's eyes. At her side, Dorran pressed his arm over his mouth as the coughing renewed. Panic had risen through Clare so gradually that she didn't realize how strong it was until it had her tightly in its grip, squeezing the breath out of her lungs and pulsing in time with her headache.

Then Beth said, "Ha."

The world ahead was a sickening dance of shadows and

ceaseless rain. Burned-out apartments clustered to their left. To their right was some kind of large structure, looking unreal in the mist.

Beth turned the bus toward the larger building. They rocked in their seats as they ran over speed bumps. A stretch of clear ground appeared to their right, intercepted by small metal shapes and towering, dead floodlights. *A parking lot.* Clare fought through the migraine to make out the building to their left. It was too big to be a home. Benches and pots of dead plants were clustered around pillars on a sidewalk. Beyond that she saw a set of large glass doors. The image clicked into place. Beth had found a shopping center.

The bus lurched again. Beth swung the wheel, a crooked smile lighting her face as she pressed the accelerator. The engine roared loudly enough to compete with the rain, and Clare barely had time to gasp as they raced toward the mall's entrance.

Broken glass and twisted metal showered around them. Dorran threw his arm across Clare's chest to keep her from being jolted out of her seat. Clare bit down on a whine as the motion sparked pain behind her eyes. Wet tires squealed on tile as the bus scraped to a halt.

Slowly, cautiously, Clare opened her eyes. The rain and thunder were muffled. The wipers were no longer battling against the downpour, and with a deft flick of her hand, Beth turned them off.

"Good, good," Beth murmured. Her eyes flashed in the low light, and Clare had the impression she could see a lot better than her human companions. The bus's overhead lights went out and the engine faded as she turned it off. "This will do nicely."

"Beth?" Clare's legs shook as she tried to rise. "I can't see anything."

"Mm. Hang on. We have a flashlight here somewhere."

Clare felt, more than saw, Beth pass her. Bags rustled, and a moment later, cold metal was placed into Clare's hand.

"Come on. I want to look around." Beth sounded breathless with excitement. The bus's door creaked as it opened.

"Beth, wait." Clare felt around the flashlight, searching for its button. It clicked but didn't turn on. Clare bit her lip and shook it. The bulb flickered, then faded again. Thunder cracked, shivering through the air and settling in her bones. She could no longer hear Beth's footsteps.

Clare held her hand out, searching. "Dorran?"

"I'm here." He found her fingers in the dark and squeezed them. Keeping Dorran close, Clare began to feel her way along the bus's length, toward the door. She could hear her own ragged breaths. She could hear her shoes scraping over the fine layer of ash on the bus's aisle. She could hear the cascading rain, punctuated by rolling thunder.

She couldn't hear Beth. Nor could she hear any other sign of life outside the bus. But that didn't mean they were alone.

Clare stopped at the top step, lungs aching and throat tight. A burst of lightning washed through the shopping center's skylights. For that second, the mall was illuminated in a viciously cold light. Faces stared at her. Wide eyes, dead eyes, pale lips. Darkness swallowed them again.

A strangled cry stopped in Clare's throat. She hit the flashlight on her thigh. The bulb flickered, then held. She raised it, panning light over the dirt-scuffed floor and over the scattered contents of a woman's clothing store.

Five mannequins faced them. Four stood; one lay on the floor, its head twisted around to face its back in an agonizing contortion. Their clothes hung askew. One was missing her arm.

Dorran murmured something indistinct, and his hand twitched. Clare's mouth was too dry to make any sound. Moving slowly, she stepped out of the bus. Dorran reluctantly followed.

The flashlight flickered again. Clare slapped it, and only let herself breathe when the light settled back to its dull glow. She directed the flashlight back to the mannequins. A wild part of her mind insisted their heads had turned a fraction in those brief seconds of darkness.

"Beth?" Her voice cracked. She kept her back to the bus as she let the flashlight's beam coast across the scene. The shopping center didn't seem large, but it was two stories. Dirty glass railings ran around the second floor's walkways. An escalator stood a few feet ahead of their bus, and Clare was grateful Beth had braked when she had. They had destroyed the front doors, though, along with what looked like a kiosk display of bags. Broken glass and merchandise marked their trajectory.

Endless surfaces refracted their light back at them, disturbingly similar to the way the hollows' eyes glinted. Clare kept her flashlight moving, trying to count the shops. No more than forty, she thought, and most of them were small.

The mall had been built on a limited parcel of land. Clare guessed it must take up a block; roads wound around it, and it was that minor separation from other buildings combined with its stone construction and fire-resistant measures that had saved it from the inferno. Not every shop had been immune; she could see several blackened interiors behind cracked windows. But the fire hadn't managed to spread any further.

It had been a good find by Beth. The mall was at the center of town and wouldn't yet have been looted. They would likely be the first humans to enter the building since the stillness. But not the first activity it had seen. Clare lowered her flashlight toward the marble floor. It was grimy, and not just from soot. Greasy footprints and handprints smeared through the surface. They seemed endless, overlapping each other, too numerous to even guess how many bodies they belonged to. The mannequins' clothes were in disarray. Grimy fingerprints dotted their blank expressions. They had been just human enough to attract the hollows' interest.

The smell was the worst. It stuck in Clare's throat as she took a deep breath. Spending so much time in close quarters with Beth had done a lot to adjust her to the scent, but it still wasn't enough to override the instantaneous panic that crashed over her.

The shopping mall hadn't just been inhabited. It had been infested.

Something heavy banged inside one of the shops to her right. Clare turned her flashlight toward it, searching for movement. Lightning flooded the scene, and for a second Clare imagined she could see eyes surrounding them, flickering bright, as the light caught on every metal surface. The lightning failed. The flashlight seemed painfully weak by comparison.

"Beth?" Every instinct in Clare's body told her to stay quiet, to not draw attention. She kept the open bus door at her back.

The noises came again: a bang, like a door being slammed, followed by the whine of twisting metal. The sound stretched out, painful, then faded until it was swallowed by the pounding rain and thunder.

Please, Beth, please let that be you.

Dorran made no sound. Except for his hand against hers, Clare could have believed she was alone.

The sounds had come from one of the larger shops. Strange shapes were stacked in the windows, bottles and boxes Clare couldn't identify. Large banners showed smiling faces. Many had had their eyes gouged out, leaving just holes in their place.

Clare directed the flashlight higher. Large block letters would have once been backlit and clearly visible, but were now a dull blue-gray against the stone wall. *Pharmacy.*

Something banged inside the store again. Clare took a step closer. Dorran didn't follow; he tugged on her hand instead, a wordless request for her to stay with the bus. She understood his concern. But she couldn't leave Beth alone in a foreign environment.

The flashlight stuttered again, fading out, and Clare hissed softly as she shook it. The flickering beam exposed sections of the pharmacy in brief bursts. Movement came from behind the displays. Dorran's hold on her was too tight. A body came toward them, weaving through the store. It was lithe and twisting, clambering over fallen shelves, moving on all fours. The eyes flashed. Clare pulled her hand free from Dorran and used it to slap the flashlight. The beam stabilized.

Beth stood in the pharmacy doorway. Her eyes were wild. She held herself unnaturally, her center of mass low, her feet braced, her back tilted. A grin spread as she met Clare's eyes. She straightened and loped forward.

"You scared me," Clare said as she came near. "We don't know this building is empty—"

"It is, it is." Beth's voice was full of mirth. "Stop worrying; we're alone here. The fire chased all of the hollows out, remember?"

The flashlight stuttered. Clare hit it again, angry and ashamed of how fast her heart beat. "We don't know that for certain."

"I do. I can tell. Stop panicking; I wouldn't leave you alone if I thought you were in danger." Beth held a hand toward Clare. She clutched a half dozen cardboard boxes. "This is what we came for, remember? I'll look after you. You know that."

"Oh!" Clare took one of the boxes and read the label. Not only had Beth found antibiotics, but she'd found the same kind Dorran had been taking. The relief was sweet. "I thought they kept prescription medicines in a locked area."

"Ha! They do. It's not locked any longer." The wolfish grin widened.

Clare passed the flashlight to Beth, then broke the seal on the box and popped a capsule out. She handed it to Dorran, and he disappeared into the bus to find water. Once again, the dose was coming a little sooner than scheduled. Clare was okay with that. The still world wasn't friendly toward routine, and she'd rather he take it too soon than not at all.

"Thanks, Beth." Clare slid the strip of capsules back into their box. Beth didn't seem concerned with lighting their environment and held the flashlight limply, so that it was directed at the tile floor. "I know you weren't keen on the detour, but it means a lot to me."

"I know." Beth turned to lean her back against the bus, grinning into the darkness. "Sentimentality is brutal, isn't it?"

Clare would call her feelings toward Dorran more than simple sentimentality, but she didn't push the point. "Did you have a next move in mind? Do you want to get back onto the road or wait out the storm?"

"Yeah, we're definitely waiting it out." Beth rolled her shoulders. "Not just because of the storm, but because this place is a gold mine."

"She's right." Dorran had returned from the bus so quietly that Clare flinched at his voice. He gave her a small, apologetic smile. "I'm not a fan of this place, but we're not likely to find another opportunity like it."

Clare glanced around the stores and understood. Clothes, medicine, and equipment were at their fingertips, and they were at no risk of being interrupted. "That makes sense. We can change over old supplies and restock our food."

"I can do one better," Beth said, her eyes dancing. "How would you like to be *clean*?"

CHAPTER 25

AT NO POINT IN Clare's life had she ever imagined herself standing in the pouring rain outside a shopping mall while wearing nothing but her underwear. And yet, that was where she found herself…and she was *grateful* for it.

The rain hadn't eased up. But it was clean. The worst of the fire's soot had been washed out of the air and what came down was close enough to pure that it didn't leave Clare feeling dirty.

Beth had raided the pharmacy for shampoos, conditioners, and soaps. Clare made use of them, scrubbing aggressively to get the black marks out from under her fingernails and getting her hair as clean as it had ever been. A broken downspout near the doors made rinsing off a fast task, even if the water was cold enough to set her teeth chattering. She didn't mind. She was just grateful.

Beth washed just a few paces away, her back to Clare, humming under her breath. Dorran showered in seclusion, having left through a door on the opposite side of the mall. When Beth had suggested washing outside, he'd initially tried to follow them, until Beth's glare had sent him backing away with quickly murmured apologies.

Clare wished he could have stayed with them. She didn't like having their group split up, even if Beth said the shopping center was safe. But the storm, and the darkness, seemed to have brought out the more erratic side in her sister. Clare had to pick her battles.

Beth shook her head, spraying water around her bare feet, then stalked back to where they'd put towels and changes of clothes under the stone arches marking the mall's entrance.

It was the first time Beth's skin had been fully exposed, and Clare couldn't stop herself from stealing quick glances to search for aberrations. She was relieved to see the ridges on Beth's back were the only significant changes. She thought her sister's knees might be more pronounced and her ribs seemed to stand out more sharply against her skin, but that could have more to do with the intermittent diet than anything else. Beth had eaten regular meals in her bunker, before she'd begun to understand how deep the mutations were. The first few days with Clare and Dorran had also ensured she ate. But since her secret had come out, she avoided food unless it was forced on her.

Clare held her breath as she dunked her head under the waterspout a final time. The deluge beat on her like a waterfall, worsening her headache, but at least it was a fast way to make sure the soap was washed away. She shivered as she jogged back to the shelter where her sister was already zipping up a jacket.

"Better?" Beth asked as she tossed Clare a towel.

"Much." Teeth chattering, Clare rushed to dry herself. She had a new outfit set out on one of the wooden benches, layers of fresh wools and cottons to keep her warm. It was so long since she'd felt clean that she could have moaned as she tugged her new top on.

Beth, grinning, lounged on the seat. She'd picked clothes that mimicked her old outfit. The dark jeans tucked neatly into sturdy boots, and the leather jacket had a high collar to disguise her neck. Even though she no longer needed to hide, Clare guessed she still didn't like having her symptoms on display. As Clare struggled into jeans, Beth gazed across the rain-drenched husks of buildings around them. "It's beautiful."

"I guess." Clare would have gone with different words. *Depressing. Bleak. Lonely.* "It's nice to not worry about being interrupted at least."

"Oh, it sure is." Beth's posture was open and relaxed. "The rain's helping, too. It'll get rid of the ash. Clean the world."

"Mm." She didn't know about cleaning the world, but Clare couldn't complain about having less ash to deal with. She squeezed her hair in the towel. Beth was letting hers dry naturally, even though it dripped onto her shoulders, and Clare supposed she didn't have much of a choice except to do the same. The shopping mall might have hair dryers, but no electricity.

Beth watched Clare towel her hair for a moment, then rose. "I'll comb your hair. Sit."

She waved to the bench she'd just occupied, and Clare obediently sank onto it. A second later, a comb grazed over the top of her head. She relaxed back, content to watch the leafless trees surrounding the parking lot sway under the deluge.

Beth half sighed, half laughed as she pulled the comb through Clare's hair. "I used to do this all the time. Remember?"

"I do." Back in their old life, before the stillness, before Clare had moved into her own home, Beth had always brushed her hair after showers. Sometimes they'd sit in the living room and watch sitcom reruns while they did it, arranged very similarly to that afternoon: Clare sitting, usually cross-legged, Beth standing behind, chatting and laughing.

"I miss that." A note of tenderness entered Beth's voice. "I missed you. After you moved out, I mean."

"Yeah. I missed you, too."

Beth chuckled. "I was mad that you moved so far away. I didn't ever tell you that, but I was."

Clare smiled. "Don't worry. I guessed."

"It was four hours. I know the houses in Winthrop were cheaper, but I wish you could have found something closer to me. Four hours was too far. There was no way for me to reach you quickly if something went wrong."

Clare took a steadying breath. "I mean, that was part of the reason I moved out, you know?"

The comb fell still. "No. What?"

"I needed to learn how to be an adult." Clare shrugged. She tried to keep her voice light and easy to make it feel like a casual

229

conversation. "You loved me. And I always, always knew that. But because you loved me so much, you wanted to help me with everything. You…you wanted to make sure nothing ever hurt me, and that was good, but…" *But it meant I never got the chance to figure stuff out for myself.*

The first six months of living alone had been brutal. Clare had needed to learn hundreds of life lessons she didn't feel equipped for. Who to call when she spun her car off the road during her first winter. How to budget. How to handle a disagreement with her neighbor. Even the most basic lessons—things that she thought she should have learned before she was ten—like how to deal with disappointment if the store ran out of her favorite brownies.

During those first six months, there had been a constant temptation to call Beth. Her sister would have gladly fixed everything. She would argue with the neighbor. She would organize for the car to be repaired. She would have driven to Clare's home and baked the brownies Clare was craving, if Clare had just asked.

But even if Beth had been able to fix every problem Clare encountered, it would have never fixed the biggest problem: that Clare needed to know how to survive on her own. She'd never told Beth about the constant frustration and stress those first six months had created. And she hadn't told Beth about the growth that had followed, either. But she *had* grown. She felt like she'd come further in her first year alone than she had in the previous ten.

"You didn't want me in your life?" The kindness in Beth's voice was replaced with pain.

Clare grimaced, mentally kicking herself. "Of course not. I love you more than anything. I just…I needed to know how to be independent. I couldn't ask you to take care of me forever."

The comb began moving again. The strokes were no longer smooth and slow; they were harsh. Beth hit a snag and Clare bit back on a gasp.

"We're family," Beth said. "And family is supposed to look after each other. They *protect* each other."

"Of course. You're right." Clare, desperate to diffuse the conversation, tried to smile. "That's why I came for you after the stillness. We're family. Moving away doesn't change that. We stick together when it counts."

The comb didn't slow. "You just proved my point."

"Beth?"

"That *maybe* you wouldn't have had to drive *two days* across the country and risk *dying* if you hadn't lived so bloody far away."

"Ah." Clare flinched as the comb scraped the top of her ear. She tried to shy away, but Beth planted a hand on her shoulder and forced her back down.

"Stop *squirming*. I'm trying to brush your hair."

"Beth, slow down—"

"Maybe if you hadn't moved so far away, we could have both been safe in the bunker. If you hadn't moved so far away, you wouldn't have had to take on this creep who barely knows how to talk."

"Stop—"

"If you hadn't moved away, I wouldn't have had to stand at my open bunker door waiting for you. If you hadn't moved away, I'd still be *human*."

The comb snagged a tangle. Instead of backing up, Beth pulled harder. Clare cried out as hair tore free. She lurched off of the bench, staggering away from her sister, until her back hit one of the stone pillars flanking the broken doorway.

They stared at each other, both breathing heavily. Beth's expression was wild, teeth exposed, lips twitching. Clare raised a hand to her burning scalp as her eyes watered. The tears weren't from pain. For the first time in her life, Clare felt truly afraid of her sister.

Beth glanced down at the comb. A clump of Clare's hair hung from it. The ferocity in her expression faded, replaced with shock, as the comb dropped to the ground. "Oh. Oh no, no. I'm sorry. Oh, Clare, I—I'm so—"

The fear faded. Clare stepped away from the pillar and cautiously wrapped her arms around Beth's shoulders.

Beth hugged her back, her body shaking with ragged sobs. "I'm so sorry. I didn't mean to hurt you."

"I know. We're okay." Clare buried her face into the damp, golden hair.

"I didn't mean to. I didn't mean for anything to end up like this."

"I know."

"It's not your fault. I shouldn't have said it was. I'm the idiot who left my bunker door open. I…" Beth moaned under her breath. "I did it because I thought you were gone. After the call disconnected, and you didn't arrive, I thought… I didn't want to go on in the world without you. And then I felt it start to infect me, and my damn survival instinct kicked in and overrode everything else. If I'd just picked a camp—alive or dead—and stuck to it, we never would have ended up here."

The lump in Clare's throat ached. "I'm so sorry."

"Not your fault." Beth repeated the phrase with conviction. She pulled back, her face wet and lips pale. "I'm just… Please, please, once this is all over, please don't hold this against me. It's not who I am."

Clare flinched as Beth's fingers grazed over the back of her head, where she'd lost hair.

Beth's lips pulled back as deep regret flooded her expression. "This isn't me. I never ever wanted to hurt you."

"I know." Clare was lost for what else to say. She felt as though she was losing Beth to the thanites one inch at a time. The volatile, violent parts hadn't originated in her sister. But they were still present. And they still *hurt*.

"I just wanted to brush your hair again." The pained edge to her voice was unmistakable. "He got to brush it yesterday. It always used to be *our* thing. I…I don't like feeling like he's taking you away from me."

Clare lifted her eyebrows, trying to get Beth to understand how sincerely she meant the words. "He's *not*. We're in this together, all three of us."

"I know that. But *he's* the one who gets to have you once this is all over with." Beth's mouth twisted into an imitation of a smile. "When we get to Evandale. I'll die and he'll have you all to himself. And it feels so…so *unfair*. Why does *he* get to keep you when I have to say goodbye? Because I left a door open a minute too long? It's so senseless."

Clare pressed her lips together, trying to repress the wave of grief that wanted to drown her. She took a moment to breathe, just to make sure her voice would be steady. "Do you want to *not* go to Evandale? Because—"

"No." Beth's smile became a little more wry. "I haven't changed my mind about that. If I could ask for anything, it would be to have more time with you, but…well, even that's going to be limited. I don't think hollows and humans are designed to cohabitate for long."

"Please stop talking like that. You're still human."

Beth chuckled. "You're trying. I can see it. You're trying as hard as you can. And I'm doing the same from my end. But it's like putting a napkin over a sucking chest wound. Just because we hide it, pretend it's not happening, doesn't mean we've stopped it."

Clare was fighting not to cry. Beth's hand patted the side of her face, where her damp hair stuck to her cheeks. "I wish I had another shot at this. More time with you. More time to make it right."

"We…we still have some time. We don't even know if there are scientists at Evandale. And even if there are, it will probably take them a while to unravel the code. It's not like we have to say goodbye at the door."

"Maybe," Beth murmured.

Her face was still full of grief and pain. She wasn't arguing, but her reply didn't hold any conviction, and Clare couldn't understand why. Reaching Evandale took them a step closer to eradicating the hollows, but it was far from being an immediate, certain end. They could still have weeks after dropping off the USB. Possibly even months. She didn't know if she could cope with the prospect of arriving so soon otherwise.

"I'm trying to be grateful," Beth said. "You won't be alone once I'm gone. And that's a good thing, I guess, even if the jealousy is eating me alive."

"Hey." Clare pulled Beth closer, so she was easier to hear over the pounding rain. "Just because I love him doesn't mean I love you any less. You know that, right?"

"Eh. Whatever. You can do better than him, you know?" Beth swiped a hand across her face, wiping away the moisture. "I'll maintain that, even in a world with a vastly reduced dating pool."

Clare choked on her laughter. "Beth—"

"All right, all right. Be nicer. I get it."

Glass crunched as something heavy moved toward them. A tall figure stepping through the broken front doors, barely visible in the lamplight. Dorran had washed and changed, like them, and craned his neck as he searched for them among the mist. "Clare? Is everything okay?"

"Hey!" Beth pulled Clare closer, her teeth bared. "What the hell do you think you're doing, snooping around while we're showering?"

He cleared his throat as he stepped back. "My apologies. I thought I heard a cry. And you were gone for more than an hour—"

"We're washing our *hair*. That's how long it *takes*."

Dorran held up both hands, placating. "As long as you're all right. Clare?"

"Fine," she called, grateful the darkness and rain masked her red eyes. She waved, smiling. "Sorry for making you worry. We'll be there in a moment."

He nodded, and the relief was evident in his posture as he backed through the door.

"What was that about being nicer?" Clare hissed.

"Eh." Beth shrugged, swiping her arm across her eyes. "I'll start tomorrow."

CHAPTER 26

WATER LEAKED THROUGH THE shopping mall's broken doors, gradually spreading in a pool across the tile floor. The wind continued to funnel rain against the walls. The skylights lit up with frequent bursts of lightning. The building didn't feel quite right when it was empty; echoes bounced through the vacant stores in strange patterns.

Despite the environment, Clare actually felt cozy. She, Dorran, and Beth sat near the minibus on their foldable camping chairs. Beth had found a new tank of gas in the camping shop, which meant they could warm their food and themselves. Clare, swaddled in a quilt and with a towel wrapped around her wet hair, was snug and warm.

Dorran placed his empty bowl aside and picked up a mug of tea from the floor beside him. "It's nice to not have to worry about watching our backs. At least for a moment."

"Mm." Beth, arms folded and feet kicked out toward the heater, watched the skylights above them. "It's almost tempting to stay a while longer. But we're playing with borrowed time. Life will start filtering back into the area, especially since the soot is being washed away."

"How long do you think that will take?" Clare asked.

Beth shrugged. "Another day? Two? I suspect the humans will come in first, looking for supplies, like we did. The crawlers won't have any interest in the area as long as it's barren and doesn't provide much cover, but if they think they can find some food here, they'll be back pretty quickly."

Clare sipped from her mug. "Even if it's just temporary, it's still nice."

"And we should make the most of it," Beth added. "The shopping center might not be large, but it's going to be valuable. We'll strip the useful bits from the pharmacy first, then take a look at what's in the other stores that we can fit on the bus."

"We have enough antibiotics, though," Clare said. "We could grab a couple of extra boxes of painkillers, but we shouldn't need much else from the pharmacy, should we?"

"*We* won't need it, but we'll still take it: inhalers, blood pressure medication, antiseizure medication. Those things are hard to come by in the outside world."

Clare exchanged a look with Dorran. His eyebrows had lowered a fraction; not enough to break the peace of his features, but enough to tell her this new direction wasn't sitting well with him, either.

"But..." Clare adjusted her grip around her mug, speaking carefully. "The thanites should have made most of that unnecessary. Right?"

"*Think*, Clare. We're the only people who know about the thanites right now. And even if other people hear about them, there will always be a group that doesn't believe it or prefers to err on the side of caution. They might not need their old medication any longer, but they'll still buy it. One inhaler might be enough to get you a jug of fuel, or three days of food, or shelter, depending on how desperate people are. We'd be fools not to take as much as we can."

To their right, the bus glittered in the burner's light. Despite the beating it had taken, it was still solid and reliable. They had fuel. They had food. They had spare clothes and blankets, all well in excess of what they needed to reach Evandale. Clare knew her sister was being practical, but her heart ached at the idea of them hoarding supplies like some kind of dragon when the next person to arrive at the shopping court might need antibiotics just as desperately as they did.

She couldn't ignore how lucky they were. Traveling across country in the bus might not be the most secure or stable way to live, but they had all of their needs met and then some. For a second, the memory of the car they'd passed flashed into her mind: the father and his two daughters, a wedding ring hung from the mirror, a camping pack in the passenger seat. They carried so little that they had to be surviving from day to day. A lot of humans were probably doing the same, fighting just to stay ahead of the hollows, to find that day's food and water, to find shelter that could protect them as they slept. Clare set her jaw. "We can take some, but we don't need all of it."

Beth, fire flashing in her eyes, opened her mouth, then clamped it closed again. She took a slow sip from her tea, then exhaled before speaking, her voice measured. "Here's the thing. You might like to take the moral high ground, but other people won't be as charitable. What would you do? Leave a sign on the pharmacy door saying 'Please take one' and hope everyone else abides by the honor system? The very next person to arrive here is going to loot everything they can carry and sell it at the highest price they can get. If someone's going to make a profit from this place, it may as well be us, right?"

This isn't Beth. It's not who she used to be. It's the thanites, pushing her to consume, to be jealous, to be ravenous.

"Let's talk about it later," Clare said.

Beth drained her mug in one go, and for a second, Clare believed that would be the end of the discussion. Then Beth slammed the mug onto the floor. The sound rang out around them like a gunshot. Both Clare and Dorran jolted.

"I don't think we *need* to discuss it." Beth stood and pulled her gloves on with sharp, jerky motions. "You can do whatever you want, but you're not my master. This is my bus, and my free will, and my time."

"Beth—" Clare half stood, but her sister had already turned and stalked toward the pharmacy. She vanished in between the display tables and gloom. Clare sighed and slumped back into her chair. "Damn it."

Dorran gave her an apologetic, tight-lipped smile. "I'm sorry. I wasn't sure if you wanted me to say something—"

"No, don't worry. My sister, my problem." Clare ran a hand over her face. "Maybe I shouldn't have even objected. This place could stay abandoned for years; I was literally arguing about a hypothetical. This is such a stupidly trivial thing to have a falling out over."

"You were arguing on behalf of compassion." Dorran's smile became a little warmer. "That is something you never lost, and I cannot tell you how glad it makes me."

Clare opened her mouth, but her words died on her tongue. A rush of lightning came through the skylights and broken door, illuminating the six mannequins outside the ravaged clothing store.

Wait. Weren't there five when we arrived?

As the sudden light faded, the figures were plunged back into darkness. Only their gas cooker illuminated the mall, and its flames barely lit the three chairs spaced around it.

"Clare?" Dorran tilted his head. She didn't dare answer him. Didn't even dare to move beyond lifting a finger to ask him to stay silent. His expression darkened.

Beth had promised the shopping center didn't hold any hollows. She said the fire would have forced them all out. The smell lingered, though, so pungent that it turned Clare's stomach. There must have been dozens of the creatures calling the shopping center home at one time.

What if not all of them made it out? What if the fire moved through the town so quickly that some had become trapped in the stores? What if they stayed here?

Another burst of lighting washed around them. Five mannequin faces stared at Clare. Her skin prickled, hairs standing to attention as her heart redoubled its rate.

"We're not alone," she whispered.

They had been lax. Clare had trusted Beth's assurance of security and left her weapons inside the bus. Their only light came from the cooker. Clare had left the flashlight beside her seat, but they hadn't even gotten around to replacing its batteries yet. They hadn't thought they would *need* to.

Clare moved slowly as she bent to pick up her flashlight. They had been in the shopping center for more than an hour without being disturbed. The hollows were too cautious to attack outright.

She could feel Dorran tensing, assessing. The bus, and its weapons, were only five steps behind them, but he refused to leave her side.

Her hand tightened around the cold metal flashlight. She pressed its button. The light didn't respond for a second, then it blinked on, forming a dull circle over a poster advertising half-price shoes.

Sounds came from the pharmacy. Beth, rummaging. Clare wanted to call to her, but she couldn't risk making that much noise. The rain continued to drum across the windows and walls. A steady dripping noise came from a leak somewhere near the door. Through all of that, Clare thought she could make out the sound of muted chattering. She tried to pinpoint it, but the high ceiling distorted noises.

Clare turned the flashlight toward the mannequins and picked out five pale, expressionless faces. She was certain she'd seen a sixth figure positioned between them, equally pale but less stoic. She continued moving the flashlight in an arc across the walls. It flickered. Something moved in its periphery. Clare twisted her light toward it, and the beam failed.

"No." She hit her palm on the flashlight. It came back on. The space, the entrance to a men's clothing store, was filled with racks of shirts. One of them swayed on its hook, recently disturbed.

Dorran touched her forearm. He bent to put his lips next to her ear. "Get into the bus."

"Beth—"

"Beth will be fine." He tugged on her, moving slowly but using enough force to let her know he was serious. "We need to take shelter. We need to be ready to go."

They were going to have to run. Clare glanced at their makeshift camp. Everything in it was valuable. Their chairs. The new tank of gas that had been intended to replace the one that had run out. A bag of food sat beside Beth's seat. On the other side of it, farthest from the bus, was the stack of antibiotic boxes. Clare tried to swallow around the lump in her throat. Everything in the camp was valuable, but they could afford to do without it for a few days. Everything except for that.

CHAPTER 27

CLARE TOOK A STEP forward. Dirt and broken glass crunched underfoot. Dorran's grip tightened on her arm. "*Clare.*"

We just need the antibiotics. Everything else can be left. But not them.

The white boxes, small and unassuming, were stacked behind Beth's chair, just a few paces away. Clare turned the flashlight across the mall, lighting up every storefront. Its glow shimmered back at her from polished metal and endless panes of glass. There was no sign of movement. She only needed a second to grab the tablets. They had time.

Clare twisted her arm to break free from Dorran's grip. He hissed her name again. She moved quickly, weeks of built-up grime crunching under every footstep. Something shifted inside the café to Clare's left. She aimed her light toward it. Overturned chairs cluttered the space. Red handprints, long dried, ran along the tile wall. Whatever had caught her notice was already gone.

The flashlight flickered, then faded into darkness. That didn't matter. She was at the chair. Clare bent, scooping up the white boxes, and shoved them into her jacket pocket. Lightning poured through the glass ceiling. That burst was closer—close enough that Clare felt the burn of electricity charge the air. Close enough that deafening thunder rolled into the building before the light even faded.

For that instant, the shopping court was illuminated. Every wall, every window, every face. Clare's heart missed a beat.

The hollows were everywhere. They hung to the railings on the upper floor. They clustered around clothing racks. They crept around the twisted metal at the broken doors.

The lightning faded. Clare was blind. She didn't dare breathe. She moved backward one faltering step at a time, toward the bus. Dorran still hadn't left her. His hand found her arm again, clenched it painfully tight.

Clare hit the flashlight against her thigh, trying to shake the bulb back to life. Something hissed to her right. A shard of glass snapped under her foot. Metal clinked as clothes were knocked off a rack.

The burner was at their back, creating a narrow ring of protection but useless to help them see beyond. Clare stopped close enough to feel the flame's heat on her thighs. The light was too weak to give more than illusionary security, but that would have to be enough. The flashlight blinked on for a heartbeat, then failed again.

More lightning poured around them, catching off scores of

eyes. Clare pressed her lips together as she tried to count the bodies surrounding them. There were far, far too many.

As long as we move slowly, as long as we stay quiet, we should be okay. They're on edge, but cautious. They won't attack without a catalyst.

It wouldn't take much to spur the monsters into a frenzy. Sudden movement. Noise. Spilled blood. Clare took agonizing care as she turned, circling the burner, to face the bus. The door had been left ajar; it would only take a second to force it open and slip inside. The crawlers would swarm the bus's outside, making it impossible to let Beth in. Clare's mind raced, trying to think through their options. *Will the car horn be loud enough to startle them off until Beth can get inside? If we have to drive out of the building, will Beth understand and know to follow us to a safer location?*

They didn't have a choice either way. They had to get into the bus.

The storm seemed to be growing heavier. Clare held her breath as she inched toward the vehicle. Dorran shadowed her, refusing to let her arm go. Then Clare froze, her pulse spiking as a raspy hissing noise echoed from ahead. She knocked the flashlight against her thigh. The light blinked, weak and erratic, but enough to catch on the six silhouettes perched on the bus's roof. The nearest one loomed down, a three-jointed arm extending to graze over the top of the door. The flashlight faded.

We could run for the bus, but we'd be dead before we reached it. I could yell for Beth, but the hollows would paint the floor red with us before she could arrive.

The flashlight was a dead weight in Clare's left hand. Her right hand, empty, flexed. She needed a weapon. She needed thicker clothes to cover her exposed skin. She needed a lot, but she wasn't going to get it.

Work with what you have. Without moving her head, she glanced at the space around them, assessing. The hollows were moving closer. She was starting to pick up the silhouettes of thin hair and long limbs at the edge of the firelight.

The fire. Clare dropped the flashlight into her pocket as she inched backward, closer to the burner. Elongated nails clicked across the floor. She whispered, just barely loud enough for Dorran to hear, "We'll need to be fast."

His head tilted in acceptance. He'd guessed her plan. He let go of her upper arm.

Clare fixed her grip around the burner's handle. Fear thrummed through her, but it was just one more sensation to blend into the overwhelming array. The acrid taste of smoke. The hungry chattering that grew less patient and more eager with every second. The rolling thunder, endless, exhausting. The bitter stench of hollows that grew stronger as they closed their circle.

She hauled the burner forward. The flames, fed by a constant stream of gas, fluttered but stayed strong. Clare carried the burner with her for a pace, holding it at her side so that it scorched the edge of her shoulder. That pace carried her closer to the bus. It built momentum. Enough momentum that, when she released the burner, it hurtled toward the hollow one towering over the bus door.

They had survived the fire in the shopping center, but they had not learned to fear it any less. Blackened lips pulled away from yellow teeth as the creatures howled, scattering. The path to the bus was clear.

Clare followed the burner's trajectory. Their portable fire hit the bus doors, the flames spiking, before falling to the tile floor with a deafening clang.

Nails grazed her shoulder. A hollow screamed as something heavy slammed into it, forcing it away. Clare shoved the bus doors open and leaped inside in one motion. She turned as she hit the driver's console, ready to pull Dorran in after her.

He carried one of the plastic chairs, and as Clare turned, he smashed it into a hollow that tried to come after him. The plastic cracked. He leaped backward, into the bus's aisle, and Clare tried to shove the doors closed.

Fingers appeared in the gap, stopping the door from locking. They squirmed, picking at the plastic and metal. Dorran joined Clare, jamming his shoulder into the door in an effort to force it closed.

"The engine," he gasped.

Clare let the handle go and reached across the wheel. Beth had left the keys in the ignition. The engine turned over and caught. Dorran had his back against the door, feet braced against the seats. She tried to count how many faces fought to be seen through the grimy window, but there were too many.

She pressed the wheel. The horn blared, deafening. The hollow outside the bus flinched but refused to back off. Clare ground her teeth as she leaned on the horn again. The door shuddered, the gap widening by an inch, as the overwhelming force drove Dorran's hold back.

Abruptly, the faces outside the door vanished. The fingers disappeared from around the seal. The latch caught as the door slammed closed, and Dorran drew a quick breath.

"Open!" Beth yelled.

Thank you, Beth. Clare made eye contact with Dorran. He gave a small nod. She hit the horn again to buy them a second of distraction. The door banged open and closed again before Clare released her hold on the horn. Beth, slightly more disheveled than she had last appeared, leaned against the bus's dashboard, her eyes flashing. The three of them held there for a brief pause, just breathing, then the scratching, scraping fingernails began to drag across the door and pry at the windows.

"Move." Beth shoved past Dorran and pulled Clare away from the driver's seat. "We need to get out of here before they block our exit. Buckle up."

Clare pulled Dorran alongside her to the seats. As long as they were out in the open, they could wait for the hollows to lose interest in the bus and leave. But they had inadvertently made camp in the hollows' nest. The creatures would not grow tired, or bored, or be easily distracted inside their home. If they didn't escape the shopping center fast, they might not have a chance to leave at all.

Clare struggled to fasten her belt as the engine revved and the bus wheels screeched on the wet tiles. Fingers pulled at the charred boards outside the nearest windows. The bus's rear shifted as something climbed over it. Feet pounded across the roof. Lightning illuminated Beth's face, tight and angry. They roared backward. With no clear view behind them, it was impossible to aim. Most of the bus passed through the hole it had already carved, but one corner clipped a pane of still-intact glass, jolting them and causing a hollow to scream as it was bludgeoned off.

"Damn it." Beth worked her jaw. She spun the bus over the curb and into the parking lot. Clare felt a spike of panic that they were about to hit one of the light poles. Then brakes screamed as Beth pulled their momentum to a halt.

Lightning washed over the entrance they had just come through. Creatures swarmed out of the shopping center. Saliva frothed over their jaws. Bloodshot eyes bulged. Some ran upright, their arms flailing, while others clambered over the broken glass and twisted metal on all fours.

"Damn it, damn it." Beth hit the accelerator. They swerved past the hollow swarm. Fists beat on the bus's roof. The hollow outside Clare's window continued to claw. "So, looks like we're not just losing the chance to loot the mall, but we've given up some of the supplies we already had to boot."

And who was responsible for making sure the mall was empty? Clare swallowed the bitter words and instead focused on maintaining her grip on her seat as the bus spun into the street. "We can make do. This won't be our last opportunity."

Beth muttered something indistinct. She took another corner tightly, relying on the bus's beaten front to clip an abandoned car out of their path. "I'm sure you're happy, at least, since you got to win the argument by default."

Don't take the bait. She's stressed, and she probably feels guilty, and the thanites are making her aggressive. You don't need to argue.

Dorran's hand moved over hers and squeezed. Clare took a slow breath, focusing on his fingers, grounding herself and reeling in her frustration and fear.

"We're not going to shake them." Beth swung the wheel to avoid a fallen tree. "Roads are too cramped to get up to the kind of speeds we need to outrun them. We'll have to power down and wait them out."

Clare hated the idea of sitting in silence for hours while the monsters crawled around the bus searching for weaknesses, but she could survive it. What worried her more was how much the bus itself might be able to survive. Beth was pushing it harder than she should. If they hit an obstacle they couldn't get past, or if the engine decided it had given as much as it could and died, she wasn't sure how easily they could get out of the town.

Beth let the bus slow to a halt in the middle of the street. She hadn't even turned the engine off when hollows clawed their way over the bus's front, blocking the windshield. Beth sent them a derisive glare, then pulled the shutters down to block them from sight.

Clare unbuckled her seat belt and felt Dorran do the same beside her. It would be her last opportunity to get comfortable for the next few hours. She would have more room to stretch out on one of the other seats, but that would mean letting go of Dorran's hand. He ran his thumb over her knuckles, tapping each one lightly, almost playfully, and Clare smiled. She was as comfortable as she was likely to get right there.

Beth exhaled as she settled back in her own seat for a long wait. Clare closed her eyes. She could see about the same whether they were open or shut. She wondering if it would be safe to try to nap. Adrenaline continued to run through her, making her twitchy and tense, but she knew the crash would come soon as it drained away.

Hollows dug around the bus's edges, chattering, hissing. She could hear one in particular; it came from somewhere behind her, its breathing ragged and wet, occasionally interrupted by thick gulping noises. A meaty, spongy fist slapped against the bus's side. Long nails scraped over the roof above her head. Meanwhile, Dorran's fingers continued to move over her hand, gentle and calming, a precious distraction. She moved her own hand in return, tangling her fingers between his, happy to fix her whole attention on tracing the lines of his palm.

The phlegmy breathing broke with another gulping swallow. It sounded closer than the others. Clearer. Most of the crawlers were muffled by the bus's walls, but that seemed almost to be coming from behind her ear. Clare opened her eyes but was greeted with pitch-blackness. Moving cautiously, trying to avoid rustling her clothes or causing the seat to creak, she moved her spare hand into her pocket where a heavy weight rested. The flashlight was nestled between the boxes of antibiotics. Clare brought it out, flinching every time the waterproof jacket crinkled. She turned in her seat.

Dorran felt her movement and tapped her hand, silently asking if anything was wrong. She couldn't answer. Instead, she aimed the flashlight toward the bus's back and depressed its button.

The light blinked on but faded almost immediately. It was enough, though. Enough to see the hollow one huddled in the back seats. Enough to reflect off its bulbous eyes and the quick dart of its tongue across its lips.

CHAPTER 28

CLARE'S BREATH FROZE AS the light died. She'd only had a second's glimpse, but that had been enough.

The creature crouched on the rear row of seats, on their bed. Four long legs bent oddly out of its waist, unpleasantly thin and elastic as the splayed toes gripped any surface within reach. The front arms seemed short by comparison. They were folded against its bare, sunken chest, fingers held limply but twitching.

We didn't think to check the bus's insides. We didn't have time.

Clare's hands shook. Her mind spun out of control, trying to understand. It must have gotten into the bus while she was distracted by the hollows coming out of the stores. Or possibly even earlier—they had left the bus unattended while they washed, assuming they were alone in the shopping mall. The door had been left ajar. It would have been easy for a curious hollow to slip inside.

And now they were trapped with it, inside a bus that felt far, far too small.

"Clare. Leave the light off." Beth's muted voice hissed around them. The hollow's phlegmy breathing hitched.

Beth hadn't seen. Neither had Dorran. They had both been facing the bus's front.

Speaking felt like too much of a risk. She didn't have a choice. "There's something in here."

"What?" Beth stood. Her boots creaked on the floor as she turned to face Clare. "We're alone. What are you talking about?"

Clare swore internally. She couldn't believe she hadn't realized sooner. Just like the hollows couldn't sense Beth, Beth's own ability to sense *them* had been dulled. That was why she'd been so certain the shopping mall was empty.

She shook the flashlight, but it wouldn't respond. Beth sighed. A button clicked, and the light above the driver's seat flashed on.

The hollow rocked from side to side, its four bent legs flexing as its torso moved. Milky blue eyes twitched against the sudden light, and the pupils tried to contract before blowing back to their enlarged dimensions.

Beth swore. Dorran took a sharp breath. He pulled on Clare's arm, tugging her close. The hollow swayed. Its tongue darted out to taste its lips.

"Hold still. I've got it." Beth reached into the compartment above her seat and withdrew a mallet. She swung it at her side experimentally, then began pacing down the bus.

"Wait," Clare said.

Beth stopped, her lips pulled back in a grimace. "What?"

The hollow continued to sway. Its hands, held close to its bony chest, twitched. But it wasn't trying to advance. If anything, it seemed to be trying to sink back into the shadows of the rear seat.

It could have attacked while we were driving. Or in those first few minutes we were sitting in the dark. It had plenty of opportunities, but it didn't, because…because…

Clare spoke to the hollow. "Hello?"

Its eyes flicked toward her, then returned to staring at the mallet in Beth's hand.

Clare's voice broke as she tried again. "Can you understand me?"

"Clare." Beth's voice held a note of warning.

She held up a hand to ask for silence, not moving her eyes from the hollow. "Do you still understand words?"

"No. Clare. What the hell are you doing?"

Dorran continued to hold Clare, one arm around her shoulders in preparation of pulling her out of harm's way, but his voice was soft, almost soothing. "It may be one of the intelligent ones. It doesn't seem to want a fight."

"Does it matter either way?" Beth, muscles twitching in her throat, swung the mallet in a broad arc. "It's a monster, whether it still has a brain or not."

"It is not that much different than *you*." Dorran took a slow breath, held it for a second, then spoke in a calmer tone. "My apologies. I simply meant that it has not tried to harm us. We should show it compassion, if we can."

"Oh." The earlier terseness was replaced with the hard angles of bitter pain. "Right. Show it compassion. Like you're showing *me* compassion, right?"

It's the thanites. Trying to make her pick a fight. Trying to make her angry. Don't respond. Clare's throat was choked by a painful lump, and she had to fight to speak around it. "That's not what he meant, Beth. Please, let's handle *this* and talk afterward, okay?"

"Fine. Whatever. Fine." Beth threw the mallet aside. It clanged as it hit the floor between two rows of seats. The hollow at the back of the bus flinched and its swaying intensified while the creatures outside the bus redoubled their efforts to dig through the metal. Clare tried to block the external noises out as she focused on the figure just a few rows away.

"We don't want to hurt you." She tried to smile, but she wasn't sure the expression came out quite right. "If you can understand me, please give me a sign."

For two painful heartbeats, the hollow continued to move in unsteady arcs, its sunken body bobbing on top of the four long legs. Then it dipped its head in an odd motion that seemed to be a nod.

Okay. Clare's hands were sweaty as she held the back of her seat. She kept her voice clear and slow. "You can't stay on this bus. As long as you don't try to hurt us, we won't hurt you. We can open the door and let you get off."

The hollow paused its watery breaths to swallow thickly. Its eyes didn't blink. Clare tried again. "Do you agree?"

Another pause. Then another odd, dipping nod.

Beth leaned against the driver's seat, her arms crossed, her eyes too bright. "This is a mistake. Let me get rid of it."

"We're…we're not going to be cruel." Clare didn't break eye contact with the hollow. "It probably only got onto the bus because it was curious. It wants to get off. We should let it."

A muffled snarl emanated from the back of Beth's throat.

Dorran turned on her. "This is for our benefit, not just the hollow one's. Attack it with a mallet, and you'll contaminate the bus. Blood is not easy to clean out of fabric."

Beth pursed her lips, but the pragmatic argument seemed to work on her better than the emotional appeals. She looked at the hollow, then at Clare, then the door. "Fine. Fine! Listen closely, monster. You will walk slowly toward the door. I'm sure that won't be a problem; you have enough legs, don't you?"

The hollow only swayed, its eyes still held on Clare.

"I'll open the door when you reach it." Beth, sounding frustrated, raised her voice. "You'll step out *immediately*. And you'll *leave*. Understood?"

The hollow gurgled sickeningly.

Clare lifted her eyebrows. "Do you understand?"

Its head bobbed. Clare released a held breath. "Okay. We can do this. Beth, you head to the front of the bus. Dorran and I will stay here. When our…guest is at the door, we'll bang on the walls to distract the other hollows and give it a chance to slip out. Ready?"

"Ready," Dorran confirmed, still not moving his arm from around her shoulders.

Beth spat something bitter as she backed toward the door. Clare waited until her sister was in position, then extended a hand toward the swaying hollow and beckoned. "Okay. You can move now."

Its tongue darted out, lapping over moist lips. Its eyes flicked from Clare's to her beckoning hand and back again. For a moment it held its position, and Clare began to doubt herself, to wonder if it had even really understood her. Then one leg extended forward.

Its toes—eight of them—fanned out from its sole, quivering in the air before finding purchase on the aisle. A second leg extended, this time fastening against one of the seat edges, the toes wrapping across the hard plastic for purchase. The torso, still swaying, moved forward.

Clare and Dorran shared a row. She was closest to the aisle, and even though Dorran held her possessively against his chest, the hollow would have to pass within inches of her in order to reach the door.

We can do this. It's going to work. Clare followed the hollow's every movement as a third leg scraped along the aisle before finding purchase on one of the seats' bases. She *needed* it to work. She needed to know there was a chance for hollow and human to cohabitate, even in a small way, even in isolated incidents. She needed *hope*.

The hollow was nearly at her side. Dorran, his chest at her back, was so still that she doubted he was even breathing. She could hear his heart, though, thundering, audible even above

259

the incessant rain and irregular scratching nails coming from outside the bus.

The creature's eyes didn't leave hers. Clare searched the watery blue orbs. They were barely human any longer; the sagging lids seemed to have recessed behind the eyes, forcing them to protrude. The pupils were dilated, blown out of proportion. The white was overridden by rivers of red veins.

And behind all of that, Clare thought she could still see a glimmer of humanity. The hollow had held on to part of its mind. Not much of it, and it was probably losing more with every day, but *enough*.

One of the elastic feet gripped the side of Clare's seat to support the body as it passed. It paused there, so close that Clare had to hold her breath against the smell of slimy skin and decay, so close that she had to fight the urge to pull away from its presence. It was the predator. She was the prey. Her body knew it, and her nerves screamed for her to run, to escape, but she remained still.

The gaze held hers. There was the same flicker of humanity. A tiny amount. Not enough.

Its jaws opened as it lunged toward her.

CHAPTER 29

THE HOLLOW'S OPEN MAW aimed for her face. Clare didn't have time to react; she'd been so focused on holding still that she hadn't been prepared to move.

Dorran had. The arm around her shoulders yanked her back, pulling her down until her shoulder blades hit his lap. In the same instant, his other hand shot forward, hitting the hollow in the center of its forehead, forcing it away.

It screamed, its neck bending at an uncomfortable angle, the hands at its chest spasming. The two closest legs left the floor as it reared up. The toes, their nails long and jagged, flexed like fingers as they reached toward Dorran.

The hollow's body rocked back as arms wrapped around it. Beth was there, fire in her eyes and her hair a golden blaze around her head. The hollow's feet hit her stomach and chest, ferocious punches that should have been painful, but she didn't even flinch. She forced it into the aisle and pinned it there, her knee digging into its bony chest until ribs cracked. Her hands fastened on either side of its head and began pulling.

The bulging eyes swiveled wildly, the jaw stretching open as it howled. The hollows outside the bus heard. They responded in kind, their voices a cacophony of screeches, their fists beating on the outside. Beth's lips peeled away from her teeth. Delight brightened her eyes. She pulled harder, twisting, and a crack rang out as the four-legged hollow's neck broke.

The screaming faded. The hollow one lay limp, its legs splayed out across the aisle and seats, its bulging eyes no longer seeing. Beth released its head and stood, breathing heavily.

Clare shuffled herself back in her seat, a hand pressed to her mouth to fight against the sounds that wanted to come out.

Beth rolled her shoulders as her features fell back into sullen disinterest. "There. No mallet, no blood, no problem."

Clare couldn't look away from the fallen hollow. A trickle of saliva ran over the parted lips. Its head rested at an unnatural angle to its body. Its retracted eyelids twitched. She recoiled, horror catching in her throat. "It—"

"It's still alive." Dorran had seen as well. He pulled her back against him.

"Eh." Beth kicked the hollow's nearest leg. "Figures. The brain's still intact and the thanites are probably already working on solutions. Unless one of the others eats it, I guess it'll be back up in a couple of days, maybe with some extra legs. I should've used the mallet."

Beth bent and picked up one of the feet, then began dragging the limp body toward the door. Clare closed her eyes. She thought she might be sick.

"Go on," Beth called. "Bang on the wall to distract them from the door."

Clare couldn't. She hugged her arms around herself as she tried to make the rushing in her ears fade. After a second, Dorran moved. He knocked his fist against the wall, moving it in a circle. The chattering, digging noises increased. The door creaked. Clare opened her eyes just in time to see Beth unceremoniously throw the hollow's body through the opening and slam it shut. Dorran stopped knocking.

Beth wiped her hands on her jacket, then sank back into her seat. "No one's hurt, right? Guess that could have gone worse. We're going to have to reset our waiting time, though, so that sucks."

A trace of coldness ran across Clare's cheek as one of the tears escaped. Beth didn't notice. Dorran's arm was still around her. His free hand came up and ran across her cheek, brushing the tear away. She met his eyes. Dark and intense. Deeply sad. Lost. He didn't know what to say.

Clare rested her head against his shoulder. After a second, Beth reached up and turned off the light. As darkness enveloped them, Clare restarted her mental countdown. Only this time she couldn't move her thoughts away from the limp body that had to be lying outside the door.

The wait was grueling. Clare's chest hurt. She knew she would feel better if she could just cry, but that would make noise. The searing pain ran through her in spasms. She compensated by squeezing her hands together until they ached.

Dorran didn't let her go, even though she sensed how exhausted he was. Twice, his coughs rose, but he bowed his head and pressed his arm over the lower half of his face as he tried to smother the sounds. Clare listened for any increased hollow activity, but she thought the rain might have been enough to muffle the coughs.

Hours passed. The ache in her chest dulled. Clare's mind turned bleary. Her headache was back; she wished she could move to get some pain tablets. She tried counting seconds in her head, but repeatedly lost her place in the mid-three-digits.

Eventually, tiredness overrode everything else. She let her eyes close as she dozed against Dorran's arm. She wasn't sure how long she existed in that fugue state, half-aware and half-asleep, before the bus's engine startled her.

Beth turned on the light above her head, her voice curt but no longer angry. "They left about a half hour ago. That's sooner than I expected. They can probably still smell the soot and want to get back to shelter, which is good for us. You ready to get back on the road again?"

Clare's mouth opened, questions dancing on her tongue. *Are you still angry? Do you want to talk about earlier? Are you going to acknowledge that twice you incorrectly told us we were safe? Is the hollow one with the broken neck still outside? Can you make sure not to drive over it?*

Instead, she just said, "Okay."

Beth retracted the metal shutters from the window and the engine rumbled as they began moving. Clare couldn't see outside, but she trusted Beth to navigate despite the near-perfect dark. For close to half an hour, they moved at a crawl, turning frequently to avoid debris, and Clare was starting to grow drowsy again when Beth reached a major road and increased their speed.

"Don't go too fast," Clare said. Beth didn't answer and she didn't slow down. Clare settled back to prepare for the long drive that would eventually end at Evandale.

Dorran slept against the window, and Clare alternated between staring at her hands and watching the dashboard clock count down the minutes. It took hours for the rain to ease. When it cleared enough to let natural light through, Clare was surprised. The ground was no longer black and the trees still held leaves. "We're out of the fire zone."

"We crossed a bridge about an hour back. Didn't you notice?"

Beth's voice was still curt. Clare tried not to let it bother her. "I guess I was napping. Well, it's good to be back on clear ground, isn't it?"

"Yep."

Clare flexed sore shoulders. "Do you know the way to Evandale, or should I get the map?"

"I know it. I memorized our route the other night."

"Well, okay. Tell me if you change your mind." Clare gave up on trying to ignite a conversation and settled back to watch the mist crawling across the rugged, rocky landscape. They were back on a rural road, with the mountains in the far distance and a ragged patch of trees spreading out toward the horizon on their right. A brisk wind snagged at the remaining spits of rain.

Beth grew increasingly restless as the afternoon lengthened. She shifted in her seat, watching the environment around them with ever-roving eyes. Occasionally, her glance would flick to the rearview mirror, but even though Clare met the look with a smile, Beth never smiled back.

The sun was still hours away from setting when she turned onto the side of the road. She barely spared enough time to pull the hand brake before springing out of her seat and kicking open the door.

"Beth?" Clare had been growing drowsy and had to shake herself awake. She detangled her arm from Dorran's and jogged after her sister. Beth strode away from the bus, then abruptly stopped in front of a massive oak tree and punched it.

Clare gasped and broke into a run. Beth pulled her arm back and slammed it into the tree again. Blood glistened on the trunk from where her skin had broken.

"Stop!" Clare grabbed Beth's arm as she pulled it back a third time. Beth turned on her, face contorted into a furious grimace. Her other hand swiped around, fingers aiming for Clare's throat.

Clare staggered back, narrowly avoiding the nails. Beth lurched away. Her breathing was ragged. Slowly, the wildness faded from her face, leaving just raw anger in its place.

"Don't...don't touch me."

Clare glanced at Beth's hand. Blood dripped from the knuckles. She opened her mouth, then closed it again.

Leaves crunched at her side. Dorran had emerged from the bus. "Beth?"

"I…" Beth's face twitched as she waged some internal battle. "It's too crowded in that bus. I can't handle it. I'm going for a walk."

She knew she was pushing, but Clare couldn't stop. "We shouldn't be alone outside."

"Or what?" Beth's voice took on a guttural note as she swung back to Clare. "Or a hollow will attack me? Or are you worried about other survivors? I would relish another round against a man with a gun."

Clare tried to speak, but her voice broke into a croak.

Beth shot her one final snarl, then stalked into the forest. Her blond hair swung wildly with each step, and it didn't take her long to vanish among the trees.

CHAPTER 30

"ANOTHER…" CLARE STAGGERED BACKWARD. Dorran was there, standing just behind her, and he rested his hand on the small of her back to steady her. Despite the grayness and the exhaustion, he'd planted his stance. A glint of metal at his side drew Clare's eyes down. He held a long, serrated knife at his side.

She let her attention move from Dorran to the space between the trees where Beth had disappeared.

She said another *fight with a gun.*

Beth had to be talking about the survivor they had disturbed in his convenience store. As she fled the scene, Clare had heard multiple gunshots, though the man didn't seem to be chasing her. She'd thought Beth was just behind, but when Clare stopped, she was nowhere to be seen. And when Beth did return to the bus, she'd brought the map—the exact kind of map they needed, one that she'd claimed had been conveniently left by the window and that she'd managed to grab on the way out. The coincidence was almost too great to believe.

No.

Beth didn't kill him.

She wouldn't have.

Would she?

Clare's stomach turned over. She couldn't stop picturing the survivor, his gun fallen uselessly against the cash register, his stomach torn open and his limbs being dismembered as the hollow ones feasted.

"I'm going back to the bus," she mumbled. Dorran sheathed the knife and followed. She hoped he wasn't thinking along the same lines she was, because her thoughts were turning desperately dark.

As he stepped back into the vehicle, he stopped, one hand gripping the door, the back of his other arm pressed over his mouth. Violent coughs shook him. Clare felt supremely helpless as she watched, waiting, counting the seconds. When his shaking shoulders finally became still, he slumped against the bus's side, sheet white. Spots of red stained his jacket sleeve. Clare's heart squeezed.

She paced through the bus and found the box of capsules. She popped one out, found some water, and returned to Dorran. He mutely took the pill.

"Have a sleep," Clare suggested. She ran her hand over his cheek. Cold and sweaty. His eyes were dull. He nodded, not even trying to argue, and passed her as he walked to the back of the bus.

Give the capsules time. They will work.

Clare sat at the front of the bus. She kept her eyes trained on the forest, watching for movement or for any sign that Beth was returning. But she kept her ears focused on Dorran. His breathing sounded irregular.

The forest on either side of the road stayed quiet. Clare couldn't stop her brain from imagining what might happen if Beth *never* returned. Beth had said she was going on a walk; she didn't say she was coming back. Clare couldn't stop watching the clock. Minutes turned into an hour. She began to shake and couldn't stop.

The sun was close to setting when a figure stepped out from between the trees. Clare bolted upright. Beth had shed her jacket and scarf. Only a tank top covered her upper half, and the thin fabric stretched over the spines running down her back. They flexed with every step. Beth's gait had changed. After spending their whole lives together, Clare was so familiar with her sister's style of walking that she could easily pick her out in a crowd. Now, Beth's stride was longer. Her body swayed and undulated with each step. She was closer to a stalking animal than a human.

Beth swung herself into the bus and slid into the driver's seat. The engine revved. Clare opened her mouth, unsure of whether it was safe to say anything, but Beth spoke first. "I'm apologizing, and if it sounds like I'm not sorry, I'll apologize for that too."

"Oh. Okay." Clare knit her fingers together.

"I'm *hungry*." Beth put the bus into gear and pulled back onto the road. "And you cannot comprehend how grating it is to be surrounded by food but unable to eat. I'm losing my temper over the smallest thing."

"I understa—"

"I love you, Clare, but for a while, I just need you to shut up."

Clare pressed her lips together. The tires screeched as the bus picked up speed. She looked behind them. If Dorran had woken, he was pretending to still be asleep.

Beth drove as night descended and the earth vanished into dark. The bus's internal lights flowed through the window, but they didn't do much to replace the broken headlights. Clare had the impression that they were floating through a void, just them and a small circle of ground around them that shifted to give the appearance of motion.

She wanted to stop. Beth's face was frozen and unwelcoming. She kept her mouth closed.

It was nearing nine when they passed through a town. The settlement held no more than a few hundred houses and a narrow strip mall. Beth didn't slow down for it. As they neared the town's other side, a figure ran out of the darkness. Clare had a glimpse of red-pocked, swollen flesh. Then the bus hit it, and a splatter of red and white matter streaked across the windshield. The bus lurched as it drove over the mass, then continued out of the town's other side.

Beth's eyes were wide and her nostrils flared. For a moment, she kept statue still, then slowly ran her hand over her face. She seemed shaken. "Let's stop for dinner. We'll have a fire."

"Oh. Aren't we close to Evandale?"

"Not yet."

Even with the delays, they should have been close to arriving. Clare wanted to question her further, but she didn't think Beth's patience could handle it. Instead, she nodded.

Beth found a clearing away from the road. A copse of small, dead trees stretched along one side, near what had once been farmland. Beth snapped branches into manageable lengths to build a fire while Clare poured fast-cook rice and canned vegetables into a pot. They worked in silence.

The night was dark. Clouds masked the sky, leaving Clare feeling unusually claustrophobic. She wished she could see just a few stars.

As Beth tended to their campfire, Clare went to wake Dorran. He was hard to rouse. Clare had to shake him repeatedly before he shifted.

"Hmm?" The bus was dim, but he still squinted against the light.

"We're cooking dinner." Clare tried to smile, but she thought the expression came out crooked. "Would you like to get up? Or if you wanted to rest a little more, I could bring you some—"

"No." He closed his eyes, exhaled, then rolled up to sit. It seemed to take significant effort. He sat on the edge of the bed for a second, brows pulled tight, then stood, only to sway dangerously. Clare swallowed her growing sense of panic as she hooked one arm around him so he could lean on her.

As they made their way to the bus's entrance, Clare snagged extra blankets from the baskets. They had lost their folding chairs in the shopping mall, so they would need to sit on the ground if they wanted to enjoy the fire's warmth. Dorran had to use her to balance as he stepped down from the bus. The fire crackled a few feet away, and Clare spread the blankets out beside it before lowering Dorran onto them.

Beth had created a pyramid over the fire with sticks and hung their pot of food from the axis. As she stirred it, her forearm occasionally dipped inside the flames. The skin was starting to blister.

Clare reached toward her. "Beth, watch your hand."

Beth's glare was frosty. She didn't stop stirring.

This is wrong. Clare turned away so she wouldn't have to watch. Dorran sat at her side, head slumped forward, eyes half-closed. He'd brought the hunting knife, she realized. He had it at his side, his hand resting over the handle.

She felt pressed on all sides. Dorran, Beth, the USB—everything was piling on, and their foundation wasn't strong enough to handle it. Beth dropped filled bowls beside Clare and Dorran. She hadn't prepared one for herself, but she sat on the ground opposite them. Clare pushed Dorran's bowl toward him. He simply shook his head.

This is all wrong.

She felt trapped, like one wrong move could snap the threads holding them together. Clare picked up her own bowl and tried to sip from it. Her hands were shaking too badly. She put it aside.

"Eat it," Beth said. Her eyes, unblinking, were fixed on Clare.

"I'm not hungry."

Something dark flashed through Beth's face. She rounded the fire, snatched up both Clare's and Dorran's bowls, and hurled them into the darkness. Then she swung back to Clare, breathing heavily. "How can you claim to not be hungry when I am so *ravenous?*"

Dorran shifted a fraction. Clare glanced down. He'd unsheathed the knife.

No. This is wrong. This is all wrong.

"Please." Clare held up a hand between herself and Beth, half-beseeching, half-defensive. "Don't be angry. We're just tired."

Beth bared her teeth. Then she took a step back and swiped her hand across her lips. The fingers were shaking. She spoke in short, stilted bursts. "I'm sorry. I need to get away. I—I'll go for a walk...be back before dawn."

She strode away, her pace fast, her motion smooth. The spines rippled under her tank top as she exited the campfire's circle of light.

Dorran sheathed the knife. He exhaled as his head sagged.

Clare put her arm around him, torn between wanting to apologize and wanting to defend Beth. "You okay? I can get you some more food."

"Just...just tired."

"Come here." She gently helped him lie down, spread out across the blankets, his head beside her so that she could stroke his hair. His eyes closed, but his breathing remained ragged. Clare let her hand slide to his throat and felt the skin. It was clammy. She swallowed and felt a lump from impending tears blocking her throat.

A cold wind slipped around them, worming into the gaps in Clare's clothes. The fire was beginning to fall low as its fuel was consumed. Mist snaked across the overgrown grass and through the dead branches at the edge of Clare's vision. She shivered. Even though Dorran was at her side, she felt horribly, horribly alone.

"Dorran?" She brushed stray hair away from his face. "Do you want to go back into the bus now? It'll be warmer there."

He didn't respond. Clare tried shaking his shoulder. His eyes opened a sliver, then dropped closed again.

Clare looked at the bus. It was close; she just had no way to get Dorran onto it herself. Until he woke or until Beth returned, they would have to stay outside. Which meant being vulnerable...to the cold and to the hollows.

Clare rose, grimacing as stiff muscles were forced to move. The fire was the one thing that could protect them from both threats, and although the flames were turning into embers, the copse of trees wasn't far away.

The cold trickled around her as she left the bonfire's circle of light. Clare kept one eye on Dorran's still form as she reached blindly into the dark and felt for branches. Dry wood scraped her palms. Clare broke off small branches and clutched them close to her chest as she turned back to their camp.

A noise came from behind her, and Clare froze. It sounded disturbingly like a sigh. *An animal? The wind?* Clare licked dry lips. *Beth?*

Clare jogged back to the fire, arms laden with wood, and

dropped it into an untidy pile. She fed new pieces into the blaze and breathed a little easier as the circle of light expanded.

Dorran didn't respond as Clare ran her hand across his forehead. He still felt cold. Clare crossed to the bus, climbed inside, and brought out their last four clean blankets. Three went around Dorran to shelter him from the wind and to warm him. Clare wrapped the final blanket around her shoulders as she watched the dancing flames.

She knew she had to stay awake. They were in unfamiliar territory and someone needed to act as guard. But she'd gone through nights of disturbed sleep, and crushing tiredness weighed her limbs down.

When she felt herself start to slip under, she stood up and paced around the fire. When her eyelids continued to droop, she pinched herself, relying on a quick shot of unhappy nerves to bring her back. She kept moving until her legs were too tired to hold her up, then she slumped to the ground on the opposite side of the fire from Dorran and hugged the blanket around her shoulders. She hoped dawn wasn't far away. Her eyes burned as though the soot had never left them, and every blink made it harder to open her lids.

She thought she saw something moving just outside the firelight. Clare squinted, but her mind was so fragmented that she couldn't separate imagination from reality.

Everything was sore. Not from exercise, but from days spent sitting in the same position and bending over the map. She wanted to lean against something to give her muscles a rest. She couldn't risk it. She couldn't risk giving in to the tiredness.

Clare groaned and rolled her shoulders. The fire crackled, and her imagination tried to say the crackling was all around her, a subtle symphony of feet across dry grass and dead leaves.

Then, she didn't know exactly when, her world shifted into a dreamscape. She was back in the farmhouse where they had taken refuge, her shoes crunching over leaves blown through the broken window. Immediately ahead, at the end of a long hallway, was the door to the master bedroom. The elastic rope was still fastened to the handle, holding it closed against a being that had no mind to open it.

She knew what she would find inside the room, but she was irrevocably drawn toward it. She reached out and lightly unhooked the rope. The handle glittered in the unnatural light.

The creature behind the door was audible. Stifled, gasping breaths. Muffled thumping noises as it writhed. She had to see it. Her fingers touched the handle.

Clare's eyes snapped open. She couldn't tell how much time had passed—a minute or an hour. She lay slumped on her side, her face and arms heated by the fire as her cheek rested on the sandy ground.

The noises had followed her into reality. Muffled gasps. The thump of writhing limbs. Clare lifted her head. Dorran lay on the other side of the fire. He was no longer still. Beth was at him. She crouched, one hand holding his head down, fresh blood running over her lips.

CHAPTER 31

CLARE SCREAMED. BETH LIFTED her head. Her eyes flashed as the lips curled back into a grin.

Dorran was moving, twisting, but sluggishly. Clare was afraid to look at him. She didn't want to see. But she had to.

Please, no, please, this can't be happening. Beth's teeth had gouged a hole in his arm, just below his shoulder. Blood streamed over his chest and soaked the blankets.

He wasn't fully conscious, she realized. Trapped in a delirium, he was powerless to fight Beth off. She pinned him in place, hunched over her feast, predatory and wild.

"No." Clare's groan stopped in her throat. She felt as though she was trapped in a nightmare, but every detail was too real, too sharp, for it to be anything but reality.

Beth tilted her head to one side. Her eyes glittered. "Go back to sleep, sweet Clare."

"No, no, stop—" Clare scrambled to her knees, her hand held out.

"Shh," Beth whispered. "This is for the best. He's become a burden."

The wildness in her eyes was horrifying. Her fingers roved across Dorran's arm, scrabbling, then began to dig into the wound. He whined.

"No!" Clare launched herself toward the blankets where Dorran had left his knife. She pulled the blade out of its sheath and clenched the handle in both hands as she pointed it at Beth's face. "Get off him!"

Beth hummed under her breath, her tongue slipping out to scoop the gore off her chin. "It's all right, baby. This is the way it was always supposed to be. We'll be together, just the two of us. And I won't be hungry anymore. You don't want me to be hungry, do you?"

"Get off him!" Clare screamed.

Dorran's movements had slowed. His breathing sounded broken.

Beth leaned over his body. The spines rippled in the firelight. One of her arms snaked out, deceptively fast, and the fingers wrapped around the blade.

Clare reflexively jerked backward. The serrated blade scraped across Beth's palm. A glut of blood dribbled out of it.

"Don't cry, baby," she cooed. "This is the way it was always supposed to be."

Beth wasn't afraid of the knife. Clare could sense she was

279

already far beyond reason. She'd tasted blood, and she wouldn't leave her feast for anything short of death.

I have to kill her. The thought came with a wave of ice freezing around her heart, solidifying in her lungs, until she could neither move nor breathe.

She pictured herself driving the knife into her sister's chest, or drawing it across her throat, or thrusting it into one of her eyes. Her body was numb. Her mind screamed, the noise trapped, reverberating, growing louder with every second.

Her limbs wouldn't move. She couldn't do it. It was the only way to stop Beth's attack on Dorran, but she couldn't. Beth's eyes, bright and delighted, turned toward the broken skin under her hands as her tongue snaked out again.

Beth didn't fear the knife. She didn't even fear her own death. But there was one thing Clare hoped she might still value enough to use as leverage. Clare pressed the blade against her own throat. "Leave him alone!"

Beth's smile morphed into concern. "Shh, darling. Stop fussing. I'll take care of you. You'll like that. Big sister Beth will care for you."

She pushed the knife in harder. The sting of steel cleaving skin was almost a relief. It gave her something to focus on. A drip of warm liquid ran down her throat, but she couldn't tell if it was residual blood from Beth or her own. "Kill him, and I die too."

The kindness was melting from her sister's features. "He's dead either way. Let me enjoy him while he's still warm."

"Get off." She tilted her head back and pushed the blade in harder. The skin burned. "*Now.*"

280

Red lips quivered around red teeth. "Are you actually siding with him over me?"

"Yes."

Beth arched her back. Nostrils flared, skin blanching pale. "You petulant, spoiled child. Do you have any idea how desperately I love you? Or what I've done for your sake? And you throw it in my face—"

The words hurt too much to speak as anything louder than a whisper. "I hate you."

Beth's eyes widened, then narrowed into slits. "No, you don't."

The phrase was having an effect, so Clare pushed on, her voice rising in volume and urgency as she clutched for the harshest words she could find. "I hate you. I *loathe* you. You're a *monster*."

Beth rose. She had never been a tall person, but at that moment, she seemed to tower. Her eyes flashed and her voice roared, red spittle flying over her lips. "Recant that!"

"Monster!" Clare knew she was pushing Beth over an edge. She didn't know what the result might be, only that her sister's tone promised violence. But it was her only option left. She couldn't make herself drive the knife into Beth. She couldn't abandon Dorran. So she used her words, and she used them recklessly. "Monster, monster, *monster!*"

Beth screamed. She seemed to be trying to drown the word out. The cry rose into a howling shriek, and Clare was suddenly knocked over. The knife skidded away. Wild, inhuman eyes stared into hers, then, in a heartbeat, they were gone.

Clare sat up. Her ears rang and her hands were sweaty. The

dancing firelight made everything seem to be moving; shadows swirled at the peripheries of her vision, but as she twisted toward them, she realized Beth was gone.

Dorran. He was no longer moving. Clare scrambled to him. His eyes were open but only halfway. Pure terror spiked through her as she held a shaking hand up to his open mouth. A faint breath ghosted across her fingers. It was cold, but he was still alive.

Blood ran from the bite wound on his arm. It wasn't stopping. Clare grabbed one of the blankets from the pile and pressed it against the cuts. Dorran twitched, but there was no other response.

Please, please, I can't lose you like this. She kept trying to tell herself that Dorran was strong, that he was resilient, that he had overcome everything else life had pushed on him, and he could overcome this, as well. She clenched her teeth as she applied pressure, knowing it would hurt him but that it was the only way to stop the flow.

Already, red liquid was starting to seep through the fabric. She tried not to look. Her eyes were blurred and her chest ached from breathing too quickly. She wished he could talk to her. He knew first aid. He would know what to do to make it better.

The fire was starting to drop low again, but Clare didn't dare leave Dorran to refuel it. She felt as though she were walking on ice, and a single wrong step would plunge them both under. Every few minutes, she leaned back far enough to check he was still breathing. His features were slack and his eyes dull. But his chest continued to rise and fall, and for that moment, that was all that Clare asked of him.

Her arms and shoulders began to ache from holding the pressure. Clare shuffled around, trying to relax the tense muscles without loosening her hold. She couldn't maintain it for much longer, she knew. She would have to ease up the pressure and see if it had been enough to stop the bleeding.

Blood had grown in a pool around Dorran's bed, soaking through his clothes and blankets. There was more of it than she'd thought one human could hold. Clare braced herself, then gingerly removed her hands from the towel and rolled back onto her heels. She held her breath as she watched.

Nothing seemed to change. She hoped that was a good sign. She clambered onto her feet and then ran into the bus and hunted through the racks to find the first aid kit Beth had been using. It was tucked behind the driver's seat. Clare pulled it out and sorted through the supplies.

The cloth bag didn't hold much. There were no painkillers, no stitches, and no antibiotics. Only a roll of clean bandages, scissors, medical tape, and a near-empty bottle of disinfectant.

Clare found the packet of antibiotics and tucked it in with the bag as she ran back to Dorran. She knelt at his side, popped one of the antibiotics out, and held it up to his mouth. "Dorran, you need to take this. Please."

There was no response. She touched his forehead. His eyes stayed glazed and half-open. His features were blank.

"Come on, please, please." She tried to push the capsule into his open mouth. He remained unresponsive. Clare swallowed hot, stinging tears as she tucked the antibiotics away.

The bottle of disinfectant was down to the last tablespoon. Clare guessed Beth had been using it on the open wounds on her back up until she'd learned that the thanites kept her immune from infection. There wasn't much left, but she hoped it would be better than nothing.

Clare gingerly peeled the cloth away from the wounds on Dorran's arm. She could finally see them clearly now that they weren't washed in blood. The bite marks were deep, exposing red flesh and muscle. She clenched her teeth, shivers running through her, and tipped the last of the disinfectant over the wound.

If Dorran felt it, there was no response. She swallowed thickly as she applied one of the cotton pads and began wrapping the bandage over the mess. She tried to move his arm as little as possible, but fresh blood began to seep out regardless.

I'm so sorry, Dorran. Please forgive me.

She'd been stupid. Dorran knew first aid. She'd had weeks in which she could have learned from him, but instead, she'd relied on him to handle every situation himself. Now that she was alone, her own knowledge was horribly inadequate. All she could do was bumble through the process and hope she did more good than harm.

His shirt was soaked in blood. Clare cut it away using the medical scissors. She threw more wood on the fire to keep him warm and, using one of the bottles of water and a towel, washed him as well as she could.

A twig snapped somewhere off to her right. Clare lifted her head and hunted through the black expanse, but if they had company, she couldn't see it. Wary, she crawled to the knife Beth had forced out of her hand. The vicious blade was still stained red. Clare wiped it clean and kept it at her side for the rest of the night.

CHAPTER 32

SLEEP WAS NO LONGER a temptation. Any time her mind started to wander, the nightmarish images returned. Beth, crouched over Dorran. Blood running. She would startle back into focus, her heart beating too fast and her stomach in knots.

She tended the fire, keeping it bright and large. Twice, she had to make the trip back to the copse of trees to find fresh wood. The trip took her away from Dorran, leaving him vulnerable for nearly a minute each time, and her mind tormented her with images of what could be happening to him while she was gone. She always broke into a run as she returned to the fire, only to feel the panic fade as she saw him lying undisturbed where she'd left him.

Blood stained the bandages around his arm, but she thought the blood in the wounds must have clotted. His breathing was shallow. She had no way to help that. His skin was gray and dry in a way that told her he was dehydrated. There was no way to help that, either, not unless he woke up, and no matter how often Clare spoke his name, he wouldn't stir. She stayed by his head, stroking his hair with one hand and holding the knife in the other as she kept watch.

Night seemed to last far longer than it should have. Clare's nerves were burning by the time sunlight brought relief over the area. Finally, she could see the hills surrounding them, the little patches of forest, and even the silhouettes of the mountains in the distance. She was grateful for the light. It chased the unseen demons away. But it was also an awful threat. They had made it through the night, but now she was forced to consider what needed to come next.

She couldn't leave Dorran where he was. She didn't think he would last long exposed to the elements, injured.

He needed a doctor. But she didn't know where to find any. She could drive to the nearest safe haven; Beth had marked their locations on her map. But they were few and far between, and she suspected they wouldn't be able to provide as much help as she needed. With strangers arriving every day, whatever medical supplies the safe havens had started with or managed to trade for would be depleted.

There was only one medical center in the area that might have hope: Evandale's research institute. Clare ground her teeth, remembering what Beth had said. They would be scientists, not real doctors. But at least they hadn't been marked as a known safe haven on the map. They wouldn't have become a destination for people seeking help. Which meant it was Dorran's best chance.

She ran her hand over his forehead. Sweat slicked his hair. She found a towel and dabbed him dry.

Having a destination was one thing. Getting there was another. Clare still had the bus, but she had no way to get Dorran into it. He was heavy, and she couldn't so much as lift him, let alone carry him.

Clare's head was foggy with stress. There had to be something she hadn't thought of. Some way to get him on board without jostling him so much that it started the bleeding again.

I need to get him inside before Beth returns.

Anytime she thought of her sister, her mind threatened to spiral. She didn't want to think of where Beth was, or what she was doing, or what she might intend.

The only truly important thing, the one thing she had to focus on, was Dorran. The research station was their only real hope. And it was close. They should have reached it the night before; it wouldn't take more than a couple of hours of driving to be at its door.

But Dorran had to come with her. She couldn't leave him alone in the wilderness, not even for an hour.

An uneasy prickle ran across Clare's back: the awful, instinctual knowledge that she was being watched. She turned carefully, trying not to make any sudden moves. A figure stood between the trees just twenty paces away. With the sun behind it, Clare couldn't see its face, but the halo of fine blond hair was familiar. Clare's pulse jumped. She reached for the knife.

"I'm not here to apologize." Beth took a step nearer.

The knife's wooden handle was damp with early morning dew. She flexed her fingers around it and tilted the blade so Beth could see the light shining off of it.

Beth stepped closer. Her eyes were emotionless as she stared down at Dorran's body. "It didn't seem wrong at the time. Even now, it makes more sense than a lot of things ever do. He's a burden. He's been sick for a long time, and you'd be better off without him."

Clare rose into a crouch. Her hands shook. Beth was close enough that a few long paces and a well-aimed strike would hit her. But still, Clare couldn't make herself move. She knew she had to. But she couldn't.

Beth tilted her head as she watched Dorran, then her eyes flicked up to meet Clare's. "No. I'm not here to hurt him. It's easier to think during the day. Easier to remember how I used to feel and what I used to believe. And I'm not here to ask to stay with you. I realize that time is gone. But I want to make some amends before I leave."

She reached toward Dorran. Clare lunged forward, the knife aimed at Beth's hand, but the blade stopped short an inch away from her fingers.

"Don't touch him," Clare hissed.

Beth didn't shy away from the blade. She tilted her hand over to show Clare the bright-red line, already knitting closed, from where she had been cut the night before. "I'm here to *help*. You need to get him into the bus. You need to keep moving."

Clare glanced toward their waiting vehicle. Beth was right; she needed help. But she was terrified of what might happen if she trusted her, even for a second. She tried to swallow the lump in her throat. "We're close to Evandale. We can't be more than an hour or two away—"

"No. You're not close at all." The eyes, familiar and alien at once, blinked slowly. "I did wrong by you. I wanted more time. We have been driving away from Evandale for more than a day."

Clare opened her mouth. Her tongue felt heavy, like it had been recast in lead. *More than a day.* Beth had to mean the aftermath of the shopping mall encounter. When she'd brushed Clare's hair, before things had started to go wrong, she told Clare the only thing she wanted was more time together. She'd wanted more time, so she'd made sure she would have it.

Beth hooked her arms under Dorran's shoulders. Clare felt as though she were paralyzed. She stared, knife still clasped in shaking hands. Her mind was too tired, too stressed, and too frightened to think, and the cognitive dissonance was brutal. Beth was a monster, but also her sister. A murderer, but the person she had once trusted more than any other human on the planet. She'd hurt Dorran. Now she'd promised to help. And she was dragging him away from the fire, toward the bus.

"Get his legs," Beth said.

It took a lot of willpower to tuck the blade back into the waistband of her pants. Clare's subconscious was screaming at her, telling her she was in the presence of a predator and that lowering her defenses would end in her being hurt. But she felt robbed of any other choice. She wrapped her arms around Dorran's feet and, at Beth's nod, lifted.

Beth went first as they carried Dorran up the step and into the bus. She bore almost all of his weight, but her face stayed eerily impassive.

Clare was breathless by the time they lowered Dorran into the bed. He was white enough to be a corpse. Clare held her hand over his mouth, and felt the thin flow of breath. She draped blankets over his prone form, trying to keep him as warm as she could. Footsteps echoed behind her. Clare stayed hunched over Dorran as Beth strode out of the bus.

Was that it? Is she really leaving? Clare brushed a strand of dark hair away from Dorran's face, then folded her arms around her torso as she followed her sister to the bus's door. Beth stood outside, early morning sunlight shining off of her hair. She faced the mountains in the distance.

"I wish I could help you more," Beth said. "But I think, right now, the most help I can give is to get myself far away from you."

Clare stopped on the edge of the step. She unfolded her arms, felt too vulnerable, and crossed them back over her chest.

Beth turned. There was no sadness in her features. "Until now, I always thought you were safer as long as I stayed with you. I could protect you, guide you, shelter you. I thought I could control my anger and my hunger for your sake. But I was losing my humanity a piece at a time, and the longer I stayed with you, the more danger I put you in."

"Beth…" She felt that she needed to say something, to try to reconcile, to give some parting words. Nothing sounded right except for "I'm sorry."

"Me too." Beth smiled. It was like looking through a veil to catch a glimpse of her old face and the person she had once been. Then the smile faded. "Drive east to reach Evandale. Don't stop for anyone. Don't take risks. Your friend will die, and you'll need to grieve, but keep moving. Pass on that code so we can end this mess, then do whatever you need to in order to build a new life."

"What about you?"

"I'll be fine." She stepped away, head held high, spines flexing under her top. "Good luck. I love you."

"Goodbye," Clare whispered. Her heart felt like it had been filed with ice. Beth walked past the remains of their campfire and stepped in between the trees, moving toward the mountains. Clare wished she could stay and watch longer, but she had already lost too much time. She pulled the door closed behind her and slid into the driver's seat.

She hadn't driven the bus before, beyond the few seconds she'd been in control after they went off the road. It felt surreal to sit in the seat she'd come to think of as Beth's. Almost as though she was intruding. The key hung in the ignition, waiting to be turned. The rearview mirror was positioned not to face the windows, but to face the bus's occupants. She could see Dorran in it, half-hidden by the shadows at the end of the bus.

Beth had said that Dorran would die. Stated as a fact, as though there was no hope left. Clare couldn't believe that. She was afraid of what would happen to her if she did. At least, for the moment, Dorran was still breathing, which meant there was still hope, and she had to hold on to it harder than anything else. She turned the key in the ignition and heard the motor rumble.

CHAPTER 33

THE TIREDNESS WAS UNBEARABLE. Clare had hoped it would become easier to cope as the sun rose, but instead of abating, the sensation merely changed, transforming into something heavy and grating, where every speck of sun dancing over her face and every bump felt like it was breaking her down.

Clare pushed them to speeds that bordered on reckless. Now that she had time to think, it was all she could do. She was responsible for what had happened. That was an underlying base truth, no matter how she tried to approach it. Dorran was dying, and it was because of her.

He'd left Winterbourne for her sake. He'd followed her down the path toward Evandale, even though he was unwell. And he'd been vulnerable to Beth because of her.

Beth had believed Dorran would turn on her when he discovered she was half hollow. And maybe he would have, Clare realized, if she hadn't pleaded with him to be kind. He'd struggled with the discovery, but he'd ultimately done what Clare asked. To make her happy.

If he hadn't...if he'd told her to leave...if he'd chased her off, like the other survivors had...

Guilt choked Clare. At every aspect, she'd failed him by ignoring the multitude of red flags in her path. She should have prioritized Dorran's safety. She should have believed Beth when she said she wasn't human.

I thought I could make them become friends. They were grating on each other this entire trip. Would Beth have coped better if I hadn't been pushing them to get along? Maybe, without Dorran to flare her frustration, she never would have lashed out.

Clare's foot was falling heavier on the accelerator. The bus rocked wildly as it passed over a fallen branch. Clare clenched her teeth and glanced in the rearview mirror. The jarring bumps would be bad for Dorran. She let her speed coast back down a fraction.

There was no need to look at the map. Their road was straight as they retraced the path Beth had taken them. She would need to drive until that evening, but then there would only be a few towns she would need to pass through to reach Evandale. She didn't intend to stop at any of them.

She was putting all of her hope in the research center. The last few times she'd put her trust in anything, people had been hurt. Ezra was dead because she'd trusted in Helexis Tower as a refuge. She'd nearly died because she trusted the hollow that had hidden in their bus. Dorran was dying because she'd trusted her sister. It seemed like goodness was spread thin in the new world.

The common denominator here is you, Clare. At every turn, you made choices that hurt the people you love. Ignorance isn't an excuse. You should know better. You should be smarter than this. You should have listened to Beth when she told you to stay at home and not take any risks. Because it's fine to risk your own life, but it was wrong to risk anyone else's.

She blinked and saw Beth crouched over Dorran, teeth sunk into his arm, her eyes alight with bliss as he twitched under her hands.

Clare screamed. The bus shuddered, throwing her against the window as they careened off the road. She tasted blood. Dust plumed around the bus's front window, and when she opened her eyes, she saw the dizzying motion had stopped. She'd hit a tree.

You fell asleep. Hopeless.

The internal voice had taken on Beth's cadence. She tried to shut her mind to it as she scrambled out of the driver's seat.

The front window had a crack running along it. The tree had been small and supple enough that it bowed under the bus's pressure, but it was a miracle they were still upright. Clare staggered down the bus's length to reach Dorran. The swaths of blankets had kept him immobile, at least. She bent close to his mouth. He was still breathing. Clare released a breath of her own and pressed a hand to her thundering heart.

The collision had jostled packets of supplies down from the overhead baskets. Clare threw them back, then dragged down a box she'd seen several days before. Inside, she found instant coffee. Clare dumped tablespoons of it into a mug and mixed in bottled water. It didn't dissolve properly and turned into an angry black sludge. She forced herself to swallow it, gagging between mouthfuls. Then she filled the mug again and slammed it into the cup holder beside the driver's seat.

The engine still turned over. Clare put the bus in Reverse and pulled away from the tree. The wheels scraped over small rocks and loose gravel as she pulled them back onto the road, then resumed the drive, counting on the adrenaline to keep her conscious until the caffeine could kick in.

She needed sleep, but that couldn't happen until she reached Evandale. Beth's detour was a crushing setback, but she thought she could still reach it that evening, as long as she didn't take breaks and kept their speed high.

She worried at her nails, chewing the skin around them until it was raw and stinging. The road was straight, painfully dull, almost hypnotic. Her eyes blurred until the path looked hazy.

Wait. It's not my eyes. It's—

Smoke rose from the bus's front, and fresh panic forced the tiredness away. "No, no, not now—"

The smoke was growing thicker. Clare scanned the unfamiliar dashboard and saw a red engine light. She grit her teeth as she eased the bus to a halt.

She glanced at Dorran through the rearview mirror. He would know what to do. He'd fixed her car, which she'd believed might be unfixable. He was good with his hands and good at solving puzzles. Clare had to hunt to find the button to open the hood.

Ever since she'd known him, Dorran had worried about not being enough—not being enough for her, not being enough for the world. The irony was that he was one of the most capable people Clare had ever known. As she climbed out of the bus and bent over the smoking engine, hot tears came, running down her cheeks and dripping onto the metal, where they fizzled away in seconds, leaving small salty deposits in their memory.

Even if he hadn't understood the technology behind the engine, he would have known enough to guess where the problem lay. To Clare, it was nothing but a maze of unfamiliar metal twisting in convoluted shapes. She knew basic car maintenance, like how to replace tires and change her oil, but complex repairs were beyond her. She touched one of the exposed pieces of metal and sucked in a breath when she burned herself.

Beth's voice returned, full of cutting sarcasm. *Congratulations, you ruined everything. Again.*

"Shut up," Clare hissed. She looked down the length of the road. The path was dirt and had been rarely used before the stillness. She couldn't see any abandoned cars. She would find one eventually, she knew, if she just walked far enough. And, if she was lucky, it would be unlocked. Then she just needed to hope it would still have its keys inside, and hadn't been damaged when it went off the road, and its fuel hadn't been scavenged by other survivors. *If, if, if…*

Clare rested a hand on the bus's side. It might take her hours to find a working car. And Dorran would be left alone and vulnerable the entire time.

What are the chances of a survivor passing the bus? Stopping? Looking inside? It's a valuable resource, with its food and medicine. If they wanted to take it for themselves, what would they do to Dorran?

Before, Beth had always been careful to park their bus somewhere hidden whenever they needed to stop. Now, it was stranded on the side of the road, in clear view. Clare's skin crawled. They didn't pass other vehicles often, but she couldn't deny that other survivors were out there, searching for any supplies or advantages they could find.

I can't leave Dorran. But I can't just stand here, either. We need to keep moving.

She turned back to the engine as emotions tightened her throat. It was just as incomprehensible as it had been before.

A faint droning noise made her lift her head. The sound, oddly familiar, seemed unreal in the stretch of empty wilderness. Clare stepped out from behind the bus and squinted down the length of the road.

A silver shape moved in the distance. A car, coming toward them.

Clare ducked back out of sight, one hand at her throat. Beth's warnings ran through her mind. *Don't trust strangers.*

Five quick steps brought her to the bus's open door. She snatched the hatchet out from its cubby beside the driver's seat. She'd kill them before she let them hurt Dorran.

The car's drone grew closer. Clare, still hidden from sight, stared at the metal weapon in her hands.

They might be able to help. Dorran lay less than ten feet away. She needed to get him to Evandale. She was incapable of achieving that on her own.

Beth said not to trust anyone. But she was out of choices. Dorran needed more help than she could give him.

He had to be her priority. She'd ignored his needs before and he'd suffered for it. She squeezed the fear into a little, tight ball in her stomach and tucked the hatchet out of sight inside the bus's door. Her heart pumped like it was preparing for a marathon and her mouth was dry. The engine was close, and it didn't sound like it was slowing down. She couldn't afford even a few seconds to gather her courage. She needed to move.

Clare stepped out from behind the bus. A silver sedan came toward her, frosted with dust, light reflecting off of its windows to hide the occupants from view. Clare raised a hand as a frightened smile twitched across her face.

The car shot past her. Clare slowly lowered her hand, the smile fading as she watched the car vanish down the road.

No. No. Please, don't leave us.

They hadn't tried to stop and loot the bus. But they hadn't stopped to help, either. As the engine faded and cold air snapped around Clare's form, she clenched her teeth, trying to hold the despair inside. Trying to hold herself together.

She slowly moved back inside the bus. Dorran lay unmoving, in his swath of shadows in the rear seats. She wanted to apologize to him, but apologies wouldn't fix what she'd done. Instead, she picked a small tool kit off one of the racks and carried it back outside.

The car's rumble hadn't entirely faded from hearing. Clare frowned as she stepped back from the bus. The silver sedan was still visible in the distance. And it was growing closer.

They turned around. Fear and hope collided in her stomach. She dropped the bag and moved toward the hidden hatchet, then reeled back. If they planned to help, she wouldn't be fostering any goodwill by greeting them with a weapon. Clare's hands felt horribly bare, so she clenched them together as she stepped around the bus.

Coming from the opposite direction, the sedan no longer had the sunlight reflecting off its windshield. Clare caught a glimpse of the vehicle's insides and a sense of surrealism flashed through her. She'd seen the car before.

A man sat behind the driver's wheel, his fawn-brown beard grown too long, his steely gray eyes intense. A golden wedding band glinted from where it was hung below the rearview mirror.

We passed him days ago. He must be crisscrossing the country.

Clare didn't know if she trusted in luck any longer, coincidence couldn't encapsulate it, and providence seemed too much to hope for. But it was *something*. Maybe a little of all three.

He gave the bus a wide berth as he pulled the car to a halt. He didn't turn the engine off and he didn't open his door, but he wound the window down and leaned through the opening, his eyes flicking from Clare to the bus's dark doorway. "If you need fuel, I don't have any to spare."

"I don't need fuel." Clare knit her hands together and took a step closer. "There's something wrong with the engine. I hit a tree and it started smoking, and I don't know how to fix it."

Again, his gray eyes darted from her to the bus. "Are you alone?"

"I have a friend. But he's hurt. Unconscious."

"I don't have medicine either," the man said, a note of warning entering his voice.

"That's okay. I don't want any. I just need the bus to run."

He shot a final, wary glance at the bus, then turned his engine off. He twisted to look over his shoulder and whispered something into the back seat. Clare followed his gaze and saw his two girls huddled there. The younger one still had a bandage over her eye. Their faces were more serious than she'd ever seen a child look before.

Then the car's locks clicked, and the man stepped out. He shut his door and locked it behind himself, squinting in the pale sunlight. "No promises. But let me take a look."

CHAPTER 34

THE STRANGE MAN BENT over the engine, but he was only giving it part of his attention. His eyes kept skipping from the bus's open door, to Clare's hands, to the field surrounding them.

He was on watch for danger. She couldn't blame him. If someone wanted to plan an ambush, a broken bus with boarded-over windows would be a great way to lure in unsuspecting victims and a perfect way to hide. He was taking a big risk in helping her. One Clare didn't know if she could have taken if their places were exchanged.

"I remember this bus," he said as he picked through the bag of tools she'd left beside the engine. "We passed it a couple of days ago. Someone else was driving."

"That was my sister." Clare swallowed. She knew the truth probably wouldn't be taken well, so she opted for a lie by omission. "She's gone now."

"I'm sorry to hear that." He lifted his head. "Your water line was crushed. I think I can repair it. Get into the driver's seat and try the engine when I signal."

Clare leaped into the bus. Hope thrummed through her. The man's car was visible through the cracked windshield. Two pinched faces pressed against its window as they watched their father.

The man waved to her. Clare turned the key. The engine spluttered, then rumbled as it came to life.

Clare keeled over the wheel, relief and gratitude overwhelming her. "Thank you. Thank you so much."

The man shut the hood and stepped back, wiping his hands on his pants. "You should be all right now. Good luck out there."

"Wait. Before you go." Clare looked over her shoulder, toward the compartments holding more supplies than she could use in a month. "Um. Do you need anything? Food, clothes?"

"We're all right for that." He was already striding back to his car. Clare knew how he must feel. Every minute away from his children was like dancing with danger.

"Painkillers?" she offered.

The man hesitated. His eyes drifted to his car's window, toward his daughter and her bandages. "We've been looking for some of those."

Clare opened her bag of medicine as she climbed out of the bus. She gave the man two boxes of the painkillers.

He accepted them with a small nod and a smile. As he moved back to his car, he called, "Owen, by the way."

"Clare," she replied, and raised her hand in farewell. "Thank you again. Good luck."

"And to you."

His engine started. Seconds later, he'd executed a U-turn, and the car was fading away from her, disappearing into the distance.

As Clare climbed back into the driver's seat, she felt as though the block of ice freezing her insides had melted a little.

Beth had been wrong. *She'd* been wrong. There was still goodness in the world. It just took some looking to find it.

The engine purred beneath her as Clare pulled the bus back onto the road. She hadn't asked Owen where he was planning to go, and he hadn't asked about her own destination. She hoped he would be all right, though. She hoped he would find a good home for his family.

The breakdown had slowed her, but not as much as she'd feared. She pushed the bus back up to speed. The road was hypnotic. Every time she started feeling herself drifting away, she took another mouthful of the coffee concoction. By midafternoon, it was giving her palpitations. Clare reluctantly pulled over to scrounge some food. She'd missed the previous night's dinner and that morning's breakfast and hurriedly chewed through two granola bars.

While she was eating, she checked on Dorran. He was unsettlingly still. She held her hand over his mouth, and every muscle in her body locked up. There was no gentle rush of air.

"No. No. Come on, Dorran." She grabbed his shoulder.

His chest rose. It was shallow and ragged, but he was still breathing.

"Please, hang on." She kissed his forehead. She wanted to be able to sit with him and watch over him, but she needed to keep the bus moving. Reluctantly, she stepped away and retook her seat.

That fright gave her enough adrenaline to keep her alert for the following hour. She couldn't stop herself from watching Dorran in the rearview mirror. The back of the bus was too dark to see him clearly enough to tell if he was still breathing. She couldn't stop herself from looking, though. Every time she tried to focus on the road, her eyes drifted back toward the mirror.

Occasionally, she thought she saw shapes moving through the trees on either side of the road. By that point, she thought there was a good chance they were delusions. The coffee-induced palpitations were growing worse. She kept drinking the concoction, though. It was the only way she could stay awake.

A crossroad appeared in the distance, intersecting their dirt trail. Clare knew it from studying the map, and a smile grew. A signpost stood on the crossroad's corner, old metal pointing in each direction. The one to the right read *Evandale*.

Clare took the turn. The shadows were stretching long. Before the stillness, house lights would have been flickering to life and acting like beacons in the distance. Clare no longer needed the coffee. Hope coursed through her veins, pushing her to drive faster as they sped into the town that she'd staked their lives on.

She'd thought it would be a small town based on how few streets were shown on the map. She was right. Like many of the settlements they had passed through, a strip mall ran down the main road. It held the staples: a general store, two cafés, a gas station, a post office, a pub, two knickknack shops, and a clothing store. It was a place for locals to run errands and for travelers to stop on their journeys. Any more serious business—including cheaper grocery shopping and specialty retail—would need to happen at the larger town half an hour away.

Clare leaned over the wheel, squinting through the streaky gore, dust, and the crack marring her window. She read each shop sign as she passed it. None of them were remotely close to a research institute. The strip mall ended quickly, then she was back among houses, and before she could blink, she'd passed through Evandale and come out the other side.

She slowed the bus, pulled a U-turn, and reentered the town. This time, she drove more slowly, examining every building she passed. Three side streets branched out at odd intervals, and she took them all one at a time. They led to more residential areas. A park. A club. A hall that advertised children's activities on Fridays and church on Sundays.

Doubt started to creep in. Clare ran through her memories of the time she'd spent with Ezra and everything he'd said about Evandale. That hadn't been much. Initially, when he was pretending to be Peter, he'd said he'd heard that the Evandale Research Institute was still running and that he intended to send the USB there to double-check his work.

A lie, Beth's voice whispered. *He never intended for the USB to leave the tower. He picked a town at random and claimed there was an institute there to give his story more credibility. Evandale has nothing. Nothing except shops and houses and hollow ones.*

The streets were rife with them. The emaciated bodies slunk between buildings, mouths gaping open and eyes glinting as they followed the bus. Clare tried not to watch them as she turned down another back road, scanning the homes. Some had signs for small businesses hung out front. Counseling. Landscaping. Painting classes. Nothing remotely like what she was looking for.

Ezra had talked about Evandale a second time, when he'd run his experiments on Dorran. Clare had asked him to give her the USB and let them leave so they could take it to the institute. His reaction had been so aggressively visceral that she turned the bus around and drove through the same back roads a second time.

He was desperately insistent that Evandale wouldn't get his research. He wouldn't have reacted like that if it was a fake institute in a made-up town. The center has to be real.

Her eyes were stinging. She turned down the same road for a third time, her shoulders aching, her mind buzzing, the shadows lengthening. Each pass through the town drew more of the hollows out of hiding. One of them launched itself at the bus. It bounced off the metal, unable to find purchase, and crept backward, hissing.

The sun was close to setting. Once it was down, Clare knew the hollow ones would grow bolder. She either needed to find the institute or get out of the town before then.

Where is it? Ezra can't have lied. The look on his face, the way he spat those words…

She was back on the main street. A sign caught her eyes. It was old and covered with dust and hung at an angle, after what was possibly a misjudged parking job had bent its pole. She slammed on the breaks, heart pounding.

The sign had been so inconspicuous that Clare had driven past it three times. Now, she read the words printed on the faded blue metal: *Whitmore Street*. And, in small letters below that, *Evandale Research Institute*.

"Yes," Clare whispered, swinging the bus around to drive down the road.

CHAPTER 35

THE SIGN POINTED DOWN one of the major crossroads that ran through Evandale and linked it to the next town twenty minutes away. Clare cruised, trying to ignore the creatures flitting around her as she scanned the houses. She'd examined them all before; none of them showed any signs of being more than a regular dwelling. Within a minute, the town had ended, and she was back into the patchy, marshy forests that filled the area between the two towns.

The research institute exists. The sign proves that. But then where is it?

She prepared to turn the bus around, then stopped herself. With the towns spread so far apart, it was possible the institute bore the town's name even if it was a good stretch outside of its bounds. She continued following the road.

The trees grew thicker until they had completely blocked out the fading light. Then, abruptly, a gap appeared in the foliage to her left. Most of the roads Clare had driven that day had been unpaved, but this one seemed like no more than a hiking trail cut through the trees. It was wide enough to carry the bus, though. Clare bit her lip as she turned onto it.

The road twisted, the trees dense enough to obscure the ground ahead before it opened into a clearing. A fence rose ahead of Clare, at least twelve feet high. She leaned forward in her seat and saw the top of the fence had been modified with slabs of metal, all fixed at an angle to make the structure impossible to climb over from the outside.

Straight ahead, the fence held a gate. Thick metal chains ran through holes in the doors, locking them together. Clare waited, hoping the car's engine would draw someone's attention, but when the gate remained closed, she turned the bus off and went to search their supplies.

Tucked behind the clothes and towels was a set of shears. Clare took them and climbed down from the bus.

The clearing was surprisingly serene. In the distance, a bird chattered. The trees still had their leaves and a cold, sharp wind rattled them. The gate creaked as the gusts pulled on it.

Clare approached the chains and clamped the shears around one link. Her muscles were drained. She had to close her eyes and brace herself before wrenching on the shears as hard as she could.

The metal snapped. Clare fastened the shears around the other side of the link and sliced through it, then dropped the shears as she unwound the metal. Once the chain was discarded, she put her shoulder against the metal and pushed.

The door clearly hadn't been opened in a long time. Dirt and leaves had built up over the runners, jamming it, and Clare had to lean her shoulder against the structure as it scraped open in patches. Once it was wide enough to drive the bus through, she stood back, breathing heavily and surveying the space beyond.

A concrete building stood ahead. It looked tiny, only large enough for one or two rooms, and it had no windows. A wide garage door covered the front wall. Near that was a small stand with a button, like the ones they used outside paid parking stations.

The rest of the ground was bare. Weeds grew unchecked, large enough to tell Clare the lawn had been neglected for months.

Ezra said he thought *the scientists in Evandale had survived the stillness. But he didn't know. They didn't try to communicate via radios, so there was no way to be sure.*

Clare looked behind her. The bird's chattering had fallen silent. She suddenly had the gut-churning sense that she wasn't alone and that leaving her back exposed was a very bad idea. Moving quickly and keeping her eyes scanning the forest, Clare jumped into the bus, started the engine, and eased it through the open gate.

She parked in front of the garage door, then left the bus again. The open gate invited danger; Clare jogged to reach it. Leaves crunched in the forest somewhere to her right as Clare fixed her hands in the metal. She lurched back, hauling with all of her strength to scrape it closed. It ground into place, and she found the chain she'd cut on the ground and threaded it back through the holes. There was no way to lock it, but at least, from a distance, the structure would look undisturbed.

Clare returned to the building. There were no handles to open the garage door. She tried squirming her fingers underneath the metal shutter, but the gap wasn't large enough. She rounded the building. It was a rectangle made of concrete, devoid of any other doors or windows. Even the roof was flat. Her loop around brought her back to the metal pole she'd parked beside. It held a red button above a small speaker and what looked like a camera. Clare wet her lips and pressed the button.

Static crackled through the speaker. Clare waited. The sun was nearing the horizon and the wind was cold. She was ready to drop. The caffeine had left her shaking uncontrollably.

Maybe Ezra was wrong. Maybe they all died in the stillness. Maybe this institute was abandoned even before the stillness. The weeds had grown unchecked. The sign in the town was old and neglected. Maybe no one has worked here in a long time.

Clare looked back at the bus. At least, if no one answered, the fence would keep any hollows out. She should be safe to sleep there that night.

But I can't sleep. Not with Dorran as bad as he is. I've traveled too far to give up.

She pressed the button again. Like before, there was a second of static, then silence. Clare let her head drop. She wanted to cry, but she had no energy left for it. So much time, so much energy, so much risk to get to Evandale. She'd lost Beth. She was going to lose Dorran. All because she'd trusted in a madman and his USB.

Clare felt in her pocket for the small metal stick and clutched it. The code was useless if no one knew how to read it. Beth had been right. She'd been too eager to grab at anything that felt like hope. And now they had all paid for it.

Wait… Clare's eyes opened. She looked back toward the fence. It had metal fastened at its top, angled to stop anything from climbing over the walls. The reinforcements were recent. They hadn't rusted like the rest of the fence. They had been built after the stillness, specifically to keep hollows out.

Her breath caught. She looked back at the box. Static crackled every time she pressed the button. That meant it had power. Which in turn meant a generator was running. And *that* meant there was someone inside.

They're ignoring me. Hoping I'll think the place is dead. Hoping I'll go away. Well, that's not happening.

She pressed the button again and held it, knowing a buzzer would probably be sounding inside the building. She didn't know how the speaker worked, whether it needed to be switched on from the other side, or whether they could hear her. She tried anyway. "Please. I need to speak with you. It's urgent. I have important information about the stillness."

There was still no reply. Clare started pressing the buzzer in Morse code. Three dots, three dashes, then another three dots, spelling out SOS.

You can talk to me, or you can live with my racket for the rest of the night. Her throat burned. Her muscles ached. More than anything, she just wanted to slide to the ground, close her eyes, and escape the world for a few hours. But Dorran needed her. She hung on to the box, mashing its button as the sun dipped past the horizon and insects began to sing.

Then a woman's voice, tinny through the speakers, yelled, "Enough!"

Clare inhaled sharply. She took her finger off the button.

"I don't know what you expect to find here, but you're wasting your time. We have armed guards who will open fire if you do not vacate immediately."

Clare almost smiled. The threat of violence didn't hold any horror for her. She leaned close, staring into the camera, and held up the USB. She knew she had a limited chance to barter for what she wanted. What she *needed*. "I have information about how the stillness was started. And I have a way to destroy the hollow ones."

The voice was silent. Clare knew the woman was still there, though. She could hear her breathing. Then she said, "Leave it outside the door."

"I'm not giving it to you." Clare's voice took on a desperate edge that she hadn't intended. "I want to trade."

Again, the voice was silent. When it spoke, it was edged with hostility. "For what?"

"My friend is dying." Clare's hand shook. Her voice shook. Her mind felt like it was shaking, too, rattling with fear and frustration and desperation. "I need you to save him."

CHAPTER 36

THIS TIME, THE SILENCE lasted much longer. Clare clung to the speaker, one hand held out to show the camera her USB. As the silence stretched on, doubts began to crawl back in.

They're ignoring me again. They don't think it's worth it. They don't want us inside their institute.

She looked at the shutter door. She wondered how reinforced it was. Whether a bus driven at full speed could smash through it. They wouldn't be able to turn her away *then*.

Twilight doused the scene in its desaturated colors. Far in the distance, a hollow chattered. Probably one of the ones that had inevitably trailed Clare's bus when she left the town. She hoped the reinforcements on the walls worked.

She was preparing to reach for the button again when static hissed through the speaker. The woman's tone was clipped. "If you have any weapons, discard them outside."

Clare wasn't in a position to argue. She unhooked the knife from her belt, held it up for the camera to see, then tossed it aside. "That's all I have."

"I am opening the door. Drive your vehicle into the parking area. Wait for me there."

The shutters abruptly shuddered, then began to rise. The metallic clatter matched Clare's heartbeat as she ran for the bus. She fumbled the key in the ignition, turned it, and glanced into the rearview mirror as she put the bus into Drive. She couldn't see much of Dorran except one gray arm, which had been jostled free from the blankets.

She eased the bus forward, through the concrete entrance. The ground tilted downward, and she had to hit the brakes to stop the momentum from getting away from her. She hadn't been looking at a building, Clare realized. She'd been looking at the entrance to an underground bunker.

There were no lights in the tunnel, so Clare had to rely on the bus's internal lights to guide her path. Concrete walls flanked an unmarked concrete floor. The tunnel continued for a ways, carrying her down at a steep angle, before curving to the right. Clare tried to guess how far underground they were. She could no longer see the shutters behind her, but she heard a distant thud as they closed again.

The passageway curved right a second time, then flattened out into a parking lot. The roof was so low that Clare was nervous it would scrape the bus's top. Large, smooth pillars interspersed the space. Clare was shocked to see other cars parked there.

It makes sense. If there are people living in this institute, they had to have driven here.

There were only four vehicles. The space was easily large enough to fit a hundred. It left the garage feeling empty and abandoned, much like everything else in the world.

At the garage's back was a double-wide door. Clare guessed that was where she was supposed to meet her host and pulled up in front of it. There were no door handles, but a pad beside the structure waited for a code to be entered.

Clare put the bus into park, her breathing shallow, and stepped outside. The air tasted stale, but it was a few degrees warmer than the surface. Still, she wrapped her arms around herself, defensive, as she waited.

It took nearly four minutes for the doors to slide open. Clare reflexively took a half step back. She felt naked without her knife.

In the doorway stood a woman flanked by two men. They all wore light-gray clothes that looked as though they might be a uniform. The woman's dark dreadlocks were tied back behind her head, and red-rimmed glasses rested high on her nose. She wasn't smiling. One of the men, tall and tanned, with a neat beard, held a rifle. He leveled it at Clare.

"What's your name?" the woman asked. Clare recognized the accent from the speaker.

"Clare," she said. "Please, my friend's sick. I'll tell you everything I know. But you have to help him."

"Where is he?"

Clare pointed to the bus. The woman nodded to her second

companion, a younger man with lightly curling, blond hair. He passed Clare and leaped into the bus. She wished she could follow him to check on Dorran, but the taller man kept his gun aimed at her.

"You said you have information about the stillness," the woman said.

Clare held out the USB. "I visited ground zero, and I met the man who created the hollows. His research is on here. It contains a way to kill them."

The man with the gun snorted and sent his companion a displeased look. She scowled back at him, then took the USB from Clare's palm.

A clatter from behind startled her. The younger man had reappeared in the bus's doorway. He gave a nervous smile, and she saw he had a gap between his two front teeth. "I'll need some help carrying him inside."

"Go on, Johann," the woman said.

The taller man glowered, then begrudgingly handed her his gun. He slouched as he followed his younger companion onto the bus.

The woman didn't try to direct the gun at Clare, but instead hooked it over her arm as she tilted her head to one side. "You look a mess."

Clare felt it. Her headache throbbed, blurring her vision and making her eyes sting. Grime was caked into the creases of her clothes. She hadn't washed her hair since their stop at the shopping center.

Since Beth combed it. Since she gave you a final warning about what she truly was.

"Ugh, he's heavy." The two men stumbled through the bus's door, carrying Dorran between them. They had kept him wrapped in the blankets to immobilize him, but he didn't respond to the movement at all. His face was slack. There was no color left in him, and Clare's heart faltered.

"Please be careful." She reached toward Dorran but pulled back when Johann, who was supporting his upper half, glowered at her. "He—he's hurt. A bite wound in his arm. And…and other injuries."

So many. I failed you so many times, Dorran.

Her pulse echoed in her ears, disorienting, and she felt herself tipping to the side. A hand took her arm. The woman's voice, clipped but not unkind, said, "Come along. Niall and Johann will take care of him. When was the last time you slept? Or drank anything?"

Clare shook her head. The hand on her arm pulled her forward. They were following in the men's wake as they passed through the doors and into a stark-white hallway.

The woman pressed, "Can you tell me what happened?"

Clare was so tired she couldn't get her vision to focus, and her throat ached with every breath. But this was the trade she'd promised. She had to give them information. Dorran's treatment relied on what and how much she could share. She started talking about Ezra's tower, his biological nanobot inventions, and his lies. She explained how the code on the USB could be used to detonate the thanites. How Ezra had tested the cure on Dorran, and how it had made him sick.

The woman didn't try to interrupt but kept one hand on Clare's shoulder as she pushed her through a maze of passageways. Ahead, the men stumbled under Dorran's weight, their hair shining in overhead lights. They turned into a room. Clare's chest ached as Dorran left her sight, and she quickened her pace to catch up. Lights blinked on. They were in a severely bright room. *A hospital,* she thought; beds with white sheets lined both walls. The men laid Dorran on the closest bed. One arm dropped free from the blankets.

Clare clasped both hands ahead of herself as she moved closer. She was scared. She needed to help him. She didn't know how. She didn't think he was breathing.

"Excuse me," the younger man said, slipping around Clare's side to reach Dorran. He held a flashlight above Dorran's head and peeled back one of his eyelids to shine the light in his eye.

"Don't...don't do that." Clare struggled to get the words out. "He needs to rest—"

The woman pulled Clare away. "Let Niall work."

Maybe he's a doctor. He could still be able to save him.

The back of Clare's legs hit the edge of a bed. She collapsed, sitting on the crisp sheets. The fear wouldn't release its grip. She didn't know if she'd done enough, if her information had been valuable enough to buy Dorran's life. She charged on, forcing her leaden tongue to recount more. When she couldn't remember anything else about Ezra, she told them about her sister. About how she'd been infected. About seeing her crouched over Dorran, blood spilling from her mouth. About how Clare had driven across the county to find them because she didn't have anywhere else to turn.

The younger man, Niall, kept moving around the bed. His fingers pressed against Dorran's throat as he searched for a pulse. Then he picked up Dorran's hand and tried to find one in his wrist. His eyes seemed grim. Clare wanted to yell at him, to tell him to stop seeming so sad, to do something to help instead. The woman was trying to push her back onto the bed, but she refused to lie down, not when Dorran needed her, not when Dorran was so sick—

The taller man, Johann, had his arms folded as he loomed. He asked something Clare couldn't hear. Niall exhaled and shrugged.

No, no, no. We came so far. We made it. It has to be enough—

Niall saw her staring. He grabbed the curtains hanging by the wall and dragged them around the bed, blocking Dorran from sight.

Clare felt herself falling, and she no longer had the will to fight it.

CHAPTER 37

CLARE'S DREAMS CAME SHARP and bitter. She ran through a forest, lungs starved of oxygen. She'd lost Dorran. He'd been sleeping beside the fire, and she only turned away for a second, and when she looked back, he was missing.

And now she had to run: to get back to him, to save him, to protect him from what she knew was coming. Up ahead, their campfire's light licked across the trees. Clare tried to call out but her tongue wouldn't move. She spilled out into the campsite.

Beth crouched near the fire. Her sister's sweet face looked exactly like the Beth from Clare's childhood, except now, blood dripped off her chin and stained her hands.

"I took care of him for you," Beth cooed. "It's better this way."

Bones surrounded her. Red bones, fresh bones, scraps of flesh still hanging from them. All that was left of Dorran.

"No!" Clare bolted upright. Blankets, sticky with sweat,

dropped away from her as she blinked at the stark-white walls surrounding her. The lights were dimmed but still bright enough for her to see the space's features. There were no windows. The floors were tile, and the walls were covered with some kind of glossy paint. Four beds filled the room, two on each wall, each with their own privacy curtain on standby.

That's right. Evandale. I made it after all.

Memories came rushing back: the drive, breaking through the chain at the gate, being afraid to look at Dorran in case she was already too late.

Dorran!

Clare turned, her voice sticking in her throat. She'd last seen him in the bed beside her. The curtains had been pulled back, but the bed was now empty, its sheets stripped off.

No.

She slowly extended her feet onto the tile floor and stood. Her body was turning numb as she stared at the empty mattress. She had to hold on to the wall to stay upright.

No.

She blinked and saw Dorran's beautiful, dark eyes, his always-gentle hands, the secret smile he saved just for her. Then she blinked again and saw Beth crouched over him, his blood running between her teeth.

No.

Beth's voice floated back to her. "He's going to die. You'll need to grieve, but you have to keep moving."

"No." This time, the word croaked out of a parched throat.

The inside of her mind was screaming. No words, no images, just a constant stream of noise trying to drown out reality.

A door creaked open. It sounded distant, like a memory. Then a voice, deep and soft and warm. "Clare?"

Standing in an open doorway leading to what seemed to be a bathroom, Dorran was bathed in gold light. His beautiful, dark eyes. His strong neck turned to tilt his head in the way Clare loved. She couldn't breathe.

This is a dream. Dorran was standing. Awake, aware, his eyes sharp and clear. He was dressed in one of the gray uniforms and his hair was swept back. The sweat, blood, and grime were gone.

She ran for him. His mouth lifted into a smile and warm arms surrounded her. Her cheek pressed against a clean cotton shirt, and beneath that, she felt the heat from his body, which was shifting slightly as he breathed. He smelled like himself again, instead of the awful scent of blood and sickness. Warm hands ran over her back and tangled in her hair.

"My dearest Clare," he whispered.

He wasn't a dream, and he wasn't a fantasy. Everything about him was real. Clare broke into deep, wrenching sobs that shook her whole body. She couldn't keep her hands still; they roved, touching every part of him that she could reach: his face, his throat, his arms, his strong, broad back.

Dorran held her, murmuring as they rocked together. Clare clutched at him. They toppled and ended up on the floor, their legs tangled. Dorran laughed. It was a good sound.

"Shh, shh." Still chuckling, he adjusted her so she could sit on his lap. His thumb brushed moisture off her face as he smiled at her. "You don't need to be afraid any longer. We are safe, my darling."

"I thought—" Clare refused to loosen her hold on his shirt. She was scared that, if she let him go, he would vanish forever.

"I'm here. I'm not going anywhere." His hands kept moving, brushing through her hair and tracing across her jawline as though he was as hungry to touch her as she was to hold him.

The awful gray shade had left his skin, but she could still see traces of the sickness. Shadows clung around his eyes. His cheekbones, always sharp, were more pronounced. He'd lost weight. She detected a slight tremor in the hand that rubbed her back.

But he was awake. His eyes held life and light in a way they hadn't since leaving Helexis Tower. When he smiled, it no longer seemed to be an effort.

"I can't believe it." Clare shivered and pressed closer to Dorran. "They really helped you."

"They did." He kissed the top of her head. "Apparently, they gave me blood transfusions. They were working on the belief that my thanites had been destroyed, and that a healthy person's blood would contain some, and that they could transplant them to me through a transfusion. And it seems to have worked."

Clare shook her head. "That's incredible. I didn't think the thanites would be powerful enough to help you in just one night."

"Ah…" His thumb nudged her chin, a tender, apologetic touch. "It was a little longer than that. You have been asleep for nearly two days."

"What? Really?"

"Mm. You needed it. Speaking of which—you will also need something to drink. Wait a moment."

Dorran gently eased her out of his lap and stood. Clare, shaky but still unwilling to let him out of her sight, followed him through the door he'd appeared in.

It led to a bathroom. Like the bedroom, it was clinical white. Large, glistening tiles framed a double vanity with foggy mirrors. A damp towel hung on a railing from Dorran's recent shower.

Dorran took a glass from near the sink and filled it. "Here. You will feel better with this."

Clare took the water. She hadn't realized before how desperately thirsty she was and downed the glass in one go. She tilted her head back and exhaled deeply as the liquid filled a craving in her stomach. "Thanks."

Dorran took the glass back and refilled it. He was trying to watch her without being obvious, and Clare detected a hint of concern in his eyes. "Unathi told me some of what you went through to get here."

Clare frowned. "Unathi?"

"She said you met her when you arrived. You gave her the USB."

"Oh!" Clare had a hazy memory of a woman with bright-red glasses and dreadlocks speaking to her in a clipped tone. "Yes. I remember her. I didn't get her name."

"She runs the Evandale Research Institute. I had a chance to meet with her briefly this morning." Clare had let her hand rest on the vanity counter while she drank, and Dorran traced his fingertips across it. He was picking his words carefully. "She told me…what happened. With Beth."

Clare's stomach dropped. Her exhilaration at seeing Dorran had dulled the pain to the point where she could almost forget what had happened. At Beth's name, it came pouring back over her like a deluge of chilled water. She tried to speak, but her voice caught. Dorran no longer smiled. He stood close, near enough that she just had to lean forward and she would be resting against him, but his eyes were sad. Clare swallowed around the lump in her throat and tried again. "I am…so, so incredibly sorry."

"Clare—"

"I put you in danger. I let you be hurt."

"Oh, Clare."

The words tumbled out of her, unstoppable. "I was selfish and stupid, and I asked more than I ever should have. You deserved better. I don't know how I'll make it up to you. I—"

His mouth was on hers, cutting her off midstream. His fingers tangled in her hair, and warm lips pressed hard, then softened, roving gently, tasting, until Clare was breathless.

Dorran drew back slowly, and as he did, he pressed his fingertips across her lips. "Let me speak."

"Sorry," she mumbled around his fingers.

He was laughing, but moisture shone in his eyes. His head tilted to the side in the enchanting way Clare had always loved. For a moment, he only looked down at her, adoring and sad. "I am so proud of you, my darling."

Clare tried to look away, but Dorran's hand moved to rest against her cheek, holding her close.

"Unathi told me what you went through to get here. What you endured. I always knew you were strong, my darling. Strong and brave. But you were forced to demonstrate that beyond what I could have anticipated or ever wanted to ask of you." His smile faded. The sadness thickened. "And I am sorry for it. For what you had to go through. For losing Beth."

Clare let her eyes close. The final memories of Beth would always hurt. And she would always have regrets over them. But Dorran was still with her, and, at least for that moment, that was everything she needed.

"You said you had a chance to talk to Unathi." Clare suppressed the waver in her voice. "What's she like? Did she say how quickly we would have to leave?"

Dorran didn't try to stop her from changing the subject. "I liked her well enough. I don't believe they intend for us to leave immediately. She wanted to know more about the code on the USB, but I asked her to wait until you were awake. You understand it far better than I do."

"Right. That's good." Clare, compelled to reassure herself that he was still solid and real, ran a hand across Dorran's chest. "It'll be good to meet her properly. And figure out our immediate future."

"She implied they wanted to hold the meeting soon, but I'm sure they wouldn't object if you took a moment for yourself first. We have access to the showers, and they left a change of clothes for you." Dorran plucked at his own gray suit. "They are perhaps not the most flattering, but they are comfortable at least."

The mirror to her side had been fogged from a shower, but the haze had gradually subsided. Clare saw her reflection and winced. Dorran must have washed her face and hands while she slept, but she still bore the remnants of her drive to Evandale: dried sweat had caked grime to her skin. Dorran's blood stained her clothes and hands. It was a small miracle they had let her into the institute at all. "Okay. Yeah. Showering's going to be a priority." Clare looked back at Dorran and realized she'd been spreading her grime onto him. "Oh no—"

"Don't worry about that. I am just happy I get to hold you again," Dorran murmured.

That was one sentiment Clare could share.

CHAPTER 38

CLARE FELT MORE LIKE herself by the time she emerged from the bathroom, running a comb through her damp hair.

"Hello," Dorran called. He carried an armful of blankets he'd stripped off Clare's bed and shrugged down at them. "I was trying to be useful by getting these ready to wash, but truthfully, I don't know where to put them."

"Ha. Maybe we can add that to the list of things to ask them." Clare wore one of the gray uniforms provided by the institute. It was comfortable, like a more formal cousin of fleece, and kept her warm. The room wasn't cold, but it was air-conditioned. Which was odd in its own right; the institute didn't seem to be trying to moderate its power usage in any way. The lights had been left on and the shower water ran hot.

Dorran dropped the sheets into a neat pile on the bed, then offered Clare his hand. "Are you ready to venture out, then?

Beyond just answers, we might also be lucky enough to gain some breakfast."

"Ready." Clare took his hand and let him lead her through the door. She'd seen parts of the institute on the night she'd brought Dorran there, but her mind had been so fractured, she barely remembered it. The halls were wide and had a high ceiling, and unlike the room Clare had woken in, they were painted in a softer, warmer shade of white. There was very little decoration except for occasional alcoves that held tasteful, modern pots of thriving plants. Dorran seemed to have a sense of the space as he turned right.

"Were you awake for long before me?"

"A little less than a day. I haven't had much opportunity to learn about this place, except for a brief talk with Unathi this morning. She gave me directions for where to find her when we were ready, though."

He took another right. As far as Clare could see, the institute was utterly deserted. They passed an open room that seemed to be designed for relaxation; comfortable chairs ringed a coffee table, and bookcases were spaced along the walls, filled with books. The building could have housed hundreds of souls, but there was no sign of anyone.

Then, in the distance, Clare caught the murmur of voices. They were muted, but then abruptly swelled before dying back down again. It sounded like an argument. Clare had a horrible suspicion she was the cause.

Dorran didn't falter, though, and he seemed surprisingly

calm. They passed a wall entirely covered in a vertical garden of ferns and came to face a meeting room. A glass wall allowed her to see the five occupants spaced around a rectangular meeting table. The woman Clare had spoken to on arrival, Unathi, stood at the table's head, hands braced on the wood, her glasses low on her nose as she peered at her companions. She looked thunderous.

"Ah…" Clare tugged on Dorran's hand. "Maybe we should give them a minute before interrupting."

Unathi's eyes met hers. She raised a hand and the murmur of conversation immediately fell silent as all heads turned toward Clare. Unathi crossed to the door and pulled it open. "There you are. I was going to send Niall to check on you if you hadn't woken by this afternoon. Come in."

Clare glanced at Dorran. He was watching her, waiting for her lead. "I hope we're not interrupting—"

"Of course not." Unathi was already halfway back inside the room. "This conversation could benefit from your input. Take your seats, both of you."

Two chairs had been left vacant, next to an older woman who had a laptop open in front of her. Clare moved to take one of the seats, but Dorran remained standing.

"Pardon us." He dipped his head respectfully. "I don't want to delay your work, but Clare hasn't eaten yet."

Clare's eyebrows rose. Dorran had always been reluctant to talk around strangers. Maybe being around Beth had brought him out of his shell. Or, she suspected, the more likely answer was that his natural protectiveness was winning out over his discomfort.

Unathi clicked her tongue. "Of course. I forgot. Can you eat while we talk?"

"Yeah," Clare said. "Definitely."

"West?"

The man opposite Clare was already out of his chair. He disappeared through the door as Unathi resumed her seat and folded her hands ahead of herself. "Well, let me introduce you to my team. They have been eager to meet you. Clare, you already briefly encountered Johann and Niall."

Clare made eye contact with the two men closest to Unathi. The bulkier one, Johann, lounged with one arm thrown over the back of his seat, his expression grim as he used a fingernail to pick at his teeth.

Next to him was Niall, the younger one with curly, blond hair. A wide grin spread over his features as he raised a hand. "Hey. I'm the doctor. I mean, I do other stuff too. Mostly cleaning and running errands. They didn't think they would actually need me to do any doctoring down here, but I guess the insurers wouldn't sign off without some medical experience on board, so here I am. Talk about luck, huh?"

A proper doctor. There probably aren't many left now. Too many of them would have been living in populated areas or working in hospitals when the stillness hit.

Niall looked young. Clare suspected the insurers hadn't cared so much about their expert's experience, only his availability and price. Still…he'd saved Dorran, and that meant she would never stop being grateful to him.

"Thank you," she managed. "So, so much."

The door banged as the third man used his shoulder to push it open, and he moved through, carrying two bowls. He was large, like Johann, but had a rounder, softer face fringed with a salt-and-pepper beard. Muscled arms placed the bowls in front of Clare and Dorran, then laid out napkins, knives, forks, and spoons, taking laborious care to line them up.

"Thanks." Clare glanced at the bowl. It held roasted vegetables, some kind of green paste, and a lump of some white substance. They had both been given a generous serving. She was ravenous and picked up her fork.

"That's West," Unathi said as the man sank into his chair. "And, lastly, Becca. She's been responsible for looking at your code."

The woman beside Clare had a pleasant, soft face, with streaks of gray running through her brown hair. She gave Clare and Dorran a thin smile and a nod before turning back to the laptop. Her fingers moved blindingly fast as she typed.

The group wasn't made up of the kinds of people Clare would have expected to find in a research institute. When she'd envisioned it, she'd pictured men and women in white lab coats, humorless and focused. But Unathi was the only one of the party who seemed to speak with authority.

"Are there many other people living here?" she asked.

One corner of Unathi's lips rose into a bitter smirk. "Just us five."

Only five. As she took a bite of breakfast, Clare looked around the table with a renewed sense of awe. She was likely looking at the last pocket of humanity in that region. "The building was so big, I assumed there would be more."

"It was intended to house many, but we were still years away from that," Unathi said. "The five of us were staying here while working on a model of an underground habitation for the eventuality of nuclear fallout, ecological collapse, or solar flares that could make life on the surface untenable."

"Like a bunker?"

"Yes, but long term. Until now, bunkers have only been designed to hold humans for a few months or years. You eventually run into the same problems: no way to produce new food or, even if you have a garden, inadequate nutrition. No sunlight means bones grow weak and immune systems suffer. Mental problems arise from a lack of stimulus. We've been developing ways to ensure humans can stay underground for decades, even lifetimes, without sacrificing quality of life."

Clare tried for a smile around a mouthful of food. "It's a lucky place to be when the stillness hit."

"It absolutely is," Niall said. He bobbed forward, switching his grin between Unathi and Clare. "I mean, we weren't actually at the point of being ready for a long-term trial. This was just meant to be for four months to troubleshoot pathogen scenarios. What would we do if a new, deadly strain of virus emerged? Would our quarantine area cope? Do we have all of the necessary precautions in place to ensure it didn't spread? And if it did spread, what would be the end outcome?"

"No real viruses involved," West added. His voice was slow and deep. "Just running different scenarios and trying to poke holes in our plans."

"Exactly." Niall pointed to a whiteboard at the other side of the room. It was littered with notes and equations. "Before the stillness, we were keeping score of our theoretical population's condition. We were only partway through the second scenario and it looked like we were going to lose that battle. It was a super bug, though, a nasty one, and we were seeing what would happen if there were no doctors left alive."

Clare frowned. "Did you have to run these experiments inside the bunker? Couldn't you have done the calculations from a desk somewhere more comfortable?"

"We could have," Unathi said, "but it would have only given us half of the picture. A place like this has so many working components that it's a fallacy to look at any one element in isolation. Being here and running the scenarios in real time, we were able to seek out complications we hadn't predicted. For instance, how does the isolation from the rest of the world impact our ability to think rationally?"

"It must have been an expensive project," Dorran said.

Unathi smiled. "Yes, yes it was. We were sponsored by Aspect. I believe they intended to modify our findings for interstellar travel. Underground living quarters could be one solution to surviving on an inhospitable planet."

Clare's heart missed a beat. The name, Aspect, was unpleasantly familiar. "That—"

"Aspect Laboratories in Helexis Tower was where you met Ezra Katzenberg, wasn't it?" Unathi leaned forward, hands folded on the table ahead of herself. "Both of our projects were sponsored by the same parent company. I believe that is how he knew where we would be. Our project was one of the biggest, and most expensive, running at the time, so it must have been discussed in his office."

"Our ship used to be a military bunker." West picked up his coffee mug, examined the dregs in its bottom, and put it aside. "When they decommissioned it, Aspect bought it up and helped us redesign it. It didn't come cheap."

Dorran paused his meal. "Your ship?"

"That's what we call her. Our own little slice of life floating out in the wide ocean. While we were in here, we weren't supposed to contact anyone outside. Preserve the integrity of the experiment. That's how you phrased it, eh, Unathi? We were supposed to act as though the rest of the world had been obliterated. I've gotta say, this current simulation is a bit too realistic for me."

Niall laughed and even Johann chuckled, but Unathi's eyes narrowed. "I would ask you to show more tact in front of our guests, West. We cannot overstate our fortune in living here. But they may not find the current situation as humorous as you do."

West shrugged, picked up his mug, and shambled toward a coffee machine near the whiteboard.

Clare put her spoon down, no longer as hungry as she had been a moment before. "How did you hear about the stillness? And does the ship have any tools to help you analyze it? Please, I want to know everything."

338

CHAPTER 39

"WE WERE ONLY DOWN here for five days before the stillness hit." Niall scratched at the back of his neck. "Because of the no-contact rule, we didn't even know anything had happened until nearly a week after."

"There were ways for people to contact us in case of an emergency," Unathi said. "But from what we've since learned, the world fell apart so quickly that it seems no one thought of us."

Through the conversation, Johann had mostly kept his eyes on the table, his arms crossed as he lounged back in the chair. Now, his lips twisted. "Because we could be holed up down here for months at a time, Aspect liked to pick people who didn't have too many family ties aboveground. That doesn't mean we didn't lose anyone. My sister and nephews were up there."

"My parents," Niall said, and his ever-present smile dipped.

"I had a husband. Greg." Becca's fingers stilled for a second, then returned to typing, more furious than ever.

West returned from the coffee machine, his mug full of a black, steaming mix. He grunted as he lowered himself into his seat. "I lost my baby. Polo. A neighbor was looking after him. I'll never forgive myself for not bringing him with me."

"Would you shut up about your damn dog?" Johann snapped. "The rest of us are grieving, damn it."

West looked hurt. "I'm grieving, too. Polo was my best friend."

"Anyway, I broke the rule first." Niall raised his voice to break up the brewing argument. "We weren't supposed to talk to anyone outside, but I was lonely and maybe a little homesick and I called my mother."

"A *little* homesick, eh?" Johann chuckled under his breath.

Niall ignored the jab. "She didn't answer the call, which was unusual for her. So I phoned my father next. Same deal. I went through every contact in my phone—and I have a *lot* of contacts—waiting for someone to pick up and tell me what was going on. At the time, I was trying to figure out what would keep people away from their phones, like maybe there was some big sports game everyone was extra invested in. Or maybe the clocks in my room were all slow and it was actually two in the morning. There's no natural sunlight, you know? It took me a while to actually go to Unathi about it."

"For good reason." She frowned at him. "You weren't even supposed to have a phone."

He shrugged and smiled. "If I hadn't, we might still be

340

WHISPERS IN THE MIST

completely ignorant and looking forward to opening the doors in two months."

Unathi sighed. "I got on the radio. It didn't take long to realize something was very wrong. Our project managers weren't answering. I tried dialing into other stations, but with no response. That's when I realized it was more than Niall accidentally breaking his phone or reception in our area being cut. Very slowly, we started to pick up on transmissions from survivors and pieced together what was happening."

Johann slouched back into his chair, jaw working. "West and I wanted to go upstairs, open the doors and have a look around, but the other three voted us out. We didn't know what had caused the stillness. We'd spent the week running pandemic simulations, and they were worried we could be exposed to some airborne pathogen."

"And as it turns out, that wasn't far from the truth." Unathi indicated the whiteboard. "Just one that was no longer active."

"It must be airtight down here," Clare guessed. "There would have been thanites in the air, but with only five of you to encourage their growth, they wouldn't have gotten out of control before the stillness hit."

"That's what we're thinking," Niall said. "I've been monitoring everyone for possible signs of mutation. So far, we seem okay."

Johann narrowed his eyes at Clare. "I think my toenails are growing quicker than they should. Is that a symptom of these nanobot things?"

She could only shrug. "I have no idea."

"Since the stillness, we've had two purposes." Unathi took off her glasses and rubbed the bridge of her nose. She looked tired. "Primarily, we had to protect our long-term survival. That was exactly what this building was intended for, but it was only equipped for the four months we planned to spend here. We've had to scramble to make it sustainable."

Clare looked around. The lights were all on, the coffee machine emitted a faint hum, and she was pretty sure the air-conditioning was still running. "Where are you getting your power from?"

"That was one of the key elements of this bunker," Unathi said. "We have a small-scale nuclear reactor. It's Johann's area of specialty."

He grunted. "It's a beauty. It can bear the energy load produced by four hundred civilians, which is what this compound is designed for. And not just necessities. Hot water, electronic entertainment, security systems, the works."

Unathi spread her hands. "I'm confident, with gradual improvements, this could be a long-term survival solution. Perhaps somewhere we could live the remainder of our lives."

Both Johann and West made faint noises of reluctance.

Unathi glared at them. "You won't be complaining if it comes down to a choice between spending your life here and not spending your life at all."

"It won't, though, will it?" Johann looked toward the other woman, Becca.

She murmured something noncommittal. Her attention didn't waver from the laptop.

Unathi sighed. "That was our second goal. Once our immediate survival was secured, we set about trying to understand the stillness. We wanted to see if we could find a weakness in the hollow ones. Once we were certain the stillness wasn't contagious and that humans were surviving aboveground, West and Johann ventured outside and reinforced the compound's perimeter."

"I saw that," Clare said. "The metal on top of the fence to stop hollows from climbing over."

"Exactly. It seems to work. So far. But making those modifications created enough noise to draw hollows out of the forest. We were forced to do the work in twenty-minute increments over the course of eight days. During that time, Johann managed to capture one of the hollows alive. We brought it downstairs to research."

Niall's smile suddenly seemed tense. "That was my job, ha!"

He held on to the edge of the table, his knuckles turning white, and Clare had the sense he was ready to change the subject, but her curiosity was too strong to ignore. "What did you find?"

"Lots of stuff that didn't make sense." His eyes darted across them without landing on any one person. "The hollow we caught was growing excess bones and excess skin. Both externally and internally. Unathi wanted to know how much it could survive. I..."

He swallowed thickly, his throat bobbing. The table was silent. When Niall spoke again, his voice was slightly quieter. "I cut it open. A vivisection. It bled, but it survived it. I started removing organs. Everything except the heart and lungs. It was...it was a nightmare in there. Anywhere there should have been fat was skin instead. All festering, some bits growing hair…"

"We can show them your report instead," Unathi said.

"No, I'm okay." He rolled his shoulders, and Clare saw perspiration shining on his face. "It survived having the majority of its organs removed. So I punctured its lungs. Somehow, it survived that. I punctured its heart. I set a timer to see how long it would take to bleed out. And…it began *healing*. It wasn't quick. But after the first hour, I thought I could see the edges of the puncture wound beginning to knit together. After the second hour, I was certain of it. But the repairs didn't look either like heart tissue or scar tissue. I took a sample and examined it under a microscope. It was growing skin cells in the wound."

Everyone else at the table would have been familiar with the results already, but they still listened with mingled curiosity and discomfort. Johann stared at the ceiling, his arms folded. Unathi sat forward in her chair, her glasses low on her nose. Even Becca stopped tapping at her laptop.

"Anyway." Niall rallied with obvious effort. "If you've been out among them, I'm probably not telling you anything you don't already know. When it became clear the heart wound wouldn't kill it, I removed its scalp and skull cap and began inflicting damage on its brain. Little cuts at first, then a puncture fully through it, imitating the type of damage a bullet might inflict. It just kept hissing at me. I became more and more desperate. The brain looked like scrambled eggs by the time it finally stopped moving."

"The thanites would have been working to repair whatever damage you inflicted," Clare said.

Niall nodded. "It was a surreal experience, let me tell you. As a doctor, you're supposed to be constantly aware of risk factors that have the potential to be harmful to your patients. Don't mix these medications; that could be fatal. Don't forget to change your gloves between patients; that could be fatal. Be on the lookout for alcohol withdrawal symptoms; that could be fatal. Everything is a minefield. And all of a sudden, I was doing the literal opposite of my job—*trying* to kill someone—and nothing worked."

"They can be killed, though," Dorran said. He'd been quiet through most of the discussion, but his eyes were bright with curiosity.

"Yeah," Niall said. "For a while I thought I might actually be dealing with something immortal, as impossible as that sounds. The brain scrambling eventually ended it. I left it strapped to my table for a full day just in case it came back like some kind of zombie, but I'm very relieved to say it didn't."

"We were trying to negotiate a second set of experiments," Unathi said. "I wanted to bring in another of the hollows and conduct more tests. They *had* to have a weakness. But Niall became squeamish after that first experience."

"I'm not squeamish. I'm fine with blood, pus, and all kinds of bodily fluids. *Just as long as I know I'm helping someone.*"

Unathi shrugged lightly. "You were. Indirectly."

"I'm not some kind of...of...*sadist.*" Niall's smile was wide

345

and his voice bright, but he was shaking. "That business…slowly dismantling a human…that's the stuff of nightmares. And all the while it was alive and hissing and writhing. The only saving grace was that it didn't seem to feel pain. But no. I'm done. If you want to torture hollows, you can do it yourself."

West sent him a sad look, then rose and went to the coffee machine.

"We were trying to understand them." Unathi's face stayed hard for a second, then softened. "I know it's not something you would have done voluntarily. But we're all working beyond our comfort levels on this."

Niall didn't agree, but he didn't argue, either. West returned from the coffee machine and placed a mug in front of Niall. Unlike West's own black coffee, Niall's was full cream and had four packets of sugar on its saucer.

"Thanks," he whispered, pulling the mug closer.

Unathi turned back to Clare and Dorran. "This new situation is beyond all of our scopes. We're specialists, but in industries that are, at best, tangential to the stillness. Niall is a general doctor, and a recently graduated one at that. Now we're asking him to analyze a mutation that has never been seen before."

"The web's down, too." His laugh was shaky. "That was, like, the only thing that got me through to graduation."

Unathi continued, "As project manager, all I can do is keep pushing my coworkers to do things they were never equipped to. My psychology degree will probably be useful once the stillness ends, if it ever does. There will be a lot of damaged people who'll need help. But right now, I can't even do much for Niall, because I have to keep driving him." She shrugged. "I'm not a good psychologist. There was a reason I got out of patient-facing work."

Clare wouldn't have guessed Unathi's background. She was clearly intelligent and perceptive, but her clipped tone didn't encourage emotional vulnerability.

Unathi spread her hands on the table. "Becca is a biologist and had some coding experience to keep the life support systems running. Working with Niall, she was able to discover the machines inside the hollows' flesh while they were scanning for viruses three days ago. We didn't know the official name for them, so we just called them bots."

"Wow." Clare looked toward the older woman with gray streaks running through her hair. "You figured it out? That's impressive."

She finally looked up from her laptop. A sad smile lifted her thin lips. "In a way. We didn't know how they got into the body, how they worked, or how to stop them. I tried electrical currents, low temperatures, and high temperatures. As long as the flesh stayed alive, the nanobots kept working."

"Your code is helping us jump forward substantially," Unathi said. "But we are still highly limited in our skills and abilities. If you need someone to design a bunker that will still be running in forty years, my team and I can deliver everything you need. But ask us to treat mutations and understand nanobots, and we're barely more qualified than you. We have no resources to consult or peers to speak to. If there were anyone else we could pass this on to, we would." She sighed. "I *wish* there were someone else to pass it on to. But I suspect we're going to have to be it."

Clare looked between the five of them, scanning their faces. Each one bore some level of resignation. "Can you do it?"

CHAPTER 40

BECCA TOOK A DEEP breath. Clare waited, hands clasped before her. Seconds ticked by while Becca stared at her laptop, mouth open. Then she released the suspended breath in a heavy sigh. "I don't know."

"She's been like this all morning," Unathi muttered. "Becca, just give us a status report."

"Well…" Becca pushed the laptop around so they could see the screen. It was split down the middle: one side had white text on a black background. The other side held black text on a white background. "Right now, I'm not changing anything Ezra Katzenberg created. I'm just picking through it and making notes. The code is complex. Sometimes it reads like pure nonsense, but then the nonsensical bits actually seem to tie back and work in a weird, convoluted way. I honestly can't tell if Ezra was a madman or a genius. And he obviously wasn't a fan of markups, so most of the time I have no idea what he's thinking."

Unathi raised her eyebrows. "But can you use it?"

"Probably. Maybe. No promises." Becca picked up her pen and used it to point at Dorran. "We know the detonation code works in some form or another because of what it did to Dorran. But that's the question: What *did* it do to him? We're assuming it destroyed his thanites, but we didn't have enough time to take blood samples to make sure. And even if it destroyed the thanites perfectly, we don't know what other damage it might have caused in the process."

"You had a whole host of issues when you arrived," Niall said, nodding to Dorran. "I was honestly surprised you were still alive. The worst was advanced sepsis, which may have been sparked by the code or may have come from any of several infected wounds. You had a low temperature and extremely low blood pressure. It's very likely there were other complications—I saw signs of massive organ failures, and there could have been clots, hemorrhages, or damage to your lungs, too. But this trial version of the ship wasn't intended to be a medical center, and we don't have any imaging equipment on board. I thought your best chance of survival would be to get some of the thanites back into you, so that's what I focused on."

"With the transfusions," Clare said, nodding to Niall. "Thank you, by the way."

He shrugged, looking pleased. "You should thank Johann and West. They donated their blood, since they were the only ones here who matched. Two units apiece."

Clare blinked, surprised. Johann had appeared so hostile that she was shocked he'd agreed to the transfusion. "Thank you, both. I can't tell you how grateful I am."

"Yes, thank you," Dorran echoed.

West beamed. Johann grunted and raised one shoulder in a half-hearted shrug.

Becca continued, "Without any test results, all we have to go on are Niall's theories and Dorran's description of how he felt. He said he was unwell from the moment the code was tested on him, so we can assume it had harmful side effects. We just don't know what. And, unfortunately, he survived, so we couldn't perform an autopsy."

Dorran made a faint noise as he tried to stifle his laughter. He shot Clare a grin. "Unfortunately."

"Oh." Becca scowled. "Sorry, that wasn't what I meant."

He shook his head, still smiling. "It's fine."

"Regardless, without knowing what damage was caused by the code, I won't know what to do to mitigate it. And I can't even talk to Ezra Katzenberg to get any insight. Working on this code… It isn't like looking at a building plan, where you can clearly see what was envisioned and what's been implemented to make it happen. This is more like…trying to add the finishing touches to an artist's masterpiece when you struggle to draw stick figures."

Unathi leaned back in her chair, her lips tight. "And there isn't any room for mistakes."

"None whatsoever. It's literally life or death for every remaining human. I wish there were some way to only detonate the thanites in hollows and not touch the ones in human hosts, but that's not how the code is written. It's all or nothing."

"What happens if we *do* nothing?" Unathi asked.

Clare realized the older woman was looking at her. She licked her lips. "I'm sorry. I really don't know much about any of this."

Unathi gestured lightly. "I only ask because, out of everyone at this table, the two of you have the most experience. You've traveled the outside world. You connected with other survivors and hid from the hollow ones and sought out supplies. These are experiences none of us have. With what you've seen, what do you think the outcome would be if we never used the code?"

They were all watching her, expectant, curious. *I see what she meant about all of us being underqualified. We're literally the blind leading the blind.*

"Ezra said the mutations would eventually destroy their hosts." Clare spoke carefully. "But he also said it would take at least twenty years for the last of them to die. That's a long time to coexist with a near-invincible predator."

Johann tapped the desk to get her attention. "If the mutations grow worse with time, will humans eventually start changing, too? We all have these, these…uh…robots living in us. Will they be trying to turn us into monsters, just at a slower pace?"

"I'm sorry. I don't know."

West chuckled. "Worried about your toenails again?"

"I'm telling you, I trimmed them just last week—"

Unathi held up her hand to silence them. She kept her gaze leveled at Clare. "The hollow ones *can* be killed, though. Humanity could regroup and begin to eliminate them. It wouldn't necessarily take twenty years to live freely again."

"Unless they eliminate us first," West said.

Clare thought of everything she'd seen. Owen, the man driving his daughters up and down the country as he tried to find a secure home for them. The way rural farmhouses had been cleared out of their necessities, forcing survivors to travel into the more dangerous, more populated towns. The safe havens that Beth had been afraid of, that welcomed any travelers with supplies to trade. She chewed her lip. "My sister, Beth, thought fuel supplies would run out within the next one or two months. Without fuel, there's no way to keep the lights on, and that's one of the few things hollows fear. And you'd need to keep the hollows away to begin producing necessities. Food could probably be grown inside compounds, but I can't see a way to mine for minerals or cut down wood for construction without being vulnerable to the hollows. Most of what we need would have to be scavenged from towns, and as long as we keep doing that, our numbers are going to inevitably drop."

"How many humans are out there?" Niall asked.

"I don't know. Not many."

Unathi asked, "Enough to feasibly win in a war against the hollows?"

"I don't know. Probably not."

The table was quiet for a moment. Then Johann shifted in his seat, looking frustrated. "Sounds like it's a roll of the dice whichever way we go. Do nothing, and we might slowly die out. Use the code, and it might turn into an instant kill for everyone still out there."

Unathi hadn't taken her eyes off Clare. "Do you think humanity could weather the storm for five or ten years, until the hollows' numbers are depleted enough that we could begin rebuilding?"

"Maybe." Clare looked up at Dorran. He seemed lost in thought, twirling his fork lightly in one hand even though his bowl was empty.

He gave a grim smile in return. "We are less than two months into the most catastrophic loss of life the world has ever experienced. It is hard to predict how we will recover, but I have the unpleasant sense that our challenges are still in their early days. Currently, the greatest risk comes from the hollows. But I am concerned for how the population will handle the escalating risks posed by human-to-human violence, starvation, malnutrition, and exposure."

Unathi, eyes narrowed in thought, nodded. "Becca, your sole responsibility from here on out is to work on the code. Please try your best."

"I can convert a room to an isolation chamber," Niall said. "We can test the code on one of us before releasing it to the rest of the world."

"Good. But testing will have to be limited. With only five members, we cannot rely on blood transfusions to save us from side effects."

"That brings us back to our earlier topic." Johann pointedly stared at Clare and Dorran.

Becca dragged her laptop back toward herself and put her head down. Niall looked uncomfortable, and West downed the last of his coffee.

"Yes." Unathi picked at an invisible speck of dust on the table. "Clare, Dorran, we need to decide what to do with you."

"The ship can't carry the extra strain." Johann shrugged. "It's nothing personal. We just can't afford it."

They assume we want to stay. Clare opened her mouth, then closed it again. *Do we?*

She'd been so focused on reaching Evandale that she hadn't thought about what would happen once they dropped off the USB. In the back of her mind, she'd pictured them ending up back at Winterbourne, Dorran's home. That was where everything had started; it had seemed natural that that was where it should end.

But suddenly presented with the idea that they could live somewhere else, Clare's mind turned blank. Did they *want* to stay at Evandale? Did they want it enough to argue their case, to make deals, to beg?

The team had been debating it before she and Dorran interrupted the meeting, which gave Clare the sense that they had a fighting chance of being accepted if they pushed hard enough. She looked to Dorran, trying to read his expression, and saw he was watching her.

Evandale represented an unparalleled opportunity. It was safe from hollows; it had power, not just for necessities but for luxuries: warm water, comfortable beds, entertainment. It was probably the closest a person could come to returning to a pre-stillness life.

By all rights, they *should* want to stay. But deep in Clare's stomach, it didn't feel *right*.

Johann seemed to interpret their silence as disappointment and slapped the table. "Look, it's not like we have a choice. If the ship were fully functional, you could stay, sure. But this is only a trial run designed to hold five people for a couple of months. We've already had to recalculate our food production goals to compensate for your unexpected arrival. And it'll only get worse the longer you linger."

"Johann, please." Unathi held her hand out toward him.

"I'm not wrong. They have to leave."

Niall fidgeted, his fingers running along the edge of his saucer. "I—"

"Stay out of this, Niall."

Unathi's voice deepened. "Johann."

"We can make room for them." Color spread across Niall's face. "Sure, it'll be a pinch at first, but it'll be nothing compared to what's waiting for them out there. Or the risk they took to get here."

Johann slouched, looking thunderous. "Niall, I swear—"

"No, let me talk." He took a shallow, harried breath. "They traveled across the country to get that USB to us. I'd be ashamed to turn them away now."

"Don't you dare take the moral high ground. She gave her terms for the trade." He pointed at Clare. "The USB in exchange for saving her friend's life. We delivered. Deal over."

The flush of color spread down Niall's neck and over his ears. "I can't believe you're going to be this heartless."

"Honestly? I wish I could be the good guy here. I wish I could put out a broadcast giving lost souls our address and inviting hundreds of them in. But what would that achieve? We'd starve within a week. This place was set up to last us just four months. The water purifier is only a temporary model. And two additional people might not seem like many, but it's nearly a fifty percent increase on our load, and honestly, this place isn't built for that. Not short term, not long term."

West cleared his throat. He looked sheepish. "I feel horrible saying this...but I think I have to side with Johann. When we figured out what was happening outside, we made an agreement. We wouldn't take on new souls, no matter who found us or how much they begged."

"Because it would be a slippery slope," Johann said. "And because we can't afford to take risks. Especially not now that we have the code, which may be the world's last hope for survival."

Niall opened his mouth, but Unathi held out her hand, silencing them both. "I feel it is extremely crass to debate this in front of our guests. Let's take our discussion down the hall. Dorran, Clare, would you excuse us a moment?"

"Sure," Clare managed.

The room filled with rustling as the small group gathered their papers and stood. Becca closed her laptop and held it close to her chest as she followed her peers. They filed out of the meeting room, and Clare watched them through the glass walls as they disappeared down the hall.

The silence following the team's departure seemed deafening.

Clare, exhausted, stared at the empty room, then turned to Dorran. "How are you feeling?"

"Ha." He leaned one elbow on the table as he rubbed the back of his neck. "I am still reeling. How about you?"

"Same."

They were quiet as they stared at the empty seats. Noises echoed from down the hall. A fist slammed into something solid as voices rose, then fell.

"It's...relieving to be here." He smiled. "To be able to sit without worrying about what might be coming up behind us and to be able to eat without being concerned about where our next meal might come from."

"Yeah." It was the first time in a long while that Clare had felt able to let her guard down. It was a strange sensation. "Would you want to stay here for the long term? Assuming they let us?"

He kept his expression guarded, but she spotted an emotion flitting through his eyes. She thought they might be on the same mental track, but Dorran hesitated voicing it, so she spoke first. "Because I kind of want to go home."

Relief spread across his features. "Do you?"

"Yeah." She didn't know exactly when the emotion had grown, but she was homesick for Winterbourne. The bunker was modern and pleasant. It had hot water on tap. The occupants seemed decent. But Clare felt as though she didn't belong there.

Winterbourne, on the other hand, was a perpetual struggle. But it was *their* struggle. She and Dorran had built it up, reinforced it, and protected it. It felt more like home than anywhere she had stayed since then.

And it might be important to salvage it, she thought. It, and its garden, might be a valuable stronghold. It was surrounded by forests owned by the hollows, but once the concealed passageways were closed, it could be defensible and sustainable. Not just for them, but for potentially hundreds of others.

"Yeah," Clare said. "I'm ready to go home."

Dorran's hand wrapped around the back of her head. He pulled her closer so he could kiss her. "I love you."

"Ha. Love you, too."

Dorran finished the kiss by resting his cheek against hers.

It felt good to be so connected to him. Clare couldn't stop herself from smiling. "Should we tell our hosts our decision before they tear each other apart?"

In the distance, voices swelled again. Dorran chuckled. "I think we had better."

It wasn't hard to find the research team. Clare and Dorran followed the voices down the hallway and discovered a smaller room at its end. Based on the comfy chairs and TV, it was intended as a recreational area. The team stood about, some with arms crossed, others with hands on hips, and Becca nestled in the corner staring at her laptop as the others bickered.

They fell silent as Clare pushed the door open. She gave a quick smile. "Hey. We just wanted to let you know—we're leaving."

Unathi, the closest, cleared her throat and lifted her chin.

"I don't want you to think you're unwelcome here. We aren't intending to kick you out so unceremoniously."

"It's fine." Clare looked up at Dorran, and he matched her smile. "We never planned to stay here once we unloaded the USB. Both of us are ready to go home."

"Oh." Johann seemed relieved; he ran his hands through his hair. "That's good. That's really good."

Niall crossed to them and placed a hand on Clare's arm. "Are you absolutely sure? I hope you're not leaving because of Johann and West, because the rest of us want you here. We could make it work."

"Thanks, but no. We made up our minds independent of all of that. But I appreciate your support."

He nodded, then glanced at Dorran. "At least tell me you're not leaving immediately. Your body was shutting down less than two days ago, and I'm worried about any possible side effects that the thanites can't handle. I want to give you a final checkup before you go."

Dorran didn't look especially enthused by the suggestion, but Clare nodded eagerly. "Could you? Just to make sure?"

"That's a good idea, and possibly a good compromise." Unathi shot Johann a glance for his approval. "Stay for a few days while you regain your strength. We'll help you equip for your journey back home, wherever it is. I'm sure we can do at least that much for them."

Johann gave a short nod. "Okay."

"That's settled. Let's say you have two additional days with us." Unathi's sharp eyebrows relaxed a little, and she rolled her shoulders back. "You can sleep in the room we brought you to on arrival. It is one of the bunker's two medical bays, but I trust it will be comfortable enough for you. Feel free to move about the ship and enjoy its amenities. I only ask that you don't touch anything that controls the system without one of us accompanying you. With that settled, shall we see about that checkup?"

CHAPTER 41

NIALL KEPT A QUICK pace as he led them toward his office. He seemed equal parts enthused and nervous to be tasked with monitoring Dorran, and kept glancing over his shoulder to make sure they were following. Unathi trailed behind them, holding a journal in one hand as she scanned her notes.

"I think I said before, we don't really have advanced tests available," Niall said, sending them a meek smile. "The final version of this place would have CT scans and blood testing facilities and the works, but most of the medical section is just empty rooms right now. If anything serious happened to us down here, we were supposed to, well, go to a proper hospital. But I can still do a physical and, I don't know, give you Band-Aids? I have lots of those. Some of them have kittens printed on them."

"The finest medical treatment the country has to offer." Clare laughed, but broke off early. The joke held a little too much truth.

"Here we are." Niall pushed open a door and stepped back so they could move inside. It looked nearly identical to every GP's office Clare had ever been in. A desk held a computer opposite two chairs, with an examination table on a wall covered with anatomical posters. There was evidence that it had been recently set up: the wall's paint was still pristine and the furniture was clean and modern.

Clare had expected Unathi to split away, but she followed them into the room, closing the door after herself. Clare thought she could guess why: she and Dorran were still virtual strangers. Unathi didn't know them well enough to be comfortable leaving them alone with one of her staff.

"Have a seat," Niall said, indicating to the examination table.

Dorran sent it one skeptical look, then opted to sit in the chair beside Clare instead.

Poor Dorran. You're not used to being fussed over, are you? She found his hand and squeezed. He responded with a tight smile. *Well, there's no escaping it as long as I'm around, so you need to get used to it.*

Niall moved through the exam methodically, noting down every detail, from Dorran's blood pressure to his temperature. He spent extra time on the cuts and bite wounds, checking the stitches and re-dressing them. For the first time, Clare had a clear look at the upper-arm injury Beth had inflicted.

Niall must have stitched the bite while Clare was asleep. It was a map of viciously red skin and black threads. Her vision blurred and her stomach threatened to overturn.

"Is it causing you any discomfort?" Niall asked, wrapping fresh bandages around the injury.

"None." Dorran's expression was calm, matching his words, but Clare knew how good he was at masking pain.

"I can give you a stronger set of painkillers if—"

"The current ones are working fine."

Clare struggled to breathe naturally. "Maybe you should take them anyway. It won't hurt—"

Dorran's eyebrows rose as he smiled at her, amused. "I promise, I am not being stubborn for the sake of it. I feel some stiffness, but the current painkillers are doing their job perfectly."

Clare nodded, praying he was being honest.

"Well, I'll give you this just in case." Niall fished one of the kitten-print Band-Aids out of his desk drawer and stuck it over the bandages.

Except for the bite, the findings were good: Dorran's temperature was still a little low, but most other metrics were within normal ranges.

"Honestly, I don't think there's much I can do except trust that the thanites are repairing you correctly." Niall shrugged as he sat back in his chair. "I have the feeling that trying to mess with what's happening will just cause more problems. So, uh, let me know if anything changes before you leave?"

"Thank you." Dorran zipped his shirt back up and rose.

Unathi, who had remained nearly forgotten at the back of the room, stepped forward. "Is he well enough to work?"

Dorran tensed. Clare knew him too well to think he was

bristling at the threat of work; instead, he was bristling at the insinuation that he *couldn't.*

Niall didn't notice. He was still focused on furiously scribbling in his notebook. "I mean, I think so. Nothing too strenuous, but some mild exercise would be fine."

"Excellent." Unathi took her glasses off and plucked a cloth out of her pocket to polish the lenses. "I'm going to make you two earn your keep. You'll help Johann in the garden this afternoon."

Niall's voice caught as his head snapped up. "What? They only just arrived. Can't you give them a chance to relax for *one day?*"

"Don't worry. Gardening sounds great." Clare looked up at Dorran for his confirmation and was answered with a gentle nod. She was fairly certain there was subtext to Unathi's words. It wasn't a demand; it was an attempt to help. Putting them to work would give them a valuable distraction from recent traumas.

And Clare was excited to be in a garden again. She missed Winterbourne's, and a part of her ached to know it must have died without anyone there to water and heat it. Gardening wouldn't just be fun; it would be healing.

"Excellent." Unathi replaced her glasses. "We still have a few hours before dinner. Come with me."

They left Niall in his office and returned to the maze of hallways. They hadn't long passed the medical bay Clare and Dorran had been sleeping in when Unathi hesitated, glancing toward a door inset into the wall. A small sign attached to the front read *Maintenance.*

Unathi cleared her throat. "I should advise you, some of your supplies are being stored in our containment room."

"Oh?" As far as Clare could tell, it was just a regular storage closet.

"While you were both recovering, Johann went through your vehicle to ensure there were no threats present. Your food and clothing were left untouched but anything deemed a weapon was confiscated. They will be held here, under lock, until you are ready to depart."

"I guess that's fair. We won't need weapons as long as the hollows can't get into the ship."

Unathi's shoulders relaxed. "Precisely. This building was designed to prevent people from seizing power through violence; excluding the rifle, which is also kept in containment, you'll be hard-pressed to find anything more dangerous than a kitchen knife."

Clare couldn't stop a faint sense of apprehension creeping through her, considering what had happened the last time they had entered a research center with no way to defend themselves.

This is different. They're helping us, unlike Ezra. They extended their trust to let us inside; we have to trust them in return.

Johann didn't seem thrilled to have company when Unathi dropped Clare and Dorran off at the entrance to the gardens, but he limited his objections to a deepened scowl as he keyed a number into a large double door. The metal panels slid back, and Clare took a deep breath.

The room was larger than a football field. Dirt paths

crisscrossed between a variety of crops. Long-forgotten scents reached her. Densely aromatic compost, the dry, dusty tang of hay, and, almost lost underneath the more dominant scents, something waxy and sweet.

"Bees!" Clare grabbed Dorran's arm as she craned to see the hives near the left-hand wall. The insects hummed as they crawled through the openings in their boxes, ferrying supplies into their homes.

"Need them for pollination," Johann muttered. "Though the honey is a bonus."

Clare couldn't stop smiling. Of all the things to make her happy, she wouldn't have expected a hive to achieve it, but her heart ached with joy as she watched the bees swirling in gentle loops as they approached and left their homes. Life was disappearing in every quarter of the still world, and it was a joy to see something thriving.

Johann took gloves off the wall near the door and passed a pair each to Dorran and Clare. "Since Unathi wants you to do something, you're going to be weeding today. *Just* weeding. Don't touch any settings, don't touch the watering cans, don't pull up anything that isn't obviously a weed. Our survival depends on you not screwing up our food source, okay?"

"No problem." Clare pulled her gloves on. She could respect Johann's defensiveness, and regardless, weeding sounded like a good time to her.

She crouched in a plot of potatoes alongside Dorran, seeking out straggles of grass and clover to expel. As she did, she scanned the rest of the plants. She counted at least a dozen varieties. Young fruit trees grew along the back wall. The corn had become so tall that it nearly reached the artificial lights above.

"This must have been growing before you entered the bunker," she said to Johann.

He stood a few paces away, running tests on the soil while he pretended that he wasn't overseeing their work. He shrugged. "Part of the sustainability trials. The teams that enter the bunker are supposed to survive off the farm. A custodian visits daily anytime the bunker is out of use. This field has been rotating crops for nearly three years."

"Wow." She shook dirt off the roots of one of the weeds. "That was fortunate."

"But it's not enough." His eyes grew darker as he shook the tube. "All it would take is a blight, a malfunction in the machinery, or a failure in one of our protocols, and we could lose it. We've started up a second farm. It's in a different room, kept a distance from this one, with no cross contamination of equipment or seeds. And I'm still worried it won't be enough."

Clare could understand. Before the stillness, a failed crop meant lost income. In the ship, it literally meant starvation.

"We're doing what we can," Johann continued. "Any excess food is being dried or canned and stored. In another month, the second farm will be producing its own crop. It's funny. Before this, we were prodding the ship from every angle, trying to find its weaknesses. Now, we're just praying we don't encounter any more."

Dorran made a faint noise. He glanced from Johann to the

plants and back, apparently weighing up whether it was safe to speak.

Johann frowned at him. "What?"

"You have a case of blight."

"What?" Johann slammed the test tube back into its box and jogged to Dorran's side. He bent over one of the potato plants, examining its leaves, then swore under his breath.

"It can be treated—" Dorran broke off as Johann uprooted the growth.

"Nope. Not chancing it." Johann held the plant like it was a grenade that might explode at any moment. "Change of plans. You're no longer on weeding duty. Swap out your gloves for a fresh pair and get searching for any more cases. We need to stop this before it spreads."

Johann was already storming toward the door, where a chute was waiting to accept trash.

"He's overreacting." Dorran smiled and shrugged. "But at least we can be useful."

The discovery had shaken Johann, but it seemed to have changed his attitude toward Dorran. As they crept between the plants, lifting leaves and hunting for the telltale symptoms, Johann didn't scrutinize their work beyond quick glances. Clare had the sense that he no longer saw them as a liability.

In the end, five potato plants were condemned to the incinerator. Johann seemed faintly relieved as he sanitized and hung up their tools, and offered to lead them back to the main parts of the ship for dinner.

CHAPTER 42

CLARE SAT ON THE edge of her bed, running a comb through her hair. Niall had come in and helped them change the sheets, and even though she'd only been awake for half a day, she was already feeling tired enough to sleep.

The ship was fitted out beautifully, but it still lacked one thing that Clare was starting to miss: windows. She found her eyes constantly roving across the walls, looking for a frame to stare out of. Some had art installed on them. They were pretty, but they didn't replace a view of the outside.

She was also missing the natural light. According to Niall, the bunker's occupants were following a strict twenty-four-hour timeline, and he was monitoring them to make sure their sleep schedules didn't start drifting. Clare could see the value in that. Already, she'd lost her sense of time. The clock on her bedside table said it was just after midnight, but it could have told her it was noon and she would have believed it.

Dorran cleaned his teeth in the bathroom. She enjoyed listened to the noises of him moving around. The sickness still left an impact; shadows clung to his face and he moved more stiffly than he used to, but for the first time, she could tell he was slowly growing better, not worse.

He seems so much happier here. Although he still spoke rarely around their new companions, he didn't have the wariness he'd shown around Ezra or Beth. It wasn't the first time that Clare had wondered if he might have a sixth sense about others' intentions. He even seemed comfortable around Johann, who had been the most vocal about getting them off the ship. Clare hoped that was a good sign.

The tap shut off, then Dorran stepped back into the bedroom. He'd changed into nightclothes—a white T-shirt he'd borrowed from Johann, and loose pants. They looked good on him.

"Would you mind lifting your feet up?" he asked. Clare lifted her legs off the ground and tucked them under herself. Dorran planted his hands on the second bed and shoved it until they bumped together.

She grinned. "Nice idea."

"I thought it would be good to stay close tonight. But I *also* thought it would be good to have room to stretch." He crawled onto his half of the new double bed and bent over the midway point to kiss Clare. His lips, featherlight, traced across hers. Clare leaned in to deepen the kiss, and he happily obliged, one hand coming up to run over her neck.

"Love you," he murmured, and pressed the light switch above their bed.

They both ended up near the center of their joint bed, hands tangling together. Tiredness abruptly fled Clare. The room was too dark. She felt as though she were drowning in the shadows. Her muscles tightened.

Dorran ran his hand across the sensitive skin on the inside of her wrist. "Are you all right?"

"Yeah," she lied. "Just trying to get my mind to slow down."

"Mm. If you're not ready to sleep, we can put the lights back on."

"No, I'm good. I just have to get comfortable first." She squirmed around a bit, hoping a different angle might let the stress drip out of her. Even if she couldn't sleep, Dorran needed rest. It was just darkness. There would be plenty more of it once they left the ship. She needed to get used to it.

The last time it was this dark was…

She saw the scene clearly in her mind. Fetching dead wood to keep their campfire alive. Stepping into the shadows in search of dry branches, leaving Dorran, unconscious, behind her.

A cold sweat rose across her skin. She tried to keep still, knowing movement would alert Dorran, but her heart rate was rocketing and her eyes were wide, staring blindly into the dark.

"Clare." His hands ran across her skin and felt how clammy it was. "Something's wrong, isn't it?"

She couldn't talk to him. Not about this. Not about *Beth*. Especially since he'd borne the brunt of her mistake. How self-centered would she sound, seeking comfort when she'd suffered the least? "Just…just can't slow my mind. I'll count some sheep. That'll work."

His hands moved away, and for a second Clare thought he was stretching, then the light above the bed clicked on. His beautiful, dark eyes glittered in the dull glow as he settled back down beside her and carefully encircled her in his arms. For a moment he just looked, his gaze moving across her face, reading her. Then he said, "Do you want to talk about Beth?"

Please, no. She closed her eyes to escape his scrutiny. "I'm so, so sorry."

A deep rumbling laugh emanated from his chest. His thumb grazed under her chin. "I asked if you wanted to talk; I didn't ask if you wanted to apologize."

She opened her eyes. Dorran's posture wasn't tense. He was languid, lying on his side facing her, his eyes heavily lidded and full of warmth. She didn't think this kind of calm could be faked. Clare wet her lips and whispered, "Do *you* want to talk about her?"

He considered it before answering. "Maybe a little. We didn't really…discuss it earlier. And I don't need to. If it hurts you too much, I won't mention her again. But…I think it might be good for both of us."

Clare wished she could take his offer and never mention her sister again. But he was right. It would loom over them, the elephant in the room, growing larger the longer they tried to ignore it. And if nothing else, Dorran deserved a chance to express how he felt. "Okay."

He waited, his posture just as peaceful, his eyes questioning. Clare felt too vulnerable. She looked away first. "You start."

"Ha." Again, he smiled. "All right. I suppose I'm curious to know where she is right now. Do you think she would keep traveling, or do you think she'd find a home to live in? I wonder if she would return to her old suburb, or whether it would be too bleak there?"

Clare choked on her words. She felt tears prickling, but she refused to let herself cry. "I don't understand how you can you be so *calm*. You must hate her—"

"Ah." Dorran's expression took on a hint of sadness. He curled forward to kiss Clare's forehead. "No, my darling. I don't hate her."

Clare frowned at him. "But…you should."

"Should I?"

Her eyes drifted toward the bandages peeking above the collar of his shirt.

"I wasn't awake for that last night, and several days before are clouded and confused." His sad smile deepened. "I'm afraid I don't have many clear memories of her."

Clare swallowed, blinking against the tears. "Well…good. That's probably for the best."

"You may need to feel a lot of things," Dorran said. "You might need to hate her. That's all right. You might need to grieve for her. That's all right, too. But I hope, with time, you can remember her for what she was before the stillness. That's how I think of her."

"Do you really?"

"As much as I can. I think about the stories you told me about her. And about how much she loved you. She might not have been a perfect older sister, but it sounded like she tried to be."

A rogue tear escaped, but Clare kept her head down so he wouldn't see it absorb into the pillow. "Thank you."

"Mm." Another kiss to her forehead. "Shall we keep the light on tonight?"

Clare was beyond trying to pretend she was fine. She nodded.

"I love you, my darling." Dorran's arms stayed around her, his fingers tracing unfathomable patterns across her skin until she finally sank into sleep.

CHAPTER 43

A HARSH, MECHANICAL WHOOPING noise blared through the room. Clare jolted, and Dorran's arms tightened around her, reflexively clutching her against him.

The fog of sleep stuck to her, and it took Clare a second to remember where they were. The blankets were in disarray around them, the light above their bed cut through the dark. Clare looked at the digital clock beside the bed. It said it was eight in the morning.

The alarm rose and fell in sickening undulations, so loud that Clare could barely hear anything else. Dorran sat up, his eyes wild, a pulse jumping in his throat. "We need to find the others."

The words broke through the paralysis. Clare swung her feet over the side of the bed and fumbled to put on her shoes. She was desperate for the alarm to stop. She was terrified of what it might mean.

Dorran snatched their jackets off the back of a nearby chair, then offered his hand to Clare. Together, they jogged for the medical bay's door and forced it open.

The siren played through the hallway as well. A red light flashed, casting a harsh glow across the white walls. Clare felt unstable, as though the floor were tipping underneath her, and clutched at the doorway to hold herself still.

Footsteps thundered toward them. West appeared, racing along the hall, but he barely glanced at them before disappearing around a corner. Clare and Dorran exchanged a look, then followed.

Clare hadn't been in that part of the ship before. The hallways were still generous but slightly narrower than the other areas, and the duller colors told her it was likely a maintenance area. Through the whooping siren, Clare thought she could hear voices yelling but couldn't make out the words.

Unathi appeared, striding toward them with long, loping steps as she dragged a jacket on over her shirt, her dreadlocks swinging behind her. She looked furious as she turned into a room. Clare and Dorran followed but stopped in the doorway. The room was crowded, with West and Johann already taking up the available space.

A dashboard was set up against one wall. Multiple screens showing security camera views of the ship's halls as well as the aboveground entrance. Lights flashed aggressively across the board, and Unathi pressed several buttons. The sirens fell silent.

Everyone seemed to breathe a sigh of relief. Unathi

straightened, turning to glare at each of them in turn. "Who set off the alarm?"

"Not me," Johann snarled.

"We were asleep," Clare said, fighting the urge to flinch under Unathi's piercing stare. "What was the alarm for?"

"Smoke alert."

West cleared his throat, looking apologetic. "I was cooking pancakes. It must have been my fault. I was trying really hard not to burn them but—"

"No, that wouldn't have been it." Unathi turned back to the screens and began typing on the keyboard. "This says it was affecting the ventilation systems across the ship. That's more than a scorched pancake can achieve. Where are Niall and Becca?"

"Here, here," a muffled voice said. Niall entered the room. He blinked bleary eyes, his curly hair lopsided from where he'd slept on it. His shirt was on backward.

Becca entered after him, looking equally exhausted, her gray-streaked hair hanging limply around her face and dark bags under her eyes. She'd brought the laptop with her, clutching it against her chest. "What happened?"

"Fire alarm." Unathi continued to work at the console. "I'm trying to pinpoint—*Oh.*"

The surveillance screens changed. They showed the garden, the plants Clare and Dorran had helped weed the day before displayed in grayscale. Smoke poured into the area.

"What?" Johann lurched forward, his face twisting. "No. No. Damn it!"

"What on earth?" Unathi squinted at the screen, nudging her glasses farther up her nose as she tried to make out where the smoke was coming from.

Johann burst past Clare and Dorran, through the door and into the hallway. Clare watched him until he'd vanished around the corner, then stepped closer to Unathi. "Has anything like this happened before?"

Her voice was calm, but her features were grim. "No. The ship was constructed to be fire-retardant. This shouldn't be possible."

"Do you have a sprinkler system?" Clare asked.

"Y-yes." Becca, shivering, stared at the screens. "But it's not water. We have a limited amount that needs to be recycled, and flooding the ship would make it vulnerable to mold and deteriorating air quality. But if we can isolate the fire's location, we can smother it with carbon dioxide."

Unathi was cycling through cameras, her jaw working. "The trick is finding the source."

"It's not in the garden?" Dorran asked.

"No. But it has to be close for that much smoke to be coming through the ventilation systems."

Johann appeared on screen, one arm pressed over his face as he ran into the garden that was steadily filling with smoke. Niall made a faint noise of distress. "Ah…as his doctor, I should mention…I have to advise against this."

Unathi leaned close to a microphone and pressed a button. "Johann, can you hear me? Get out of that room. We won't be able to rescue you if you pass out from smoke inhalation."

On the screen, Johann raised one hand as though to acknowledge the order but continued on his course between the plants.

Clare thought she could see where he was heading. The smoke was coming from the back of the room, where massive fans were set into the wall to circulate air. Sure enough, he didn't stop moving until he'd reached a blinking panel next to the right-most fan.

The six of them crowded into the surveillance room were so quiet that Clare thought she could hear her own thundering heartbeat. They all craned to see the screen, watching Johann as he pulled a metal panel off the wall and buried his hands into the wires underneath. The smoke was so thick that it almost obscured the camera's view.

Unathi pressed on the microphone again. "Damn it, Johann, get out of there."

He held his position, and Clare bit her tongue, silently urging him to hurry. Then, abruptly, he turned and began sprinting back to the door. Unathi released a heavy breath. "Thank mercy."

She began typing again, bringing up a map of the compound. Flashing red lights littered the image. Clare didn't know the building well enough to guess where they were on the maze of lights. New sections lit up as the alarm spread.

"Ah," Unathi whispered. "Found it. Mechanical fire, air-intake system. Something must have jammed. Becca?"

The smaller woman stepped forward, still clutching her laptop in one arm, and began typing on the dashboard with her spare hand. Command boxes flashed up on the screen and disappeared before Clare had the chance to read them.

The door thumped open as Johann barged into the cramped room. He was wheezing, breathless, and as he entered, the scent of toxic, plastic-laced smoke filled Clare's nose.

"I shut off the ducts so that the smoke doesn't kill the garden, but that means it's going to be building up in the ventilation system. You need to cycle it back outside."

"That's a problem." Unathi indicated the dashboard, where Becca's quick taps were turning lights from red to flashing yellow. "The fire came *from* the intake. As far as I can make out, something blocked it and caused it to overheat."

Johann pulled his lips back from his teeth, narrowed eyes darting from Unathi to the screen. "But…the external intake wasn't even supposed to be running. We're a closed system. That's how we survived the stillness, right?"

Becca carefully stepped away from the board and pressed her back to the wall. "Fire's out. And, yes, we were supposed to be a closed system, but I had to deactivate that protocol when we allowed Clare and Dorran's bus through the shutter door. Then we were so busy, I forgot to reactivate it. I'm so sorry."

"At least we know the cause." Unathi traced her fingertips across her jaw as she scrutinized the ship's map. The blueprints changed: the white hallways faded into gray, and blue lines appeared, detailing the air filtration system. Flashing red exclamation marks lined many of them. "At least with the vents closed, the smoke will be contained."

"That's only a temporary fix, though, isn't it?" West tugged on

381

his beard, a nervous tic. "Closing the ducts isn't a perfect seal; the smoke will still be seeping out, just more slowly."

Johann tapped one of the screens. "The intake is positioned behind the aboveground entry. If we can clear whatever's blocking it, we should be able to reverse cycle the system and blow the smoke back outside. I'll head aboveground and fix it."

"Wait a moment," Clare said. She turned to Unathi. "Can you find out what caused the blockage?"

Unathi pressed more buttons, and the screens changed from the blueprint to aboveground cameras. One faced the front entry to the compound and the shuttered door Clare had driven through. She thought it might be the camera attached to the speaker system. Grass swayed in the breeze, and in the distance, the chain-link fence glittered in the early morning light. Unathi pressed another button and the screen switched to a different angle of the entrance. "We don't have a view of the intake."

Johann sighed. "Then I'll take the low-tech approach and go see it for myself."

"I don't like this," Unathi said.

"Hell, Chief, neither do I. That's why I'm gonna *fix* it." Johann wrenched open one of the cupboards at the back of the room and brought out the rifle.

Unathi shook her head. "No, I mean...I don't understand how the filtration intake could become blocked. It's supposed to be maintenance free."

"Well, congrats, we found one of the kinks we were put down here to discover. Now we gotta fix it, because that smoke will continue seeping out of the ducts every hour we wait, and I don't think Aspect is going to send a repairman anytime soon."

"I'll come," West offered. "In case you need backup."

Dorran stepped forward. "I can help as well."

"You stay put." Johann pointed a finger at him. "Not to appear ungrateful, but West and I have this covered."

Dorran gave a short nod. Clare let her shoulders relax. Even though the cameras showed outside the bunker was empty, she appreciated not having the stress of being separated from Dorran.

"Stay in communication," Unathi said, forcing a small gray transmitter into Johann's hands. "Be cautious. Remember, the hollows are attracted by noise."

"I know." He took the transmitter, hefted the gun over the crook of his arm, and disappeared through the door, with West close behind.

Unathi ran a hand over her face while she continued to stare at the screens. As the footsteps faded down the hallway, she murmured, "How the hell could it become blocked within three days?"

"They should be safe, though, shouldn't they?" Niall hung near the back of the room, arms crossed as his eyes darted from the screen to his leader and back. "The hollows can't get over the top of the fence since we put up those reinforcements."

Clare's breath caught. She grabbed Unathi's shoulder. "I cut through the chain on the gate when I brought the bus in. I threaded it back through so it would look locked, but it isn't."

Unathi switched to the second camera. The gate was visible in the distance. The definition wasn't great, but Clare could still see the gate was closed, and the chain remained threaded through the holes.

"Looks like it hasn't been touched," Unathi said. "Maybe dead leaves or a stray plastic bag blew into the intake. Or maybe the system malfunctioned. Johann should know how to fix it."

Clare bit her lip. She kept scanning the camera's view. There were no hollows in sight—either inside the compound or out. That didn't make her feel any more comfortable. Dorran's hand rested over her shoulder, partially to comfort her, and she suspected partially to reassure himself. Niall stayed in the room's corner, eyes tight as he watched the screens. Becca remained near him as she clutched the laptop close, like it was a baby she didn't dare let out of her sight.

The console's speaker crackled, and Johann's voice came through. "We're at the doors, chief, open sesame."

Unathi pressed a button. The massive shutter door ground up, and a moment later, Johann and West emerged through it. West gave a thumbs-up to the camera as he followed his companion around the rectangular concrete block.

Audio continued to float through the speakers: crunching footsteps interspersed with heavy breathing. Johann and West must have run through the ship, Clare realized. It wasn't a short trip to the entrance.

They disappeared from the camera's view as they turned the corner. A moment later, Johann's voice broadcast through the speakers. "We're at the intake. The grate has been removed."

Unathi leaned forward, eyes narrowed. "What? How long has it been like that?"

"Did anyone check it before we entered the ship?" Niall asked. "Someone should have—"

Johann swore. There was the scuffle of hurried footsteps. West muttered something inaudible.

"Report," Unathi snapped.

"There—uh, there are hollows in the intake filter—" Johann's voice sounded strained. "At least a dozen. Hell. No wonder it was blocked."

"Retreat. Don't engage." Unathi's voice betrayed her stress.

For a few painful seconds, all they could hear was Johann's labored breathing. Then he said, "Nah, I think we're okay. They're dead. I'll pull them out. Gimme a hand, West."

Clare's mind was racing. *Hollows. Inside the compound. But how could they get in without disturbing the chain? Unless...*

Clare grabbed Unathi's sleeve. "Get them back in."

Unathi hesitated, eyes flicking over the screen, from the locked gate to the undisturbed trees outside the compound.

Clare shook her. "It's a trap! Get them back in!"

Dorran's hold on Clare's arm was almost painful. He was thinking the same thing. The filtration system's failure hadn't been an accident. Hollows wouldn't have piled themselves into an intake without cause.

Unathi bent forward, her eyes hard. "West, Johann, return inside. That's an order."

Johann laughed. "This isn't the army, Chief. You don't have the authority to give orders. I doubt we're even getting paid anymore now that the world's ended. Gimme one more minute and—"

A muffled cry came from West. Then scuffling noises, followed by thumping footsteps.

"They're on the roof!" Johann yelled.

West swore.

The two men reappeared on the camera, running like death was on their heels. Clare squeezed her hands together, silently begging them to hurry.

They weren't the only movement. Hollows scuttled down the structure's walls, pouring off the roof like insects as they raced toward the ground. Toward the open door.

CHAPTER 44

UNATHI'S HAND HOVERED OVER the button to close the metal shutters. Johann and West were still at least twenty feet away. The first of the hollows hit the ground and immediately turned toward the opening, disappearing into the black pit that led down to their compound.

"Shut the door!" Johann bellowed.

"But—"

"We can make it. Shut the door!"

Unathi hit the button. The shutters ground into action and began to descend painstakingly slowly. Clare could hear the mechanical rattling through Johann's receiver.

She could hear other noises, too. The hissing. The chattering. Gooseflesh rose across her arms.

Johann lifted his rifle and fired toward the swarm without breaking stride. The shot went wide. The hollows didn't react to the noise. More disappeared into the opening.

They're being controlled. There's a leader somewhere. One of the smart hollows. One that has found a way to exert control over the others, just like Madeline Morthorne.

Dorran bent close to her ear. "Stay here. Lock the door. I love you."

"Dorran—"

He was gone before she could argue, disappearing into the hallways, the doors slamming closed behind him.

Clare took two strides toward the door to follow, but a tinny scream caused her to freeze. She swiveled back to the screens. Unathi staggered away from the console, a hand pressed to her throat.

The shutters were nearly closed. Hollows continued to scuttle through the gap. Johann lowered his head and held the rifle out ahead of him like a spear as he charged into their midst. He disappeared inside, the shutters scraping his shoulders.

"Where's West?"

Clare's question was met with silence. The shutters clicked down, locking into place, sealing out the rest of the monsters. They pressed their pale bodies against the door, open hands slapping the metal as they looked for a way in.

But not all of the creatures were focused on the doors. A clump of them had gathered near the building's corner. They swarmed, writhing over each other in a frenzy.

Then Johann's voice bellowed, crackling through the speakers: "West? West!"

Unathi's hand covered her mouth. She shook her head, swaying.

"No!" The sound of a fist beating on the shutters echoed through the speaker. "Open the door! I've gotta get West!"

Unathi reached out. She stopped, her hand poised over the button, but didn't press it. The weight of the decision was written across her features in deep, horrified creases.

"Open the door!" Johann screamed.

Another voice, faint but familiar, followed it. "Behind you," Dorran yelled, followed by the *swoosh* and *thwack* of a weapon connecting with a hollow's skull.

Unathi's hand stayed poised over the button. The fingers shook. A tear slid past her lower lid and ran down her cheek, but still, she didn't lower her hand.

Niall shoved past Clare. She grabbed for him, trying to pull him back, but he was too fast. He reached around Unathi before she could react and slammed his open palm into the button. Then he was moving past them, aiming for the door, his blond curls whipping in his wake.

No. No. You'll let them in. There are so many. Dorran's there.

A muffled choking sound came from Unathi. She stared down at the button, then looked back up at the screen. The shutters were lifting. Hollows were pouring through the gap.

"Close it again!" Clare began running. It was too late to stop the hollows from getting in. She needed to find Dorran—find him and keep him safe.

She moved through the hallways at a painful speed, hitting walls as she took corners too fast. As she ran, she scanned for any kind of weapon. The ship's minimalistic design restricted her. There was nothing long enough and strong enough to be effective against the monsters. The knives in the kitchens were all small. If she could get to the gardens there would be farming implements, but they were on the other side of the ship—

Her eyes landed on a fire extinguisher. She grabbed it and wrenched it out of its holder. It was metal and heavy enough to do some damage. Clare kept moving, retracing her steps to the door that would connect to the outside world.

Chattering noise came from behind her. Clare twisted just in time to avoid the teeth snapping at her face. A hollow scuttled along the hall behind her. It had grown three mouths, each filled with too many molars, all gnashing at her in a sickening rhythm. Clare swung the fire extinguisher and smashed it into the face, sending teeth scattering. The hollow tilted back but didn't fall. Clare pushed into it, bringing the metal down again and again, until its head was a pulp. She didn't spare any time to admire her work. She gave herself just enough leeway to draw a fresh breath, then turned and continued down the hall.

A figure came out of the passageway to her left. Clare gasped and reeled back, raising the extinguisher. She didn't need to. Dorran scraped to a halt. Blood ran down one side of his face and saturated his jacket. She reached a hand out, and he clasped it before she could touch him.

"Not my blood," he said, then glanced behind them. "The ship's overrun. Get back to the surveillance room, lock the door, and keep the others safe. I'll find you as soon as I can."

"Johann—"

"We were separated. I don't know where he is. I'm looking for him."

"Niall's out here somewhere, as well."

"I'll do what I can." He pressed her hand, then gave her a shove in the opposite direction. "Be safe."

"Dorran—"

"Trust me." He swung the object in his other hand, and Clare saw he'd torn a pipe off a wall. Its end was covered in gore. "I'll come back for you."

He disappeared back down the hall, toward the entrance. Clare muttered furiously under her breath and turned back. Dorran was right. With the ship compromised, the best they could do was gather and find shelter. She and Dorran had experience fighting the hollow ones. She couldn't say the same for anyone else from the ship.

As Clare ran, a cacophony of discordant sounds disturbed the hall's normal serenity. Her own footsteps were the loudest, but they were joined by faint, indistinct noises, the clang of metal impacting bone, and the endless, maddening chatters and hisses of dozens of hollows.

Unathi stood in the control room's doorway. Her glasses had slipped down, and she made no move to push them back into place. Sweat slicked her face as she stared down the hallway.

The extinguisher was dripping with blood, and Clare threw it aside. "Is the external door shut?"

Unathi's mouth opened, but wouldn't form any words. *Shock.*

Clare grabbed her shoulders and forced her back inside the

maintenance room. Becca stood near the back wall, shaking, knuckles white as she clutched the laptop. Clare shut the door behind them, then crossed to the console.

The screen still showed the shuttered door. It was open. There was no motion outside. Every hollow that had been a part of the ambush had found its way inside, but that didn't mean more wouldn't be coming. Clare pressed the button to shut the door, then flicked the switch to activate Johann's radio.

"Johann, can you hear me?"

"I'm here. I'm here."

"Where are you?"

There was a grunt, followed by a wet cracking noise. Then Johann returned, breathless. "Trying to find a way back to the door. Hollows are everywhere."

"Johann, get to the surveillance station. We're reconvening here."

"I've gotta get West."

Clare's eyes moved to the screen. The place she'd seen the hollows gather was empty. The lump in her throat made it painful to speak. "West is gone. You have to come back. We're not going to survive if we don't stay together."

Johann swore. "I'm not leaving West!"

"It's too late for him. Please. Think of the others. Becca and Unathi are here. They need you."

Another obscenity. The way his voice cracked made Clare think he might be crying. "I really screwed up, didn't I?"

"That doesn't matter. Just come back."

The chattering grew louder outside the door. Clare crossed to it in two quick paces and flipped the lock. A normal hollow wouldn't know how to turn the handle, but not all of them were normal.

One of them is smart.

It had been a concentrated attack. The hollows had been brought into the compound, and then the gate's chain had been reaffixed so it looked as though it hadn't been touched. They had hidden on the roof, out of view of the cameras. Bodies had been sacrificed to block the intake vent, knowing that someone would come out of the bunker to repair it. And even then, instead of directly targeting the two nearest bodies, the hollows had swarmed through the open door, because their leader knew that was where the greatest feast would be found.

And now Dorran, Johann, and Niall are out there with it.

Clare flexed her hands at her sides. Flecks of hollow blood clung to her left-hand palm, making it tacky. She hoped Dorran knew what he was doing. She needed him to be safe.

Unathi took a shuddering breath. She leaned her back against the cabinets, her eyes staring sightlessly at the wall opposite her. "We're going to die, aren't we?"

"No." Clare spoke with an almost wild conviction. "You're going to be fine. But I need you to focus, okay?"

She gave a shaky nod.

The scratching at the door grew louder. Fingers, digging into the edges, into the gap underneath, the brittle nails fracturing. Clare fought the urge to press her hands to her ears. The sound seemed to come from every side, unrelenting.

The speakers crackled as Johann reopened his communication link. "Bloody things are in the ducts. That's how they keep appearing behind me."

Clare's eyes flicked to the ceiling. Two simple grates were set high in the walls. Her heart plunged.

The scrabbling *was* coming from every direction. The dry scrape of nails against wood barely masked the tinny tap of bones against metal. The door was only a diversion.

"We need to go."

Her two companions looked terrified. Clare remembered her fist experience fighting the hollow ones. Fear and shock had dulled her reactions, slowing her, making her limbs weak.

We need weapons. Something long and sharp. The gardens have hoes and shovels. They will do.

Clare pointed to the screen. "How do I get the map back?"

Unathi stumbled forward, her shaking fingers finding the right buttons. The blueprint flashed up.

Clare leaned close to the screen, hyperaware of the growing clatter in the ducts. "Where are we?"

Unathi tapped a room. Clare blinked, trying to visualize the rest of the ship around them. She barely knew the paths; trying to translate them into an aerial view was disorienting.

"Garden?" she asked.

A gesture drew her attention to one of the largest squares on the other side of the map. Clare tried to trace the twisting path they would need to take. It wasn't a short hike.

If they're in the ducts, nowhere is safe. We need to get weapons quickly. Quicker than running to the gardens. Something simple enough for Becca and Unathi to use. What else is there?

Clare ran through her memories of the building, scanning each of the rooms she'd visited in her short stay. The kitchens had knives, but nothing long enough to be a ranged weapon. The offices were bare of anything sharper than a letter opener. The fire extinguishers had a good weight, but she doubted either of her companions were in a physical or mental state to bludgeon anything.

Which left…*the storage closet.*

It was full of the supplies from the bus. The hatchet, the bat, Beth's favored rebar, and a spear. And it would be close.

Clare rushed to trace their path to it. Just one corridor and a corner to traverse. That was doable. It had to be. They were out of time. A small key icon hovering over the room indicated it was electronically locked. Clare took a guess, pressed the key icon, and was rewarded as the symbol vanished.

Fingers poked through the duct slats above Becca. She gasped and staggered away from it. Metal screws squealed as pressure was applied to them.

"Stay close," Clare said. "We're going to make a run for it."

"No." Unathi's pupils were pinpricks as they swiveled toward the door. Shadows danced through the gap underneath it as fingers clawed. "They're right outside—"

"They're a distraction. There won't be more than two of them." Clare searched for a bulky object she could lift and settled on a folding chair. She raised it and stepped toward the door. "Open it."

Unathi shook her head, the horror and denial stark on her features.

Clare tilted her head forward, pouring force into her words. "Open it!"

She obeyed, grasping the handle and wrenching the door open before flattening herself against the wall with a gasp.

The hollow ones spilled in.

CHAPTER 45

CLARE LURCHED FORWARD TO meet the creatures. She had guessed right; only two waited in the hallway. The nearest one reared its head, a flap of fat as large as a watermelon hanging from its neck. The chair's legs hit its torso hard, thrusting it back into the hallway, and Clare reeled her makeshift weapon back to slam it into the skeletal hollow that followed. Bones fractured like dry kindling being crushed.

Smoke flooded the hallway, cloyingly thick. Most of the lights were gone. Deliberately, Clare thought, spotting shards of glass scattered across the floor. The only remaining light came from the emergency beacon; it flashed intermittent beats of red across the scene.

"Follow me!" Clare launched into the hallway, bringing the chair down to slam the first hollow back into the floor. She staggered, her balance compromised, as the chair's back fractured under the impact.

The two women remained frozen in the maintenance room, their wide eyes catching the flashes of red from the alarm's light. Then the telltale squeal of compromised metal rang out from behind them as the surveillance room's duct cover popped free.

Becca yelped, jumping over the skeletal hollow's grasping arms to join Clare in the hallway. Unathi ran after her, clearing the creature in a long bound and hitting the opposite wall.

"Stay close." Clare threw the broken chair aside. The hollow with the tumorlike growth was already regaining its feet to clamber after them. She couldn't afford to stay long enough to kill it, even if the chair hadn't broken. They had made enough noise to summon every monster in that quarter of the ship.

One hallway. One corner. We can make it.

Clare split her attention between the path ahead and making sure her companions were keeping up. Unathi had regained some of her poise. She clung to Clare like a shadow, her paces long and purposeful. Becca was starting to lag, though. She clutched the laptop to her chest, her breathing shallow and too fast as she began to hyperventilate.

Hang on, Becca. We're almost there. Almost—

They were nearly at the corner. The two hollows she'd knocked down with her chair were gaining on them, accompanied by at least five more from the duct. One was so tall that her bowed head grazed the ceiling and her strides carried her five feet at a time.

Clare took the corner at speed, praying the new corridor would be clear. It wasn't. A shape loomed out of the gloomy smoke. Clare checked her momentum, arm thrown out to shield herself as the creature raised its weapon.

No... hollows don't use weapons...

"Stop!" Clare cried. The weapon missed her by a fraction as the figure tried to swerve its attack. The spade's gore-painted tip cut a chip out of the wall. The alarm light above them flickered, a split second of harsh red revealing Johann's ashen features.

"Hell," he snapped. "Nearly brained you."

Clare didn't spare the time to respond. She shoved him back the direction he'd been coming, toward the storage room. Unathi and Becca followed her, and a second later, hollows spilled around the corner.

Johann yelled in shock, staggering back, swinging his shovel. The nearest hollow balked at the weapon, its lips peeled back from elongated teeth in a furious hiss.

Clare felt for the closet door. She knew it had to be close, but in the gloom and with her eyes burning from the smoke, she was as good as blind.

Sparks exploded as the tallest hollow's head smashed into the alarm light, cracking it. In that split second, the light reflected off a metal handle. Clare lunged for it, wrenched the door open, and dragged the closest body, Becca, inside.

"Get in!" she called.

Unathi darted after her, but Johann didn't seem to hear. He backed away from the creatures, the shovel shaking as he brandished it at the growing crowd.

Clare lunged, grabbing his shirt, and leaned back, using her weight to drag him off balance. He staggered into the closet, and Clare slammed the door behind them. She didn't even have time to draw breath before the scrabbling noise began as countless fingers dug at the wood.

She had never imagined a darkness as deep as what the room afforded. Her other senses struggled to pick up signs from her companions. Deep, ragged breaths from Johann. Gulping sobs from Becca. A faint whistle as Unathi breathed through her nose. Clare clung to the door handle as it was rattled from the other side.

Then a click, and suddenly, the room was flushed with light. Unathi stood by the switch, eyes wide as she stared at them.

Clare scanned her small team just long enough to make sure that no one was hurt, then looked down at the handle. It contained a lock. She turned it and stepped back as it continued to rattle.

"We're going to be okay." She rotated in a slow circle, examining the walls and ceiling. Like she'd hoped, the storage room was too small to warrant any ducts. The only vulnerable point was the door. She didn't like how flimsy it seemed, but at least for that moment, it was holding. "We're safe in here."

Becca shook her head in a sharp, barely perceptible motion. Her graying hair stuck to her face as frightened despair leaked out in her voice. "It's all gone. The ship. Everything. It's gone."

Clare touched her forearm and felt how cold it was. "Don't worry about that right now. We're alive. We're together. We can get through this."

Johann ran the back of his hand over his chin, which was dotted with flecks of red. "Where's Niall?"

"He…went out after you."

Johann swore and swung away, fingers digging into his hair. Clare swallowed, trying to center her own emotions. Niall had gone not just for Johann, but for West. She'd seen the desperation in his face. He'd wanted to save them. It didn't bode well that Johann hadn't encountered him.

Or Dorran.

Dorran is strong. He's smart. He'll be coming back for me… No. He's going back to the surveillance room.

She closed her eyes, trying to fortify herself. It was hard to think while the hollows continued to dig at the door. The sound of splintering wood sent chills into her core. "We need to find a stronger place to hide. Somewhere without air ducts and with a solid door."

For a beat, the only sound came from the hollows outside. Then Becca took a stuttering breath. "The surgery. It's airtight. Metal doors."

"How far away is it?"

"Not…not far."

"Good." The bus's weapons were arranged on the shelves, where Unathi had said they would be. She searched through them and felt a rush of relief as she found two items she'd been hoping for: the fencing masks. As she picked them up, she caught sight of a glass object behind it. Johann, overcautious, had brought their battery-powered lamp inside, too. Clare pressed its switch and was relieved to see the batteries still had enough power to light it up. It would be invaluable in the dim hallways.

The sound of fracturing wood grew louder. A hole appeared at the door's base. An eye pressed against it, peering in at them, before twitching hands pulled it away again.

"Grab a weapon," Clare said. "Something with reach. You need to either decapitate them or crush their heads—and I mean really crush it, not just dent it."

Unathi reached for a knife. Johann adjusted his grip on the shovel. Becca was frozen in place, so Clare chose for her, pressing the rebar into her hand. It would be light enough for her to carry without becoming winded and was simple to use.

More wood splintered. Clare leaped back as an arm reached through the widening hole in the base of the door. The gray limb thrashed, feeling blindly.

We're out of time.

Clare took a sharp breath. The sounds outside had changed. Metal hit metal, and one of the hollows screamed. The hand reaching under the door retracted, and a human snarl joined the feral noises.

Dorran.

Clare undid the lock and threw the door open.

The flashing alarm light revealed the scene in horrible snapshots. Dorran leaned into his attacks, the pipe swinging with deadly force as he bludgeoned hollows away. He was painted in red, teeth bared and eyes narrowed. Shadows crept up behind him, and he lunged out of the way as grasping fingers tried to snag his jacket.

He can't see.

Clare dropped into a crouch and shoved the lamp along the slick floor. It skidded to a stop near the fray, bathing the hollow ones. Dozens of eyes caught in the glow, their bared and bloodied teeth sparkling. A cacophony of wails went up as the nearest creatures retreated from the light. Dorran straightened, swiping a hand over the red across his features.

"Clare?" he called, snatching up the lantern and backing toward the open door. "All right?"

"Fine. Johann's here. Did you find Niall?"

He shook his head, and Clare's heart sank. She braced herself, pulling the helmets out from under her arm. "We were planning to go to the surgery room. It's airtight and has solid doors."

Dorran kept his back to her, facing the hall, swinging the pipe as a hollow crept too close to the light. It darted back, chattering. "Good. I'll go first. Johann, guard the back."

Clare pulled Becca up to her side. "The helmet will keep you safe," she whispered as she pushed it into place, folding the cloth down around her neck and tucking it into her jacket's collar. "Just follow me. We'll watch out for you."

She hefted the second helmet, aiming for Unathi.

"Clare." Dorran pointed his pipe at her. "Put that mask on."

She glared at him as she closed the distance between herself and Unathi.

"Clare, no."

Ignoring Unathi's confused recoil, Clare pushed the helmet on over her head.

"You are infuriating," Dorran said. Then, as though he wasn't able to stop it, the corners of his mouth curled up. "I am so in love with you."

"Same back at you. Let's go."

Dorran passed her the lamp to keep his hands free. Clare held it high to illuminate their group as she followed close behind Dorran, hatchet at her side, switching her attention between the hallways around them, watching for any hollows that were creeping too close.

Dorran kept the pace brisk but didn't try to break into a run. He continuously glanced back to check that they were holding together. Johann brought up the formation's rear, weapon swinging in slow, threatening loops.

The monsters' fear of the light was fleeting. Already, they were creeping closer, teeth snapping and bony hands stretching forward. Dorran's pipe broke one of the grasping arms with a well-aimed swipe.

"Take the right up ahead." Becca's voice sounded wheezy, like she was close to being sick. Clare knew the cloistering mask couldn't be helping.

A hulking creature blocked the path. It ducked underneath Dorran's pipe. He lifted his foot and kicked its face, twisting the head back and forcing it into the wall. Another blow from the pipe brought it to the floor, and he kept moving. Clare put herself between the others and the twitching crawler. As she did so, her swinging lamp illuminated the two other hallways branching off from the intersection. Its glow cut through the twisting smoke and illuminated a distant figure.

Her heart missed a beat. Niall stood in the hallway, twenty paces away. With smoke coiling around him, he seemed ethereal, as though he were more ghost than human. His freckles stood out starkly against his white face, which glistened with sweat. The lower half of his body vanished into the smoke. He reached a hand out toward them, his eyes wide.

"Niall!" The word escaped Clare as a scream. He was real. He was terrified. She didn't know how long he had been lost in the darkness, chased by phantoms he couldn't see, but it had left him dazed from fear.

Shapes moved behind him. Clare's stomach turned. She lurched forward, a warning on her tongue. She was too late. Niall fell as hands grasped his legs and dragged him back.

CHAPTER 46

"NIALL!" JOHANN BROKE PAST her, a clip from his elbow sending the lantern swinging. The hollows that had been following him set up a chattering wail as they lunged forward.

Clare lashed out, reverberations running along her arms as she beat the creatures back. Dorran appeared next to her, joining the battle, one arm nudging her behind himself. "Get to the surgery!"

Her mouth was dry, her legs locked. A deep, overwhelming nausea rose up, and at the same time ice poured down her spine.

Niall was screaming. Not from fear or from shock, but from pain. Gut-wrenching cries forced out of him against his will.

She blinked and saw the memory of Beth, crouched over Dorran's unmoving form, firelit blood running from her lips. She blinked again. Dorran was streaking down the hallway, so fast and sleek that he seemed to blend into the smoke. Niall was no longer visible. A pile of hollows swarmed, dozens of them, jaws stretched and eyes rolling with ecstasy.

Clare moved to run after Dorran but forced herself to stop. Unathi and Becca clung to her, shaking. They would be easy prey if she left them. Dorran was right: she needed to get them to the surgery.

Movement came from her left and she swung blindly, clipping a monster that had darted forward. It snarled at her, then turned, racing down the hall to join its companions and their feast.

Screams flowed around them. Clare thought she would be sick if she didn't block her ears. Becca was crying openly, the sobs barely audible under the onslaught of noise.

Dorran and Johann were in the middle of the fray, fighting with a fury she had never seen before. Part of a hollow's skull flicked down the hallway, leaving a trail of blood as it skidded into the wall. More hollows were closing in on them. But even more were converging on Clare's group. Clare dropped the lantern, praying the distant light would be enough to help Dorran and Johann see, while still lighting her path.

"Go!" she yelled, grabbing Becca and Unathi's shoulders and pushing them down the hallway. They moved stiffly, as though they had forgotten how to walk. She could see two large metal doors up ahead.

Niall's screams had faded. Clare grit her teeth to keep her own cries inside. She shoved her companions, forcing them to move faster. Two hollows snaked past them, ignoring her group in favor of the smell of blood down the hallway. They were at the door.

Clare grabbed the handle, but it wouldn't turn. A keypad stood beside it. She swung toward Unathi. "It's locked."

The masked face stared back at her, silent and unresponsive. Clare grabbed her and wrenched the helmet off. Unathi stared blankly, unseeing, her lips opening and closing without making noise.

There was no time for gentle coaxing. Clare pushed her closer to the keypad. "The door! Unlock it!"

"Oh…" The word sounded wheezy. She punched in a series of numbers that must have been muscle memory by that point. The door hissed and the metal panels slid open. The room inside was pitch-black, but the air was clean, void of either the stench of blood or the musky taint of hollows.

"Get the lights on." Clare forced the two women past her, then turned back to the hallway. Blood sprayed across the walls. Bodies lay in clumps. The fighting was worse, though. More of the creatures had joined the fray. Clare felt sick. *Just how many are there?*

A figure emerged from the turmoil. It was too far away to see its features, but the broad shoulders belonged to Dorran. He carried something.

Clare stepped into the hallway, a hand held out to guide him forward. He put his head down and broke into a run. As he passed the lantern, Clare caught a glimpse of his burden.

Niall was limp. In Dorran's arms, he looked more like a child than a man. His clothes hung in scraps, and a glimpse of the flesh underneath made Clare's heart flip.

Hollow teeth, dripping red, grinning. Beth.

She forced the sickness down, forced the image of her sister away. Ringing filled her ears. She relished it, grateful for the dimming of the monsters' cries. She stepped aside as Dorran reached the door, allowing him to move through without breaking step.

Someone had turned the light on. Clare hadn't even noticed. But now she saw the surgery for the first time. It held a large surgical bed in its center, surrounded by stainless steel drawers, surgical lights, and baskets.

Dorran made for the bed and gently laid Niall down.

The chattering was growing closer. It was deafening. Clare turned back to the hallway and lifted her hatchet. Johann was coming, breathless and dripping with sweat and blood, the horde close on his heels. Clare reached for the button to shut the doors. She poised one hand over it, palm itching, nerves taut. Johann put his head down and leaped through the doors. Clare slammed her fist into the button as he passed, then darted toward the door, weapon raised. She screamed at the approaching hollows, a deep, broken bellow that hurt her own ears.

The nearest faces contorted in response to the noise. Their bloodlust was too strong to be deterred, but the shock was enough to break their momentum. That second of hesitation was all Clare needed. The doors slid shut. Bodies hit the metal and rebounded.

Clare, breathing heavily, dropped her weapon. The doors were thick enough to block out the worst of the hollows' noise.

Shrieks, laced with frustration and hunger, whistled through the metal, but it was thick enough to mute the chattering and the clawing.

Johann staggered toward the surgical table, his steps unsteady as the shovel trailed behind him. One hand reached out. "Niall? Buddy?"

Shivers ran through Clare. In the new quiet, she could hear Niall breathing. Shallow and pained, each inhale seemed to cost him dearly.

Her eyes drifted toward his legs, and she pressed her hand to her mouth to keep a moan inside. His legs had been the first part of him to be dragged into the horde. They were shredded.

Dorran moved in sharp, blindingly fast motions. He wrenched drawers open, scattering their contents. He had some medical experience, Clare knew; he'd spent time training under his family's doctor.

"Tell me what to do," Clare said.

He was blanched white, his eyebrows pulled so low that he looked terrifying. He didn't lift his attention from his work. "Look for medicine to aid clotting. It might be an injection or a gel."

Clare ran to the drawers at the other side of the room and started opening them. The surgery was well stocked. She rifled through endless gauze and implements, then found a row of drawers full of cardboard packets. One in particular caught her eye. It showed a large, illustrated drop of blood with a medical cross where the light would catch. The packet read *Medical coagulant.*

"This?"

Dorran was at her side in a second. He took the packet out of her hand, then snatched the rest out of the drawers. "Yes. Good. Turn the lights on."

At first, she didn't understand. The room was already lit. Then she looked back toward the surgery table and realized he meant the massive, suspended bulbs. She hurried to them, feeling around them to find the switches. The lights burst on, washing the scene in a blindingly harsh light.

Dorran wrenched packets open, using his teeth to tear into them. Inside were syringes full of a clear liquid. He bent over Niall's legs, pushing the needles into the deepest gashes. When he injected the liquid, the ooze of blood stopped.

Johann stood at Niall's head. He was shaking as he brushed the other man's sweat-slicked hair away from his forehead. "Wait… uh…you're meant to use gloves."

"The thanites will take care of infection." Dorran didn't lift his head from his work. "We don't need to treat him. We just need to keep him alive."

Clare forced herself to look at Niall. He'd been so quiet that she'd thought he was unconscious. It was a jolt to see him awake and aware. Blue lips were parted to take weak, gasping breaths. Bruise-like circles underlined his eyes, which were moving, alternately glancing down at his body and then looking away again.

"Hey, hey, focus on me," Johann said. He kept brushing Niall's hair back. "You're going to be fine, buddy. We've got you."

Dorran moved quickly as he tried to stem the flow of blood. The vivid red liquid already drenched the surgical bed, dribbling over its edge to drip onto the floor.

Clare grabbed one of the unopened boxes and ripped the seal to access the needle. "Dorran, do I need to do anything special, or just inject it where there's blood?"

His glance was brief and searching. "Are you up for it?"

"Yes." She put conviction into her voice.

"Inject it into the source of the flow. A quarter of a needle in each location, or more if it won't stop bleeding."

Clare snapped the plastic cap off the needle and bent over Niall's other side. She had to push blood-soaked scraps of clothes aside. Parts of the fabric had become embedded into his wounds. She tried to pull them free, then remembered what Dorran had said. Infection and contamination didn't matter—at least, not yet. All that counted was keeping him alive. She pushed the needle's tip in and depressed its plunger.

Dorran discarded another needle, then pulled out a strip of gauze and used it to tie off a large slice. "Does anyone here match Niall's blood type?"

Johann blinked sluggishly. "Yeah. Yeah, I do. I'm a global donor. I've got plenty more blood. Take it."

Dorran remained bent over Niall's legs. "Can any of you perform a transfusion?"

Clare clenched her teeth. *I've spent weeks with him. Why didn't I ever ask him to show me how?*

"I can," Unathi said.

Clare had almost forgotten she was present. She and Becca were near the room's back. Becca held on to her laptop, rebar, and helmet, eyes round as she stared at Niall. She looked like she wanted to turn away but was physically incapable. Unathi stood tall, chin lifted, her expression firm.

Dorran gave a short nod. "Start one. Directly into him; don't bother drawing into a bag first."

Unathi stepped toward the drawers and began hunting through them for needles and a plastic line.

A sudden noise shook Clare. She looked up. The doors had done an admirable job of blocking out the hollows, something she was only grateful for. But now, a new noise entered the room. Fingernails clattering across metal. She scanned the ceiling and saw half a dozen ducts.

"Becca." She swung toward the other woman, her pulse jumping. "You said the surgery was airtight."

"Ah…right. Hang on." Becca slid down the wall, legs extended ahead of herself, and unfolded the laptop. She used the trackpad to click several times, then her fingers flew across the keypad. The tapping sounded so much like hollow chatter that uneasy prickles rose across Clare's skin. She turned back to Niall, doing her best to focus on her work and ignore the growing sounds of danger converging on their location.

Then a scraping noise rang around them, seemingly coming from all sides. The ducts above them turned as they closed off. A hollow one howled, the sound echoing through the blocked passageways.

"Focus on me, focus on me," Johann whispered. "You'll be fine, buddy."

Niall's voice croaked. It sounded horribly faint. "I'm really sorry. I couldn't save West."

CHAPTER 47

CLARE STIRRED. HER NECK ached from the angle she'd rested it at. A low headache thrummed, the product of prolonged stress and mild dehydration.

She sat up, and a surgeon's gown slid to the tile floor. Someone must have draped it across her after she fell asleep. Dorran, she was pretty sure.

Clare brushed her hair out of her face. Her fingers caught in flecks of dried blood. She didn't know how long she'd been asleep, but based on her stiffness and the fogginess around her brain, it had been at least a few hours.

The surgery was almost perfectly silent. The only sound came from the steady breathing of her companions. Becca sat on the floor in the room's corner, legs extended, fingers typing on the laptop that Clare had begun to think of as an extension of the woman. She made eye contact with Clare for a second, the glance empty and emotionless, then looked back at her screen. The code was a form of escape for her, Clare thought. A way to take control in a world that had suddenly left her feeling very powerless. Unathi stood in the corner near Becca, staring down at her laced-together hands.

She looked in the other direction. Dorran sat with his back against the wall, bloodied hands limp in his lap. He looked wrecked. The efforts to save Niall had gone on for nearly six hours. He'd been active for all of them, constantly moving, barking instructions, even as exhaustion began to paint crevices across his face and slur his words. He'd only stopped twice, while trying to suture wounds closed, when his hands shook too badly to point the needle. He'd put his equipment down, stepped away, and closed his eyes for thirty seconds. That was the only break he'd allowed himself before returning to the table.

Clare rose and picked up the surgical jacket to hold it around her shoulders like a blanket.

Johann rested in a chair at the bed's side. His legs were splayed awkwardly under himself, shoulders hunched, one arm and his forehead resting across the bed's top, not far from Niall's head. His skin had taken on an unnatural shade of gray. He'd given what must have been liters of blood, and refused to let the cannula be taken out of his arm, even when Dorran began to grow concerned.

Clare pulled the jacket tighter around herself. Her throat, too dry, ached. Niall lay on the bed, features slack. He looked more like a skeleton than a man, with his hands curled into claws over his chest, the freckles making an odd contrast against his off-color skin.

Johann lifted his head. His eyes were bleary, but the ghost of a smile tugged at his lips. His voice had developed a crackling rasp. "He's asleep. That's got to be a good thing, right?"

"Right," Clare agreed.

Niall's chest rose in barely perceptible movements. Clare hated how small, how vulnerable he looked. She pulled his blanket slightly higher around his chin, then retreated to Dorran.

Dorran's eyes followed her, though nothing else about him moved. Clare lowered herself to sit at his side and leaned her head against his shoulder. She whispered so that she wouldn't disturb the room's other occupants. "I'm so proud of you."

"Mm." His lids fluttered. "Hope it's enough."

"Come here." Clare pulled him over so his head rested in her lap. She ran her hands through his hair, thick, black locks that always looked a little messy, but were significantly worse after that day. She felt a warm sigh against her leg.

"That feels nice."

"Sleep," she whispered.

"Wake me if Niall grows worse. Promise."

"Of course." She kept her hands moving in soft caresses. It didn't take long for him to go limp. Clare leaned her own head back against the wall. She felt like the emotions from the day were just starting to catch up to her, but she wasn't ready to handle them.

We saved Niall. But West is gone.

She bit the inside of her cheek. There had been enough warning signs that the blocked filter was a trap; she should have recognized them sooner. If she had, Johann and West would have never gone outside. They wouldn't have been cornered. The ventilation system might still be broken, but at least West would be alive.

Movement disturbed Clare's thoughts. She cracked her eyes open and saw Unathi had approached. She lowered herself gingerly to kneel in front of Clare. Her composure was back in place; she'd tied her dreadlocks into a bundle and had smoothed her clothes. A spot of blood lingered on her shoulder, a memento from the night. She fixed Clare with a searching look over the top of her glasses. "What's our next step?"

The implication was clear. Clare had led them into the surgery room, and she was expected to lead them out somehow. *The ship is compromised. There were so many of them...dozens, maybe hundreds. How can we possibly reclaim the rest of the building?* Clare shook her head. "I have no idea."

"I only ask because you'll know better than any of us. We have been in this room for close to ten hours. We will need water soon, and food not long after."

The room had a sink in its back wall. Clare nodded to it. "Doesn't that work?"

"No." To her surprise, Becca answered. The older woman remained bent over her laptop in the room's corner, her voice seeming eerily fragile as she tapped. "The airlock protocol involves shutting off the water as well. The surgery was designed to be completely isolated in case of the emergence of an aggressive disease. Which is lucky for us."

"Very lucky." Clare glanced at the closed air vents. That presented a new risk; with six of them in the room and no fresh air circulating, oxygen levels would begin to run low. She tucked a strand of hair behind Dorran's ear as she frowned. "We'll need to leave eventually. But they'll know we're here; they'll be waiting outside the doors."

As soon as the words left her, she realized she was wrong. Even though the doors were thick, they couldn't block out every trace of the hollows' persistent clawing. Clare remembered the faint noises following her into sleep as she finally lay down, exhausted. Now, the hallway outside the door was silent. The air vents no longer held the echo of scuttling bodies.

Becca's shoulders hunched. "Um. Actually. Maybe they won't."

"What did you do?" Unathi asked.

"Johann gave me the idea. In a roundabout way. He was really worried about the garden being killed by the smoke when the ventilation system broke. And I thought…the hollows are strong and good at healing themselves, but ultimately, they're still human. They need to breathe. So I cut off the oxygen and pumped the ship full of carbon dioxide."

Unathi's lips pursed, then opened, then shut again. At last, she said, "You can do that?"

"Well, yes. It was implemented as a way to put out fires. But by overriding the natural safety locks, I was able to drop our entire carbon dioxide load through the bunker's ventilation system. That's a huge security flaw, by the way. What if one of the citizens went rogue and hacked into the system to poison the rest of the ship? We might not even know until it was too late."

"Thanks." Unathi's tone was dry. "I'll pass that on to the team in charge of research and development."

"Sorry," Becca mumbled.

"Why didn't you raise this with me first? What if the gas got into our room? You could have killed us."

"Well, I was pretty sure it would work, and the room really is airtight, and besides, everyone was busy helping Niall... You know I'm not good with blood. So I figured I'd do what I *was* good at, which includes maintaining the ship's life support systems. Though I guess I did the opposite of that, didn't I?" She broke into feeble laughter. When no one else joined in, the sound quickly petered into silence. "Sorry."

"Don't be!" Clare had to fight to keep her voice to a whisper. "That's incredible, Becca. Will the hollows all be dead?"

"They should be." She turned her laptop to face them. The screen was open to a security camera looking down a hallway. Crumpled shapes were visible. It took Clare a beat to recognize a three-jointed arm. Becca pressed a button, and the view changed to a different hallway, displaying a similar scene. Everywhere she looked, Clare saw dead hollows.

"It really worked," she murmured.

Becca looked pleased for a second, then her smile faded. "I'll need to flush clean air through the system before we can leave the surgery."

"How long will that take?" Unathi asked.

"An hour."

"Can we begin now?"

"It should be safe." Becca clicked through the screens again. "I've been watching them. I haven't seen any movement in a while."

"Good," Dorran mumbled. "Want a shower. Want a proper bed."

Clare pressed a hand over his eyes. "Shh, you're supposed to be asleep."

Becca returned to typing. Her shoulders remained hunched, but Clare thought she looked brighter than she had before.

Unathi folded her arms, her gaze directionless. Clare didn't like the melancholy in her features and cleared her throat. "We were lucky the surgery was so well stocked."

She shrugged. "We never thought we would actually use it. This test run was considered so relatively safe that the surgery and the presence of a doctor was to please the insurance company and legal team more than anything. If it had been left up to me, it would be minimally stocked. But Niall was given his own operating budget and maximized it. Theoretically, any unused purchases could be used as starting stock for the official launch. No one else believed Niall was anything except insurance pacification." She chuckled. "West and Johann used to joke about visiting him for mosquito bites and splinter removals. Despite that, he always took his responsibility seriously. Thank goodness. It's probably what saved his life."

Clare glanced at the small man on the table. He'd admitted he had never been the best in his class. He'd seemed overwhelmed by the position as the bunker's doctor. But Unathi was right: despite his inexperience, he'd never shown any sign of shirking his responsibility.

The irony of the situation wasn't lost on her. In the new world, he would be one of the very few doctors left. His knowledge would be invaluable, no matter how untried he was.

Time passed slowly. Despite his exhaustion, Dorran slept fitfully. Whenever he seemed to be dipping toward deeper sleep, he jolted awake, first glancing up at Clare, then toward the surgery table, before finally lowering his head and closing his eyes again.

Niall didn't stir. Clare kept watch over him as best she could from her position on the floor. The harsh surgery lights had been turned off, allowing more natural shadows to fall over him. She ran her tongue around the inside of her mouth. It was dust dry.

"The air out there should be breathable now." Becca stretched, rubbing the back of her neck with one hand. "I can unlock the doors anytime, just say the word."

Her companions were all staring at the door, wary, and she thought the same question must be running through their minds: *Is it really safe out there?*

She stroked Dorran's head a final time, then gently eased him off her lap. "The rest of you stay here. I'll have a look around, make sure there are no more living hollows, and bring back some water and food."

Dorran pushed himself to sit up, blinking against the light. "I'll come with you."

"Not this time." She found his hand and squeezed it. "You should stay in case Niall needs you."

He frowned through his tiredness. "Don't want you out there alone."

"I'll go with her," Johann said. He rolled off his seat and shambled toward where they had dropped their weapons near the door. "I figure I've got the measure of this monster-bashing business by now."

"I can join you as well." Unathi gave Clare a quick nod. "I was very little use last night. At least I can provide some assistance now."

"Very well." Dorran sighed, though he still looked uneasy. "Don't stray too far from the surgery. Yell if there are any problems."

She kissed his cheek. "We'll be fine. See you soon."

CHAPTER 48

"OH," CLARE SAID.

Becca had retracted the surgery's doors. As the metal drew back into the walls, a small cascade of corpses tumbled into the room.

The hollows had spent their last moments clawing at the surgery's doors. There were at least thirty of them, and they had piled on top of each other as they hunted for an advantage. In death, they created a blockade. Clare scanned the pile, searching for any sign of twitching limbs or swiveling eyes, but they were lifeless.

"Ugly things," Johann grunted. He stepped forward and applied his boot to the bodies, shoving them back into the hallway. They fell stiffly, hands held ahead of themselves, necks twisted back, and mouths open in a representation of their final breaths. "What're we going to do with them?"

"They'll need to be disposed of," Unathi said. Her eyes narrowed. "It's going to be a monumental task to carry them back aboveground."

"What about the furnace?"

"That might work. It should be hot enough to burn bone."

Johann cleared a walkway between the creatures. Clare stepped out first, carrying the hatchet. It was one of the few weapons that hadn't been stained by blood the previous night. Unathi moved at her side, a bat held loosely. Johann stalked behind them. He swung his shovel.

At Clare's nod, Unathi pressed the button to retract the surgery doors, sealing Dorran, Becca, and Niall inside. Dorran had returned to his position beside Niall's bed, his dark eyes watching Clare until the last moment. A small rush of affection for him made her smile. He worried about her just as much as she worried about him.

She sobered as she returned her focus to the hallway. "We need essentials. Food and water. We should also get towels and blankets. Anything else?"

"That will be enough for a first trip," Unathi said. "We can always come back for more later."

Everywhere they looked, they encountered dead hollows. Clare marveled at how many there were. The attack had been an enormous undertaking.

They would have been controlled by one of the smart ones. But why did it bring so many of them down here? Did it assume there would be enough people here for them all to eat?

She passed a cluster of contorted bodies and swallowed. Maybe the leader had been motivated by something beyond its own hunger. *Resentment against humans, like Beth had begun to develop? Did they feel pity for their starving brethren? Or simply madness?*

She doubted they would ever know. If the leader had come into the bunker—and Clare was sure it had—it would be dead, one of the countless bodies they passed, indistinguishable from its mindless counterparts.

They turned into the kitchen. It was comfortably large and clean, except for the hollows' activity. Stainless steel pots hung above the stove and the chopping block full of sharpened knives. West had obviously taken pride in the space. Clare caught sight of a framed photo on top of the cupboards and her heart ached. A small dog, covered in black and white splotches and with its tongue lolling, grinned up at the camera.

Johann took a shuddering breath. "He loved that damn dog. I wish…I wish I hadn't been so mean about it."

"It's all right," Unathi said, removing her glasses and polishing them furiously. "I think he knew you didn't really mean it."

"At least they'll get to be together again." Johann swallowed as he stared up at the photo. "Polo, take good care of him for me, won't you?"

Clare rested a hand on Johann's arm. He was shaking. They would all need to grieve, but she couldn't afford to let them sink into melancholy, not when the others in the surgery were waiting for their return. "Johann, does Niall have a favorite food?"

"Huh?" The big man blinked. "I mean, yeah. Anything with sugar. You'd think a doctor would avoid it, but he has the biggest sweet tooth of anyone I know."

Clare chuckled. "That's good. Why don't you see if you can find something he'll like? We'll bring it back as a treat for him."

"Yeah." Johann, revitalized, began looking around the kitchen. "Let's do that. I'll see if I can find him some chocolate. That's his favorite."

"Unathi, can you help me collect the water?"

"Of course."

Clare opened cupboards under the sink and found two large pitchers. With the hollows gone, it would theoretically be safe to open up the surgery's air ducts and water pipes again, but Clare preferred to play it safe, at least for a few more hours. She focused on filling her pitcher next to Unathi at the double sink. As the water swirled closer to the top of the glass jug, Clare's skin prickled into goose bumps.

Something's wrong.

She turned, surveying the room. The counters, the spotless metal pots, the open pantry doors, and a closed door leading into a room for long-term storage. That was where most of the preserved fruit and vegetables had gone, Clare knew. Johann dug through the open pantry, a simple closet with wide shelves. He muttered under his breath as he searched its contents.

Nothing seemed out of place. The crawler horde, not hungry for human food, had left the kitchen fairly intact.

Something's wrong.

She blinked and saw herself back by the fire, struggling to wake up, her skin prickling as her subconscious tried to warn her about what Beth was doing to Dorran.

Something's wrong.

"Clare?" Unathi asked.

Her pitcher was overflowing, the water gurgling down the drain. Clare held up a hand to ask for silence. She couldn't see anything wrong, so she focused on her other senses. The musk of hollows lingered everywhere. *Is that what I'm reacting to? The smell?*

She turned to her ears, holding her breath to listen. Water drained down the sink, unchecked. Metal and glass clattered as Johann moved through the cupboard. Unathi breathed. Johann breathed. And a third being breathed along with them.

Clare reached for her hatchet. The sound was close. She tilted her head, trying to pinpoint it, and fixed on the long-term storage room. Unathi opened her mouth to ask a question, but Clare lifted her hand again.

Johann swung away from the pantry, holding up a block of chocolate. "Look what I found! We weren't technically supposed to bring processed food. I bet Niall snuck this on board for a bad day. Well, I guess that's today, huh?"

He noticed Clare's expression and his smile vanished. His eyes darted to the hatchet in her hand. He placed the chocolate on the counter, then reached for his own shovel.

Clare stretched a hand toward the storage room's handle. The breathing coming from inside was rapid but shallow. It was trying to avoid detection. She lifted her weapon, set her stance, and turned the handle.

The monster inside burst out.

CHAPTER 49

CLARE LUNGED AWAY, SWINGING her hatchet. The blade hit a bag of flour and sent a plume of white spiraling across the space.

The hollow lurched forward, emerging from the storage room one horrible vertebrae at a time. Its round skull was nearly completely hairless, bearing just a few thin strands. Its jaw receded. The neck stretched on. Clare's first glimpse of it made her brain recoil from the shock. The neck, articulated and twisting like a snake, stretched nearly two feet long.

Johann bellowed as he charged forward, shovel raised. The hollow neatly wove out of his way. Lidless eyes followed Johann as he tumbled past, into the storage room. Clare held her hand out. She had no chance to stop it. The hollow one stepped out of the room and slammed the door behind itself, locking Johann inside.

"You killed my babies."

The words sent chills through Clare. It was the barest imitation of human speech. Like a dog trying to mimic its owner's voice, a stale and lifeless series of syllables forced through an ill-suited larynx.

The creature's body had been twisted badly. Nubs that might have been the beginnings of new limbs poked out of its torso and thighs. It had dressed itself in strips of fabric woven around its body. The colors hinted at a desire to be beautiful, but the application represented the state of the creature's mind: broken beyond repair, an echo of what it once had been.

It reached toward the chopping block. The beginning of two new fingers wriggling from its wrist. The sight nearly froze Clare. It was only when she saw the glint of a silver knife being drawn free that she forced herself into action.

She raised the hatchet and lunged forward. The head bobbed ahead of her, and she angled her weapon for it. A fraction of a second before her blow landed, the head pulled away. There was nothing except for the storage room's door behind it. The hatchet embedded into the wood. Hot pain arced down Clare's shoulder. She twisted away, leaving the hatchet behind.

Again, the awful imitation of a voice rang through the room. "You killed my babies."

Clare's pulse thumped in her ears, almost in time with Johann's fist on the storage room's door. The head bobbed just out of Clare's reach, taunting. The lidless eyes rolled toward Unathi. Her own eyes were wide with fear as she lifted her bat.

"No!" Clare yelled. "Get back!"

The elongated neck gave it a distinct advantage. It held its head forward, almost like an offering, a red flag waved in front of a bull. As soon as it was attacked, its flexible neck retracted the head, leaving the attacker charging at thin air. They couldn't go for the obvious target. They had to attack the slower body.

Clare grabbed Unathi and dragged her back, out of the hollow's reach. It held the knife at its side, unthreatening, but Clare knew the blade would rise as soon as she moved closer. Her own hatchet was embedded in the storage room's door behind it. Her eyes flicked around the room, searching for a weapon.

She grasped the nearest pot, a thick bronze object that was large enough to heat a meal for six. Keeping Unathi behind her, she set her pose, preparing to spring. The hollow extended its neck, bobbing its head before her like an easy target. She kept her eyes firmly on it but switched her focus to her peripheral vision…and the body two feet to the head's left.

Clare lunged forward, feinting for the head. The neck retracted with the lithe speed of a striking snake. This time, she was ready. Her trajectory carried her toward the body, and she slammed her pot into the reedy bones just above its torso.

She'd hoped to break its neck at the lowest vertebrae. Her aim was slightly off, and she hit one of its collarbones instead. The creature fell onto its back, and Clare didn't give up the advantage but planted herself on it, legs straddling its squirming chest, bringing the weapon down again and again.

The head wove, avoiding her blows. The hand with the knife rose. Clare saw it out of the corner of her eye and knew she had to move but couldn't bring herself to give up the slim advantage she'd gained. It sliced into her shoulder. Clare hissed as hot pain dripped down her arm but didn't retreat. The knife pulled back for another attack, then abruptly dropped from the hollow's grip, tumbling to the floor, as the bat smashed its hand.

Unathi stood at Clare's side, shaking and with sweat dripping down her nose. She pulled the bat back and brought it down across the neck. The hollow screeched, arms coming up to grasp at Clare.

"Quick!" Unathi shouted. She pressed the metal across the monster's throat below its chin, holding its head still. Clare raised the pot and brought it down. Two teeth vanished from the monster's gaping jaw. Clare grimaced but kept moving, beating the pot down again and again until the reverberations left her arms numb and the pot's base was dented so badly it would never cook again. The grasping hands dropped away, limp. Clare didn't stop until she saw the gray of brains across the tiles, then lurched backward, breathing heavily. Unathi staggered back to rest against the nearest counter, bat dropping to the floor with a clatter. The room was silent.

Johann's voice, tight with fear, came from the storage room. "Unathi? Clare?"

"We're fine," Clare called. She shook her arms out and crossed to the door, unlocking it to let Johann out. He stumbled into the kitchen's light and blanched white. A quick glance took in the hollow's crushed head, then he turned his eyes toward the ceiling, lips pressed tightly together.

Clare paused in the storage room's doorway. Bags of flour had been carried up to the door. She shook her head. "That was the leader. The smart one."

"It talked." Unathi swiped her hand across her forehead, unable to take her eyes away from the fallen monster.

"Badly, but yeah. The smart ones sometimes remember how." Clare indicated the bags of flour. "When it realized the ship was being filled with carbon dioxide, it hid in the storage room and used those to make it airtight. It probably planned to stay hidden until we let our guard down. I should have been more careful."

Johann made a faint choking noise, still keeping his eyes averted from the broken skull. "I don't know about you two, but I'm ready to get back to the surgery."

"Yeah," Clare said. She crossed to the sink, turned the tap off, and lifted the pitcher of water. "Someone get cups and some food. Don't forget the chocolate."

The walk back to the surgery doors was completely silent. Johann carried armfuls of supplies, including blankets from the nearest recreational room and towels from a bathroom, as well as Clare's hatchet. She carried the pitchers of water. As the adrenaline faded, she felt the cut in her shoulder more acutely. It was like a line of fire running through her skin and into her muscles. She bit her tongue. The thanites would deal with the cut. She just wished they would deal with the pain, as well.

Unathi typed the code to open the surgery's keypad. The murmur of conversation inside the room fell silent as the doors opened. Dorran's expression relaxed as he saw Clare, and a smile rose across his features. "Everything all right?"

"Yeah," she said, as he took the pitchers from her. "They're all dead. We found the leader, the smart one, hiding in the storage room, but it's dealt with now, too."

"It cut her," Unathi added.

Clare grimaced. *Traitor.*

The relaxation fled Dorran's features. He moved around her, fingertips brushing across her arms and back until he found the gash on her shoulder. A hiss escaped clenched teeth. "Does it hurt?"

"Not bad."

"Come here. I'll dress it." He pulled up the seat from beside the surgery's bed and settled Clare into it, then began digging through open drawers. "I should have come with you."

"We did all right," Clare said. "And at least now it's dealt with, and we won't have it killing us in our sleep. So that's good."

A raspy laugh drew her attention to the bed. Niall was awake.

Clare lurched forward, a smile growing. "Hey. How are you feeling?"

"Grateful to be alive." His skin still looked ashen and sunken around his eyes, but Clare was encouraged to see some life returned to his features. His smile faded as his gaze moved toward his legs. They were covered by blankets, but Clare remembered what they looked like underneath.

"Those will heal," Dorran said to Niall as he pushed the chair back behind Clare and nudged her to sit down. He used surgical scissors to cut the top's shoulder, so he could access the skin underneath. Clare fought the impulse to flinch as a swab touched the broken skin.

"I'm really sorry," Niall said. His smile vanished entirely as his eyebrows pulled low. "I opened the doors. That was so stupid. So...*so* stupid."

"Don't feel that way," Clare said. "We were all under pressure and just trying to do the best we could in an ugly situation. You were trying to save West. I can't blame you for that."

"West is dead, isn't he?"

Clare's stomach turned.

Niall's voice had dropped to a whisper. He watched her, pleading. "No one will tell me, but he's dead, isn't he?"

The room was silent. Clare didn't want to have to be responsible for delivering the news. He was in so much pain already. It seemed cruel to add to it.

Unathi spoke instead, her voice soft but dispassionate. "Yes. West is dead."

"Okay." Niall turned away from Clare. He'd already guessed as much, but the confirmation seemed to steal some of the life from him.

Johann swiped the back of his hand across his eyes, then snatched up the block of chocolate from the table. "Hey, hey, look what I found for you. You like this sugar garbage, right?"

Niall stared toward the ceiling, eyes shining, lips pressed together as he tried not to let any emotions out.

"Don't tell me you're not hungry." Johann's fingers shook as they fought to unravel the foil. "I fought an actual monster to get this for you. Come on. Just a piece."

"I messed up so bad," Niall said.

"We all did." Johann choked on his laughter. "You weren't even outside with him. I thought he was behind me. I guess he was…until he wasn't. But…but the rest of us are alive. And that's more than I expected."

"The whole thing was a mess," Unathi added. She glanced at Clare, then looked aside. "When we heard the broadcasts explaining what had happened outside, and when we realized we were isolated against a swarm of something that was no longer human, I instigated drills."

Johann chuckled. "Yeah. What to do if one of them got inside. I would have my gun. We would all proceed to a safe room in an orderly fashion—"

"And they did us absolutely no good," Unathi finished. Her smile was wry. "Not one iota. I fell apart almost immediately. Johann wouldn't listen to my instructions. West was gone. Then everything was out of control…"

"You're still alive," Clare said. *Focus on what's important. Don't fall into melancholy.* "And as of this morning, the ship is secure again."

"Yeah. Could be a hell of a lot worse." Johann broke off a piece of chocolate and waved it in front of Niall's head. "C'mon. Have a bit. It'll make me happy."

Niall hesitated, then opened his mouth and accepted the chocolate. He frowned as he chewed it. "Did you really fight a hollow just to get this?"

"Hell yeah, buddy. Can't leave you to suffer without your sweet fix."

CHAPTER 50

DORRAN FINISHED WASHING, STITCHING, and bandaging the cut on Clare's shoulder. Unathi found her some painkillers. As she tipped two tablets out of the bottle, she said, "We could get you something stronger, if you think you need it. Opiates."

"Thanks, I'll be fine with this." *Better to save them for Niall.* He'd managed four pieces of chocolate and a glass of water before lapsing back into unconsciousness.

The rest of them shared the food and the water Clare's team had brought back, and then took turns washing their faces and arms in the sink at the back wall. Clare longed for a proper shower, but she was sticking to her principles: they couldn't separate until they were certain the ship held no more surprises. She pictured fighting a hollow one in a shower cubicle while she was slippery with water and soap, and the mental image was so horrible and hilarious that she broke out into laughter.

They laid the blankets and pillows across the floor. Johann volunteered to keep watch and resumed his seat beside Niall. Dorran finally dropped into a proper sleep, his arm thrown over Clare as she dozed at his side. Unathi napped against the opposite wall. As Clare drifted under, she was aware of the steady tapping coming from Becca and her laptop in the corner behind her.

When she woke, she felt like she'd barely closed her eyes, but the tackiness in her mouth and the fog in her head told her she must have slept for hours. Dorran was gone. She reached out, searching for him, then caught his voice coming from behind her. She rolled over and saw he was at Niall's side, rewrapping one of the bandages on his arm. She rubbed sleep out of her eyes and sat up. Becca's laptop was silent. She and Johann slept along the wall Unathi had occupied.

"Hey," Clare whispered, rolling to her feet to join Dorran.

He smiled as she neared him. "How is your shoulder feeling?"

"Fine." The pain tablets were wearing off, but she didn't think she would need another dose for a while yet. "How're you doing, Niall?"

He gave her a bandage-swaddled thumbs-up. "I'm feeling really good, thank you so much for asking. Morphine is amazing."

Unathi came up on the bed's other side. She'd managed to clean up, washing her face and tidying her hair, though her shirt was still creased. She nodded to acknowledge Clare. "Becca stayed up until nearly two, watching the cameras. There is no sign of motion in any of the hallways."

"Two…in the morning or the afternoon?"

Unathi blinked, quietly stunned. Then she began to laugh. "I don't know. I didn't ask."

Clare chuckled, shaking her head. "I guess it won't matter much unless we go aboveground." Her laughter faded. "We'll need to do that anyway. Sooner, rather than later. One hollow realized the gate was compromised and got in. I don't want any more discovering that same trick."

Unathi's lips twitched. "What if they're already in the compound? The cameras don't see behind the entrance or on its roof."

"We know their weak spots now. We can be prepared." Clare squeezed Dorran's arm. "Dorran, Johann, and I will go up."

"Johann and I will," Dorran corrected. "You went last time—"

"*All three* of us will go up," she repeated, narrowing her eyes at him.

He sighed and tried to look irritated to hide his amusement. It didn't work completely.

"Safety in numbers," Clare continued. "We'll make sure the compound is empty before locking the gate. Do we have any more chains?"

Unathi nodded. "We should. Johann will know where."

"Wha?" Johann stirred against the wall as he heard his name. "Johann will what?"

"Sorry," Clare said. "I didn't mean to wake you. You must be tired."

"Nah, nah, I'm up now." He got to his feet, staggered, and pressed a hand against the wall as he rubbed his knuckles into his eyes. "Whatcha need?"

"Chains to lock the gate."

"Oh hell, I forgot about that." His head snapped up. "Yeah, we gotta get that secured. Can we go now?"

Clare glanced at Dorran for his feedback. He tied off the bandage on Niall's arm and nodded. "I'm ready."

Just minutes later, carrying chains retrieved from the garden's storage, they set off to reach the surface. Clare, Dorran, and Johann all carried weapons as they moved through the ship, though Clare hoped they wouldn't need them. She pressed the back of her hand across the lower half of her face, breathing through her mouth as her eyes watered. The stench from the hollows was growing worse. She'd never been trapped in enclosed quarters with dead hollows before; they smelled so much more than their living counterparts. She guessed that would only grow worse as decomposition set in.

Dorran made sure Clare hung at the back of the group as they stopped before the massive metal shutter that led outside. Johann spoke through his communication link to Becca, who activated the door. They hunched, muscles tensed for an attack. A sliver of sunlight poured through the growing gap.

Fresh air rushed around Clare. Sounds—the sounds of the *real* world, birds, leaves, and insects—reached her. She'd grown used to the air inside the bunker, but now she realized how much she had been missing out on. The outside air tasted *real*. She moved forward, slipping around Dorran's protective arm, desperate to feel the sun on her skin.

Heaven help any hollow that disturbs this moment. She tilted her face up toward the sky. A featherlight blanket of heat rested over her as the sun hit her skin. Dorran released a deep breath beside her.

The field of long, weedy grass swayed ahead of them, its edge marked by the chain-link fence reinforced with slabs of metal at its top. Beyond that was the forest. A bird sang somewhere in the branches.

Focus, Clare. Make sure you're safe before you lose yourself too much.

She turned to face the concrete building and backed up, looking for any creatures on the roof. She couldn't see any, but she knew they could be hunkered down, hiding.

"Dorran, can you lift me?"

He crouched and wrapped his arms around her legs. Clare gasped as she rose off the ground and clutched at his shoulders to hold on to her balance. He chuckled as he lifted her higher. Dorran was tall to begin with. Their heights combined was plenty to let her see the building's flat concrete roof.

"It's empty." Clare gasped again as Dorran dropped her back down. Her arms shot out, prepared for the impact against the ground, but he neatly hooked a hand across her back, swinging her until he held her like a child. He kissed her forehead, then set her feet back down.

Clare couldn't stop the smile from entering her voice. "Okay. We'll check around the back, then we're good."

Johann swung his shovel in arcs as he led them around the concrete structure. Fifteen feet away from the building, almost completely disguised in the long grass, was a metal grate opening into some kind of faintly whirring machine. Johann swung the grate up, and Clare saw a mash of limbs underneath.

"Ugly beasts," Johann said, then crouched to pull the hollows' bodies free. There wasn't enough room for all of them to work at clearing the intake, so Clare paced in a slow circle and watched their sides. Once the last torso was hurled aside, Johann shut the grate, and they circled back around the building, picking up their length of chain along the way, and aimed for the gate.

Clare's attention was pulled toward the ground nearby. A patch of the long grass had been crushed. Her step faltered as her mind connected the events from the previous day. Brown stains marked the damaged plants, sticking to them like paint.

Her skin prickled. She forced her face to maintain a neutral expression as she turned back to face the fence. She didn't want Johann to see. He was struggling enough as it was.

He'd noticed her falter, though. His squinted eyes roved from Clare to the crushed grass. His mouth opened, then closed, then opened again. When he spoke, it sounded less like a word and more like a croak wrenched out of sick lungs. "Oh."

He swallowed, swayed, and then began to move toward the tainted area. Dorran reached out, seemingly wanting to pull him back, but stopped short of touching him. He sent Clare a helpless glance. She shook her head in return.

Johann came to a halt at the edge of the churned-up ground, his features slack as he gazed across the uprooted grass, the claw marks in the dirt, and the dark stains.

443

"There's nothing left." He sounded incredulous. "They didn't even leave us anything to bury."

Dorran placed a hand on Johann's shoulder. His voice dipped into the more formal style that he tended to adopt under stress. "Come now. Let us secure the fence. We will see to a funeral after."

"A funeral?" Johann blinked furiously. "Can we?"

"Of course." Clare came up on his other side. She and Dorran helped Johann away from the scene. "We won't forget West just because he's gone."

"'Kay." Johann swiped his arm across his eyes, then set his features into something fierce as he stared at the gate. "Gimme the chain."

It took them less than a minute to secure the fence. Dorran and Clare stayed outside, surveying the area, while Johann returned to the ship. He emerged fifteen minutes later carrying two additional shovels, and with Becca and Unathi following in his wake.

There was nothing to bury except the bloodstains, but Dorran and Johann turned the dirt over, entombing the grass in a shallow grave. When they stepped back, the scene of violence had been transformed into a layer of fresh dirt.

Clare held Dorran's hand as the survivors stood around the grave. Johann spoke, his voice choked. "I hope your dog's waiting up there for you, buddy. I hope he's as happy to see you as you'll be to see him."

Metal clattered behind them. A hollow, attracted by the noise, had emerged from the trees and began to climb the chain-link fence. The group held motionless, watching, as it scaled the twelve feet toward the slats of metal installed after the stillness. It reached the flat surface, hands splayed as it fought for purchase, then tumbled back to the ground. It stayed down for less than a second before beginning its climb again. A second figure moved out from the gloom behind it, chattering through a fractured jaw.

"We should return inside," Unathi said.

Slowly, they moved back toward the open shutter door. Johann lingered behind. Clare and Dorran stopped by the door, watching as he pulled a wooden spoon out from the folds of his jacket and embedded it in the fresh dirt.

"Best damn cook I ever met," Johann said, then put his head down as he followed them back inside the ship.

CHAPTER 51

THE HALF HOUR CLARE had spent outside, with sun on her skin and fresh air around her, had been a beautiful reprieve. As the shutters ground shut behind her and the howls faded, she let herself sigh.

The bunker was an excellent invention. It served its purpose well and had protected its occupants impeccably until they had opened the doors. But the fern walls and soothing paintings were no substitute for the outdoors.

"I'm going to check on the garden," Johann said. His voice still sounded tight, and Clare guessed he wanted to be alone more than anything.

Becca rubbed at the back of her neck. "I have free time now. Should I keep working on the code?"

Unathi looked from Clare to Dorran, silently asking their approval. Clare nodded back to her, signaling it was Unathi's choice.

Unathi nudged Becca's shoulder. "I would say so, yes. Make it a priority."

"I should go back to Niall," Dorran said. He glanced at Clare. "Will you come with me?"

"Actually…" She wrinkled her nose at the nearest hollow one. It was starting to shrivel as its body dehydrated in the air-conditioning. Hands turned into talons, jaw gaping wide, eyes melting into their sockets. "These delightful additions to your home are getting riper. I thought I'd start on the cleanup efforts."

His eyebrows pulled up. "Are you—"

"Sure I want to do this?" She laughed. "I decidedly don't. But I'll regret *not* doing it more."

"If you wait a few minutes, I'll check on Niall and then come to help."

"I'll do my share, as well," Unathi said. Her cool eyes surveyed the bodies around them. If they revolted her, she didn't show it.

Clare asked, "We decided to incinerate them, right?"

"That's probably the cleanest option. There are degradable bags in the kitchen. I'll find some gloves."

The rest of the afternoon was spent attempting to purge the ship of hollows. Six chutes spaced around the building fed down to the incinerator. Clare, wearing rubber cleaning gloves that rose up to her elbows and with a roll of bags tied to her waist, set to removing the bodies.

The smaller hollows could be bagged and shoved down the chute whole. To her disgust, though, some of the taller, more spindly ones needed dismantling. A saw from the gardens cut through their brittle bones, and the bodies had been dead long enough for the blood to congeal.

Dorran seemed to have a sixth sense about when she needed to hack apart a body and moved in to take over the work in most cases.

"You're a saint," she said the third time he intercepted her.

He slipped in long enough to steal a kiss, then pulled back, grimacing. "Sorry. Not the most romantic scene. I'll wait until we're both showered and no longer smell like death."

Clare chuckled as she shook out one of the black plastic bags, and let Dorran drop severed arms into it.

She was coping better than she had expected. The sickening, overpowering smell was everywhere. Some of the bodies—the ones filled with more fat than lean muscle—had started to ooze.

The bodies they had fought and killed before escaping to the surgery were worse. They had crushed heads, severed limbs, and blood and bone fragments scattered across walls and floors. Clare could only handle them for a couple of minutes at a time before backing off, bent over and breathing through her mouth as her stomach threatened to revolt.

But for all the horror the scene contained, it was not as bad as Clare had expected. Music—probably controlled by Becca—piped through speakers. It had a quick, upbeat tempo, and Clare was surprised at how much it helped to keep morale up. Every cleared hallway was a small victory. Piece by piece, the ship began to look more like the calming environment it had been before the invasion. And with every bag dumped down the chutes, Clare repeated a small truth inside her head.

We survived. The hollows sent the worst they had, but we still survived.

The evening shower was the best part of the day. Clare stayed under the hot water so long that her fingers and toes began to wrinkle. She shampooed her hair three times in an attempt to scrub the nauseating stench out of it and mostly succeeded.

She could have slept in a proper bedroom that night, except that Dorran was staying in the surgery to watch over Niall. The soft, clean blankets looked almost seductive, but Clare hated the idea of being alone. She compromised by dragging blankets and pillows off a bed and carrying them into the surgery. The smell lingered there, just like it lingered everywhere, and the lights were a little too bright, but at least she was near Dorran. He chatted with her and Niall, and the gentle talk soothed her raw nerves until she fell asleep.

They cleaned the last of the hollows out of the building the following day. Some had tried to hide, crawling into narrow chutes or wedging themselves behind doors, and Clare had to go through the building three times to be certain there were no more corpses waiting to surprise her. She became well acquainted with the maze.

Then began the scrubbing. The hollows' stench was finally muted under the burning odors of bleach and soap. The scrape of bristles against tile became a familiar song.

Dorran joined her shortly after lunch, pulling on his own set of gloves and a face mask. As he knelt beside her and dipped a brush into a bucket of discolored, soapy water, he said, "I changed Niall's bandages this morning."

"How's he looking?"

"Horrifying. But improving." His dark eyes followed the sweep of his brush as he erased blood spatter from the floor. "Do you remember how Johann was worried his nails were growing faster than they should?"

"Oh, yeah."

"There may have been some truth there. Even though the bunker was airtight, I suspect its occupants had a heavier dose of thanites than you or I did. That is why their blood transfusions improved me so rapidly. And it is helping Niall begin to heal."

"Thank goodness for that," Clare said. "He might not have lived through the night without them."

"No, I suspect not. While changing the bandages, we stitched some of the largest lacerations to help them heal. And I mean *we*. He wanted to do it himself."

"Was he able to?"

"Surprisingly well. We sat him up and numbed the areas, and he did the bulk of the work himself. He has sensation in his legs and some motion, which I believe is a good sign. He was particular about how we stitched them." Dorran laughed through his mask. "I would prefer to do it the way I was taught, but I cannot argue. They are *his* legs, after all."

Clare dunked the brush back into the water, then returned it to the tiles. "So he can treat himself. That's helpful."

"Yes. And it is what I came to tell you. With Niall's condition stabilized and the ship's threat averted, we could leave at any time. If you wanted."

Clare set the brush aside and sat back on her haunches. They had already stayed longer than they had intended. It had been unavoidable: the bunker couldn't have afforded to lose them without risking its safety and increasing the burden on its surviving members. But now, the environment was stable. Cleaning would probably continue for weeks until every last trace of the invasion was purged, but none of it was urgent.

She didn't know what the food situation was like. Johann had been splitting his time between cleaning, cooking—he had taken over West's role, though he wasn't as talented at it—and working furiously in the garden. Whenever she asked him how the plants were doing, he gave vague, noncommittal answers. That worried her.

Clare suspected that if they asked to stay in the ship, the others would make room for them. But that half-hour taste of the outside when they'd secured the fence had told her something. She didn't want to spend weeks, let alone months or years, underground.

She stripped her gloves off and pulled down her face mask. Dorran mimicked the motion, and she was glad to see the rest of his features. She wanted to make sure she was giving weight to his feelings, too. "Do *you* still want to go home?"

Yes, his eyes answered, even though his mouth said, "Only if you do."

Clare grinned. "I'm calling it home. That probably tells you how I feel."

451

He took her hand. Warm fingers massaged hers, then threaded through them as he held her hand against his chest. His smile dropped. "The trip back will probably be dangerous."

"We did it once. We know what to expect now."

"And once we return home, I cannot promise it will be safe there, either."

"But it's home." She looked at her hand, her fingers encased in his, and nodded. "I'm ready."

He kissed her. "Thank you."

They finished cleaning that hallway and tipped the buckets of brown liquid back into the water reclamation system. It would be filtered, then fed to the gardens or—Clare shuddered to think of it—diverted to shower or drinking water. Even though the filtration should leave it completely pure, she still didn't like the thought of swallowing it.

As they neared the surgery, the tenor of quiet but urgent voices reached them. Dorran sent Clare a look, then tapped the code to unlock the door. The voices fell silent as the metal slats slid back.

The entire crew had converged in the surgery. Niall sat on the edge of his bed, cloth-swaddled legs hanging over its side. Someone had brought a table into the room. Becca sat at one side, laptop's glow highlighting her face in blue. Unathi sat at the other side, a pen poised over her notepad. Clare couldn't read the tight cursive, but she saw a series of numbers whittling down into calculations that made her head hurt. Johann had been pacing but stopped at Clare and Dorran's entrance.

"Hey," Clare said. The silence was uncomfortable enough to make her want to squirm. "Are we interrupting?"

"Of course not." Unathi turned the notepad over. "Come and have a rest. We were going to find a pack of cards and play a few rounds of poker, if you would like to join."

There was no sense in delaying the announcement. Clare took a deep breath. "We were thinking of leaving soon. We've already stayed longer than we meant to."

"So you did hear us." Johann swore and resumed pacing. "We can make it work. Don't worry about that. We'll figure something out."

"What?"

"It might take a couple of weeks of rationing, but it won't be too bad." He waved his hands. "If we need to, I can go to town and see what I can find in the houses there. So don't you worry."

"Oh." Clare's eyes flicked back to the hidden notepad of calculations. She found a chair and drew it up near the table. Dorran stood behind her, his hand on her shoulder. "Is this about the garden?"

Unathi met her gaze, serene. "The hollows got into it. They didn't eat anything, but many of the plants were trampled. Johann has done what he can to save them. And we have some long-term stores. Not as much as I would like, but—"

"I've got the second garden going." Johann spoke eagerly. "There are enough plants in there for all six of us. We just have to wait for them to grow enough…but it'll be fine."

Clare chewed on the corner of her thumb. She addressed her

question to Unathi. "Do you have enough food for four people to survive on?"

Unathi flipped the notepad over. She'd already done the math. "Not at full rations. But at eighty-five percent, which is enough for us all to function on until the secondary garden begins cropping. If three of us drop to eighty percent of our caloric intake, the fourth could have full rations."

Niall frowned, catching the implication. "I'll be eating the same as you."

"No, you won't. You're healing; you need fuel."

"I'm a doctor. I *know* what I can take."

"And I'm your boss. My word is final."

"What would you do, fire me?" Niall's face broke into a grin. It gave Clare a rush of relief. Since the breach, Niall had looked like a shadow of himself. He'd been too thin, too pale, and too weak. That smile held the enthusiasm and joy that had been missing. Dorran had said Niall would be all right, and for the first time, Clare really believed it.

She turned back to Unathi. "I don't think it's a good idea for any of us to go into town unless it's absolutely necessary. If you think you will be all right on those restricted rations…"

"No. We're not making you leave." Johann swung back toward them, hands held out. "We're not in the business of sacrificing our friends."

Clare gave him a fond smile. "I seem to remember you were the one who wanted us gone the most."

"Look, I'm sorry about that. It wasn't personal." He wrapped his

454

arms around his torso, his steps becoming faster. "I was just trying to look out for my team. But…but *you're* my team now. We're not going to make you leave. No way, not even if I have to fight every hollow between here and the city. We can make it work."

"Johann. Thank you. You're a good guy. I know why you were taking a hard line back then. It was the smart thing to do." Clare glanced up at Dorran and matched his smile. "But this choice isn't motivated by survival. We were going to leave even if you had food falling out of every cupboard. We're ready to go home."

Johann finally stopped pacing. He looked heartbroken as he glanced between his small group, as though silently asking them to object.

"You're absolutely sure?" Niall's eyebrows pulled together. "Johann's right. We could make it work."

"Thanks. But we're sure."

Unathi snapped the cap back onto her pen. Clare couldn't remember the last time she'd seen the older woman smile, but she smiled then. "You'll be missed."

"And we'll miss you."

"Thank you for letting us stay so long," Dorran said.

"And thank you for keeping us alive." Unathi indicated Becca. "What time is it?"

"Late," she said, glancing up from her screen. "Nearly midnight."

Clare almost laughed. Time stretched strangely in the bunker. If she'd been asked, she would have guessed it was shortly after lunchtime.

"Don't leave while it's dark," Unathi said. "We want to give you the best journey out we can. Stay the night, then in the morning, we can check over your bus and make any repairs it needs, and give you a little extra food to help you reach home."

CHAPTER 52

CLARE KNEW SHE NEEDED to sleep—that it would make the difference between a safe, sane drive and a painful one—but she felt too alert to drift off. The permanent day inside the ship had upended her body clock faster than she could have anticipated.

She and Dorran had opted to spend the night in the surgery again, using the blankets and pillows Clare had brought in the previous night. No one had actually voiced their motivation, but Clare knew the others felt it as much as she did. They didn't want to be apart on that final night together. Unathi, Johann, and Becca stayed as well, each building their own little nest.

Dorran slept well, his breaths slow and deep, one arm cast across Clare as though he needed to hold her close even in his dreams. Clare tried to relax, but every time she closed her eyes, anxiety began to creep in. The room still had light—a lamp from Unathi's office had been left on in one corner—but the pale glow wasn't enough to stop the darkness from clawing at the edges of Clare's nerves.

She rolled over, trying to find a better position without waking Dorran. Something shifted close by, then a voice whispered, "Clare, you awake?"

"Yeah. Can't sleep." She squinted up at Niall. He'd lifted his head from the pillows, and his messy hair was turned into sparkling gossamer strands by the lamplight behind him.

"I can't, either. Everyone here expects me to rest, but I think I'll go mad if I don't do something. Do you want to have a game of cards?"

Clare grinned. "Absolutely."

She gently, carefully, worked her way out from under Dorran's arm. He murmured as she left him, so she tucked her pillow in at his side to keep him warm. He relaxed again.

Clare tiptoed to Niall's bed as he slipped his legs over its edge. She pulled the table up next to him, then found the pack of cards perched on one of the medical trays. Clare had to smile as she slipped the cards out of their holder and began to shuffle them. The surgery had lost any claim to being a sterile environment thanks to the past few days. "What do you like to play?"

He cast a glance at their sleeping companions. "How about rummy?"

"Good for me." She began dealing cards.

Bare feet padded over the tiles behind them, then Becca appeared at Clare's side, rubbing her upper arms as she blinked owlish eyes. "Can I join you?"

"Of course." Clare moved her chair back to make room for Becca. "I'll deal you in."

Becca smiled, but the expression didn't extend past her mouth. She took the cards Clare handed her and stared at them with unfocused eyes. Niall played first, but when it reached Becca's turn, she didn't react. Niall lightly nudged her arm, and she looked up, lips trembling. "I think I figured out what to do with the thanites."

"Oh?" Clare lowered her cards, her heart spiking with hope.

"I've been going over that code again and again, looking at it every which way, trying to understand it. It's been madness."

Niall gave her a sympathetic smile. "I'm glad it's you and not me."

She chuckled, but it came out awkwardly. "I don't do well with pressure. And this...it's like the most pressure I've ever had. The fate of humanity, resting in my palm. Part of me hoped I would get eaten by those hollows just so I wouldn't have to deal with it any longer."

Clare hadn't even suspected Becca was feeling that way. The older woman had been consumed by her laptop, but Clare had assumed that was just her personality, not a symptom of anxiety.

"But I think I finally figured it out. And it's so, so simple, it seems crazy." Becca gave a nervous smile, shuffling her cards in her hands, then placed one on the pile on the table. "We can assume the code basically works. It destroys the thanites. But it has side effects we don't yet understand."

"That's about right," Clare said.

"I kept returning to one idea. What if there was a way to

destroy the thanites that lived in the hollows, but not humans? It would be the closest to a perfect solution, except there's no way to do that. The code doesn't distinguish between hosts. I couldn't stop thinking about it, though, and that train of thought eventually led to my solution."

Niall placed a card on the pile without looking at it. He'd put a queen of spades on top of a five of hearts. Clare didn't try to correct him; she was too riveted by Becca.

"I can't differentiate between hosts, but I *can* restrict the number of thanites destroyed. It's a simple snippet of code... Each thanite flips a metaphorical coin. Half of them detonate. Half aren't affected."

"Oh," Clare said, starting to understand.

"With no new thanites being manufactured, there's a finite supply," Becca said. "If we destroy half of the machines, every person will feel the side effects, but they'll still have the remaining thanites inside of them to heal any damage. Just like what happened with Dorran, except without the need for transfusions."

"I think I get it," Clare said. "It won't stop the damage, but it leaves a way to heal. That might work."

"Then, after a few weeks, I can run the code again. Another half of the thanites will be destroyed, with a quarter of the original supply left to repair the damage. And again, and again, until the remaining thanites are so negligible that we can wipe them out completely without any ill effects."

Clare nodded. "And the hollows..."

"The hollows are a nightmare. You've seen them. Open

wounds, organ damage, severe mutations that would kill a normal human. The only thing keeping them alive is an absolute swarm of thanites constantly making repairs. Reduce the thanites and they'll die from infection. The worst ones will probably go down with the first run of code."

Clare's pulse thrummed. She placed a two of diamonds on top of Niall's queen, and no one cared. "That's smart, Becca. Really smart."

Becca put her head down, a nervous smile growing. "It's not foolproof. But...I think it's our best shot. I'll still need to go through the code carefully and look for any compatibility issues it might cause. But it's somewhere to start."

Clare looked over her shoulder, toward where Dorran slept. His features were relaxed, his breathing deep and even. She whispered, "Hey, Dorran, are you awake?"

He didn't stir, except for his lips tugging up at their corners. "I am."

"You're too good at faking sleep. I can't trust you at all."

He chuckled, a deep, rumbling noise that felt oddly good in Clare's soul.

"You lost your thanites once. You'll know what it feels like better than any of us. Do you think Becca's plan will work?"

Dorran rolled onto his back and frowned at the ceiling. "It sounds as though it might. After the encounter with Ezra Katzenberg, I felt...weak. Not just in my muscles, but in my bones and in my core. As though I had been diced into a million pieces and put back together. But once I had some thanites replaced through the transfusion, that sensation began to recede."

"I think it sounds like a plan," Johann said. He was still tucked into his bed against the opposite wall but stroked his beard. "Weaning people off them might be a better approach than doing it all at once. People are going to have cuts and infections. If we can warn them in advance, tell them they'll only have the thanites for a limited time, they might have a chance to patch themselves up before they lose the robots."

An irritated sigh floated out of the room's other corner. "Is *anyone* actually sleeping?" Unathi asked.

Clare bit her lip. "Sorry. Didn't mean to wake everyone."

"I'm honestly mad that you didn't try to," Johann said.

"None of this is anything that can't be discussed in the morning," Unathi grumbled. "Just go back to sleep, all of you."

Clare gave Niall an apologetic smile and stacked the cards back into their pack. She slid off the chair and returned to Dorran, who pushed the pillow out of the way so she could resume her spot at his side.

As she lay in the dark, listening to her companions toss and turn around her, Clare wondered if they felt the same way she did. Like a giant clock was counting down. Too soon, it would chime that morning had arrived, that it was time for her to leave the safest location she had found since the stillness. But its countdown wouldn't stop there. It would continue ticking, invisible hands moving, clawing time in with painful reliability as it pulled them toward an inevitable resolution.

They were going to end the war against the hollows.

CHAPTER 53

JOHANN AND DORRAN MOVED in and out of the bus, boots thumping every time they leaped down from the step, ferrying armfuls of supplies in each direction.

The bus's external structure had held up reasonably well, but the insides were a mess. None of the blankets or clothes had been washed. The bus had sat in the ship's parking garage for days, undisturbed and festering, and when its doors opened for the first time, Becca gagged.

"We'll only need to be in it for a few days," Clare had said, trying to reconcile herself to the idea.

"You cleaned our home," Johann responded. "Let us return the favor."

Bottles of bleach and upholstery cleaners had been brought in. The basement's elevator dinged every couple of minutes as supplies were ferried in. The old blankets—the ones stained with blood and caked in dirt—disappeared into the ship, either for the laundry or the incinerator. Fresh blankets were brought to replace them. Johann filled up their empty cartons of water and reorganized their food stores.

"You should have enough for ten days," he said, shoving the last box back into place.

"We won't need that much," Clare said with slightly more conviction than she felt. "The trip back can't take more than two or three days. You should keep the extra food."

"Don't even think about it." He gripped her shoulders, turned her around, and pushed her back out of the bus. "We've got enough to last us until the garden is back up and running. I'd rather know you two aren't forced to take too many risks."

Dorran worked on the engine, moving through every component with meticulous care. Johann scrubbed the outside, tightening the bolts on the plywood window covers and cleaning the fractured front window.

Niall came down to the garage to see them off. Clare thought he shouldn't have been moved, but his stricken look made the rest of the group relent. Unathi had brought him down in a wheelchair, blankets wrapped around his pale limbs. He watched the activity keenly, not fully able to hide how much he wanted to join in.

When the bus was finally up to Johann's standards, he stepped back, looking pleased. "That'll make the trip home nicer."

Clare realized they were finally on the cusp of leaving. She blinked at the four surviving researchers, and a lump appeared in her throat. "Thank you for taking us in."

"No, thank you," Unathi said. She carried something small under her arm, which she offered to Clare. "This can't transmit, but you'll at least be able to listen to what's happening. I've tuned it to our own station. Keep an ear out; we'll begin broadcasting when we're ready to enact Becca's protocol."

Clare took the radio and bit her lip. "Are you sure? Don't you need it?"

"Technically, we weren't even supposed to have it." Unathi sighed. "But *one* of us smuggled in a significant quantity of contraband that would have ruined the experiment."

"My bad," Niall said, fidgeting and unable to hide his smile.

The four friends moved in, hugging Clare and Dorran in turn and murmuring goodbyes.

"You're a good guy," Johann said, clasping Dorran's hand, then pulling him in for a brief bear hug. "Take care out there."

"Same to you," Dorran said.

"Listen to the radio," Unathi said. "It might take us weeks. But we will be here, working on the code, working to reverse this, and we'll tell you when we're ready. I'll open the shutters for you in a couple of moments. Safe journey."

They stepped into the bus. The doors creaked shut behind Clare. Dorran stepped into the driver's seat and Clare took up position in the seat beside him. The engine started with a rumble, and as the bus circled around the massive concrete pillars to face the ramp, Clare watched their friends in her mirror. The four of them raised their hands in farewell and stayed, waving, until they were out of sight.

The bus entered the ramp, suspension bouncing as Dorran navigated the narrow passage. They followed the two bends in the path, then stopped at the shutters leading to the outside world. Clare faced the wall so Dorran wouldn't see how hard she needed to blink to keep her face dry.

His fingers grazed her arm, a gentle caress. "Are you sad?"

"They gave us too much food," Clare said.

A hint of a smile lifted Dorran's lips. "Are we going to leave some for them?"

She drew a hopeful breath. "Can we?"

He put the van into park and pulled two cases off the racks above the seats. Clare opened the bus doors, and he dropped the boxes outside, lined up neatly against the wall.

"I love you," Clare said as he stepped back inside.

He smiled, took her hand, and pressed a quick kiss against it as he slid back into the driver's seat. The door ahead of them rattled as it opened. Dorran coaxed the bus out, then pulled up next to the speaker box Clare had used on the night she arrived. She wound her window down, reached across the distance, and pressed the button. "Hi, Unathi, are you there?"

The box crackled. "I am. Are you ready for me to shut the door?"

"Go for it." Clare waited until the shutters started to clatter down behind her, then said, "We left a couple of boxes in the hallway. Something to fill out your rations."

Unathi sighed heavily. "We had a plan. Why does *nobody* ever stick to the plan?" A trace of fondness bled through the frustration.

Clare grinned. "We'll miss you, too."

Voices followed Unathi's: Johann, Niall, and Becca, all blending over each other.

"Be safe, all right?"

"I hope we can catch up again, sometime when the world isn't such a mess."

"Thank you for everything."

Clare blinked back tears as the bus rolled forward. It only took Dorran a moment to unlock the chain on the fence, and Clare took over the wheel to move the bus through the opening while he sealed it again behind them. Hollows began to chatter in the distance as the noise attracted them, but before they had a chance to get close, Dorran was back in his seat and the bus was moving along the trail and toward the main road.

"Your time to shine, map reader," Dorran said, smiling at her. "Where to?"

ABOUT THE AUTHOR

Darcy Coates is the *USA Today* bestselling author of *Hunted*, *The Haunting of Ashburn House*, *Craven Manor*, and more than a dozen other horror and suspense titles.

She lives on the Central Coast of Australia with her family, cats, and a garden full of herbs and vegetables.

Darcy loves forests, especially old-growth forests where the trees dwarf anyone who steps between them. Wherever she lives, she tries to have a mountain range close by.

THE FOLCROFT GHOSTS

EVERY FAMILY HAS ITS SECRETS.

When their mother is hospitalized, Tara and Kyle are sent to stay with their only remaining relatives. Their elderly grandparents seem friendly at first, and the rambling house is full of fun nooks and crannies to explore. But strange things keep happening. Something is being hidden away, kept safely out of sight...and the children can't shake the feeling that it's watching them.

When a violent storm cuts off their only contact with the outside world, Tara and Kyle must find a way to protect themselves from their increasingly erratic grandparents...and from the ghosts that haunt the Folcrofts' house. But can they ever hope to escape the unforgivable secret that has ensnared their family for generations?

For more info about Sourcebooks's books and authors, visit:
sourcebooks.com

THE CARROW HAUNT

THE DEAD ARE RESTLESS HERE.

Remy is a tour guide for the notoriously haunted Carrow House. When she's asked to host guests researching Carrow's phenomena, she hopes to finally experience some of the sightings that made the house famous.

At first, it's everything they hoped for. Then a storm moves in, cutting off their contact with the outside world, and things quickly take a sinister turn. But it isn't until one of the guests dies under strange circumstances that Remy is forced to consider the possibility that the ghost of the house's original owner—a twisted serial killer—still walks the halls. And by then it's too late to escape…

For more info about Sourcebooks's books and authors, visit:
sourcebooks.com

THE HAUNTING OF
ROOKWARD HOUSE

SHE'S ALWAYS WATCHING...

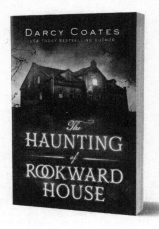

Rookward House may be hours away from its nearest neighbor, but its newest owner can't escape the feeling that he's being watched. Still, Guy decides to camp in the crumbling old mansion while he does repairs. Surely nothing too bad can happen in the space of a week.

But there's a reason no one lives in Rookward House, and the dilapidated rooms aren't as empty as they seem. Forty years ago, a deranged woman tormented the family that made Rookward its home. Now her ghost clings to the building like rot. She's bitter, obsessive, and fiercely jealous…and once Guy has moved into her house, she has no intention of letting him go.

HOUSE OF SHADOWS

SHE'LL NEVER ESCAPE ITS SHADOW.

Sophie's world is shattered when disaster bankrupts her family. She's still reeling when she's offered an unexpected solution: Mr. Argenton, a wealthy stranger, has asked for her hand in marriage. Marrying Mr. Argenton will save her family, but it condemns Sophie to a life in Northwood, a vast and unnaturally dark mansion situated hours from civilization. Still, she has no choice but accept the offer and hope the darkness won't swallow her whole.

It's a struggle to adjust to her new position as mistress over the desolate house. Mr. Argenton's relatives are cold, and Mr. Argenton himself is keeping secrets. Even worse, the house is more than it seems. Day by day, Sophie is inevitably pulled toward the terrifying truth: Northwood's ancient halls are haunted, and the man she married—the man she's coming to love—is hiding an unforgiveable truth about his ancestral home...and the spirits that now haunt them both.

HOUSE OF SECRETS

SHE'LL NEVER SURVIVE ITS SECRETS.

Sophie and Joseph Argenton have survived the impossible...for now. But their escape from Northwood is short-lived. The beast that haunted their ancestral home survived and has attached itself to Joseph's young cousin. Desperate, they travel to meet her father at Kensington, a long-abandoned mansion overlooking a dead town. The house offers a small hope: its original owner had dedicated her life to researching the monster that now possesses Elise. There's a chance that here they will find a way to kill the creature without harming the girl. But Kensington has its own dangers, and once it has Sophie and Joseph within its grasp, it may never let them leave.

Trapped inside the ancient building's collapsing walls, Sophie and Joseph are forced to confront the horrors that hide within. Shrouded figures stalk them from the shadows. Whispers echo through the night. Unmarked graves dot the property. And the dead are not as restful as they seem...

VOICES IN THE SNOW

NO ONE ESCAPES THE STILLNESS.

Clare remembers the cold. She remembers dark shapes in the snow and a terror she can't explain. And then…nothing. When she wakes in a stranger's home, he tells her she was in an accident. Clare wants to leave, but a vicious snowstorm has blanketed the world in white, and there's nothing she can do but wait.

They should be alone, but Clare's convinced something else is creeping about the surrounding woods, watching. Waiting. Between the claustrophobic storm and the inescapable sense of being hunted, Clare is on edge…and increasingly certain of one thing: her car crash wasn't an accident. Something is waiting for her to step outside the fragile safety of the house…something monstrous, something unfeeling. Something desperately hungry.

For more info about Sourcebooks's books and authors, visit:
sourcebooks.com

SECRETS IN THE DARK

YOU CAN'T OUTRUN THE STILLNESS.

Winterbourne Hall is not safe. Even as Clare and Dorran scramble to secure the ancient building against ravenous hollow ones, they face something far worse: Clare's sister has made contact, but she's trapped, and her oxygen is running out.

Hundreds of miles separate Clare from Beth. The land between them is infested with monsters, and the roads are a maze of dead ends. Clare has to choose between making a journey she knows she might not survive, or staying safe in Winterbourne and listening as her sister slowly suffocates. At least, whatever her choice, she'll have Dorran by her side. And yet there are eyes in the dark. There are whispers in the mist. There is danger lurking in the snow, and one false step could end it all…